THE QUEEN OF
SINISTER

Also by Mark Chadbourn

The Kingdom of the Serpent:
Jack of Ravens

The Dark Age:
The Devil in Green
The Queen of Sinister
The Hounds of Avalon

The Age of Misrule:
World's End
Darkest Hour
Always Forever

Underground
Nocturne
The Eternal
Testimony
Scissorman

For more information about the author and his work, visit:
www.markchadbourn.net

THE QUEEN OF
SINISTER

MARK CHADBOURN

an imprint of **Prometheus Books**
Amherst, NY

Published 2010 by Pyr®, an imprint of Prometheus Books

Inquiries should be addressed to
Pyr
59 John Glenn Drive
Amherst, New York 14228–2119
VOICE: 716–691–0133
FAX: 716–691–0137
WWW.PYRSF.COM

14 13 12 11 10   5 4 3 2 1

Library of Congress Cataloging-in-Publication Data

Chadbourn, Mark.
    The queen of sinister / by Mark Chadbourn.
        p. cm. — (The Dark Age ; bk. 2)
    First published: London : Gollancz, an imprint of Orion Publishing Group, 2004.
    ISBN 978–1–61614–200–1 (pbk.)
    1. Mythology, Celtic—Fiction. I. Title.

PR6053.H23Q44 2010
823'.914—dc22

                                                                            2010006205

Printed in the United States

For Elizabeth, Betsy, and Joe

CONTENTS

ACKNOWLEDGMENTS

Allan Beacham, Labhras de Faoite, Alanna Morrigan, Faith Peters, and the other regular visitors to the Mark Chadbourn message board, and all the many people who've e-mailed me or written to me during the course of the Age of Misrule; Greta for discussions about balance and the Craft; Howard's House Hotel, Salisbury; and finally to the staff of Salisbury Cathedral, who answered all my impertinent questions with good grace.

For more information on the author and his work, please visit:

www.markchadbourn.net

CHRONICLES OF THE FALLEN WORLD

One night, the world we knew slipped quietly away. Humanity awoke to find itself in a place mysteriously changed. Fabulous Beasts soared over the cities, their fiery breath reddening the clouds. Supernatural creatures stalked the countryside—imps and shape-shifters, blood-sucking revenants, men who became wolves, or wolves who became men, sea serpents and strange beasts whose roars filled the night with ice; and more, too many to comprehend. Magic was alive and in everything.

No one had any idea why it happened—by order of some Higher Power, or a random, meaningless result of the shifting seasons of Existence—but the shock was too great for society. All faith was lost in the things people had counted on to keep them safe—the politicians, the law, the old religions. None of it mattered in a world where things beyond reason could sweep out of the night to destroy lives in the blink of an eye.

Above all were the gods—miraculous beings emerging from hazy race memories and the depths of ancient mythologies, so far beyond us we were reduced to the level of beasts, frightened and powerless. They had been here before, long, long ago, responsible for our wildest dreams and darkest nightmares, but now they were back they were determined to stay forever. In the days after their arrival, as the world became a land of myth, these gods battled for supremacy in a terrible conflict that shattered civilisation. Death and destruction lay everywhere.

Blinking and cowed, the survivors emerged from the chaos of this Age of Misrule into a world substantially changed, the familiar patterns of life gone: communications devastated, anarchy raging across the land, society thrown into a new Dark Age where superstition held sway. Existence itself had been transformed: magic and technology now worked side by side. There were new rules to observe, new boundaries to obey, and mankind was no longer at the top of the evolutionary tree.

A time of wonder and terror, miracles and torment, in which man's survival was no longer guaranteed.

chapter one
CROW LIFE

"Life is the saddest thing there is, next to death."
Edith Wharton

Two storms. Without, the night torn asunder by the kind of jungle-beast weather that always marked the passing between winter and spring. Within, a storm of death and despair.

Bodies were heaped around the village hall with the sickening confusion of a medieval charnel house, on parquet flooring that had felt the celebratory tread of weddings and birthdays and anniversaries, and in the annex, obscuring trestle tables that had served a thousand meals and more. Not even the kitchen's no longer sterile work surfaces were free of bodies.

At first, they had been placed in reverent rows, a futile attempt to impose order on an incomprehensible chaos. Eventually, when the full magnitude of what was happening became apparent, they were simply tossed in piles in one corner or another. Before the storm had started, the plan had been to dig individual graves, but those efforts had soon been outpaced. Now there was no hope of catching up. Occasionally their minds turned to the practical options—pit or fire, fire or pit—but the horror was too consuming for rational thought. A part of them knew the corpses would have to be disposed of quickly to prevent the spread of disease—the stench already left them breathless and reeling—but that would mean facing up to what lay around them, seeing and knowing and accepting.

It wasn't just the stink of decomposition that fouled the hall. The corpses leaked a yellowish greasy pus from the suppurating sores where the swellings had blackened and burst like alien fruit. It pooled on the floor and became sticky underfoot, smelling like rotten apples dusted with sulphur. They all had per-fume-soaked handkerchiefs tied across their faces, but that did little to protect them. Worse, they felt as if they were becoming inured to it, the stench becoming, through repetition, as irritating and ignorable as exhaust fumes on a foggy morning.

The storm swirled about them, detaching them from their humanity. Only the moans of the nearly dead, lined up on camp-beds against one wall, reminded them that they were still on earth, not in hell.

There were five of them. Caitlin Shepherd was in charge. She was twenty-eight, but felt as if she'd lived for at least seventy years, her body fragile with weariness, her mind worn by too many nights without sleep, too many days of labour and struggle and heartache from dawn to dusk. The others—the former chairman of the parish council, a teenage boy with a bad case of acne, and two elderly sisters who used to run the post office—were the only ones from the village who were prepared to help. Everyone else still standing had locked themselves in their homes with their families, threatening violence to those stupid enough to come calling.

Caitlin pulled the rubber band from her hair and refastened it. It had become a nervous act, subconsciously distracting her from the futility of what she was doing. The woman on the table in front of her had just expired with a phlegmy rattle. Caitlin had seen her every morning in summer tending her garden, but she couldn't remember her name.

"How many is that tonight?" she asked. It made it easier for her to think in terms of numbers rather than people.

Eileen, one of the sisters, placed a hand on Caitlin's forearm. "Best not to think about it now, dear. You could do with a break."

"How can I take a break?" Sparks flashed across Caitlin's vision and she had to steady herself on the edge of the table.

"You're not going to help anyone by running yourself into the ground," Gideon noted. The council chairman, who no longer had any council members left, had a disgusting smear of dark bodily juices down the front of his shirt that made him look as if he'd been stabbed. "And if we haven't got our doctor, we're nowhere."

In the grim surroundings, Caitlin's laughter sounded even more damning than she had intended. "A doctor's no good if she doesn't know what she's doing. I've never seen this before. It's not in any of the textbooks. As far as I can tell, it's something completely new. I have no idea how to begin treating it . . . antibiotics don't work. All I can do is make people comfortable before they die." And they did die. Always. The initial appearance of the tiny black spots was a death sentence.

She glanced up at the few boxes of medicine left on the shelves. Soon it would all be gone, and with no one manufacturing new drugs in the crisis that had gripped the country since the Fall, they'd be down to bunches of herbs and wishing.

"It's still important to make people comfortable in their last hours," Eileen said gently. "That's a good deed."

"It's not enough." Caitlin tore the useless handkerchief from her mouth and rested her eyes behind her hand. "We'd better get this . . . this lady . . ."

"Mrs. Waid," Eileen prompted.

"Mrs. Waid . . . we'd better get her moved."

"I'll do it," Gideon said. "Timothy, give us a hand!"

The teenager stood shell-shocked, staring out into the rain-lashed night. "There'll be floods along the river," he said, as if it were important.

While Gideon and Timothy carried the blackened, seeping body to the latest pile in the main hall, Eileen gave Caitlin a brief hug. Caitlin was surprised by how comforting it felt.

"You should take a break . . . go back to your husband and son. Family's even more important at times like this," Eileen said.

"I don't know . . ."

"Go on. You said yourself you're not doing anything we can't. Have a good rest, and when you come back we can arrange some kind of rota system."

Caitlin looked into the elderly woman's face, as if seeing her for the first time. "How do you do it?"

"What, dear?"

"Keep going . . . not start wallowing in despair."

Eileen didn't seem to comprehend the question. "It's just what we do, isn't it? There's no point in giving in to it . . . that doesn't do any good at all."

Caitlin took a long, juddering breath. "I think I will go home. Just for an hour or two."

"You do that, dear." Eileen gave her another hug, and this time Caitlin didn't want to break it.

The moment was disrupted by a thin cry from Daphne, Eileen's sister. She was staring at her hands with a shattered expression.

Caitlin knew instantly what it was. "Oh God—"

They rushed to Daphne's side and sure enough the telltale black spots that marked the first appearance of the disease were visible on the wrinkled webbing at the base of her fingers.

Daphne looked up at them both with tearful eyes. "Oh dear . . ."

Eileen wiped away her own tears, but the two of them remained calm. It wasn't as if the development was unexpected—they all knew the risks of contracting the disease. It didn't strike everyone; sometimes just one person in a family, sometimes all of them. Caitlin had no idea of the pathology, but it was a reasonable guess that extended exposure increased the chances of contraction.

Caitlin stared impotently at the thin collection of medicines. Eileen sensed her thoughts. "Don't worry, dear—you go."

"I can't leave now!"

"You know there's nothing you can do, Caitlin." Daphne gave a weak smile, a tear trickling down her cheek.

Daphne was living, breathing, feeling, talking, but she was already dead. Within hours, the fever would hit. She'd lose all contact with the real world, imprisoned in dreams and memories of frightening intensity while the disease worked its insidious route through her system. The spots made strange patterns across the skin before reaching the glands, which swelled, turned black, and filled with pus. Death would come three to four days later without the patient regaining consciousness.

Caitlin felt as if she was being torn apart by her inability to do anything worthwhile. All her years at medical school, in the surgery, all worthless.

"I don't want to leave you to all this," Daphne said pitifully to Eileen, her frail voice betraying the wealth of emotion behind the simple statement. They'd been together all their lives, never married, supported each other through hard times, enjoyed the best, never even known a day apart for decades. And now it was all coming to an end.

Caitlin gave Daphne's arm a squeeze, silently cursing the impotence of the gesture to convey all the razor emotions but not knowing any other way to express them.

"I think we'll have a little time alone, dear," Eileen said, her eyes brimming. She led Daphne away to a quiet corner where they crumpled into each other.

Caitlin watched them with feelings so raw they made her throat burn. That one symbol summed up everything she had felt over the past year: the suffering and the strength, the heartbreak and the hopelessness. The humanity.

Too exhausted to cry, Caitlin pulled her battered all-weather parka on tightly and forced her way out into the storm. The rain was cold and hard, the roaring wind buffeting her. Yet she felt swaddled in cotton wool, and that the harsh, uncompromising world was just a dream.

The sense of unreality had been growing since the Fall. It had started with the government's unspecified announcement of some threat on the home front and the subsequent imposition of martial law and a media blackout. Travel had been limited, and with the telephone network down, the only available information was always leavened with an unhealthy dose of rumour, gossip and downright lies. Newcastle had been wiped out. The Royal Family was in exile. Nuclear disaster, a military coup, an attack by some rogue state—never identified—an epidemic of some awful bioengineered disease. She'd always discounted that last one, but the evidence of the past week had made her think it was probably the truth, or part of it. Perhaps the Fall had been caused by some conglomeration of all the rumours.

Whatever the answer, life in the intervening months had been too hard to give it too much consideration—the first weeks of near starvation when the shops and supermarkets stopped being stocked, the slow crawl to set up the distribution of locally supplied food, and even more months on subsistence level while new sources were established. But slowly, slowly, they had got back on their feet . . . until the plague had come.

She didn't know whether it had swept the country or if it was a localised phenomenon. It had come too fast, too hard, to comprehend.

She bowed her head into the gale and attempted to dodge the puddles, but without streetlights it was a struggle to see. They had some power during the day thanks to a wind turbine erected by a local engineer and solar panels scavenged from a nearby health farm, but it was conserved at night. The national grid hadn't come back online; the nights remained black, friendless, and frightening, filled with all the stories she had heard from the more superstitious residents.

It was just a short walk along the High Street, but then she had to negotiate the winding lane to their barn conversion; she wished they'd bought a place in the centre of the village. When she reached the rutted track, it was even darker than the built-up area, where at least a few candles had glimmered through the window panes. The trees, just coming into bud, pressed tightly on either side, the hedgerows wild and untrimmed.

Before she stepped into the lane, she couldn't help succumbing to the primal desire to glance behind her. It was then that she saw something strange and disturbing. They'd kept the electric lights on at the village hall since they had started using it as an infirmary-cum-mortuary and from her slightly elevated position she could now see the bright windows clearly above the rooftops of the houses at the lower end of the village. Yet when she had turned back, briefly those windows had been obscured. No swaying trees lay in her line of sight; something had passed in front of the hall, but from her perspective she knew it would have to have been something much larger than a person. It was a simple thing, barely worth comment, yet inexplicably it touched a nerve, triggering a ratchet of fear. She hurried along the lane, overhanging branches reaching down to grab at her hood.

The lane was half a mile long, doglegging to the left before rising sharply to the ridge on which the converted barns rested. On the slope it became more exposed to the elements and she had to struggle to make progress against the gale which thrashed the trees on either side. Nothing could be heard above the maelstrom of the storm, yet she couldn't shake the feeling that there had been footsteps, or hoofbeats, on the road behind.

It was irrational, stupid even, but it pulled tingling sparks up from the pit of her belly. She looked back again, and saw nothing but darkness and the movement of shadowy vegetation.

Get off the road! a voice in her head said. The notion was so powerful and so unexpected it was shocking. There was no reason for her to be scared, but then an overwhelming sense of presence came upon her from nowhere, a feeling so frightening that she fought the urge to run. *Someone was behind her.*

She looked back again. The storm rushed all around. Stupid. She was getting as superstitious as some of those villagers who had come to believe there were ghosts and devils and mythical beasts away in the countryside.

When she returned her attention to the path ahead she was startled to see a big black bird standing in the centre of the lane. It was a hooded crow, bigger than any she had ever seen before. That it was there at night, in the middle of a storm, was discomfiting enough, but the way it kept one beady eye fixed on her brought a chill to her spine.

Caitlin took two steps forward to shoo it away, but it still didn't budge. She had never experienced anything so unnatural. Everything about the bird frightened her. She had the uneasy feeling that it wouldn't let her pass. Hesitating, she gave in to her irrationality despite herself and clambered over a gate into a field before moving into the trees that lined the road.

Peering over the hedge, she saw that the crow was no longer there. *Typical*, she thought, uncomfortable as the wet undergrowth soaked her jeans. *That'll teach me to be childish.* Yet the feeling that something was coming up the lane behind her was still growing; goose pimples ran up and down her arms.

Caught in the wind, the trees, bushes, and grass moved with an eerie life of their own. She forced her way through the dripping vegetation, the wind slowly dropping as the storm finally began to move away, the staccato drip of rain from branches the final percussive reminder.

Caitlin realised she was holding her breath; her instinct was responding to something beyond her senses, but whatever was out there gradually crept into the edge of her perception. At first she thought the wind was picking up again, until she noticed that there was structure to the sound.

Whispering, she realised with a strange chill. People talking in rustling voices, yet making no attempt to remain unheard. The conversation floated amongst the trees, insinuating itself within the *drip-drip-drip* of rain, growing louder as it approached.

It sounded so bizarre. Caitlin wondered who would venture out at that time of night in such a fierce storm. The lane only led to four barn conversions and Caitlin couldn't imagine any of her neighbours talking in such a strange manner.

Yet as the whispering intensified, Caitlin realised it was not becoming any more comprehensible. It seemed to her a foreign language, at times like Russian, something northern and guttural, at others incorporating the florid clicks and glottal stops of an African tribal dialect. The hairs on her neck grew erect.

With a feeling of rising dread, she quickly dropped to her haunches, holding her breath tight in her chest. The road was just about visible through the hedge.

The whispering surrounded her like icy fingers playing along her spine. Although she couldn't understand the words, it carried with it an air of menace, cunning and, floating underneath it, something profoundly despairing. The complex sounds did not appear likely to have been formed in a human throat.

The Whisperers were accompanied by a heavy tread that she at first took to be horses, but as the ground began to vibrate at each fall, it became clear something much larger was approaching.

Thoom-thoom-thoom. It made her think of some enormous machine as the tremors ran up into the pit of her stomach.

Nearly here now, she thought. The whispering insinuated into her mind, set her teeth on edge, made her think black thoughts. She was surprised at how scared she felt; not the fear of disease or starvation, but something more profound and unfocused.

Her instinct told her to take no risks of being discovered, but she had to look. Steadying herself with one hand on the sodden ground, she peered through the gaps in the hedge just as movement entered her frame of vision.

She could only perceive glimpses of the whole, a jigsaw puzzle of disturbing fragments that her conscious mind put together despite warnings from her subconscious to leave well alone. There were indeed two riders, but their mounts, though like horses in form, were clearly not: they were much larger, hugely powerful, and appeared to have a scaly hide and cloven hooves. Caitlin tried to rationalise what she was seeing, but could find no context.

She saw even less of the Whisperers, yet obliquely the threat increased. Their legs were unpleasantly thin, as if only bones lay beneath the fluttering rags wrapped around them. What she saw of their clothing only added to her impression: broken chain mail, corroded gauntlets, worn, rotten leather. The heavy aroma of loam hung in the air, as if they had scrambled their way, mounts and all, from beneath the earth.

The sibilant whispering floated all around. Caitlin didn't move, didn't swallow, barely breathed, praying they would pass quickly and take the overwhelming atmosphere of dread with them. Yet just as they were about to move on, they stopped. The whispering died away, and somehow the eerie silence was even worse.

They could sense her. She was sure of it in some instinctive way she couldn't comprehend. Her heart thundered.

The heavy hoofbeats sounded again, this time coming toward the hedge behind which she was hiding. Could they see her? Surely it was impossible in the dark.

The horses that were not horses drew close. Soon the first rider would be able to peer over the top of the hedge. And what awful thing would she see when she looked up into that face?

Desperately, her gaze darted around. She could attempt to run through the thick trees that would preclude the mounts pursuing her, but sooner or later she would have to cross open fields.

Just as she prepared to launch herself into the undergrowth, wild activity erupted further along the lane. It was difficult for Caitlin to comprehend what was occurring: a blood-chilling screaming tore through the night, rapid movement flashed in shadow form, only partially glimpsed through the hedgerow. The Whisperers paused in their advance. It was the crow, Caitlin guessed.

For an agonising moment, Caitlin remained frozen. Then, when she thought she couldn't bear it any longer, the Whisperers guided their grotesque mounts away from the hedgerow into the centre of the lane, and advanced toward the source of the disruption.

Caitlin crouched there shivering for fifteen more minutes before she finally dared move. Keeping low, she followed the hedge for as long as she could and then headed across the dark fields toward the house.

There was no sign of the Whisperers, or of the strange hooded crow.

Caitlin burst through the door as if the Devil were at her heels, locking and bolting it in one fluid movement before hurrying to peer through the curtains into the fading storm. A distant flash of lightning half-illuminated what appeared to be a figure standing amongst the trees just beyond the drive. She had the odd impression that it was a man, yet also that there was something bestial about the figure; in her fleeting glimpse she had seen something that reminded her of a boar's head. Yet as her eyes grew accustomed to the dark after the lightning she could see only a gnarled yew on the spot. An illusion?

"What's going on?" Grant emerged from the kitchen, clutching a tea towel and a dinner plate. He looked tired, the hardship of life since the Fall making him seem older than his thirty years.

She blurted out what she had seen in the lane without taking her eyes off the dark countryside.

"There are nuts all over the place," Grant said with a dismissive weariness before returning to the kitchen. In the midst of her fear, his reaction irritated her, but she understood it: there was only so much energy to go round. What with learning a new trade as a carpenter so that he could contribute to the local economy and earn them food, preparing defences in response to the increasing lawlessness in the countryside and trying to bring up Liam, Grant was almost drained.

Caitlin waited for another couple of minutes and then convinced herself that whatever she had seen out there had moved on. She trailed after Grant, feeling washed out in the come-down from the adrenalin surge. The flickering lanterns gave a dreamlike feeling to the warm kitchen.

"How are things?" Grant replaced the crockery without waiting to hear her response. "I kept some stew for you on the Aga. You know, just in case you ever came home."

The bitterness in his voice sparked a dull flame of anger. Did he think she wanted to be away from her family? Risking her life, under massive stress, getting no rest for days on end? She bit her tongue, knowing nothing good would come from responding.

"This is lovely," she said, dipping into the saucepan with a wooden spoon to taste the stew. "Thanks for making it. I'll get to it once I've seen Liam. He's still up, isn't he?"

"He's in his room." Grant continued putting the crockery away until a restrained thought slipped its leash. "He's missing having you around, you know."

On the surface, it appeared to be such a throwaway comment, but it brought tears to her eyes and a burning to the back of her throat. "I'll see to him." She hurried away before any more turbulent emotions tipped out.

Liam lay in bed in his *SK8board* pyjamas, flicking through an old Digimon annual. With popular culture effectively dead, at least in the short term, old favourites had taken on a new resonance. They'd attempted to keep his bedroom as *normal* as it had been before things had gone so spectacularly wrong: posters on the wall, PS2 on the side, now dormant like some antique radio set.

He jumped up with an energy that made her feel old and weary. "Mummy!" With the overstated passion of the young, he threw his arms around her, and she held him tight, feeling his hair against her cheek, and his warmth and smallness and hardness, blinking back tears, desperately trying to hold in all the things she needed to do to remain a grown-up.

"You're working too hard!" he said. "Daddy says you're going to wear yourself out." He moved over so she could get in bed next to him. "Under the quilt, Mummy. It's all snuggly then." He burrowed in beside her.

"There are a lot of people who need me to help them," she began. "It's Mummy's job and they'd be very sad if she wasn't there to make them better." The hollowness of her words rang in her ears.

"But we need you too, Mummy—Daddy and me."

"I know you do. And I'm here for you, too. Look, I'm here now." She gave him a mock-crushing hug and then let him fight his way free. "Do you want me to read to you?" She picked up the dog-eared copy of *The Hobbit* they'd slowly been making their way through. Caitlin thought she enjoyed it more than Liam; the escapism was even more poignant compared to the world beyond their home.

"No, not tonight," he said, to her disappointment. "Tell me a story."

The rain had started again, pattering insistently against the window. It gave her a false sense of security as she huddled in the warmth beneath the quilt with Liam pressed close beside her, his innocence heady and hopeful. She closed her eyes and dreamed.

"OK," she began, "once upon a time, there was a great and powerful kingdom, where people worked hard and enjoyed themselves when they weren't working, and believed they were the masters of everything. They had great scientists who could see deep into the universe and right down to the smallest atom, and businessmen who could make millions of pounds for the kingdom's coffers, and soldiers with terrible weapons that could destroy any enemy. Or so they thought. And the people were sure that things would keep getting better and better."

"But they didn't, did they?"

"No. One day they woke up and found everything had changed. They weren't the masters of everything anymore. More powerful people had turned up in the night and changed all the rules. The scientists weren't important anymore because suddenly there were things they couldn't explain. And the soldiers discovered that their weapons weren't so powerful after all."

"Who were they? Aliens?" Liam's voice was growing sleepy.

"I suppose you could call them that. Nobody knew what they were really, but they'd been around for a long, long time. They'd been to this . . . this kingdom . . . before, many hundreds . . . thousands . . . of years ago . . . and then everyone thought they were gods. You know, like in Hercules."

"Uh-huh."

"And they brought with them all the magical creatures that children heard about in fairy tales. Everyone had thought those things were made up, but they weren't, they were real . . . only they weren't quite like the stories said. The simple folk of the kingdom had written stories and told tales to try to understand these creatures all those years ago, but the stories had got changed in the telling, with made-up stuff and real stuff getting all mixed up."

Liam's breathing was regular, but Caitlin could feel the faint movement of his facial muscles against her arm as his eyes flickered in response to her words.

"It looked as if the kingdom was going to be destroyed. The government fell apart, and the soldiers were beaten in battle after battle, and nobody knew what to do at all, and nobody even knew how things worked anymore because there was all this . . . magic . . . flying around that they didn't understand. But in times like that—you know, disasters, crises . . ." She was talking to herself now, lost to the images that flashed like jarring lightning strikes across her mind. ". . . it's not the big, important people who save the day—the kings and queens and politicians and generals—it's the normal people. The people who believe in themselves, who believe in good things so much that they'll fight against any danger. And so, five men and women came from nowhere to attack the . . . the . . . gods. Their names were . . ." She struggled to recall the details of the wild story that had been told to her by those superstitious villagers she used to tease. ". . . Church and Ruth and Laura and Ryan and Shavi. And some say they won.

At least, the kingdom wasn't destroyed completely and those gods went off into hiding, but the heroes . . . no one knows what happened to them.

"But things could never be the same again. People still hadn't learned all the new rules, and everything they believed in had been thrown up in the air. They had to start from the beginning once more, trying to make a new . . . a better kingdom for themselves. But it was very, very hard and many hoped—and prayed—that those five heroes . . . if they really existed . . . would come back from wherever they had gone to help again."

A gust of wind against the panes shook her out of her reverie. "That's how the story goes, anyway. Some of it might be true, some of it might be made up, but that's the way with stories." She looked down at Liam and saw that he was fast asleep. *Stories to make the world better*, she thought. *To make us understand the truth behind what's going on.*

Suddenly her thoughts rushed back to the moment of his birth, in St. James's Hospital in Leeds, with Grant there and the sun streaming through the windows. It had been the last time she recalled truly living in the moment, when the experience of what was happening wiped out all conscious thought. The concentrated hope of those few hours, the unshakeable belief that things could only get better, was still so profoundly affecting that she could feel the burn of nascent tears.

Liam had come at a difficult time. She had barely started out on her medical studies, the long road of late nights, dull books, and no spare time stretching out ahead of her. The soul searching and intense debate had overwhelmed them from the moment the home pregnancy test kit had dropped into the waste bin: should Grant's studies as an architect take precedence over her ambitions? Who would give up their dreams to look after Liam? The thought that Liam wouldn't be there was not an option. The length of studies for both their chosen careers meant there would be no going back on the decision; it was a once-only life-defining choice, a sacrifice and a commitment that would have to be forever or lead to a shattering bitterness in later years.

Caitlin had already decided that she was going to give up her path when Grant had called her on her mobile and asked her to meet him in Roundhay Park, where they had gone for their first date, away from the stink of Leeds city centre and the incestuous gossip of the university campus. She had found him sitting in the summery morning sun on the same blanket he had brought to that first picnic, with a basket of bread, cheese, cold meat, and mineral water.

There was something about that moment—the quality of light, the smell of warm vegetation, the enigmatic turn of his smile and the openness in his eyes— that had crystallised her feelings, and she knew that she loved him and there would be no need for anyone else, ever. It would be just the two of them, just the three of them, and it wasn't frightening at all; it felt right.

"I'm doing the baby stuff," he had said before she could sit down.

"No." She had tried to wave him silent. "I've already decided—"

"I knew you'd try to talk me out of it, which is why I've already sold all my books and drawing equipment and officially quit. No going back."

"Grant!" she had said, horrified.

"Let's face it, Caitlin, the most I'll ever be is average. You're brilliant. It has to be me."

She had looked him in the eyes, dumbfounded. "You wanted it more than me. You know you did."

"Then you owe me big time." He had smiled, opening the mineral water, which fizzed loudly, sparkling in the sun. She'd shed a few tears, which she'd hidden away from him to avoid his merciless teasing, but for the first time she had been convinced that everything was going to be just right.

When Caitlin slipped out of Liam's bedroom, Grant was sitting at the kitchen table with a glass of homemade beer, looking exhausted. She felt drained herself, but after the brief respite with Liam, the harsh reality of the plague crowded her thoughts once more. Since the Fall, the local community had come to rely on her more than she had ever dreamed when she was a simple GP. In a world suddenly chaotic, she was a symbol of stability, a wise woman who could offer advice while curing all their ills. They demanded more of her than she could possibly give—as the only doctor working the area she was on call 24/7—but her sense of responsibility overrode every desire she had to escape from the position.

In the lounge, she plucked a pile of medical textbooks from the bookshelf and took them to the table where the lantern flickered. Over the last few months she'd amassed quite a library to fill the gaps in her education, but nowhere had she managed to find any reference to an illness that resembled the symptoms of the plague. Some aspects reminded her of what she had read about the bubonic plague, yet the speed and the black discoloration were more reminiscent of the septicaemic plague, which had been much rarer during the Middle Ages but was transmitted by the same *Yersinia pestis* bacterium. Like the current outbreak, it had a near one hundred percent fatality rate and, worryingly, no treatment had ever been found.

Yet the septicaemic plague's discoloration, which gave the Black Death its name, was caused by disseminated intravascular coagulation, visible over wide areas of the skin and certainly not in the remarkably regular lines of this disease. Caitlin could find no evidence for the cause of that symptom in any of her autopsies.

She wondered if it was some obscure tropical illness—certainly, the ferocity of its assault on the human system matched that of the Ebola virus—but even if she could identify it, there was little she could do without access to a lab or scientific expertise and the minimal medication she had at hand.

It had appeared in the village as if from nowhere. She had been called out in the early hours of one morning to treat a farmer who had gone down with the warning-sign black dots and raging fever. The farmer had been away at a market in Fordingbridge trying to organise another branch of the food-distribution system, but had not mentioned anything to his family about illness on his return.

Within a day, incidences of the disease cropped up rapidly throughout the village. Caitlin had attempted to track the spread, but it was soon apparent that it was striking down people who had had no contact. The only explanation was that it was airborne—a worst-case scenario that was devastating in its implications. With no national communication system available since the Fall, outside information was thin, but by that time she was knee-deep in the dead and the dying and she had no time for anything but disposal.

"What are you doing?"

She started. Grant was at the door, holding his glass of beer. She couldn't see his face in the shadows. "Just some research. If I could pin down the genotype of the plague it might point—"

"We haven't seen you in days. Can't you give it a rest just for tonight?"

She recognised the tone in his voice and knew what was to come. "Grant—"

"No. Don't give me all the excuses again. You're barely a part of this family—"

"I've got responsibilities!" Her voice snapped and tears of frustration sprang to her eyes. She'd told herself she'd remain calm and she'd barely lasted a few seconds; the unbearable stress she was under forced everything up against her skin, trying to break out of her.

"You've got responsibilities to us." Grant was cold and distant, but anger bubbled just beneath the surface.

Caitlin stared at the textbook illustration of a virus, something so deadly stripped down to a cartoon. She'd heard the argument so many times recently in so many different tones, from despairing to furious, that she really didn't have the energy for such a futile exercise.

"Yes, people need their doctor," Grant continued. "But we need you, too. You're never here anymore. You never even think about us when you're out—"

"How do you know what I think?" She winced; too combative—it would only notch the argument up to another level.

"I know. I can see it in every part of you . . . in everything you do. We're just here in the background. You don't give us any time, you don't give us any thought. We're not important. Why can't you forget about your job for a while?"

"Because people are dying out there!"

"People are dying in here . . . getting older . . . time running away . . ." Resentment rose up in him, old arguments running round and round in a Moebius strip, never answered or explained.

"You know what I mean," she replied sullenly.

"We never even have sex anymore—"

"Oh, God, if I hear that one more time—"

"I'm not just talking about the sex! It's symptomatic of everything else. It's about intimacy, being close to someone you love . . ." He slammed the glass down on a table, slopping beer everywhere.

"I'm too tired to have sex!" The emotion burst out in a tidal wave. "I'm worn out by everything . . . too frightened . . . too . . . oh, it doesn't matter!"

The brief silence that followed her outburst was filled with her guilt, and then anger that she'd given in to her emotions.

"What's happened to us, Caitlin?" Grant's voice was like glass. "We never celebrate what we've got . . . we just exist. Before, we used to celebrate all the time—"

"Before, before, before, that's all you ever talk about!"

"Listen to me!" he snapped. "We've got to do something to put this right, or—"

"Or what?" She slammed out of her chair and stormed across the room. "Or what? You'll leave me? Go on, then!"

She pushed past him, snatched up her coat, and marched out into the night.

Distant flashes of lightning burst intermittently across the sky. There was no rain, but the wild wind still made the trees around the barns sway and moan as if they were alive. Caitlin threw herself into the gale, lost to emotions that felt as if they were tearing her apart. She didn't even think about what she had glimpsed in the lane earlier, or the plague and the suffering.

Ten minutes later she realised where her subconscious was driving her. The windows of Mary Holden's house were aglow with the ruddy light of a fire. The white cottage stood on the edge of the village, camouflaged by several years' growth of clematis and surrounded by a garden so wild it clamoured on every side as if it was trying to break into the warmth.

Caitlin felt bad about calling at so late an hour, but Mary had proved a good friend throughout the difficult months since the Fall and would understand.

Mary answered Caitlin's knock quickly and ushered her in. "What are you doing out in weather like this?" she said. Mary was in her early sixties but looked much younger: her long grey hair had a lustre and was tied into a ponytail with a black ribbon; she wore faded blue jeans and a too-large white T-shirt that looked as if it had been in the wash with the colours. "Have you run out of supplies?" she continued. "I've got a new batch of herbs in. Haven't had a chance to dry them yet, though."

"No, it's just . . ." Caitlin suddenly couldn't stop the tears from streaming down her cheeks.

"What is it, love?" Mary put an arm round Caitlin's shoulders and led her toward the pleasant heat of the wood fire. The house had an exotic spicy aroma from the herbs and wild plants Mary collected to turn into potpourri or incense, her dining room packed to the brim with jars of the dried produce. Mary knew everything there was to know about their medicinal uses and regularly supplied Caitlin with mysterious bunches of crispy vegetation to boost the surgery's dwindling medicinal stocks. The remarkable success rate of remedies made up from her scrawled notes had led Caitlin to come to trust her judgment.

At first Caitlin couldn't get her words out—the tears wouldn't stop, her throat appeared to have closed up—so she sat on the old, comfy sofa in front of the hearth while Mary went into the kitchen to make her an herbal tea.

"Here you are." Mary offered a cracked mug. "Probably tastes like shit, but you won't get much better anywhere else these days."

"Sometimes I wonder why I carry on," Caitlin said. "There's no point. To anything."

"Now you know that's not true." Mary stretched out next to her like a cat. "There's a point to everything, even if you can't see it. But that's not what you want to hear, is it? What's wrong?"

Mary radiated an atmosphere of peace that Caitlin found eminently comforting. In a way, Mary was her equal in the eyes of the community. Most of the villagers had found their way to Mary's door at some time or other, and with increasing regularity, seeking wisdom or herbal remedies that they couldn't get from Caitlin. Finally, it was Caitlin's turn; and so she spoke about the plague, and her fears that it could wipe out the population, and her guilt that she couldn't do anything about it. And against her better judgment, she talked of Grant and the growing gulf between them, and how their relationship appeared to be sliding away, though neither of them wanted that to happen.

Mary listened intently, nodding at the right points. When Caitlin had finished, Mary smiled a little sadly and said, "You've got it all on your plate, haven't you? Stronger women than you would buckle under that kind of pressure. You mustn't feel bad about taking a few knocks."

"Well, I do. People are relying on me."

"You're not Supergirl, you know." Mary's black cat startled them both, leaping onto her lap from the shadows beside the sofa. Mary had named him Arthur Lee after some sixties singer she admired.

"What am I going to do?" Caitlin asked.

"I hate to say this, but I agree with Grant."

Caitlin eyed her suspiciously.

"This life is all about maintaining a balance. You're completely out of whack at the moment. Too much yin, not enough yang. You're not going to do anybody any good by running yourself into the ground."

"I feel too worn out—"

"Then you'd better unwear yourself. These are hard times, Caitlin, but they've been worse . . . not for us, but in the past. It's easy to give in to all the misery, when what we really should be doing is enjoying life. Because we still can." Mary chewed her lip in thought for a moment before adding, "And if you don't mind me sticking my nose in, you should start sleeping with Grant again."

Caitlin looked up sharply; she hadn't mentioned that aspect to Mary.

"Come on. It's obvious." She cracked her knuckles like a docker. "Sometimes it's hard to find the energy, but it rewards you if you can. Sex is the glue of relationships, Caitlin, and it's what life is all about. It's the opposite of death, of giving up, of getting swamped by . . ." She waved a hand toward the window. ". . . what's out there. See it as symbolic."

"That's one line the boys never used."

They laughed together, wrapped in the firelight and the warmth, the wind bucking with irritation at the panes.

"I appreciate this, Mary. At this time of night—"

"You know you're the daughter I never had," Mary said sardonically.

"No, really."

"I'm a sucker for waifs and strays." Arthur Lee settled in her lap so Mary could scratch behind his ears. "We have to pull together, in a way we never did before."

Mary was serious and thoughtful, and Caitlin felt calmer simply being around her. Mary was one of those people who felt so much bigger than the actual space they filled. "You really think it's worth it?"

"The clock's been set back. We've got a big opportunity to put things right this time."

"You're saying all the death and the suffering are worthwhile?"

"That's the wrong word. But we can't see the big picture—we're too close to it. I know this: the world we had before wasn't all it was cracked up to be. People just . . . existed. They weren't really happy. They worked, and got more possessions than their parents had, and lived a few years longer, but they weren't really happy. Everything in society was just geared toward maintaining that system . . . keeping the *status quo* . . . because there were a lot of people who *really* benefited from it. Everybody else just drifted along. Is that living?"

"Tell that to the bodies stacked up in the village hall. I bet they'd prefer a touch of the old life, however dull it was."

Mary smiled, but not in agreement. She pushed Arthur Lee off her lap and went to a cupboard containing a row of dog-eared vinyl records. "They're all useless now," she said, "but I keep them for what they mean . . . good mojo." She laughed as she flicked through the rack and selected one, which she handed to

Caitlin. It was called *Forever Changes* by some band called Love and the cover featured a collection of psychedelically coloured heads against a white background.

"Never heard of them," Caitlin said, not quite understanding the point. "The last music I remember hearing was *doves*."

"They were around in the midsixties," Mary said. "They had an underground following but never really broke through into the big time because they refused to get involved in all the corporate bullshit. They were quite brilliant. Anyway, there was a quote about them that's always stuck in my mind. It said something like, 'Love perfectly captured the combination of beauty and dread that was around in the sixties.' That's what we've got now, beauty and dread."

"Not so much of the beauty."

"It's there, if you can see past the mud and the shit and the dying. In a way, this time is a lot like the sixties." Caitlin's disbelieving expression made Mary laugh. "It was a crucial time . . . when everything was poised. Young people, for once, were on the brink of shaping society. Not old farts like me. Young people—younger than you. There was a move away from repression toward freedom . . . hope and optimism. The occult—magic, if you like—was back in the mainstream, and a real honest-to-goodness spirituality came with it. For a moment it seemed as if that was the way things were going to go . . . toward a new Golden Age."

"Then human nature kicked in."

"Oh, you are a cynic," Mary chided. "No, it wasn't that. Human nature is basically what I've just told you—good stuff . . . hope . . . freedom . . . people looking for magic in their lives. But there's a tiny group who always manage to worm their way to the top. You wouldn't look twice at them in the street—they're boring, fade into the background. But they're cursed with having no imagination, and that's a terrible thing. If you've got imagination, you worry about people's feelings because you can put yourself in their shoes, you worry about your place in the world . . . in history. These people somehow know they're lacking because they've got no imagination, so they try to fill in what's missing with power—and because they've got no imagination, they'll do anything to get to the top. No scruples."

"Is this your conspiracy theory?" Caitlin said with a wry smile.

"No conspiracy. They stand there in plain sight, but you never think badly of them because they're so boring. They were the ones who killed Kennedy—both of them—Martin Luther King, John Lennon, gave Charlie Manson the wrong direction, blew apart all the protests against the Vietnam War, ruined the hippie movement. They're the ones who killed the sixties."

Caitlin waved her away with a chuckle.

"You can laugh, my girl, but it's true. Those people don't like all the positive things, all that light and freedom and hope, because in that sort of atmosphere they can't exist. They're shown up for what they really are. With the country upside down . . . the government nowhere to be seen . . . we're at a point where we can go in that right direction again, if a few good people lead the way. But those shadow-people are only lying low, and I'm betting you they'll soon rear up their ugly, boring heads and try to stop us getting some good out of all this shit."

Caitlin looked into the heart of the fire, smiling. The more she learned about Mary, the more she liked her. Mary was an odd mixture of hardness from her days as a psychiatric nurse, and optimism, which she often hid in order to maintain her tough image. Caitlin could listen to her talk all day. But when Caitlin looked up to see Mary watching her with concern, it was clear that Mary had only set off on her impassioned discourse to take Caitlin's mind off her problems.

"I saw something earlier." Caitlin struggled to find the words to describe her chilling experience in the lane. "There were two men on horses. I got the impression they were hunting." She eyed Mary cautiously. "Only I'm not so sure they were men. Or horses for that matter. I know it sounds stupid . . ."

"The world's gone crazy in a lot of different ways, Caitlin." Mary went over to the window to peer out into the turbulent night. "Some of the things out there . . ."

"You believe all that stuff—all the superstitious rubbish people keep going on about in the village?"

Mary turned back to her; for the first time her face was impossible to read. "Don't you?"

"No." Caitlin broke her gaze and returned her attention to the fire, unable to accept what she saw in Mary's eyes. "It's just a human reaction to all the upheaval. When you're trapped in chaos that makes no sense, it's easy to return to childish ways, believing it's all the result of some supernatural power . . . God, gods, angels, ghosts—"

"What did you see tonight?" Mary asked pointedly.

"I don't know."

"You do, Caitlin. It's not rational to deny the evidence of your eyes."

"Really, I don't know what I saw. It was dark, stormy . . . It just didn't feel right . . ."

Mary fished a bottle of Jack Daniel's from the sideboard. "Gary Smedley offered it to me in return for dispensing something to help him sleep. So who am I to say no," she said wryly. She poured two shots and handed one to Caitlin before joining her on the sofa. "Look," she began, "I know you're a down-to-earth sort, so there's no point me testing your credulity with all the wild and woolly theories as to what caused this whole mess. But you can't deny that people have been seeing things—"

"I don't deny that people *think* they've been seeing things."

"You really do have a poker up your arse, don't you?" Mary knocked back the shot. "At the risk of souring our friendship, then, let me tell you that my family always believed they were gifted with what they called the *sight* . . . second sight."

"Oh, they could see the future." Caitlin smiled superciliously. "Did they win the lottery?"

"Not just the future, missy. Ooh, you really are asking for a clip round the ear." She poured herself another drink. "They . . . *believed* . . . they could see things happening at a distance, too, and the past . . . Anyway—"

"And you've got it." Caitlin laughed. "Do you want to read *my* palm, too?"

There was silence for a few seconds, and when Caitlin looked up Mary was deathly serious. "I can do a lot of things you'd be surprised about."

"Go on, then." Caitlin shrugged. "I could do with some entertainment."

Mary shook her head, thought for a moment, and then recanted. She disappeared toward the kitchen and returned with a large glass bowl half filled with water that shimmered in the firelight. Despite herself, Caitlin was growing intrigued.

"Have you heard of scrying?" Mary asked.

"What's that? A new sport?" Caitlin poured herself another drink, enjoying the fuzzy edge of detachment that the Jack Daniel's gave her.

"It's a trick to contact the subconscious. You stare into a bright, mirrored surface—in this case, water—and try to reach a trance state. And then spout whatever rubbish comes to mind."

"How will I tell when you're under?" Caitlin teased.

Mary waved her silent with mock-weariness, then placed the bowl on a coffee table in front of the fire. "I use it sometimes to try to . . . understand what's going on with this world." Caitlin was puzzled to see a shadow cross Mary's face. "We might find something that would comfort you." She winced. "That's probably not the right word . . . something that might give you a bit of perspective, perhaps."

"You're serious?"

"No talking now." Mary gave a smile, but there was a weight behind it that made Caitlin obey instantly.

Silence descended on the room beyond the crackling of the fire; even the gale at the window seemed to abate. Mary leaned over the bowl and stared into the depths of the water. Caitlin watched her for a while until her attention drifted to the fire and then to the patterns made by the occasional raindrops trickling down the panes. She thought of Liam, snuggled up in his bed, and then of Grant. The lucidity surprised her; she saw past the last few years and was overcome with a surprising rush of warm memories, all the reasons why she had fallen in love, the gentleness, the humour, the way she always felt secure around him. It left her with a deep regret that she had run out in such a temper. She'd make it up to him when she got back; perhaps they'd even have sex. If he was asleep, she could wake him . . .

"I see something." Mary's voice was dreamy. Her eyes flickered in the depths of a trance. "I see . . ." Her words floated languidly.

Caitlin leaned in closer, curious to hear what she had to say.

"I see . . ."

At first Caitlin wondered if Mary was playing a joke to distract her; it was the kind of thing she would do. But there was a strange cast to her face, muscles held in an unnatural position, that suggested it was real.

"I see a dragon," Mary said dreamily. "Lying in the land. It stirs . . . a trail . . . blue . . . so blue."

Her words brought a tingle to Caitlin's skin. Though she couldn't explain why, she felt a strange connection.

"It's rising . . . on powerful wings . . . above the land now . . . changing . . . changing . . . becoming . . . Caitlin . . ."

Caitlin shivered. Instinctively, she was sure there was some meaning hidden in it.

"And now changing again . . . Caitlin becoming the dragon once more . . . and flying . . . flying over the land . . ."

A spasm crossed Mary's face. After the stillness it was like a bolt, jerking Caitlin out of her intense concentration.

Mary's voice dropped to the barest whisper. "Something is watching . . . in the night sky . . . like a hole in everything . . . so deep . . . it goes on forever . . . it's sending out . . . things . . . to hunt . . . the dragon . . . Caitlin . . . to destroy her . . ."

Mary threw her head back as if someone had grabbed her shoulders and hurled her against the sofa. Her mouth sagged, her eyes wide and staring, fixed on some spot on the ceiling. She didn't look like Mary at all.

Caitlin jumped in shock. "Mary . . . ?"

Before she could act, Mary began to speak. At first it was just a mumble, barely audible. But as Caitlin leaned in to hear, the words came out loud and clear. Yet it wasn't Mary's voice. A deep masculine rumble reverberated through it, distorted as though it came from the depths of a well. Caitlin's blood ran cold. It was no trick.

"You have been noticed." There was a long pause as phlegm rattled in Mary's throat. "It is coming."

Caitlin shivered at the growling old-man voice. *Who had been noticed?* Her second question made a cold shadow move in her heart: *And what was coming?*

Mary turned her head slightly so that her staring, unseeing-yet-seeing eyes were fixed firmly on Caitlin. "The Lament-Brood is stalking. They smell your soul." Another phlegm-rattle. "They will have you, Sister of Dragons. There is no running."

Drool ran from the corner of Mary's mouth as tiny tremors rippled through the muscles of her face. Caitlin grabbed Mary's shoulders, afraid that she was on the brink of a fit.

There was an instant when Mary's body went rigid, but then she relaxed, her head sagged, and a cloudy, frightened consciousness surfaced in her glassy eyes. She tried to speak, but the words caught in her throat.

"Just take it easy," Caitlin said, not really understanding what had happened.

Mary shoved her aside with one flapping arm and reached for the Jack Daniel's bottle. She poured herself a shot with shaking hands and downed it in one go.

"What was that?" Caitlin asked once Mary had calmed a little.

"It's never been that strong before," Mary said weakly. "Things have been more focused since the Fall, but that . . ." She took Caitlin's hand firmly. "I think there's trouble coming."

"You mentioned my name." Caitlin's thoughts were too jumbled under the geological layers of stress of numerous tensions. She collapsed back into the sofa, trying not to cry. "I can't take any more. Really." The pity she saw in Mary's face made it even worse.

"Have another drink."

Caitlin shook her head. "What just happened?"

"Nothing. Just . . . silliness." Her expression gave the lie to her words.

"Nothing makes sense anymore." Caitlin dried her eyes with the back of her hand and stood up. "I'd better be going. I have to call in at the . . . the village hall." She'd wanted to say surgery, but had almost said morgue. "They need my help."

"I need to . . . think about what just happened, Caitlin," Mary said gravely. "But I'll come looking for you when I've worked out what it all meant."

Caitlin forced a smile. "It'll wait till morning, I'm sure. I'm not going to stay at the hall for long. I want to get back home."

Mary saw her to the door, but just as she was stepping out into the gale, Mary gave her a fierce hug in an unprecedented show of physical affection. "Look after yourself," she said. Then, "Be careful."

It sounded like a warning.

As Caitlin entered the foul atmosphere of the village hall, Gideon greeted her with a sad expression and nodded to one of the side rooms. Through the gap in the door, Caitlin could see Eileen sitting hunched beside her sister, holding her hand loosely. Daphne was lying on a table, already comatose and sleek with sweat. The black mottling was visible in contours on her face and forearms like some Maori tattoo. Caitlin couldn't believe the speed with which the plague attacked the body.

Was this the end of the world? she wondered. Humanity wiped out in a matter of weeks, nature clearing the decks ready for the next phase? It seemed so unfair after all they'd endured during the last few months: they had escaped the bang, only to be done for by the whimper.

There was nothing she could say to Eileen, so she left her to her grief. No more new patients were being brought in, so she retired to the office, grateful for a moment of privacy to try to make some sense of the illness. Frantically scrawled notes on sickeningly stained paper were scattered all over the desks, while charts and graphs were pinned to the cork board next to a yellowing announcement of some pre-Fall Best-Kept Village contest.

Caitlin still nurtured a desperate hope that if she kept turning over all the details, sooner or later she'd hit upon some startling insight that would reveal the plague's true nature. But the mechanics of transmission escaped her; the whole epidemiological nature of the disease was a complete mystery. Were some people genetically predisposed to contracting it? Perhaps even for those like herself who appeared immune, it was just a matter of time.

She tried to focus on the positive, but everything pointed toward the unthinkable: at best, humanity stripped back to a handful of survivors. At worst: the end. She stared at the mass of notations and scribblings and felt the waves of despair break against her. It was all chaos. All too much, with no time to make sense of it.

Liam was still in his bed. Grant was fast asleep, too. Relieved, she went into the kitchen and poured herself a glass of beer. She hated the taste of it, but at least it anaesthetised her. Finally, she had calmed enough to go to bed. She would wake Grant, she thought, and they would make love, and the world and all its hideous threats would be forgotten.

Her desperation for something life affirming made Caitlin as drunk as the alcohol. She slipped into the dark bedroom and pulled off her clothes, her awkwardness dissipating in the heat of her rapid arousal. Grant was dead to the world, but she knew how to wake him. She found his chest and moved her hand toward his groin.

It took a second or two before the sensations told her something was wrong. Grant's skin felt waxy and feverish, and there was a puddle of sweat near his belly button. For the first time, she listened to his breathing: it was shallow and laboured.

"Grant?"

Her mind became a mad jumble of thoughts: flashes of worst-case scenarios, quickly suppressed, prayers, memories, oddly settling on the time when he had proposed to her, when everything had been perfect. Deep in her heart, she knew the truth, and she thought the rush of brutal emotion would drive her mad.

She jumped from the bed, cursing the lack of electricity, and raced to fetch the candle from the hall. Shielding it with her hand, she closed her eyes briefly before she dared take that first look. The pain was as sharp as if she'd been physically struck. In the candlelight, Grant's skin looked hoarfrost-white, only emphasising the black mottling running in lines all over him. Pretending she was doing something worthwhile, she checked his pulse and then opened his eyelids.

He wouldn't regain consciousness. She'd already felt his final kiss, shared her last words with him—and what had they been? The bitterness and anger of their parting brought another stab of pain. Amidst the cold depths of her despair, she felt a burst of self-loathing, but it only had a second of life before another thought struck her, just as terrible. And then she had the candle and was into the hall, hovering outside Liam's door, whispering, "Please, God, please, God, please, God," not daring to go in, thinking she might actually go mad there and then from the sight she was projecting.

But the reality was much, much worse. Liam lay in his bed, the sheets tucked up, just as she had left him, just before the goodnight kiss. His skin was white. And black.

The storm outside had broken, but the one within would rage forever.

chapter two

ALONE AGAIN OR

"Parting is all we know of heaven,
And all we need of hell."
Emily Dickinson

T he night never ended.

All thoughts and fears, grief and desperation were purged from Caitlin as she lost herself in the constant round of mundane tasks necessary during the last few days: the sheet changing, the bed washing, the administration of what sparse painkillers she had to hand, but most of all the talking. She would sit at their bed-sides for hours at a time, letting the words come from the depths of her mind and heart, a trance state in which she had no idea what she was saying. Part of it was a simple attempt to impose order on a situation that had none, a discussion of the mundane chores as if Grant and Liam were both up and about, just out of sight, ready to respond once they had finished whatever they were doing.

And she talked and talked so they wouldn't have the opportunity to respond; if they couldn't get a word in, there was still the possibility that they might. And at other times, she spoke of her love for them both, that deep, deep well of emo-tion that she hadn't visited for a long time, and which surprised her with the volume it contained.

And there was the tragedy, for it shouldn't have surprised her at all. She didn't know if they could hear her, didn't really know if it was for their benefit or her own, but she hoped and prayed, and talked.

And on the fourth day, they died.

The first hour was one of utmost peace, a chrysalis state of numbness and nothing. Caitlin was gone; her life was over. Afterward, she sat by Grant and thought of what had been lost, never to be regained; and then she sat by Liam and considered what might have been and now never would.

Then she retired to the kitchen and brewed herself a pot of the infusion they laughingly used to call tea as the thin light of a cold, grey dawn gradually leaked through the windows. Hunched over her mug, she saw Grant and Liam's shoes next to the back door, muddy from their last walk together as a family. The image hit her with an inexplicable power, and then she was sucked away in an uncontrollable torrent of grief that dashed her on the rocks of her own bitter sorrow.

*

Shortly after noon, in a light rain with the clouds shimmering like silver, Caitlin took a spade into the garden they had all tended in the days before the Fall. At the end, underneath the gnarled oak where Liam had climbed and Grant had built a tree house, she dug. The topsoil went down for two feet and then she hit the thick, yellow-grey clay, water-sodden and dense. Her muscles burned and her joints cracked and complained, yet she forced herself on, relishing the pain. The rain plastered her hair against her head and soaked through her clothes so completely that she felt as if she were wearing water.

Grant, holding her hand when the tiny, warm bundle of life was placed on her sweat-streaked chest, saying, "We're in this together. You never have to stand alone again." Holding her on New Year's Eve, watching the fireworks light the sky.

And when she had finished one hole, she started on the next, a smaller one.

Liam, three years old, at Christmas, putting out a mince pie for Santa. Waking her up on her birthday with a present he'd wrapped himself and a home-made card. Kissing her cheek when he caught her crying . . .

Three hours later, the job was done. She returned to the house in a dream, where nothing could touch her, and was content with that state. But the moment she attempted to lift Grant from the bed, she realised it was only transitory. His skin was cold and he didn't respond when she said his name; he would never answer. It looked like Grant, but it didn't feel like him, not warm, not loving, not laughing anymore; it made no sense, and that only made things worse.

The tears came again, this time squeezing out silently to run into the corners of her mouth, where the saltiness made her feel sick. He was too heavy for her to carry. She fell twice, smashing his head against the bedside cabinet. His arms and legs wouldn't go where she wanted. With a tremendous effort, she managed to get him half onto her back, and then she dragged him from the room, crying out every time some part of him cracked against a door jamb or piece of furniture, as if he could still feel.

Outside, she slipped and dropped him on the wet lawn. After all her struggling, it was the last straw. She knelt down and sobbed as if it were the end of the world. But once those tears had gone, she began again, struggling to get him up, slipping and sliding in the mud of the churned-up turf, falling again, twisting her ankle. At one point his cheek rested gently against hers, and the rain running down his face made it feel as if he was crying, too.

Her mind began to fracture into unconnected fragments of thoughts, so that it seemed as if time was no longer running correctly. She was on the grass with him, staring up at the clouds. She was at the end of the lawn with Grant hanging from her back. She was standing at the edge of the grave. She was looking down at Grant's jumbled body at the bottom of the hole, thinking, "Why doesn't he get up? I'll never get the clay out of that shirt."

And then she went back for Liam, and he was easier to carry. But at the grave, she couldn't bear to drop him in. She hugged him to her breast, kissing him repeatedly, and she would have stayed there forever if the universe hadn't told her what needed to be done.

The edge of the grave crumbled and they tumbled into the hole together, crashing into the pool of muddy water at the bottom with a great splash that filled her mouth and nostrils. The clay covered her from head to foot so that she resembled some wild prehistoric woman. And still she held Liam, his body so small, his clothes soaked, and she prayed that she would feel some warmth, that the world would turn back, that everything would fall apart and drift away.

She stayed there, while water puddled in the bottom and slowly worked its way up her legs, as the barely light day faded and darkness crept in from the east. Her thoughts continued to shred. Nothing was worse than what she had endured. The rest of the human race could all die, scythed down by the plague; she didn't care. Nothing was important anymore. It should all come to a stop.

Fragments . . .

At some point, when the night was riven by lightning, she crawled out and found the spade. Every time she thought she'd endured the worst, something even more terrible would rise up. Seeing the first shovelful fall on them broke her into even smaller pieces. It was her husband and son and she was sealing them beneath the earth. The soil landed with a hollow thud on an unmoving chest. She waited for a complaint—"*Mummy, what are you doing?*"—but none came.

Lying on the wet, packed mud, the rain splattering over her, taking everything away.

Another crack of lightning, dragging her from the nothing. A strange sensation: weight on her chest. Opening her eyes so that the rain sloughed off from where it had settled in the hollows. A large hooded crow, oddly familiar, sat on her breastbone, its beady black eyes glimmering only inches from her face. Talons dug into her skin. The blue-black beak was long and cruel. Did it think she was dead? Was it searching for carrion? It only had to lean forward to peck out her eyes.

But instead of attacking, it only watched. Was she dreaming?

It shuffled back and pecked her chest, not so hard that it hurt, or perhaps she was just too numb to feel. Only it didn't stop; the pecks continued rhythmically, as if it were trying to crack her open. It was so large that the weight of it was making it difficult for her to breathe. She should wave it away, only there was no point.

She closed her eyes, drifting into the rainfall once again.

Mary had a bad feeling. For three days, the cards had hinted at something dark: an ending, or a new beginning—both the same as far as the universe was concerned. She wished she could get whatever powers she was tapping into to see things from the low-down human perspective once or twice: they might look the same, but they certainly didn't *feel* the same.

She'd tried scrying, but had found it difficult to reach the trance state, and for some reason her thoughts kept coming back to Caitlin.

On edge and unable to settle, Mary swigged back the whiskey with blatant disregard for its rarity in the new world, but she knew she wouldn't be able to rest until she'd been to see her friend. She threw another log on the fire to keep it going until she returned, and then put on her anorak. She was sick of the damp weather; it felt as if it had been raining for months.

The weather affected her mood badly. She had always been prone to depression, Churchill's black dog following her wherever she went, but in the dark, dismal days it was worse. She couldn't stop her mind from turning to the past, what was and what might have been. Would things have been different if she'd settled down with someone? Or would she still have disliked herself so much, and in doing so made her partner's life a misery too? She'd always thought she was best on her own—save wrecking another life—but she missed a touch, a word on awakening, the warmth of another mind, little comforts as much as the big ones.

She still marvelled at how life can pivot on one simple event. How arrogance could turn to guilt, youthful optimism to self-loathing, all in the blink of an eye. Sometimes she liked to blame her childhood religion for programming her to carry her suffering with her, but her inability to get over who she had been didn't have one source; it was an accretion of tiny failures. A life, to all intents and purposes, wasted. Her first religion had told her everyone had a reason for being. She was the example that gave the lie to that little fantasy.

As she searched for the old miner's Davy lamp that had belonged to her father, she heard a noise outside. It could have been the wind gusting at the shed door or the broom falling over at the back of the house, but her spine tingled nonetheless. Any visitors—and she had many, wanting advice and help at all hours of the day—would come straight to the front door. The sound had come from the side of the house.

Her nerves went on edge. With the breakdown in law and order, there were plenty of threats that wouldn't think twice about attacking a woman on her own.

The village had its own Neighbourhood Watch patrolling during the night, but it had been devastated by the plague, might even have gone completely.

From next to the door, she grabbed the brush handle with the carving knife strapped to the end. One she could probably see off; any more and she would have to run. Cautiously, she approached the side window.

The night was too dark, the storm bending the trees and hedges toward the cottage, the fields beyond impenetrable. She waited patiently for any hint of movement. Nothing came.

Just as she had convinced herself that she had been mistaken, a lightning flash exploded everything into white. A large figure was standing beneath the old hawthorn tree just outside. It had been watching her looking out.

She swore in shock, backed away, and almost fell over the armchair. The darkness concealed the figure once again.

Mary moved to the centre of the room, turning back and forth in case the watcher came through the front or the back. A heavy knock sounded at the door.

"Who's there?" she shouted defiantly.

"I was sent to see you." The voice was loud, confident, educated with a hint of arrogance.

"Why are you skulking around outside?"

"I wanted to be sure I had the right place." Exasperation, a hint of annoyance; Mary eased a little. He didn't sound like a threat, but then who did? "Will you open this door?" he snapped. "I've been walking for hours and I'm cold and I'm wet."

Holding the homemade spear ahead of her, she leaned forward and turned the key. Standing on the step was a tall, big-boned man in a sodden overcoat and a wide-brimmed felt hat that had almost lost its shape in the rain; he was carrying a knapsack and a staff. He was in his late fifties, with long, wiry, once-black hair and beard, now turning grey and white. The skin of his cheeks had the leathery, broken-veined appearance of someone who enjoyed a drink, but his eyes were beady, black, and unfriendly.

Mary prodded the spear toward his chest. He looked down at it contemptuously.

"Are you the witch?" he said curtly.

"What—?" Mary was taken aback.

He pushed the spear to one side and forced his way past her. "A tree told me," he added gruffly.

Mary readied herself to herd the visitor out, but he was already stripping off his overcoat and shaking the rain across her living room. He gave up, threw it to one side, and marched to the fire to warm his hands. Mary advanced with the spear.

"You can put that pigsticker down for a start," he said, watching her from the corner of his eye.

"If I put it anywhere, it'll be right up your arse." She considered giving him a prod just to hear him squeal. "Who are you?"

He drew himself upright, shaking his head wearily as he flung his hat on top of his coat. "The name's Crowther. Frank, if you want to be chummy." His eyes narrowed. "Though you probably don't."

"And—" she prompted, shaking the spear.

"And I am here to see you," he interjected with exasperation. "I presume."

Mary chewed her lip for a second, then used the spear to motion him toward the chair. "Just don't go making everything wet while you tell me about it."

He flopped into the chair, weariness etching deep lines into his face as his head lolled onto the chair-back. With his eyes closed, he began, "I would hope I don't have to begin from first principles. We can accept that there is an element of what used to be called the supernatural in the world, can we not?"

"Go on."

"I have been known, from time to time, to communicate with those other powers. Recently, they've been getting in a bit of a state. Something's up, apparently. A rather big and extremely troubling something, though as usual, trying to get any useful detail from them is like trying to carry water in a sieve. It seems, however, that it's linked to this damned plague." He flapped a hand. "Anyway, that's by the by, for now. The important thing is that something can be done about it. Apparently. And it seems I have a part to play, and you, because I was guided here. Frankly, I can think of better things to do, but I presume the survival of the human race is a pressing matter."

"Who told you this?"

"The Wood-born." He watched her quizzically.

She nodded. "The tree spirits."

He tutted. "Don't make them sound like fairy-tale stuff. You get on the wrong side of them and you won't live to regret it. I saw a man once with a hawthorn bush bursting out of his belly. He'd somehow swallowed a fragment of the wood and they'd made it sprout inside him."

"He probably deserved it."

"How very humane of you."

Despite his appearance, Mary didn't feel a sense of threat from Crowther: she was usually good at judging people, but that didn't mean she liked him either. He carried his arrogance like a badge, reminding her of intellectuals she'd met who couldn't help but look down on the common herd.

"Why should I trust you?" Mary asked.

Crowther pondered this for a second or two and then a deep sigh shook his large frame. "The simple answer is that you probably shouldn't. God knows, if I were in your position, I wouldn't trust me." The weariness permeating his features appeared to be born from days on the road.

"You've come a long way," Mary stated.

He nodded. "From the West Country. There's a college there, newly founded after the Fall. It aims to pass on long traditions of studying nature and the heavens and how it all interacts, the wisdom of an age-old group called the Culture, though everyone knows it by a different name. A mystical college. You've heard of it?"

Mary shook her head.

"I'd spent all my days in academia—avoiding having a life, I suppose—so it was only natural I ended up there. Couldn't do anything else productive. I'm a professor, which used to mean something, I suppose. Various disciplines came under my aegis—a little psychology here, some archaeology and anthropology there. I was at Oxford for a while—"

"Married?"

"Wife dead, I'm afraid." His features remained impassive; Mary had no idea how much she could believe of what he was saying. "Children, I don't know where. They're old enough to have minds of their own. No ties, you see. The college sounded enticing . . . and it was. Except it's run by one of the most miserable, bad-tempered old bastards you could ever imagine." His eyes narrowed. "And one of the Five."

Mary's breath caught in her throat. "They exist, then?"

He nodded. "Not a myth, though they're rapidly turning into one. Five people who saved the world when things were going pear-shaped. A shaman, the one in Glastonbury. A warrior—who turned out to be a traitor, killed in the Battle of London. A human-nature-spirit hybrid . . . or something, I'm not quite sure. A leader, missing, presumed dead. And one of your own."

Mary sat on the arm of the chair, staring into space. "I'd heard the stories, like everyone, but I hardly dared believe. Are they going to come back?"

"To save us?" He laughed bitterly. "They've done their bit. It's down to us now."

"Then this college is somewhere quite special."

His eyes took on a distant cast. "The things I learned there . . . amazing things . . . worlds beyond our own . . . the existence of beings we'd always considered gods . . . magic . . . a new, deep philosophy about the way everything is tied together . . ." He brought himself down to earth sharply. "But that's not important. This is."

"You came all this way because the Wood-born told you to." Mary felt secretly pleased when she saw Crowther flinch slightly beneath her unwavering gaze. "Out of the goodness of your heart, to help humanity. You don't seem like a good Samaritan."

"I never said I was. I'm a part of humanity too, whatever others might think, and I have a vested interest in its survival."

"And the tree spirits told you about me?" Mary grew more suspicious the more she considered his words.

"Not just them. There were rituals, other communications, once I knew something was amiss. And, yes, I was pointed here because of one very special reason, something that shines out like a beacon to those kinds of beings who have a feeling for all this."

"And that is?"

"I am quite prepared to sit down and tell you all about it. But first, is there any chance of a brew before we decide exactly what we're supposed to do?"

Without gratifying his request with a friendly reply, she turned to go to the kitchen. But as she did so, she noticed something very strange about him in the flicker of the firelight when he bent forward to warm his hands again: there appeared to be holes just beyond the line of his hair and beard, as if something had drilled into his skull.

When Mary returned with two mugs of the herbal infusion, Crowther had his boots and socks off and was wiggling his toes in front of the fire.

"You really are a disgusting pig," she said, handing him his drink.

"Thank you. I see an ability to offend as a mark of unique status." He slurped on the brew before nodding appreciatively.

"So," Mary asked after a few moments, "did you have any more information or are we supposed to glean something from that load of old cobblers you just told me."

"Yes, the key to it all is some girl . . ."

Mary stiffened.

Crowther saw her response. "You know who I'm talking about?"

"Put that tea down," Mary snapped. "We have to go out."

When Mary's call echoed throughout Caitlin's house, she feared the worst. They'd already checked the village hall, but even if Caitlin had gone out on a call, Grant and Liam should still be around at that time of night.

Crowther stalked off to check the bedrooms, returning with a curt shake of his head. A jarring banging led them into the kitchen, where the back door swung back and forth in the wind. Outside, Mary saw movement at the end of the garden. Running down anxiously, she found a figure so slathered with clay and mud it was at first impossible to tell it was Caitlin. She was knee-deep in a hole, frantically shovelling earth out onto the lawn.

Caitlin looked up at Mary with big, staring eyes, made whiter by the filth caked around them, and shouted, "I've got to get them out!" She didn't seem to recognise Mary at all.

Caitlin dug wildly, spraying mud all around, then threw the spade to one side and dropped to her knees so she could claw at the sodden earth. Mary glanced at the growing hole, and at the mound of earth nearby and knew what had happened.

"Oh, lovey." Her voice trembled with pity.

"I've got to get them out!" Caitlin dug like a woodland animal, thrashing madly as Mary tried to ease her out of the grave.

In the end, Crowther and Mary between them managed to calm Caitlin enough to get her away from the hole, and once it was out of her sight it was almost as if it was forgotten. Her face grew blank, her eyes empty. She trudged in a dream state toward the kitchen, holding Mary's hand.

They sat her at the kitchen table, but Caitlin made no attempt to respond to any of Mary's questions, didn't even acknowledge anyone else was with her. Her chin lolled onto her chest as she stared hollowly at the table. She looked like some relict human hiding out in the depths of the jungle.

Crowther surveyed Caitlin dismissively. "If this is who we came for, I wouldn't put money on us coming out on top."

"Shut up," Mary snapped. She moved in close to Caitlin and said gently, "You don't need to worry about Grant and Liam any more, dear. They're in the Summerlands now, happy, content, waiting till they can see you again."

The words hung in the stillness of the kitchen, and then a faint light came on in Caitlin's eyes before they flickered toward Mary. Curiously, Mary didn't recognise what she saw there.

"I know you." Caitlin's voice was of a higher pitch than usual, almost child-like, with a faint singsong swing.

"Of course you do, lovey. It's Mary." She put her hand comfortingly on the back of Caitlin's.

Caitlin's eyes continued to search Mary's face. "I'm Amy."

Mary flinched. "No, you're Caitlin."

"Caitlin's here, but I'm Amy."

Crowther leaned forward and said a little gruffly, "How old are you, Amy?"

"Six."

"And how many of you are there?"

Caitlin sat back in her chair and mouthed the numbers as she counted off on her fingers. "Five," she concluded. "Me, Amy. Caitlin. Brigid. Briony. And . . . and the one we don't talk about." A shadow crossed her face.

In a somewhat unseemly manner, Crowther was enthused by what he'd heard. "Multiple personality," he mused, "or dissociative identity disorder, to

44

give it its proper name. Some debate in psychological circles about whether it actually exists."

"The poor girl," Mary said. "Is there anything we can do?"

"A few decades of therapy and a strict drug regime."

"I don't like it here. It's scary. There's something frightening in the garden," Caitlin/Amy said, glancing in a scared, childlike manner toward the back door. "I want to leave. I don't want to come here again."

"Don't you worry." Mary put on a brave face. She helped Caitlin to her feet and slipped an arm around her shoulders. "We'll get you somewhere nice and warm and safe."

Crowther grumbled as he followed. "Well, that's torn it."

The journey down the rain-washed, wind-torn lane was like a funeral procession, with Caitlin trailing spectrally behind Mary and Crowther taking up the rear in his oversized coat and hat. Halfway along the lane, though, the wind blew the clouds away and the bright, white moon emerged like a spotlight, casting the scene in silhouette and shadow.

Mary felt instantly on edge. She knew that she had half-seen something from the corner of her eye, registered only by her subconscious. Turning slowly, she saw black shapes moving along the ridge a mile or so to her right, picked out by the moonlight as if nature was informing her of something important.

She came to a sharp stop, cold and disturbed. "What's that?" she said. Caitlin didn't look, but Crowther came in close, pushing up the soggy brim of his hat so he could get a better look.

Two figures moved relentlessly along the back of the ridge. At first glance it looked as if they were riders on horseback, except in silhouette the horses were oddly misshapen, too large, too long and bulky, as if they had been crossed with some kind of giant lizard. The eerie sight brought a shimmer of fear to Mary, and she could tell from his rigid stance that Crowther was disturbed by it, too.

"Do you recognise them?" she asked. Crowther shook his head.

"The Whisperers," Caitlin/Amy muttered, still without looking. Mary and Crowther stared at her for a long moment, then hurried her along the lane.

In the cottage, Mary locked and barred the door before throwing another log on the fire. Crowther had become more stoic, which manifested itself in a degree of politeness he hadn't exhibited before. He carefully hung his coat and hat on the back of the door while Mary stripped off Caitlin's clothes in the kitchen, washing her face and hands and wrapping her in an old dressing gown. Once she was in the chair in front of the fire, Caitlin sagged back and instantly fell asleep, as if a switch had been thrown.

"I don't see that we can do anything with her," Crowther said. Weariness emerged from behind his arrogance and brought lines to his face that added years to his age.

"Give her time," Mary said. "She's had a big blow, but she's a tough kid." She went to the window and looked out; everywhere was still now that the storm had passed. "Things are going from bad to worse, aren't they?" she said, almost talking to herself.

"This plague is a bit of trouble, certainly," Crowther agreed. "But if not for that, I don't really know how I feel about it. We seem to have lost a lot of things that were holding us back. We've reset the clock, I think. Time to get it right this time. Which is, I know, very Darwinian, but there you go."

"So what do we do now?"

"I don't know. I was only guided to find you. Somehow the three of us have to find a cure for this plague. Somehow . . . I don't know . . . I'm sick of all this vagueness." He sighed. "I need to contact the other side."

Mary knew why there was such an edge to his voice. Such contacts had a cost, sometimes in a transfer of energy, sometimes in something much, much higher. After the first time, she had decided to avoid them. One other question struck her, and it was such a conundrum that she couldn't begin to find an answer. "Why us?"

Crowther gave a bad-tempered shrug. "I suppose we won the lottery."

The hot coals in the brazier sent out a dull heat that only dispelled the cold in a tiny circle in its immediate vicinity. Beyond, the Ice-Field rolled out immeasurably, consumed by the infinite blackness of a night where no stars twinkled. They sheltered in the nook of a small rock formation, the only feature on that flat, endless plain. It was crescent-shaped, barely twelve feet high, but enough to keep the chilling wind at bay. Snow was frozen hard against it so that it glistened in the ruddy firelight.

Perched on a boulder beside the brazier, Caitlin shivered, her arms wrapped around her, not thinking, not feeling.

Amy stood beside her, tugging at Caitlin's sleeve. The little girl had a powerful innocence about her that made her appear brittle. She peered into the night with wide, frightened eyes. "Something's coming," she whimpered. "It'll be here soon. Then we'll all pay."

"Shut up!" The shrill voice came from a neurotic-looking woman in her late thirties, too thin and angular, her face bearing the mean expression of someone who felt they had suffered too much unnecessarily. Briony lit a cigarette and sucked in the smoke, her eyes watering. "It doesn't do any good whining, you little brat."

"Leave her alone. You know she's right." Brigid was so old she appeared like a gnarled, wind-blasted tree, her bones barely holding on to her flesh. Her hair was a wild mane of white, knotted and greasy. "We have to get her moving." She nodded contemptuously toward Caitlin. "That's the only hope."

"You could let me out."

They all grew rigid at the rasping voice. Slowly they turned to the dense area of shadow at the back of the shelter. In the deepest part of it, two red eyes burned.

Across the Ice-Field, the wind howled mercilessly. The night grew a shade darker.

Mary jumped at the cry reverberating throughout the cottage. It contained physical pain, but also a soul pain that filled her with dread. Crowther had retired to her bedroom to carry out whatever ritual he used to access the powers that gave him information. He had insisted on secrecy, though she had offered to help him keep the threats at bay.

He emerged ten minutes later, shaking and drawn as though he were suffering from some debilitating illness. Mary offered him a glass of whiskey, which he knocked back without thanks.

"Did it work?" she asked.

"After a fashion. As usual." He steadied himself against a wall.

She could see from his face that whatever he had learned had disturbed him greatly. "What is it?"

"There's no cure for the plague in this world."

Her heart fell. "No cure?"

"*In this world.*"

The stress he gave to those words made her skin prickle. "What are you getting at?"

"There's a place that exists side by side with ours . . . the ancient Celts called it Tir n'a n'Og—"

"The Otherworld," Mary breathed.

"The place where the dead go. The Celts' land of their gods. The source of all supernatural influence, of dreams and imagination . . ." He was flushed, his breath short. "It exists. The cure is there."

"You believe what you were told? You know they don't always say what we think they say."

"I know," he snapped irritably. "But this time I think it's right."

Mary sat on the sofa and covered her face wearily. The blackness of the depression she'd fought all her life was snapping at her heels. "What are we supposed to do, then?"

"There are places where one can cross over."

She looked at him slowly as the implications began to dawn on her.

"Historically, they've always been known as *thin places*, where, if you know the right way to go about it, you can open doorways. The ancients understood this clearly. It's knowledge that's been lost to us, like so much of importance." Crowther hauled himself to his feet. "We can't stay here. Those riders . . . they want to stop us."

"Why? Who are they?"

He shrugged and gave his overcoat a shake before sweeping it on. "I was simply told they were pursuing us."

Mary had difficulty coming to terms with her life suddenly taking a right-angled turn. But she understood obligation, and however apprehensive she felt, there was a job to do. "Let me get some things together."

"Not you." Mary stopped and stared at him, puzzled. "Just the girl, and me."

"I thought you said you were led to me because I had a part to play?"

"You have. You've got to get that girl *compos mentis* . . . at least enough for me to travel with her." He shook his hat, then put the soggy mess on with a grimace.

Mary couldn't explain why she felt uneasy, but so much was happening that she didn't have time to think. She dropped to her knees in front of the fire and took Caitlin's hand. It was so cold that at first Mary thought she'd died. Slowly, Caitlin stirred from her deep sleep.

"Come on, lovey. Come to me."

Caitlin's lips moved in her dream state. Mary couldn't make out the words, but she thought she could just hear the susurration of different voices, the timbre and intonation changing as if Caitlin were holding an internal dialogue. It was so unnatural that it brought a chill to her spine.

"Caitlin," she stressed. "We need you here."

"She won't go." The voice was sharp, not Caitlin's at all.

Mary rocked back on her heels, shocked, before composing herself. "Caitlin," she said firmly. "It's Mary. You have to come *now*."

There was a brief silence and then Caitlin's eyes flickered open. Mary saw in them the Caitlin she knew. The young doctor leaned forward and covered her face. "What's happening?" she said weakly. Then, "Grant . . . Liam . . ." She started to cry silently.

"I know, I know." Mary felt like her own heart was breaking as she hugged Caitlin to her. In recent months, Caitlin's family had almost filled that awful gap in Mary's life, that loss from all those years ago, when Mary proved what an awful person she was. Mary had taken such joy in seeing Caitlin with so much, knowing her friend was, despite the stress and the strains that arose from it, so fundamentally happy. It wasn't fair that Caitlin should have to suffer such a loss, someone who had always tried to do her best for other people. Not like herself, Mary thought; she had turned selfishness into a fine art.

"It's my fault," Caitlin croaked to herself. "If I'd been there for them—This is my punishment—"

"Don't say that." Mary choked back her emotion. "Don't you go blaming yourself. You're a good person . . . these things happen—"

When Caitlin looked up at her it was with eyes that Mary didn't recognise. "I'm a doctor. I'm supposed to help people. And I couldn't help the most important people in my life." She bit her lip until blood started to flow. "The last time I spoke to Grant we were arguing. That was the last thing he'll remember . . . the last thing—"

"Hush now." Mary stroked Caitlin's hair. Everything she said sounded so useless. How could any words make the slightest difference in a situation of such tragedy?

"I didn't even say good-bye to them. Now they'll never know . . . they'll never know . . . how I felt . . ."

"They know, honey. I'm sure they do. Wherever they are, they'll know your heart."

Crowther watched all this impassively. Mary wondered how he could be so cold. Yet for the little she knew about him, she felt the inherent truth in what he had told her, about the warnings from beyond and the hope that there might be a cure somewhere for this damnable plague. Perhaps she was expressing the naïvety of a child, but if Caitlin could be instrumental in bringing back a cure, her young friend might find some kind of salvation from the terrible thing she had experienced.

For the next hour, Mary sat with Caitlin in her arms while the younger woman grieved quietly. Caitlin wasn't herself—at times her voice would change inexplicably, or her words would become incomprehensible—but the depth of her feeling was unmistakable.

Finally Caitlin subsided into an aching silence.

Mary waited for a moment, not sure if she'd done enough, and then left Caitlin to her grief. Crowther hovered near the door. "You be careful with her," Mary cautioned. "Remember what she's been through. Don't you dare hurt her."

"I have no intention of hurting her," Crowther said with irritation. "She's of vital importance to what has to be done. Without her, there's no hope."

It wasn't quite the reassurance Mary had wanted, but it would have to do. She turned and helped Caitlin to her feet. "Listen, lovey, you've got to go with Professor Crowther now. He's going to take you somewhere safe." Mary winced at the lie. "Don't ask questions. Just do what he says until you're away from here. Do you understand?"

Caitlin nodded, lost to her grief, but at least once more the Caitlin that Mary knew. Mary wrapped her in an old anorak and led her to the door. Once Caitlin had stepped out into the night, Mary caught Crowther's arm. "I don't like you and I don't trust you," she hissed, "but I'm going on instinct here. You'd better do the right thing with this girl or I'll hunt you down, cut your bollocks off, and make you eat them."

"Oh, you *are* a charming lady," Crowther replied. "Don't worry. I'm putting myself at risk too, you know."

Mary gave a snorting laugh to show how much she was concerned about that fact.

Crowther stepped out behind Caitlin, then half turned. "One other thing. If I were you, I wouldn't wait around here. Those hunters may decide you're too close to all this to live."

"Where am I supposed to go?"

He made a couldn't-care-less gesture. "Not my problem."

And then he put his hand on Caitlin's shoulder to guide her, and they went down the path, into the lane, and away.

chapter three
THE LAMENT-BROOD

> *"The human heart is like Indian rubber: a little swells it,*
> *but a great deal will not burst it."*
>
> Anne Brontë

The New Forest had grown dense and in some areas impassable in the months since the Fall. Without access to petrol, roads were mainly travelled by horse and cart, and on foot, and so vegetation had crowded in or forced its way through the cracking asphalt. In the Forest it was even worse. The ancient broad-leafed trees thrived in a silent world that rebelled at the fall of a human foot. If not for necessity, Crowther would never have ventured into the thick greenwood.

Caitlin had slipped in and out of a daze as they walked, but there were signs that she was becoming more lucid. Yet he was surprised to hear the sound of crying coming from her. He didn't know how to react, hated any show of emotion. Hesitantly, he asked, "Are you all right?"

When she looked up, the pain in her tear-streaked face made him wince. "It's not fair," she said desperately. "I loved them so much."

The sound of her sobbing carried with it the weight of complete heartbreak. Crowther rested against a nearby tree, surprised at the overwhelming pity he felt. He had thought it was beyond him. Perhaps there was hope for him yet.

As they continued on their way, Caitlin was, for the most part, lost to her own shifting thoughts, but occasionally she would speak either to herself or to ask him a question. Often Crowther was disturbed to hear that the voice was not her own. He'd read accounts of dissociative identity disorder, but experiencing it at firsthand was unnerving. He knew some research had shown that the separate identities, referred to by experts as *alters*, could exhibit differences in speech, philosophies, mannerisms, whole character traits—even gender. They could also have different physical states, such as allergies, whether they were right- or left-handed, and some were even short-sighted when the main personality had twenty-twenty vision. There were psychologists who denied the existence of DID, claiming that the personalities were simply fantasies of the patient, but if he had any doubts, here was the evidence.

"Brigid says you're scared." Caitlin's voice surprised him.

He looked away quickly. "Does she now."

51

"Brigid knows things like that. She's very wise. What are you scared of?"

He laughed hollowly. "What am I scared of? I'm scared of everything, as all wise men would be. I'm scared because we were taught to live in a world of Reason, and there's no reason anywhere anymore. We don't have the tools to thrive here. And I'm scared because we're so far down the food chain, we're just above the bovine."

"Brigid says you're hiding something in your coat."

He flinched. "Brigid should mind her own business."

"There's a village up ahead." Caitlin switched the topic of conversation with ease.

"How do you know?"

"I can smell it."

He sniffed the air but couldn't pick up anything beyond the forest scents, although he knew some people with mental disorders had heightened senses.

Several yards further on, the sickeningly fruity smell of decomposition was unmistakable. Bodies left in the open to rot was a clear warning sign and Crowther was already preparing to skirt the area when Caitlin caught his arm. She had seen something beyond his range.

Fighting his natural instinct, Crowther allowed her to guide him. She ducked low, crawling through the vegetation until they had a view of a sixties-style bungalow. The ruddy glare of fire rose up behind one window, followed by thick black smoke pouring out of every opening. The front door burst open and out came two men clutching a box of food, a shotgun, and a few other objects Crowther couldn't make out. They were both wearing some kind of strange uniform, black T-shirts bearing a scarlet V from shoulder to navel.

As the looters hurried away, Crowther edged ahead to get a better view. Further down the street he could see more of the oddly dressed men—some kind of gang, he guessed—coming out of other houses with their swag. They moved quickly and efficiently, taking only what they needed, and left the village in wagons parked at the far end of the main street.

"Well, we certainly don't want to be tangled up with those," Crowther mused. There was a rustling beside him and before he could react, Caitlin had emerged from hiding and was sliding down a grassy bank into an overgrown field that bordered the main street. "Wait," he hissed, but she paid him no attention.

She skipped through the thistle and grass and clambered over a five-bar gate before checking up and down the road. Crowther waited for a long moment to see if she would be attacked, then reluctantly followed. He was weighing the advantages of tying her up for the remainder of the journey when she hailed him from a large detached house that must once have been considered desirable. The front garden was now heavily obscured by a tangle of undergrowth and it didn't look as if any repairs had been made to it since the Fall.

"You don't want to go in there," he said, pointing to the red X painted roughly on the front door.

"I heard something inside."

"It's a plague house."

"This isn't the Dark Ages, Professor," she said.

"You'd think, wouldn't you?" He turned back down the weed-clogged drive, then sighed as he heard the front door open. This time he wasn't going to follow her. There were limits.

The stench inside the house was overwhelming. Caitlin covered her mouth, fighting the urge to retch, not sure why she was in there, though she guessed it had something to do with the strange voices that occasionally surfaced at the back of her head.

She moved through the hall, with its damp, peeling wallpaper, and pushed open the door into the room where she thought she'd heard a noise. The sight that greeted her was horrific, but she felt only overwhelming pity.

Bodies marked with the unmistakable scars of the plague lay all around. At first some attempt had been made to stack them, but the last few had been thrown on the pile haphazardly.

That thought brought a succession of jarring images: the first case brought into her surgery, the sudden realisation, the mounting horror as the bodies piled up in the village hall. The faces . . . her friends . . . acquaintances . . . good people, undeserving people . . . and then Grant . . . and Liam . . . She rammed her fists into her eye sockets to drive out the terrible pictures, the sickening smell of clay and the clammy feel of wet clothes.

The sound was barely audible, but it jolted her out of her emotional state. Something was in the room, alive. *Rats?* The arm of one of the corpses dropped suddenly and made her jump. Behind it she saw movement—too big for a rodent.

"Come out." She could barely believe someone was hiding underneath those suppurating bodies.

Vibrations amongst the cadavers suggested a brief struggle was taking place, and then the corpses fell away as a boy of around nine or ten pushed his way out. He was black, his hair shorn to a bristle, and a little overweight, but he had big, expressive eyes that made him seem much younger. He blinked once, twice, his gaze filled with hope.

"Don't worry," Caitlin said, shocked. "I won't hurt you."

There was a sudden rush of falling bodies and another figure emerged: a girl of about sixteen, also black, her features street-smart and hard. "Don't come any closer," she said menacingly. She was brandishing a switchblade.

Caitlin held up her hands. "It's OK."

The girl's cold eyes searched the room and the hall beyond. "You're not with them?" she said, without lowering the knife.

"The gang with the V-shirts? No. I just got here as they left."

The girl scanned Caitlin's clothes and came to her own conclusion. "You'd better not try anything," she said. Despite appearances, her voice had an educated inflection, but her attitude was unmistakably dangerous. Yet behind it Caitlin could see a hint of fear in the mirror of her eyes.

"My name's Caitlin. I'm a doctor."

This piece of information reassured the girl enough for her to lower the knife, but it didn't remove the iciness from her face. "Got here a bit late, didn't you?"

"Come on, let's get out of here," Caitlin said gently. "It's dangerous."

"Everywhere's dangerous." Hardness came to the girl's voice easily, but she still indicated for the boy to follow Caitlin out.

Crowther waited in the shade of a tall ash, watching the empty street cautiously. As Caitlin led the new arrivals up to him, his face showed weary annoyance at another complication.

"I'm Caitlin and this is Professor Crowther."

The girl made no attempt to venture her name in reply until the boy gave her a little shove. "Mahalia," she said. "Jackson."

Crowther raised an eyebrow. "Like the singer."

"Like me," Mahalia replied.

Caitlin knelt before the boy, warmed by his open, honest features. "And what's your name?" she said.

"He can't speak." Mahalia's body language was defensive of her charge. "Actually, I think he *can* speak—he just doesn't choose to. Don't ask me why."

Caitlin looked into his face for confirmation, but all he gave was a broad, warm smile. His eyes, though, showed such depths they made Caitlin shiver.

"His name's Carlton Breen. He wrote it down for me."

"Where are your parents?" Caitlin felt a jab of anxiety. Mahalia snorted and looked away. "Is this your home?" Caitlin pressed.

"We're from Winchester. At least I am. I don't know where Carlton's from. Have you got any food?"

"No, but we can probably find something—"

"Why don't we go shopping for clothes while we're at it," Crowther snapped.

"We can't leave them here alone," Caitlin replied.

"We can't take them with us. Do you have any concept of what we're going into? Believe me, they'll be far safer here."

A sharp pain stung Caitlin deep in her head; she felt as if she was falling back into a dark tunnel.

"If you don't take them with us, I'm not going!" Mahalia and Carlton's eyes widened at the petulant child's voice coming from Caitlin's mouth.

Crowther swore under his breath. "All right. For a little while." He marched down the drive. "Though you do realise having a nursery tagging along is going to be the death of us."

They found some vegetables the looters had missed and cooked a brief, bland stew before setting off again. Striding ahead, Crowther made no attempt to hide his aversion to spending any time with the others; he was already plotting ways to jettison Mahalia and Carlton when an opportunity arose.

Once it had been confirmed that the two children were coming with them, Amy allowed Caitlin to resurface. "What happened to you back there?" Mahalia asked suspiciously as they trudged amongst the trees. "With that creepy little-girl voice?"

Anxiety coiled inside Caitlin. "I don't want to talk about it."

"Fine," Mahalia said with a dismissive shrug. "This should be an interesting journey. On the road with a grumpy old man and a crazy old woman."

"Have you been on your own for long?" Caitlin asked.

Mahalia clearly wasn't used to small talk. Her suspicious eye suggested she was waiting for Caitlin to ask something of her. "Since the Fall. Wandered across the south coast after skipping my school . . . just trying to stay alive like everybody else."

Caitlin could hear the intelligence in the girl's well-spoken voice. "And there's nobody else to look after you? No family?"

"I can look after myself well enough."

"You shouldn't have to try to survive on your own. Everyone needs somebody."

For some reason this comment annoyed the girl. "I've got Carlton and he's got me, and we've done all right so far. We don't need you. We're going along for the ride, for something to do. But we can walk away at any minute. Don't forget that."

She marched ahead so she wouldn't have to talk to Caitlin any more.

They picked their way across patches of heath and through dense woodland for five miles, attempting to stay out of view as much as possible. The countryside had grown wild more quickly than they could have believed possible and at times the going was hard, but by early afternoon the last remaining clouds were finally blown away and the brilliant spring sunshine took some of the edge off their journey.

"But you've got to have some idea where you're going!" Mahalia said in disbelief after quizzing Caitlin about their destination.

The question troubled Caitlin. There was an existentialist peace in simply walking; to consider any more meant facing up to what lay behind her. "I'm just following the professor." She winced at how pathetic that sounded.

Mahalia turned her attention to the professor, who was attempting to keep several yards between himself and the others. "You know where you're going. I've seen you looking at the sun to keep a check on your direction."

"Aren't you a clever girl."

"If you don't tell me, I'm just going to keep asking until you're sick of me."

"I'm sick of you already."

"Where are we going?"

Crowther made an angry sound in the depths of his throat. After a few seconds of reflection, he said, "We're going to find a cure for the plague."

Caitlin looked down at her feet, her face strained. Mahalia considered Crowther's response thoughtfully. "So you know somewhere that's got a vaccine?"

"Not quite."

"Then where are you going?"

"There's no point explaining it to you, you wouldn't understand," Crowther said as patronisingly as he could manage.

Mahalia grew flinty. "Try me."

Crowther rounded on her as his irritation peaked. "All right, little girl. There's no cure for the plague in this world—no hope at all. So we're going to cross the dimensional barriers to *another* world, and hopefully we'll find the answers we seek there."

Mahalia's thoughts played out clearly on her face: at first she was sure he was mocking her; second that he was as insane as the girl clearly thought Caitlin was. But then a strange thing happened that gave Crowther pause: Carlton tugged on Mahalia's arm to get her attention and nodded assent. The girl instantly acquiesced.

"OK," she said. "Tell me about this other world and how we get there."

Now it was Caitlin's turn to exclaim in disbelief. "Another world?"

"Not *some* other world. *The* Otherworld," Crowther said as he clambered on to an overgrown stile. "It's been a part of legend here for millennia . . . the land where the ancient Celts believed their gods lived. And it actually exists, not in myth but in reality, and those selfsame legends were our ancestors' way of preserving that knowledge for posterity—part information, part warning. There are people who have been there, and I have spoken to one of them."

"Whatever." Mahalia winked at Carlton in a manner that annoyed Crowther intensely.

"I'm actually warming to the prospect of taking you across to that place," Crowther said. "It's the source of every nightmarish thing that has found its way here since the Fall, and believe me, there's a lot worse waiting over there. I think you'll have a wonderful time meeting them all."

"Well, we're going to come whether you like it or not," Mahalia said blithely. "What do you think, matey?"

Carlton nodded his head eagerly.

"I thought I understood the depths of the stupidity of youth until I met you," Crowther said. "Really . . . thank you for the enlightening experience."

"We're leaving this world behind?" A light began to dawn in Caitlin's face. "We can really do that?"

The notion pleased Mahalia, too. "But how are we going to do it?"

"Just wait and see," Crowther said brusquely.

He ignored any further questions for the next five miles and then brought them to a halt with a raised hand. Through the trees they could see a pretty village of red-brick Georgian cottages, dominated by a grand building.

"Is this where you've been leading us?" Caitlin asked.

"The National Motor Museum," Crowther said. "We're going to get a car."

As he led them forward, Mahalia noticed that Carlton was hanging back.

"What is it?" Caitlin asked.

"He's scared." Mahalia dropped to her knees in front of the silent boy. His expression was troubled, his eyes scanning the trees that clustered tightly around the village. "What's wrong, Carlton?" Her genuine concern was a stark contrast to her normal demeanour.

"What's the point in asking him questions if he can't answer?" Crowther said with irritation.

"Carlton's right. Can't you feel it?" Caitlin had tilted her head to one side, not just listening but sensing the atmosphere. There was an edge of tension, slowly rising.

"The birds have stopped singing," Mahalia observed.

Crowther grew tense. "I fear they've caught up with us again. Come on."

"Who's after you?" the girl asked.

"Something not of this world," Crowther said. "Another reason to get out of here as quickly as possible."

The museum lay just beyond the Great Gatehouse of a fourteenth-century Cistercian abbey, the boundary fence overgrown with creepers and the once carefully kept grounds quickly returning to the wild. They located the entrance and scaled the security gates, with much blowing and cursing on the part of Crowther.

"Why did you come all this way just to get a car?" Caitlin asked.

"Because time is of the essence and we have a long way to go," Crowther replied. "And to be honest, anything that lessens the time I have to spend with you—and now those two—is a good thing."

"You don't think they'll all have been looted?"

"Only if there's a classic-car collector in the area. Nobody else would be interested in these museum pieces. I'm taking the gamble that most people won't have realised that there must be some kind of fuel depot on the site. We can fill up and be away, and whatever's behind can choke on our exhaust fumes."

The explosion made them all jump. A nearby branch splintered and fell.

"Somebody's shooting at us," Crowther exclaimed incredulously, a second before Caitlin knocked him to the ground.

"Clear off, you bastards! I'll kill you all!" A wild-eyed man with grey hair rising up like a sunburst around a bald pate stormed toward them from the direction of the museum. He wore a threadbare overcoat and mud-splattered brown trousers, and he was brandishing a musket so worn and rusty it looked as if it would fall apart if it were fired again. "This is my place!" he yelled. "You can't come in here!"

Another burst of grapeshot rattled over their heads. The gun was so inaccurate that they were more likely to die from accidental fallout than any specific shot. "Into the trees!" Caitlin shouted, looking around for the others. Carlton was there, but Mahalia was missing.

Their attacker set about the laborious task of reloading the musket—shot, gunpowder, tamping it down. Caitlin seized the opportunity to haul Carlton toward cover while Crowther scurried on his hands and knees behind them.

Once they were hidden, Caitlin frantically searched for Mahalia. Had she run for the boundary fence?

The answer came a second later. Mahalia appeared like a shadow rising from the ground behind their assailant. She was so silent that he was oblivious to her presence until she knocked the musket from his hands and entwined her arms around him, a knife at his throat.

The three of them rushed over just as the man stopped struggling in response to whatever Mahalia had whispered in his ear. Blood trickled down his neck from the knife point.

"Don't hurt me," he whimpered. Tears of fear trickled from his eyes; in them was a hint of the madness of isolation.

"What are you doing?" Crowther raged. "You could have killed us!"

"This is my place," the man said pathetically. "You can't come in."

"Do you want me to kill him?" Mahalia's cold voice chilled Caitlin.

"Kill him?" Crowther said incredulously. "Are you insane as well? We don't go around killing people!"

"You leave him free, you might regret it," Mahalia continued.

"Oh, shut up." Crowther pulled her knife hand roughly away from the man's throat. The prisoner sagged and then began to sob.

"Mad as a bloody hatter," Crowther said. "He's probably been living up here since the Fall, shooting anyone who came near like some hillbilly. Whatever happened to resilience? The first sign of hardship and everyone starts going insane." He flashed a glance at Caitlin.

Behind them, Carlton was growing agitated again. As Caitlin turned to comfort him, he pointed fearfully toward the gate.

Five shapes had emerged from the tree line beyond the boundary fence. The moment Caitlin laid eyes on them she felt as if her life was draining away. It was the Whisperers, she knew that without a doubt. They had faces that would haunt Caitlin's worst nightmares, a forensic study of a human head once the skin had been removed, though the musculature was white as snow, dry and parchment-like, the teeth needle-long and sharp, like those on luminescent fish caught in the furthest depths. Their eyes exuded a smoky magenta light that drifted around them in clouds as if they burned inside. They were tall and gaunt with limbs so thin they looked as if they barely had the strength to lift themselves, their bodies almost lost in their odd combination of armour—winged, spiked helmets and breastplates, all of it rusted a muddy brown—and fluttering black rags. On their backs or hanging from their belts were a variety of rusted metallic weapons—swords, spears, axes, and some things that just looked like long spikes. Their mounts were a disturbing mixture of lizard and horse, their scaly skin a desiccated grey. The hazy purple light wreathed all around them.

Mahalia, Crowther, Caitlin, and Carlton were all rooted before the terrible sight.

Beneath the rustle of the wind in the newly formed leaves, a whispering rose up that carried with it notions of terrible, depressing things even though no words were clear.

The Whisperers dismounted and drifted like ghosts to the boundary fence, where they stood motionless.

"Why aren't they trying to get in?" Caitlin asked.

"They can't come in here," the hermit moaned. "Nothing can. Sacred land . . . old, sacred, monastic land."

Crowther dropped down and placed the palm of his right hand on the soil.

"What's he talking about?" Mahalia said.

"The Blue Fire," Crowther said to himself. "I wish I could feel it."

"You're bleeding." Caitlin noticed the thin trickle running from Crowther's nose just as the iron filings taste dribbled into the edge of her own mouth. She dabbed at it and checked the stain on her fingers. "What are they doing to us?"

"Come on," Mahalia said insistently. "You're standing around as if you're in a dream." She picked up a rock from nearby and smashed it against the back of their prisoner's head. He pitched forward, unconscious. "So he doesn't get in the way."

Caitlin was too distracted to be horrified by the girl's action. Images scurried through her head that were not her own thoughts, a flickering of consciousness as contact was made—the face of one of the Whisperers loomed before her, and though its mouth formed no human syllables, the words made perfect sense: *Give up now. There is no hope . . . no point in running. Everyone must die. No point in anything. You could take your own life. Illness will claim you . . .* The message hid a secret virus that infected her mind like poison in the blood: despair. The emotion was almost painful.

Suddenly Caitlin was back in the Ice-Field and Briony was shaking her roughly. "Brigid says they're in your head. You have to get out of here."

Caitlin came out of her trance to realise that she was walking slowly toward the boundary fence alongside Mahalia, Carlton, and Crowther. She moved quickly, punching Crowther so hard in the face that his lips pulped against his teeth and blood splattered into his mouth.

The pain disrupted the mental image. "You stupid cow!" Crowther roared.

But it was enough. Caitlin grabbed Carlton while Crowther picked up Mahalia and then they were hurrying toward the museum buildings.

They realised they'd exceeded the range of the Whisperers' sickening influence when Mahalia suddenly yelled, "Put me down, you creep!" and lashed out wildly. Crowther dropped her hard on the floor with what Caitlin thought was a little too much relish.

Caitlin took one last look at the drifting purple haze where the withering atmosphere of despair hung along the boundary fence and then forced them to pick up the pace.

"What are those things," Caitlin asked, "and why are they hunting us?"

"Sport or food are the obvious answers," Crowther muttered, but his expression suggested that the questions troubled him immensely.

It took them a while to gain access to the vast display halls; the previous occupant had effectively blocked every entrance. They eventually managed to smash open a side door, and once inside it felt odd to be walking alone amongst the gleaming archaic vehicles that now provided a haunting reminder of the world they had left behind. One vast echoing hall led on to another, all filled with the smell of oil and rubber and leather upholstery. Every car they had ever seen or heard of stood side by side, their pristine paintwork shimmering in the half-light.

"In centuries to come, when this place is overgrown and forgotten, this will be like Tutankhamun's tomb to a future generation of archaeologists," Crowther said in hushed tones. "Of course, that's if the human race is still around."

Crowther bypassed the oldest vehicles, which looked as if they would barely have outrun a horse, and instead stopped at a display of seventies sports cars. He finally selected one, a 1974 Ferrari Dino 246 GT.

Mahalia laughed. "I bet you always wanted one of those."

"And never had the money," Crowther said. "One advantage of the Fall . . . everything's there for the taking."

"If you're strong enough," Caitlin added pointedly.

Crowther examined the display sign. "Actually, I chose it because it's really just a two-seater and we can shove the children in the tiny space behind the seats where I won't have to be bothered by them for the whole journey. Should be fairly uncomfortable." He proceeded to read aloud: "2418 cc V-6 engine, twelve over-head valves, 195 b.h.p. at 7,600 r.p.m. and a max speed of 150 m.p.h. That should do the job. Now we just need to fill it up." He opened the door, then paused uncomfortably. "I don't suppose any of you know how to hot-wire a car."

Mahalia pushed by him roughly and dipped under the steering column. A few seconds later the throaty roar of the engine echoed around the display hall.

"Oh, why am I not surprised." Crowther slipped behind the wheel with obvious relish. "Looks like there's enough in the tank to get us out to wherever the fuel depot is."

"'Thanks' would have been nice," Mahalia said sourly.

The fuel depot lay behind the display halls. High winds had camouflaged it with plastic sheeting, broken branches, leaves, and other vegetation. Crowther uncovered several cans filled with petrol and smiled as he filled up the Ferrari's tank. "Isn't it funny," he mused to himself, "I'd forgotten what it smelled like."

Carlton stood off to one side, eyeing the treetops uncertainly, his head cocked to one side. "I think Carlton knows a lot more than he shows," Caitlin said. "It's as if he can sense them."

"I don't care if they're about to tap me on the shoulder," Crowther said as he screwed the cap back on, "they don't stand a chance of keeping up with this machine."

Once they were all in, Crowther revved the engine and drove around to the exit gates. The purple mist that signified the Whisperers' presence drifted through the trees, but Crowther didn't wait to look at them.

The car hit the gates at speed. The impact jolted their teeth, but the gates burst off their hinges and then they were away down the winding service road.

"We did it!" Caitlin said in disbelief.

Carlton reached over the back of the seat to give the professor a hug. "Get off me!" Crowther roared.

"You can thank me when you're ready," Mahalia said, positioning herself so that Crowther would see her every time he looked in the rearview mirror.

The professor grunted. "You're not completely useless."

He pulled the car out onto the main road and hit the accelerator so hard they were all thrown back into their seats. "I wish we had some music," he said.

Euphoria gripped them as they made their getaway. Only Carlton peered back to watch the purple mist drifting slowly in their wake.

Mary had battled with a feeling of unease ever since Caitlin had left. Part of it was worry for her friend's safety. The first time they had met, three years earlier, they had disliked each other: Mary, the herbalist and alternative practitioner, and Caitlin, the rational GP, could see little common ground. But over the weeks and months as they came into contact more and more, they saw past the superficialities. Mary had learned to admire so much about Caitlin. The young doctor's strength of character and ability to sacrifice her own needs for the good of others were in stark contrast to how Mary saw herself. If her past mistakes had not been so great, Mary might have found a partner she could love, and they might have had a daughter. She would have been proud if the child had turned out like Caitlin.

But Mary's uneasiness also came from the certain knowledge that not all the trouble had moved on with Caitlin and Crowther. There was something in the air; she could *feel* it.

As the glass of whiskey caught the light from the fire, she felt a twinge of guilt that she'd only had breakfast half an hour ago. But then, life was more painful than anyone ever imagined, and what was wrong with something that took the edge off the cutting blade? At least she wouldn't be able to indulge it to the point where she ended up hanging around the village hall doing jigs for anyone who passed. No nipping down to the off-licence to replenish her supplies. The powers that be had seen fit to enforce a period of sobriety.

The community had managed to survive another winter of long shadows and harshness. But then the plague had come with the spring. Existence certainly had a taste for irony. Where would it all end?

Arthur Lee bounded in from the kitchen with an urgency that shook her from her dismal thoughts. He was unsettled. With his fur bristling, he tried to bury himself in her calf muscles, body rigid, and he was not a cat prone to fear; indeed, being more than cat, he existed in a state of contempt for everything. Mary's spine prickled in response.

This is a warning, Mary thought.

A quick slug of whiskey fired her, and then she moved from window to window, searching the countryside now bathed in early morning light. Trees and shrubs were budding; she could smell the season changing. Nothing disturbed the peaceful scene; no figures moving, no shift of vegetation in opposition to the wind. She let her senses envelop her, but all she could feel was that constant background unease.

"What's frighted you, then?" She dropped to her knees to look into the cat's gleaming eyes, but he was too anxious to stay still long enough for her to see. A drop of moisture splashed onto her cheek. Puzzled, she glanced up at the ceiling to search for the source. Absently, she wiped the droplet away, but then grew still when she glimpsed her fingertips: the stain was dark.

In the mirror, she saw a thin scarlet trickle running from each ear.

Thoughts of disease and death flashed across her mind, but she barely had time to consider them, for at that moment the phone began to ring; and it had been dead, like all phones, from the time of the Fall. Her heart began to pound.

Everything shifted at once; shadows in the room altered their position slightly, the light became strangely harsh, the barely perceptible sound of her feet on the carpet now buzzed loudly in her head; heightened sensations were twisted into something a step aside from reality. With a queasy sense of dislocation, Mary approached the phone.

She hesitated, rigid with apprehension, and then plucked up the handset. "Hello?"

There was a moment of fizzing static and then a hollow emptiness that reminded her of space. Out of it came a questioning voice that was faintly mechanical. ". . . Sshhh . . . hsss . . . Are you there? Can you hear me? . . . hssss . . . over. Do you hear? . . . sshhh . . . not over. It is not over. You have to—"

Mary threw the phone across the room. After a moment, fighting an irrational dread, she marched across the room and picked up the receiver: the phone was dead once more. She stared at it for a second or two while Arthur Lee flattened himself under the coffee table, and then a hammering at the door jolted her alert.

Don't answer it, a shrill voice said at the back of her head.

And she had every intention of obeying it, but then her hand was mysteriously on the handle, pressing it, pulling it. Her breath caught in her throat.

A large dark figure stood on the threshold. Oddly, she couldn't make out the face that terrified her so much; it was filled with shadows that moved like smoke. The figure entered and she seemed to float back before it.

Finally, she saw that it was a man, but that provided little comfort. His face had an odd plasticity that hinted at a mask, made worse by the burning, dreadful eyes stretched wide and staring through that masquerade. Yet everything else about him was thoroughly ordinary: his appearance resembled that of someone who had spent a long time on the road—mud-spattered jeans, faded T-shirt, worn jacket, long, greasy hair tied in a ponytail.

"Mary Holden." The voice appeared to come from some other part of the room; a disturbing ventriloquism, a party trick with added menace.

"Who are you?"

"I come from a place of quicksilver and lightning." He stood stock-still, arms at his sides, and the light and shadows circled him, or seemed to, from her perspective.

The dread in Mary's heart twisted until she thought she would be sick. "What do you want with me?"

"It is not over."

For some reason, the words terrified her.

"You shall not walk away." The eyes peering through the mask burned into her head. "The girl will need you."

"Caitlin?"

"Something has woken on the edge of Existence. It has seen you, and everything you are, and everything you will be, and it is moving even now to prevent your awakening."

Mary's thoughts were cotton wool, swaddling his words so that the sharp meaning could not be felt. But she struggled with them until some semblance of understanding emerged. "We're in danger?"

"A time of frost and fire approaches."

"Why do you care?" She jerked, not meaning for her words to sound so emboldened. When he didn't answer, she said, "What do you expect me to do?" though she feared the answer.

"Nothing is as it appears. You will need new eyes." He reached out, and his arm appeared to stretch like melting rubber. Fingers that were not fingers scratched the centre of her forehead and Mary's vision fragmented in jewelled images and starbursts. When she could finally see again, the stranger had raised his arm and was pointing out of the door. "Go. See."

She found herself at the village hall without any memory of how she had got there from her cottage. She still had on her slippers, but didn't have a coat, and she shivered in the early morning cold. Dreamily, she made her way into the hall.

Her hand flew to her mouth at the choking stench. Gideon, the chairman of the parish council, and some teenage boy whose name she didn't recall dozed in chairs, worn out by futile caring. She tried not to pay any attention to two unmoved bodies that lay blackened by the plague in the centre of the room, and instead made her way to the side room where lay those still clinging on to thin life. But the instant she stepped across the threshold she was shocked rigid.

Tiny figures as insubstantial as smoke danced and twisted above the heads of the woman and young boy lying on the tables. Black-skinned, with a mix of human and lizard qualities, their twirling tails and curved horns reminded Mary of nothing more than medieval illustrations of devils. A malignant glee filled every movement as they soared and ducked, pinching and stabbing their unfortunate hosts. And where they touched the woman and boy, blackness flowed from them into the strange meridians the plague left on the bodies of its victims.

As Mary clutched the doorjamb in disorientation, the devils appeared shocked that she could see them. Their malignancy returned quickly, though, and they silently jeered and mocked her with offensive gestures, knowing she could do nothing to stop them.

Mary grabbed a yard brush from the wall and swung it to swat them away, but it passed straight through them; they weren't there, not in any sense she understood.

Staggering back into the main hall, understanding swept through her. Now she knew why the medication didn't work, why the plague was like none seen before; it wasn't of the world at all. And after that, other thoughts surfaced in a mad rush of release, but the most important was this: Caitlin had gone in search of a cure without realising the plague's true nature. She may well have been sent to her death.

chapter four
ON THE EDGE OF FOREVER

"Remember me when I am gone away,
Gone far away into the silent land."
Christina Georgina Rossetti

The Oxfordshire countryside was coming alive. Buds were bursting on all the branches and overgrown hedgerows, and burgeoning wildlife scurried everywhere Caitlin looked. The already crumbling roads were camouflaged with thistle and yellow grass. Caitlin fought back a wave of grief at the realisation that Grant and Liam weren't there to experience it with her. Sometimes the despair came from nowhere, like a storm at sea, and she had to battle to keep in control. Other times she was simply numb.

To distract herself, she turned her attention to Mahalia and Carlton while Crowther drove.

"Where were you going when we met you?" Caitlin asked.

Mahalia thought for a moment, then said, "To meet you."

Caitlin didn't hear any sarcasm in the comment, but she couldn't be sure. She still hadn't decided whether she liked Mahalia, or if the girl's sullen attitude was simply a defence mechanism.

Mahalia saw what was going through Caitlin's head and gave an annoyed shake of her head. "Carlton saw you in his dreams. Yeah. Really. He was determined that we should come after you."

The boy looked up at Caitlin with wide, innocent eyes that made him seem even younger. She saw in them something of Liam and instantly wanted to hug him. "He dreamed about me?"

Mahalia read Caitlin's expression and threw a protective arm around Carlton's shoulders. "He's special. Aren't you, mate?" He giggled silently as she squeezed him. "I didn't believe it at first, but he soon showed me. He sees things."

"Visions?"

"I suppose. He knows all sorts of stuff that he shouldn't. Sometimes he has trouble making me understand exactly what he's saying, but I get most of it. He's got us out of a few scrapes. There was a time in Southampton . . ." She shook her head to dispel the sour memory. "I wouldn't be here now if not for him."

"But why me?" Caitlin said.

Mahalia's contemptuous expression said that she had no idea either.

"What is it, Carlton?" Caitlin asked gently. But all the boy would do was smile.

"He does that sometimes," Mahalia said. "He'll tell you in his own good time."

"So when were you going to tell me this, Mahalia?"

"Oh, soon," the girl replied lightly.

Caitlin didn't fall for it. She wondered what else lay behind Mahalia's diamond-hard exterior that the teenager wasn't revealing.

They made their way through picturesque villages that belied the advent of the Fall. In many of them, life appeared to go on as normal: wisps of smoke floated up from the chimneys of stone houses and washing fluttered on lines in back gardens. Villagers out on their errands would stop and stare in amazement as the car roared by, wondering what the apparition signified. Other lanes were blocked by horse-drawn carts transporting produce from one village to the next, the drivers yanking the reins tight to prevent their horses from shying at the unfamiliar beast.

Eventually, reaching a minor road along a windswept ridge on the edge of the Cotswolds, Crowther pulled up against a mass of vegetation that had once been the verge.

"We're here?" Caitlin said, looking for some sign of a specific destination. All she could see were untended fields turned wild, and burgeoning hedgerows and copses.

Crowther grunted something incoherent in response and set out along the road without waiting for the others, his staff clattering an insistent rhythm. Mahalia and Carlton crawled out from behind the seats, stretching aching muscles. It was still and peaceful, with insects flitting over the long grass and birds singing in every tree.

As Caitlin, Mahalia, and Carlton hurried to catch up with the professor, the chattering at the back of Caitlin's head grew louder as her inner selves became feverishly excited.

Mahalia could feel something, too, for the contempt had left her face to be replaced by an out-of-place uncertainty. "Where are we going?" she asked. Carlton gave her hand a supportive squeeze; of all of them, he appeared the most at ease.

Crowther pointed to a weatherworn rock rising up in a field to their left. Rusty iron railings imprisoned it. "Well, there's part of it," he said gruffly. He turned swiftly through a gate concealed by overgrown vegetation and led them past a small hut with yellowing pamphlets in a dirty display case. And then they were there.

Surrounded by trees and hedges on three sides was a small stone circle forty strides across. Only a few of the pockmarked, eroded limestone pillars still stood tall. The majority were broken stumps. On the fourth side, two gateway stones opened out onto sunlit fields rolling down into a valley.

"The Rollrights," Crowther intoned. "A Neolithic stone circle."

"This is where we get to that other world?" Caitlin asked.

"Where we'll make the attempt to cross over." Crowther led the way cautiously, his darting eyes searching amongst the trees.

They paused on the edge of the circle, which Crowther defined with a wave of his hand. "These are known as the King's Men." He turned and pointed in the direction of the stone now hidden behind the hedge across the road. "The King Stone." And then away across the fields to the east, where they could just make out four upright stones and one fallen. "The remains of a chambered long barrow, now known as the Whispering Knights. Legend says they are a king and his knights turned to stone by a witch. Some of the locals say the stones come alive at midnight, performing strange ritual dances . . . they even go down to Little Rollright Spinney over there to get a drink. Stories like that are one of the hidden sources of information I spoke of earlier. The suggestion of transformation and magic tells me the ancients believed this place had a special power—that's what we need to tap into, the reason why we're here."

Caitlin expected Mahalia to make some sneering comment, but the girl remained on edge and watchful.

"I'm not sure I like it here," Caitlin said.

"You're responding to the atmosphere. This is a special place," Crowther replied.

"What do you mean?"

"It has a unique ambience, a confluence of subtle alterations to the quality of the light, the scents of the vegetation, the temperature . . . and on an unseen level, patterns of background radiation, ultrasound, anomalous radio signals. What you're feeling is the shock of a new experience. It's quite . . . destabilising. You'll get used to it."

Mahalia didn't look convinced. She put her arm around Carlton again and led him away to one side where she whispered to him insistently, flashing occasional urgent glances at Caitlin.

Crowther moved to the tallest of the nearby stones and held out one hand, as if to touch it. But then he hesitated, as if he were about to plunge his hand into water that could be freezing cold or boiling hot. He steeled himself, then clamped his palm on the surface before smiling. "Power, you see. Infused in every molecule."

"What kind of power?" Caitlin asked.

"Ah, that's the question. Something science never quite got to grips with. This place is like a battery . . . no, like a node on some national energy grid." He removed his hat and leaned forward until his forehead was gently touching the cool rock. "There was a research group called the Dragon Project working here in the late seventies, early eighties, looking into the notion of some kind of telluric energy—earth energy. Airy-fairy, you might say." He laughed. "New Age nonsense. But then a Geiger counter picked up sudden surges of radiation, something that only seemed to happen at megalithic sites. And then they found pulses of ultrasound, strange radio signals, short bursts, like a homing beacon. They never did get to the bottom of it."

Caitlin realised that Crowther was right: she was starting to feel better, attuning herself to the subtle energies of the place. The chattering voices had quietened, and an abiding peace rose in her heart. She breathed deeply, tasting the trees and grass and rock. But there was still memory, tugging her back. "How long have we got?" she said.

Crowther looked at the sky, an ages-old shaman divining the wind and clouds. "Not as much time as I'd like."

"You don't think the Whisperers will leave us alone?"

"No. Do you?" He eyed her cautiously before deciding not to let it spoil his mood. "It's going to be a lovely day. Make the most of it."

The morning passed slowly. They lit a fire on rough ground beyond the hut and cooked up a meal of eggs and herbs, stolen by Mahalia from a farm they had passed during the night. Caitlin's plea that they in some way pay for the produce had been cut short by the angry farmer and his sons chasing them furiously away.

The day was warmer than they could have expected for that time of year. Caitlin and Mahalia took turns keeping watch while Crowther busied himself with things he insisted were necessary for whatever ritualistic endeavour he had planned for sunset, though Caitlin was convinced he was simply trying to avoid doing any real work.

It was during her third watch in the early hours of the afternoon that Caitlin became entranced by sparkling lights high up in the trees. Just the pleasing play of sunlight in the branches, she thought, until she realised that the glimmering moved of its own accord. She watched the glitter trails with distracted curiosity, lost in the dreamy peace that had crept over her since she had become accustomed to the Rollrights' peculiar atmosphere. Even the sickening undertow of grief in the pit of her stomach had abated, and though she still thought of Liam and Grant every few moments, it was with the warm remembrance of happier times, not the sense of loss that physically hurt. Perhaps the lights were another manifestation of whatever caused the odd sound and radiation effects Crowther had mentioned earlier, she speculated.

But after five minutes, she realised with a growing sense of amazement that she could make out tiny forms at the heart of the lights—little people, with wings. The discovery filled her with a pure, innocent wonder that she had not experienced since she was a child. She watched them for a few more minutes until one appeared to notice her and swooped down. The figure hovered on gossamer wings, barely six inches high, its androgynous features incredibly beautiful. The skin itself exuded the golden light.

She reached out to it, but it always stayed a few inches away from her finger-tips, examining her with a deep curiosity as if it was reading the depths of her mind. Eventually its puzzled face broke into a sympathetic smile and it dived forward to trace its fingers across her forehead before darting a few feet away. Its touch felt like the wings of a moth, but then a strange syrupy warmth flowed through Caitlin and in an instant even the last vestige of her grief disappeared. The being's smile became broad and warm. It waved to her once, and then soared back up to rejoin its companions in the treetops.

Caitlin could barely believe what had happened. In a rush of excitement, she ran from her lookout to tell the others what had happened.

Crowther was nowhere to be found, but Mahalia and Carlton had just returned from an exploration of the surrounding countryside. She gushed out a description of the event, ending with a passionate admission: "It cured me! Of my grief, I mean! I'm sure it'll be back . . . I know it will . . . but for now . . . amazing!"

Mahalia merely nodded and said, "Good for you."

"You're not surprised? I mean, I'm talking about, you know, fairies or something . . ."

The girl shrugged blithely. "I've seen things. Anybody who goes out on the road has—in the countryside, the wild areas."

Caitlin had a sudden true perspective of the girl's age; Mahalia acted so much older than she was. "What happened to your family, Mahalia?"

"None of your business."

Caitlin didn't need to quiz her further to guess the true picture. She knew how bad things had been in the cities—the breakdown of communication and food supplies, the riots and looting. In some areas, she'd heard tell there had been death on a grand scale. They'd all thought society had been so strong, but in the end it was as fragile as a human life.

As they made their way back to the campfire, Caitlin asked, "Why are you coming with us? You know it could be dangerous."

Mahalia's laugh was so bitter, Caitlin winced. The girl pulled her jacket to one side to reveal a harness of belts she'd strung together herself. It held various weapons—knives, straight razors, screwdrivers, and other things that looked homemade but nonetheless lethal. "You haven't seen what it's like out there."

"No, I haven't. But I can guess . . ."

"No, you can't. Nobody could, because everyone had been fooled into thinking we're all such cosy, caring people. But take away a few home comforts and the truth really comes out."

"I know some people—" Caitlin began in disagreement.

Mahalia laughed again. "Listen up. I'd been hiding out in the country but couldn't find any food during that first winter, so I went into Southampton. Big mistake. All the rich folk had built a nice little compound where they'd stock-piled food and they'd found enough shotguns to keep everyone else out. The poor were left to fend for themselves in the city centre. And that's just what they did. There were gangs—young, old, black, white—all fighting for their bit of turf. They didn't care what was going on in the rest of the world, they didn't care about decency, they just cared about getting through the day. That's what hap-pens when it comes down to survival. You'll do anything just to stay alive."

"No . . ."

"Yes! I got picked up by some creepy old guy the first time I wandered in beg-ging for food. He hit me round the back of the head with a lump of wood and dragged me back to his place, locked me in the attic with a bunch of others. He'd got a nice little business going, trading people for food . . . girls, boys, women . . ."

"For sex?"

"For anything . . . sex, work, stealing. I spent four nights in there—ten of us in a space as big as a van. No toilet, no light, a few crumbs of food every now and then, a few drops of water that tasted like he'd pissed in it. One woman in there . . . she'd got a baby. She'd been in longer than me. The kid was crying all the time, and she'd hardly got any milk. She was in a bad way. Then suddenly there wasn't any crying anymore."

Caitlin had a vivid impression of Liam in his pram. "It died."

"She killed it. Smothered it, because she needed all the energy she'd got just to stay alive."

"Oh, no . . ."

Mahalia snorted dismissively. "That's the way it goes. I got sold on soon after. But I wasn't anybody's property for long. I learned to look after myself. I've taken a man's eye out with a spoon, watched it bounce across the floor, then squashed it with my boot in front of his good eye. And you know what? I let him off lightly— I should have had both his eyes out. I've stabbed a screwdriver into somebody's ribs while they were sleeping to collapse a lung. But I've never been raped! I'm proud of that. All the sick bastards out there, and nobody's ever took me."

Carlton shook her shoulder roughly; he had tears in his eyes.

"I'm sorry, mate." Mahalia gave him a squeeze, then said to Caitlin, "This place is hell. People make it hell. It can't be any worse where you're going."

Caitlin drew patterns in the soil with a twig while she weighed Mahalia's words. Finally she said, "I've seen terrible things happen—not like that, not things people do to each other but . . . bad things. And you mustn't ever let yourself think that the bad people are everything. Yes, they exist, but the best of humanity is out there, too. People helping each other . . . making incredible acts of sacrifice. I honestly believe most people are good."

"We'll have to agree to differ there." Mahalia suddenly jumped to her feet, pulling out a knife from under her coat.

Caitlin whirled to see a figure coming toward them out of the glare of the sun. It was a man, but not Crowther.

"Don't come any nearer," Mahalia said.

He held up his hands, then moved slightly so that the sun was behind a tree and they could all see him. He was in his early thirties, good looking with blond hair and blue eyes that reminded Caitlin slightly of Leonardo DiCaprio; a sensitivity was embedded in his features that made her instantly warm to him.

"I didn't mean to scare you . . ." he began.

"You don't scare us," Mahalia said. "We just don't like you."

"You're going to try to cross over, aren't you?" He fixed his attention on Caitlin.

Mahalia shifted suspiciously, looking to Caitlin for a lead.

"You don't have to answer—I can see it in your faces." He lowered his hands slowly. "I want to come with you."

"Who are you?" Caitlin asked. "And how do you know what we're doing here?"

"Matthew Jensen. Matt. Architect by trade. I know what you're all thinking—'Let's get him on board—that's a skill we *really* need.' But it could be worse. I could be an estate agent. How do I know what you're doing here? You mean, how do I know all about *crossing over*, and that there is actually somewhere to cross over to? Well, long story."

Carlton watched him curiously but openly, then motioned toward the fire.

"Carlton wants to know some more," Mahalia translated. "Me, I think, why would we need you tagging along? But I'm reasonable . . . I'll give you a chance to convince us. You've got five minutes."

"Five minutes? I can give you my life story in half that." He headed for the fire and sat down.

Caitlin had already warmed to his self-deprecating manner, but she couldn't see any advantage in him joining their motley crew. If she hadn't been so unstable at the time, she probably wouldn't have been eager to encourage Mahalia and Carlton to go along with them. "So how do you know what we're planning?" she asked, sitting next to him. The question came to her in the screeching tones of Brigid, who seemed to have taken an interest in Matt.

"Simple. You wouldn't be here for any other reason," Matt replied. "The countryside's too dangerous to be wandering around alone. If you had any sense you'd be holed up with your community. And this place . . . all these kinds of places . . . the stories that build up around them keep everybody away. It's not exactly a top holiday destination." He motioned to the haunting stones. "During the Fall, I met someone who told me that all these ancient sites were doorways to the place where the gods came from. You know about them, right? You heard the stories . . . what happened to London? So, the nutter alarm went off. You smile and nod and shuffle away. But then I saw the lights over the stones at the solstices, the shapes passing through—not human, you know?—heard the music—God, the music!" He gave a faintly embarrassed smile. "Sorry. You had to have heard it for yourself to understand, I guess."

"So why would we want to go to that place?" Mahalia asked. Caitlin could see that she wasn't warming to Matt. "And what makes you think we know how to?"

"I don't know if you do, but I do know a lot of people would like to find a way through to that place, for a whole load of different reasons. My reason? Simple." He looked openly into all their faces, laying himself bare before them. "I think my daughter's over there."

A bird cry, low and mournful, made them all jump; Caitlin realised she had been hanging on his words. "You think your daughter crossed over?"

"I think they took her . . . something did." He took a deep, calming breath. "It seems to me that place and the things that live there are responsible for all our old stories and legends. We've been misidentifying them for thousands of years—angels and devils, fairies, UFOs—I don't know, Men in Black. And you know the old stories about changelings? How the fairies would take human babies? Do you know how many people go missing every year? Tens of thousands in Britain alone. Every year. And I reckon some of them end up over there . . . for whatever reason." He looked away from them into the trees, but he couldn't hide his concern.

"How old's your daughter?" Caitlin asked.

"Eight. At least, she would be now. She's been gone nine months. Somebody from the village saw her up here just before she disappeared, even though she knew she was supposed to keep well away from this place. I've searched every-where—every ditch, wood, lake . . ." He shook his head. "This is my last chance."

"I'm so sorry," Caitlin said. "I know what it's like . . ." She caught herself. "Is your wife coping OK?"

"She left a long time ago, when Rosetta was two. I haven't seen her since." He reached out his arms toward them. "If you know a way over, take me with you. Please. The way I see it, there's safety in numbers. I'm fit. I can look after myself."

"So can we," Mahalia said.

"I'm sure you can, but one extra person to keep watch at night can only be a good thing, surely."

Caitlin didn't have to think; how could she refuse him? "Of course you can come," she said, "if we *can* get over. I'm still not convinced."

He smiled. "Thanks for trusting me."

Mahalia clearly didn't want to hang around the adults any more than she had to, so Caitlin and Matt went for a walk through the waist-high grass of the adjoining field. They felt safer out in the open away from the clustering trees where there always seemed to be something lurking, just out of sight.

Though she knew little about him, Caitlin felt a connection between them. He had a sharp wit, but she could sense something much more troubling just beneath the surface. She wanted to find out more about him, but he was the one who asked the first questions as they walked.

"Are you OK?" he asked. "Because there's something . . . I don't know . . . sad about you. Or is that just me being my usual imperceptive self?"

The familiar swell of grief hit her so hard that she almost gasped. The usual response was to damp it down into that area where Brigid, Briony, and Amy could wrap the harrowing pain in cotton wool until it felt as if it was just a dream, and everything that caused it had never happened. Yet this time was different. After a brief, choking hesitation, she began fitfully to tell Matt all about Grant and Liam. She couldn't hold back the tears and Matt didn't appear to mind, so she let them flow. The racking sobs made her chest feel as if she'd crawled out from under a landslide.

Matt waited for them to subside and then said, "I'm sorry. I feel like such a fool talking about my problems when you've been through all that—"

"No!" Caitlin said, horrified. "Don't ever say that! All my life's in the past now. You've got a chance to save Rosetta, that's the important thing."

"There isn't a thing I can say that won't sound like daytime TV advice, but don't talk about your life being in the past—"

"Well, it is." They reached the jumble of stones that Crowther had called the Whispering Knights. Iron railings protected them from prying fingers, but Caitlin desperately wanted to touch their cool surface. "When I started out on the road to this place, I was in a terrible state . . . didn't really know what I was doing. When I finally came to my senses and the professor told me what he planned . . . well, if I was a sane, rational woman with everything to live for, I would have walked away there and then. I can still barely believe that this mythical Otherworld really exists, but the professor is convinced. If it doesn't, we've got nothing to lose. But if it does, we're going to a place filled with dreams and nightmares . . . a place where humans aren't supposed to exist. How long do you think we might possibly last there?"

"But we've got to try, haven't we?"

Caitlin reached across the railings and just managed to touch one of the stones; her fingers tingled in response. "Yes, you've got to try for your daughter, and if there's a chance of finding a cure for the plague, as Professor Crowther seems to think there is, then I've got to try, because, you know, better me . . ."

"I wish you wouldn't be so fatalistic. It might be catching." He stared across the sweep of the field to the trees hiding the Rollrights. "I'm keen to meet this professor. He seems to know a lot of stuff. What is he, like Doctor Who or something?"

Caitlin laughed at the idea. "Just wait till you meet him."

"You trust him?"

"He seems OK. I don't think he tells the whole truth. He doesn't lie, exactly, it's just that he doesn't give you the whole picture." Caitlin realised that Matt was staring intently back toward the standing stones. "What is it?"

"I don't know. Probably nothing. I thought I saw something . . ." He gave her a tight smile. "Look, you wait here. I'll check it out and then come back for you."

Before Caitlin could protest, he was loping away through the grass. She waited for an uncomfortable moment, but there was an eerie atmosphere now that she was standing all alone in the wide open space and she decided to set off after Matt.

She'd only gone a few paces when there was a crack of thunder, though the sky was clear blue. A smell of burned iron rose up around her and she had the sense of a sudden, crackling light at her back. She spun round to see the Whispering Knights shimmering as if she were looking at them through a heat haze.

And then a figure emerged from behind them and rapidly began to move toward her. Her first, shocked impression was that it was some black-skinned monster with the head of a pig. Her second notion gave her a true picture: it was a knight in gleaming black armour, a sword hanging from his belt, but his helmet was in the shape of a boar's head.

"Get away!" Briony screamed from Caitlin's mouth as the knight marched implacably toward her. She turned and she ran, trying not to stumble over the uneven ground, and she knew that this was what she had seen from her window on the evening Grant and Liam had contracted the plague. It had followed her from there to here, and even in the Ice-Field that thought filled her with a powerful dread.

"What is it?" Matt had run back and caught her shoulders; she fell into his arms.

"He's coming!" Briony screamed.

Matt peered over her shoulder, then slowly turned her round. The field behind was empty, save for the Whispering Knights keeping their lonely vigil.

Back at the campfire, Matt managed to comprehend Caitlin's mental state with the aid of Mahalia's less than sympathetic descriptions. As she calmed, Briony receded and Caitlin returned. She was happy to see that Matt still treated her in the same friendly manner.

"I did see somebody," Caitlin said.

Mahalia twirled a finger at the side of her head before winking at Carlton. But the boy didn't join in; his dark eyes suggested only the deepest sympathy. Caitlin smiled at him and nodded her thanks.

"Who the hell is this!" They all jumped as Crowther marched up, roaring as he jabbed a furious finger at Matt. "Good Lord, don't you stupid people understand what we're about! Why don't you summon up every thug and bandit in the area—"

"I'm not a bandit," Matt said, standing up and extending a hand. "I prefer the term desperado. I've always had a cowboy thing going on."

"Ahhhhh!" Crowther roared, throwing his arms into the air as if he were going to attack Matt. "Get out, damn you!"

Caitlin jumped up to throw herself between Matt and Crowther. "Professor, just a minute, I asked him to stay—"

"Is that supposed to calm me down? Someone with a tenuous grip on her own mental health finds a kindred spirit? I should beat you all to death with my staff now and be done with it!"

It took Caitlin a good twenty minutes to convince Crowther. He raged about waifs and strays and hangers-on compromising their security, and in the end Caitlin had to call on the services of a shrieking, neurotic Briony. Only then did Crowther back down, unable to cope with her psychosis.

Realising he was powerless to change anything, Crowther retired to the other side of the stones to brood, while Mahalia climbed onto the roof of the hut to throw stones at the wildlife. Carlton sat with Caitlin and Matt, listening to their conversation and smiling easily. Matt was surprised to hear Caitlin's stories of the intensity of the plague—he'd heard a couple of rumours in the local village but had seen nothing. That gave Caitlin some hope that its spread wasn't as fast as she'd feared.

It was Mahalia who spotted the professor sneaking off, from her vantage point on top of the hut. She dropped down and encouraged the others to follow him, but somehow he gave them all the slip. Half an hour later, his anguished cry rang across the valley. Their blood chilled, fearing the worst, Matt led Caitlin into the field, but they found the professor staggering toward them, looking haggard. Blood trickled down either side of his face.

"What happened?" Caitlin said. She reached out to examine his wounds, but Crowther knocked her hand away. Yet the action shifted his hair and she saw, or thought she saw, a hole drilled into the side of his head. "Who did that to you?" she asked, concerned.

"Nobody did it to me," he snapped. "I've been finding out the information we need—someone has to." He barged past them, but despite his demeanour they both saw his hands were shaking uncontrollably.

Back at the camp, he sat next to the fire to warm himself, though it wasn't particularly cold. "I know how to cross over," he said in a thin voice. "I had an idea before, but now I know it all." He jabbed a finger toward Caitlin. "You're the key."

"Me? But why me?"

"I presumed you were," Crowther continued as if she hadn't spoken. "And I know where we have to go for the cure once we get to wherever it is we're going. Somewhere called the House of Pain."

Matt laughed, eliciting a glare from Crowther. "It couldn't be called the House of Fun, could it? You're making this up."

"I'm going to ignore you," Crowther said, "and just talk to her." He indicated Caitlin. "I was told—"

"Who told you?" Caitlin interrupted.

"That doesn't matter." His voice was wearier now. "But the road will be long . . . and hard."

The shadows stretched out as the day drew to a close and soon Crowther was ready to begin his preparations. He took them to the centre of the circle where they could watch the sky for the exact moment of sunset. None of them were prepared to back out, despite Crowther's ominous information; even Mahalia was insistent.

"So you really know what you're doing?" Matt asked in a tone that suggested he didn't think the professor knew at all. Crowther ignored him, but Matt persisted. "People always said these stone circles had something mysterious about them," he continued. "Everybody thought it was just superstition."

This time Crowther couldn't resist. "There you have it. The clues have been before us for centuries, but in our arrogant belief that earlier people were ignorant, uneducated, superstitious barbarians, we ignored the truth that was hidden away in the old stories. Things that seem inherently stupid on the surface are metaphor and symbol. The stones coming to life, moving around, that means . . ."

"I'm not so sure that's a metaphor," Caitlin whispered.

Everyone followed her gaze to the stones, which now appeared to have a thin blue light limning their edges in the setting sun. The stones themselves had taken on a ghostly quality, which could well have been a trick of light and shadow, but made it seem as if they were in one place, then another, then back again.

"The stones are dancing," Caitlin said with Amy's voice.

"What's going on?" Matt asked.

"Reality warp," Crowther said in a hushed voice. "This is where we got the legend that the stones here could never be counted correctly . . . different answers on different days. Reality here is thin, warping with the stresses of the energies concentrated in this spot."

"What kind of energy?" Matt asked. "Radiation?"

"Earth energy, spirit energy—it's called the Blue Fire, and it's in everything. If I could see it, it would be so much easier to find the patterns that would help us to open the door," Crowther complained.

"People can see it?" Matt said.

"Some. Those who've learned, or who have special abilities. You need to manipulate the Blue Fire to break through to the other side, but most normal people don't have the perception to do that." He delved into the depths of his knapsack and pulled out a small plastic bag of some dark substance.

"What's that?" Mahalia asked suspiciously.

"*Amanita muscaria*. The fly agaric mushroom. These are from Mexico. You wouldn't believe the trouble I had tracking them down."

"Magic mushrooms?" Matt said.

"I'm not eating those," Caitlin/Amy whimpered. "It's poison!"

"There are dangers involved in everything," Crowther said curtly. "Ancient Siberian shamen used these mushrooms to induce out-of-body experiences and mystical and prophetic visions. There was a cult of the sacred mushroom in Mexico. The pre-Columbian Indians, *circa* 1500 BCE, called it *God's Flesh*. Academics have even stated that *Amanita muscaria* was a significant part of the founding of Christianity alongside Jesus Christ himself. All our religions . . . civilisation itself . . . would not have come about if not for this tiny fungus."

"I knew a girl in Southampton who freaked out on them," Mahalia said.

"They're not meant for everyone." Crowther opened the bag and poured the shrivelled mushrooms into his palm. "It's special because it activates the 'God zone' in our brain and allows us to contact the divine, the place where higher forces live, the home of dreams, visions, and imagination . . . the Otherworld. We're going to open the doors of perception."

Mahalia shook her head. "I don't like drugs. They stop you keeping an eye on the world. They're a luxury for the weak and the lazy."

"We're not talking about hedonism, little girl," Crowther said witheringly. "We're talking about the only possible way we have of getting from here to there. Well, for you and me at least—she'll be fine." He nodded to Caitlin, who shied away in a little-girl manner. Crowther leaned toward her. "I'm not going to make you take them," he said loudly and insensitively. He turned over the fungi thoughtfully. "One codicil: Aldous Huxley said, 'once the doors of perception are unlocked, the path to hell is as open as the path to heaven.'"

"Oh, give it here if it'll shut you up." Mahalia grabbed some of the mushrooms and stuffed them into her mouth. Carlton watched her chew and swallow, then followed suit. Matt was next, a little reluctantly, and then Crowther took his portion.

"What now?" Matt asked.

"Now?" Crowther grabbed Caitlin and made her stand in the focal point of the circle. "You wait there," he said to her, "and do what I say the second I say it." To Matt, he said, "Meanwhile, we wait for the hallucinogen to take effect . . . and we hope."

A sense of awe had descended on the entire stone circle, pregnant with possibility. No birds sang; the trees barely stirred in the breeze. The sun slipped to the horizon, bringing gold to the face of the stones, ploughing long shadows into the heart of the ring.

"A fairy circle," Mahalia said in a whisper, the first stages of the trip evident in her voice.

"Exactly," Crowther said. "Metaphors and symbols, all hiding a deeper truth." They listened to the silence for a few moments and then the professor added, "We are Psychonauts, embarking on a journey beyond reality. Few have been this way before us."

"Let's hope we come back," Matt said.

"Look." Caitlin/Amy pointed past the shimmering ethereal stones to a hazy area in the field beyond. Ghostly but unthreatening figures appeared and then faded, walking through their echo-lives oblivious to Crowther and the others.

"The dream zone," Crowther said. "Reality is thinning."

Caitlin glimpsed people in ancient dress, images she distantly recalled from storybooks, some dressed in clothing styles she didn't recognise, others that looked barely human. And briefly she saw five people staring back at her—a man with dark hair, another whose torso was covered with tattoos, a thin Asian man, a woman with brown hair, and another with dyed-blonde hair. They appeared to be trying to communicate with her, but they were gone before Caitlin appreciated their presence. Caitlin looked round; Mahalia had seen them too.

"Magic," Matt said dreamily. "Everywhere."

"In the local stories, this place was supposed to be the favourite haunt of Oxfordshire fairies and Warwickshire witches," Crowther said. "The last Oxfordshire fairies were seen disappearing down a hole under these stones in the eighteenth century. It was reported, written down—an eyewitness account. Amazing."

The air had grown unseasonably warm, and a hazy, cosseting feeling enveloped them all; they felt at peace yet excited about what lay ahead. Distant music floated in and out of their hearing, merging with the sound of the wind.

But just as they began to enjoy the warm, joyful atmosphere, Carlton began to whimper. Caitlin didn't have to ask what was wrong because she could feel exactly what Carlton was sensing: a dull psychic warning of impending danger. If they hadn't been in that spot, tripping, they would never have perceived it, but now it was like an alarm bell tolling.

"What's going on?" Matt asked fearfully.

"Don't get worked up," Crowther cautioned. "The drug will magnify your emotions. You'll panic."

"Don't get worked up?" Amy was gone, and now the neurotic, frightened presence of Briony dominated. "You know what's coming."

"What is it?" Matt said, urgently.

"Things have been tracking us," Caitlin said. "Tracking me. They won't give up."

"Stay calm." Crowther laid a heavy hand on Caitlin/Briony's shoulder.

"What things?" Matt searched the area. The sun was now just a thin line of red at the horizon, and the shadows surged everywhere amongst the trees.

"The Whisperers." Caitlin/Briony hugged her arms around herself.

"Can you feel that?" Matt stood up, ready to roam to the edge of the circle to search the growing dark until Crowther grabbed his jacket and pulled him back down.

And then they all could feel it: a wave of black despair washing across the land, rising inexorably up to the higher ground where the stones looked out. The Whisperers were coming.

"What are they?" Caitlin/Briony asked desperately. "How can they make us feel this way?"

Mahalia grabbed Crowther's arm and said ferociously, "How much longer before this thing works?"

"I don't know. I don't know if it *will* work."

Mahalia whirled around. "We're too exposed here. We need to find shelter . . . somewhere we can defend."

"They shouldn't be able to step into the circle," Crowther said. "The Blue Fire will keep them out."

"But if we don't cross over, they can just wait outside the stones until we starve," Mahalia said.

A thin purple light was visible far away down the valley, but drawing quickly closer.

"Come on!" Caitlin screamed. It felt as if all her occupants were struggling to gain control.

The remaining sun was just the slightest sliver, as if the sky was cut and bleeding. Yet oddly the blue glow edging the stones was growing brighter, running in veins and capillaries down the very rock as if infusing them with life. The air became charged with magic.

A ragged breathing rose above the stillness. Mahalia drew one of the knives from her harness and turned in the direction of the sound. Purple mist drifted languorously through the trees and soon after a figure came stumbling through it. But this was not one of the Whisperers. It had the shape of a man, though the purple light was leaking out of him as if he were a fractured steam pipe.

Carlton whimpered; Mahalia crouched low to the ground, ready to fend off any attack.

The figure reached the edge of the stones and they recognised him as the hermit who had tried to drive them away from the Motor Museum. But he was no longer as he had been.

"My God! What have they done to him?" Crowther breathed, transfixed.

The man could barely be called that anymore. Bones protruded through his skin as if it had been broken and the frame had torn through, but without blood; instead there was that purple light. His skull shimmered in a spot where there should have been hair and scalp; an eye stared out of a harsh orbit. He somehow managed to lurch forward even though a thigh bone was cracked and exposed. The numerous ridges and furrows of exposed bone made him resemble some kind of walking dinosaur.

And as he moved, he moaned, a thin whine of pain and despair that provided a backdrop to words that could not have been his. "There is no hope," he said with an unsettling, otherworldly sibilance. "It ends here. You end here." Rusted sword blades emerged from both of his hands where they had been embedded in the bone.

Behind him came the dark, lumbering shapes of the Whisperers on their mounts, black against the shadows but their eyes lit with purple. The colour itself had begun to make Caitlin feel queasy. They were approaching the circle on every side, drawing in their ring of terror.

And if they couldn't enter the circle, their herald had no such qualms. He crashed across the barrier, swinging those sword blades wildly. Mahalia ducked at the last moment, narrowly escaping the loss of her head. Carlton scampered on all fours to the other side of the circle where he was feverishly aware of the Whisperers just a stone's throw away.

The man turned on Crowther, his crazed attacks unpredictable.

"LET ME OUT!" The terrible voice roared at the back of Caitlin's head: the Fifth, the one the others all feared. "LET ME OUT! LET ME BRING MY FURY TO BEAR!"

"No!" Caitlin told herself. "Never, never, never."

Matt threw himself forward, knocking Crowther out of the path of the killing blow. The sword drove into the soft earth.

"Life winds down to decay, then death," the herald continued. "All things are ending, always."

The drug was slowly working its magic in all of them, spinning up the spiral dance of the trip. The visual hallucinations were taking over from the auditory and emotional twists. The world within the circle was like a dream of bursting flowers and life, while the darkness howled at the stones from without.

"Now!" Crowther yelled at Caitlin. "Slam your hand on the ground! There! There!" Frantically he pointed to a spot near her feet.

Caitlin did as she was told and instantly lines of Blue Fire ran from each stone toward a focal point in the centre of the ring. The coruscating energy crackled, rising up like liquid, then forming odd geometric shapes. A massive structure of shimmering sapphire was forming over them.

The herald turned on Caitlin. He pointed one of the swords toward her throat, then drove it forward. She was rooted.

Matt knocked the blade away at the point when Caitlin closed her eyes in acceptance that it was all over. The rusted metal tore through the flesh of Matt's forearm, but still he turned and smashed a fist into the herald's jaw. The attacker stumbled, off balance. Before he could right himself, Mahalia appeared between his legs, thrusting a screwdriver up into his groin. Like a rat, she darted underneath him and came up, bringing a knife in a sideways motion across the herald's throat. Purple light was everywhere, mingling with the blue luminescence until they were all lost in colour.

As the herald went to his knees, Crowther yelled with a raw throat, "Get to the centre! Where the light is strongest!"

They all scrambled to the place where music swirled all around like a tornado and a rush of excitement came up through the ground and into their heads. Crowther made some strange gesture with his hands, whispered a word they couldn't comprehend, and then there was a sound like thunder and the world rippled and fell away.

chapter five
IN THE FOOTSTEPS OF INFINITY

"There are fairies at the bottom of our garden."
Rose Fyleman

The new world came up at them in a flash of white and they hit it hard, crashing to their knees and sucking in a huge gulp of air as if they had fallen from a high place. A fleeting memory of somewhere wonderful and blue slipped from their thoughts the moment they tried to catch it. Yet the sensations came too thick and fast for reflection on the transition. Snow lay thickly all around and a blizzard roared with such force they had to hunch against it like old men, yelling so their disbelief and amazement could be heard. Within seconds they were shaking with the bitter cold.

Despite their situation, Caitlin's eyes sparkled with wonder. "I can't believe it! We're . . . we're . . ."

"In Fairyland," Crowther said wryly. Good humour transformed his face. "For those who have studied the Kabbalah, this is Yesod, land of dreams, first staging post for the dead. We all go here in our sleep sometimes." He looked around, scarcely believing it himself.

"This is . . . just . . . amazing." Even though he was buffeted by the blizzard, Matt stretched out his arms so he could fill his lungs. "The crossing was so . . . wild." He struggled to find words to describe the experience. "I felt like I was filled with energy . . . like my thoughts were electric . . . like they were spinning around the universe. And here, it's . . . magic."

They all knew what he meant. The very essence of reality was heightened, as if they had walked through the screen into a movie. Colours were brighter, textures more evocative, aromas unbelievably heady, sounds so vibrant they had to stop and listen in amazement to the music the wind made. Suddenly there was no such thing as mundanity and boredom. Magic burned in even the smallest thing and anything was possible. The sheer wonder of it made their heads spin.

"It's like a drug," Caitlin said. "You could lose yourself in it." She thought for a moment and then added, "Who'd want to go back after experiencing something like this?"

"Who indeed?" Crowther said.

The cold was too much for them to wallow in the experience. "We have to find shelter before we freeze to death," Matt yelled. He took in their position in a second. At their backs were the loftiest mountains any of them had ever seen, the peaks snow-capped and filled with the dreams of childhood, solid against a sky of threatening slate grey cloud. Protecting his eyes from the stinging snow, he motioned down the slope.

The snow was knee-deep and it was hard going as they trudged downward, but at least the gale was at their backs. Soon Matt spotted a gully filled with boulders as large and misshapen as mythological beasts. He led them directly into it, relishing the protection it gave them from the wind and the worst of the snow.

Once in the shelter, they relaxed a little, but after the initial exhilaration, worries surfaced. Mahalia checked back up the slopes, the haunting images of the Whisperers still echoing through her mind. "Can they follow us?" she asked.

"I don't know," Crowther replied, "but I have no intention of waiting around to find out."

Caitlin was still dazed by the crossing. More than for the rest of them, the lure of the blue world they had passed through so quickly remained strong. "What did they do to that poor man?" she said. "It was as if they'd tried to turn him into one of them."

"He looked like some kind of zombie," Mahalia said.

"Maybe that's what they do—take people over." Matt was checking his arm.

"What is it?" Crowther asked.

"The hermit guy wounded me. Pretty badly." Matt held up his arm to show them. "But it's healed."

"A quality of the Blue Fire," Crowther said. "It has strong healing properties—"

"That blue, blue world . . ." Caitlin said dreamily.

Carlton started suddenly, his eyes wide.

"What is it, mate?" Mahalia hurried to his side and followed his gaze, but there was only the thick snow running along the edge of the gully and the grey sky beyond. The boy shook his head, unsure.

"He's probably disorientated," Crowther said. "Understandable. We've done something remarkable here—travelled between worlds to a place that has influenced our dreams for millennia—"

"Oh, stop being so pompous," Mahalia said. "Carlton's probably dealing with it better than you. Don't forget—"

"I know," Crowther said, adding in a childishly mocking voice, "he's *special*."

Mahalia shook her head in disgust at the professor's immature manner before leading Carlton gently away. "Don't worry, mate," she said gently, "we'll keep a good lookout."

They continued to pick their way along the gully, their teeth chattering. The gully ridge and the boulders obscured any view of their exact location, although it was clear they were on the lower slopes of the monolithic range.

As they edged their way around a rock as big as a house, Matt threw an arm across Crowther's chest to stop him and pointed to the thick snow at the gully ridge. Two red spots blazed like hot coals. They disappeared, came back again, and then there was a flurry of snow and they were gone.

"Eyes," Crowther said in shock.

"Something's tracking us." Mahalia remained cool as she eased one of the knives from beneath her jacket. Carlton huddled close to her. "Don't worry, mate, I'll look after you," she whispered comfortingly. She eyed Caitlin coldly, fending off Caitlin's attempt to move in to comfort Carlton herself.

"Come on, Prof," Matt said quietly, "you're the expert here. What kind of predators should we be looking out for?"

Crowther's laugh was not comforting. "Think of your worst nightmare, then expect something ten times more hideous. This is the land where anything is possible, good or bad. If we thought we were slipping down the food chain on our world, here—"

"I get the idea, Prof. Thanks for putting my mind at ease." Matt continued to lead the way, but his eyes never stopped searching the surroundings.

Eventually the gully opened out onto a small, exposed plateau where the snow lay thickly. Beyond it, the land gradually fell away again and the snow soon gave way to another mass of the enormous boulders. "Looks as if we're nearly in the foothills," Matt said. "Should be easier going if we can get across this bit." He didn't need to give voice to his fear that this would be the place where whatever was tracking them would attack; there was no cover, no place to run. At least they would be able to see it coming.

The snow was calf-high as they lurched into it, crunching underfoot like gravel. But they hadn't gone far when the two red eyes appeared suddenly on the ground six feet ahead of Matt. He half turned, ready to urge the others to sprint back to the gully.

Something rose up from the ground, as white as the snow that had concealed it. At first glance it resembled an enormous jellyfish with a crab-shell head from beneath which the two eyes glowed. But then they saw that beneath the strangely shaped skull it had a human form and what they had taken for the jellyfish-like drifting appendages were glistening white clothes hanging from its shoulders in tattered rags.

"I search for the Cailleach Bheur," the thing said in a voice that sounded like glass breaking. "She may release the Fimbulwinter."

Everyone in the group was struck dumb by the terrifyingly strange apparition looming before them. It swayed from side to side in a manner that suggested it was uncomfortable and they realised it couldn't quite understand the effect it was having on them.

"We ... we can't help you," Crowther replied eventually, his mouth dry. "I'm sorry."

"What are you?" Caitlin asked in the frightened voice of Amy.

The thing moved forward as if blown by the wind until it stood in front of Caitlin, and those frightening red eyes burned into her face. "I see ice in you?" it said, puzzled. Then, as if realising it had acted impolitely, it stepped back and held out arms swathed in the white tatters. "I am Moyaanisqi, known as the White Walker. I roam across all worlds. My home is the great wilderness, the frozen plains, the chill peaks. But what," it added curiously, "are you?"

"We're ... humans," Crowther replied awkwardly.

"Humans?" The White Walker thought for a moment, then exclaimed, "Fragile Creatures! I have seen your kind from afar when I have wandered the great mountain ranges of the Fixed Lands in search of the Cailleach Bheur, but never so close. Fragile Creatures!" There was wonder in its voice, as if *they* were the fantastical beings.

"You've been to our world?" Caitlin asked.

"Many times, though my long quest has made me solitary and wary of contact with others. I roved the high places and the white wastes for a time, leaving only the prints of my feet behind, finding nothing. And so I moved on, here, to the Far Lands. Perhaps my journey will take me further afield again."

"Then you have seen many things." There was a gleam in Crowther's eye.

"Many things."

"We are searching for a place called the House of Pain, though I suppose it may have another name. Could you direct us to it?"

The White Walker thought long and hard, then shook its strange crab-head slowly. "It may lie in the burning places where I cannot pass. But if that is so, then you may encounter the Djazeem who abide in the great sand deserts. There is a word of power I know that will make them do your bidding. Whisper it to them and they will be empowered to take you to your destination." It looked intently into all of their faces and then returned to Caitlin. "You. For in you there is not only ice, but also the fire that does not burn. You will carry the word of power."

Caitlin/Amy shied away, but the White Walker moved rapidly to whisper into her ear. Whatever it said, it affected Caitlin profoundly, for she fell to her knees, dazed.

"You will not recall the word until you need it, but it is there. That is my gift to you." It stared at them, shaking its head in amazement. "Fragile Creatures!" Then it drew itself up and turned to go. "Now I must continue my search, for the Cailleach Bheur never rests and the worlds must not come to an end."

Crowther called out one more question. "Who should we ask for guidance?"

The White Walker waved its tatters toward the lowlands. "Follow this path to another gully and then to the plain. I have heard tell there is a place nearby where live many who were once Golden Ones, but are no longer. They may know more. Farewell."

Before they could answer, it was gone, perfectly lost against the snowy background.

"What," Matt said in a state of extreme awe, "was that?"

"In the Dyak dialect of Borneo, there is a word," Crowther mused, "*ngarong*. It means a secret helper who appears in a dream. And, my friend, you will soon learn that this is very much a dream."

They made their way into another gully below the snowline. The way was uneven underfoot, and they had to pick their way carefully so as not to plunge onto the jagged rocks that lay all around. Broken-backed, skeletal trees pointed their way down the mountainside, at once cosily familiar yet somehow eerily alien. Such was the confusion of outcroppings that they couldn't measure their location against anywhere beyond their immediate surroundings.

Eventually, the rocky mountainside gave way to gentler slopes where wild grasses and flowers grew in abundance, and the trees became sturdier and thick with leaves. The temperature increased several degrees, but they still couldn't get their bearings or even tell the time of day, for a thick fog hung low, the air infused with fine droplets of moisture that soaked them to the skin within minutes.

Caitlin had the odd sensation that the scenery was creating itself just beyond her perception, shaping itself to fit her expectations. And if she allowed herself to dwell on that notion, she then had the disturbing feeling that there was an intellect all around her, in everything—the grass, the fog, the stones beneath her feet. She walked on the face of an infinite god, which could open its mouth and gobble her up in an instant. The notion set the voices at the back of her head chattering like monkeys in the jungle.

They broke the journey for a while and slept, possibly for hours, but it was difficult to tell because it was still daylight when they awoke. When they set off once more, Crowther strode on ahead, using his staff like a rudder to steer them. Caitlin and Matt followed closely at his heels, with Mahalia and Carlton bringing up the rear. After her initial euphoria, Mahalia had returned to her brooding, continually watching their surroundings with suspicion, which Caitlin decided was not a bad thing. But Carlton was bright and excited, skipping here and there to examine each new landmark as if he were on the holiday of a lifetime.

"I didn't realise you were such a fighter," Caitlin said to Matt as they waded through waist-high grass that rippled around them like a green sea. "You were a natural back at the Rollrights."

Matt shrugged uncomfortably. "It's amazing what you find inside you when you really need it."

"Well, I'm glad you're here."

"I want to prove my worth. I still feel like a hanger-on. Professor Crowther . . ."

"Ignore him. He's grumpy about everything. Whatever he says, I bet he's secretly glad you're along for the ride."

Matt shifted uncomfortably, then said, "There's no easy way to put this, but . . . are you feeling OK?"

"You mean the voices? I don't want—" Shards of glass were suddenly being driven into her brain. Her hands shot to cover her eyes.

"I'm sorry . . ."

But his question had released some of the pressure and words came out unbidden. "There are four of them, apart from me, all sitting in an Ice-Field, looking out into the night." She approached the image hesitantly, like a sleeping jungle beast.

"You're aware of them?"

"All the time."

"How does that feel?" He looked uncomfortable at his probing, but couldn't help his curiosity.

"Like they're all me, but not me. I know that doesn't make any sense, but I can't describe it any other way. There's a pressure in my head, as if they're all jammed in, each one trying to force themselves forward. Me . . . Caitlin . . . I'm a little stronger, so most of the time I can stay at the front. But if one of the others became stronger . . ." She really didn't want to consider that. "In a strange way, they help."

"How's that?"

"Most of the time they stop me thinking about Grant and Liam." Two graves, a stormy night; her mind shifted with a tempest-driven lurch. "Even mentioning their names, I know . . . I could go mad if I allowed myself to think about it." She laughed bitterly. "Mad! Madder . . . maddest . . . My sanity is hanging on a cliffedge by its fingertips, and the slightest thing could send it plunging into some big black hole, never to return. The others . . . it feels as if they're keeping all my thoughts and feelings chained up, keeping me steady. If it wasn't for them, I wouldn't be here." She chewed her lip until it hurt. "I'd probably be dead."

"Don't say that."

She was surprised by the concern in his voice. "I can't help it. Sometimes I wonder what's the point in going on. It's just misery all around us and misery waiting for us in the future. Sometimes I try to fool myself with optimism, hope, but the truth is always there, casting a shadow over anything. I wish I could feel pure again. I wish I could feel happy."

She had the impression that Matt wanted to put his arm around her shoulder to comfort her, but he restrained himself, and while a part of her was glad he did, another part just wanted to feel some human comfort. "How are you holding up?"

"You cope, don't you?" he said. "There's nothing else to do. Everybody's been trying so hard to hold things together since the Fall. It made us a third world country overnight. Yeah, we've been clawing our way back—the interim government in Oxford is doing a good job . . ."

"Government? I never heard about that."

"The news hasn't fanned out yet. You know what communication is like. I thought when Rosetta went, that was it. After Jan left, I was only really doing things for her—you know, getting through each day, making sure food was on the table, for what it was worth. But then I saw how everybody else was pulling together and I thought I was just being selfish for thinking about giving up. Now, more than ever, we need each other. I've got a part to play, however bad my personal situation."

Whether he intended it or not, his words struck a chord with Caitlin. Their conversation dried up as she retreated deep into herself where the cold winds of the Ice-Field blew.

By the time they'd got through the fog, night swathed the countryside and a heavy rain dampened their spirits.

Mahalia increased her pace until she was beside Crowther and then gripped his arm forcefully. "I'm cold and I'm wet and I'm tired and I'm hungry," she said. "Where's this city?"

"They don't really make maps of this place," Crowther replied with irritation. "Now shut up—you sound like a whining brat."

"Are you sure we're up to dealing with the things we're going to meet in this place?" Matt asked. "The White Walker was about the most bizarre thing I could imagine, but at least it was friendly. We may not be so lucky next time."

"I don't think we really have a choice, do we?" Crowther replied curtly.

Carlton began to tug on the professor's sleeve. Crowther rounded on the boy, then caught himself when he saw Mahalia and Caitlin's glares. "What is it?" the professor said in clipped tones.

Excitedly, Carlton pointed across the sweeping grassland into the dark rainswept distance. Gradually the others picked out flickering lights that they had first taken to be twinkling stars.

"I don't want to go there." The tiny, frightened voice of Amy chilled them all.

The fortress city rose up the side of one of the foothills into the dark, vast even in the part they could see illuminated by the light of the torches that blazed along the ramparts. A jumbled mass of towers and spires, domes, vaults, steeples, and the pitched roofs of myriad smaller dwellings, all of them crammed so closely together that the city resembled some third world sprawl, the layout so confused and organic that what lay beyond the light could have stretched on forever.

The city walls at the front rose up two hundred feet or more, the lowest part of them constructed from gargantuan boulders, as if the city had grown naturally from the earth. An ebony gate six storeys high was set in front of a rough road that wound across the plain. On either side of it, roaring flames hissed in the rain.

If they hadn't known better, they would have said the city itself was alive, for it exuded an oppressive, brooding presence, and as they stood before those massive gates they couldn't escape the feeling that it was surveying them with a forensic eye to decide if they were worthy to enter.

For the first time, Crowther was so disturbed that they all thought he might turn back, but after a moment's hesitation he marched forward, held up his fist for one cautious instant, and then hammered on the gate. The pounding that rang out from his knock was distorted beyond all reason into a deafening alarum that made them cover their ears. Beyond the gates, the thunderous warning ran along winding streets into the heart of the city.

"At least they heard us," Crowther said. The humour fell flat. Caitlin/Amy clutched on to Matt's arm and whimpered. Carlton, however, held his head high and walked forward to stand beside Crowther. He appeared more curious than anything.

They waited in unbearable anticipation as the echoes rang out, eyeing each other fitfully. After long moments, they heard the clunk of some locking mechanism, and then the gates slowly ground open. There was no one on the other side.

It took a while for them to pick out the detail of what lay beyond the shadows clustered under the arch of the gate; not because it was dark, for torches burned everywhere, but because their eyes appeared to mist over, or because their brains took an unusually long time to piece together an image from the information they were receiving.

Eventually they agreed that a cobbled street wound up the hillside into shadow amongst houses of varying styles—most prominently medieval and Tudor—clustering so hard against the road that they threatened to swallow it. The claustrophobia was palpable.

All five of them hesitated, unsure if they should enter, until figures emerged from the shadows. They were men, barely more than five feet tall, clad in leather and steel that was not quite armour but not quite clothes. They had long hair and beards, but their eyes were the most disturbing thing. Flat and cold, they showed no personality, nothing human at all.

Crowther made a strange, nervous noise in his throat and stifled it with embarrassment. "We are visitors from the Fixed Lands," he began. He'd practised the words a hundred times in his head, as he had learned in the college, but they still sounded strange. "Do you accept us freely and without obligation?"

The cold, unnerving stares of the guards did not waver, but after a few seconds a slightly taller guard stepped forward from the group. Crowther was pleased to see a little more life in his eyes. "Is that a Sister of Dragons I see before me?" His gaze was fixed on Caitlin.

Crowther followed his stare, unsure how to respond. "If you say so."

The chief guard nodded thoughtfully and motioned for them to enter. Matt began to step forward, but Crowther held him back with an arm across his chest. "Do you accept us freely and without obligation?" Crowther asked again.

The chief guard eyed him slyly. "We do. Now follow me."

Caitlin/Amy buried her face in Matt's shoulder as they walked into the city and the gates boomed shut behind them.

They were led through the steeply winding cobbled streets for nearly half an hour. Houses, inns, and shops pressed oppressively on either side and leaned in over their heads so that only a thin sliver of sky was visible. Occasionally they would glimpse strange faces peering at them through bottle-glass windows that distorted the inner torchlight into starbursts. Sometimes they would hear whispered comments that they couldn't understand, but which disturbed them immensely.

Finally they rounded a corner into a small cobbled square with a mildewed fountain, no longer working. The water in the stagnant pool around it was stained with green slime. On the far side stood a threatening building that towered over the surrounding rooftops. It echoed the construction of the city itself, monolithic walls soaring up into the darkness, devoid of ornamentation, like a slab of granite.

The leader of the guards turned to them with a strange smile. "We bid you welcome to the Court of Soul's Ease."

Inside the enormous building—which they had decided was a palace or a city hall, though it contained none of the opulence one would have expected to find in either of those places—a chill exuded from the stone walls that penetrated deep into their bones. Impenetrable shadows lay all around and even the flickering torches that lighted their way did little to dispel them. The pervading atmosphere was one of waiting for a terrible event that could never be deflected.

The five travellers were led along interminable corridors, occasionally glimpsing vast vaulted halls through half-open doors where only the echoes of footsteps lived. But as they progressed deeper into the heart of the building, they saw more of the strange small people, flitting across their path carrying secretive bundles or gossiping conspiratorially in pairs, hidden in alcoves, hands raised to cover their mouths. They would watch the procession pass with intense speculation; Caitlin couldn't tell if they were fearful or threatening, or simply contemptuous. There was an overpowering sense of intelligence moving through the shadows, of plotting and waiting, of secret treaties and backroom murders.

"I don't think I've breathed since we crossed over," Matt whispered, possibly to himself.

Caitlin came forward from the cold hiding place where she had been watching events through Amy's eyes, distanced and protected. "We never dreamed," she said. "Or perhaps we did dream . . . but we never believed."

"I wonder how differently we would have lived our lives if we had realised all these things existed just behind the scenery," Matt continued. The whites of his eyes occasionally gleamed from the shadowy pools of their orbits. He noticed Mahalia was walking so close to him that her shoulder occasionally brushed his arm. "Don't be scared," he said.

"I'm not scared." She glared at him scornfully and then ostentatiously dropped two steps back, but Caitlin saw her right hand sneak under her jacket, ready.

"What are they?" Caitlin asked uneasily.

Crowther glanced back, his entire face lost in the gloom beneath the brim of his hat. "They're the source of all our myths and legends—they're our gods." He laughed bitterly. "Fairies. Elves. All the old stories and the abiding tales, from the campfire to the library. Everything that bursts from the wellspring of imagination. Crossing over into our world, darting back before we could really be sure we'd seen anything. Sometimes staying for a little simple torment. Jung was right, though I venture he never imagined it quite this way."

"It's hard to see them as gods," Matt said.

"They didn't always look this way. They've been . . . diminished," Crowther replied.

Crowther's attention returned to the guards as they took a sharp left into a large room where the only light came from a blazing log fire in an enormous stone fireplace. As their eyes adjusted to the hellish glow, they saw shapes around the room, sitting in high-backed chairs talking in hushed tones, hunched over a map resting on a large oak table, more whispers, more plots, but in this room there was a feeling of sleeping power.

The chief guard stepped forward. "My Lord," he said into the half-light, "here are Fragile Creatures, washed up at our door on this night. And a Sister of Dragons."

The residents of the room stiffened as one. Goose bumps ran up Caitlin's arms. What did that phrase mean? Was it linked to the vision Mary had, when the world had been a different place? And why did it haunt her so?

"Come closer." The voice was the source of the power they had sensed. It came from a chair near the fire, where a small man with long black hair and beard and pointed ears glanced up from the flames. His eyes gleamed red in the firelight, red and thoughtful.

The others made to approach, but the guards raised short stubby swords to hold them back so that only Caitlin was allowed to move. The four presences squirmed at the back of her head, but she held them back; she would be brave.

"I'm Caitlin," she said.

He looked her up and down. "A Sister of Dragons."

"I don't know what that means."

"No. You never do." He surveyed her intently, then said with a strange note to his voice, "You are the Broken Woman." Caitlin didn't know what to say to that, and after a moment's silence the lord returned his gaze to the fire. It may have been the way the light made the shadows fall on his face, but he appeared to be carrying a tremendous burden. "In the days of the tribes, your kind would have known me as Lugh, though few from that time would now recognise me. On occasion, I fear the cycles are repeating, that I will grow smaller and smaller until . . ." He looked up sharply with a flash of anger, as if Caitlin had hurt him. "Why have you come here?"

Caitlin's mouth was dry, but she forced the words out. "My people are dying from a plague. We were told that the cure is here, on this world somewhere . . ."

"And you seek it?" He gave a dismissive shrug. "Small battles fought by a small people. As always, you are unaware of the great sweep of events."

"Can . . . can you help us?" she ventured nervously.

"Perhaps."

"Please, we're in a hurry," Caitlin pleaded. "If we don't find a cure quickly . . ."

"Time has no meaning here," Lugh interrupted. "You are fortunate to have found your way to the Court of Soul's Ease. Other courts would not have been so welcoming."

"Some would," a bitter voice called from the back of the room. "In some places, they would have been raised up on high."

Cold laughter rustled through the shadows. Caitlin grew frightened.

"We remain neutral," Lugh said. "For now."

"Are you waiting for something?" Caitlin changed the subject, worried that the conversation was going in a dangerous direction.

Lugh glanced her way briefly. "Yes, we wait. We wait for war." He waved her away morosely. "You will be shown to quarters. Move freely through the court, but avoid the low town. Some . . . undesirables outstay their welcome there. We will talk again."

Before Caitlin could press her case further, the guards had ushered her and the others back out into the oppressive maze of corridors.

They were shown to windowless rooms that offered little comfort apart from a wooden bed and hard mattress, a coarse blanket, a reed rug on the flags, and a bedside table on which stood a stubby candle.

Hunger nagged at them all, and the chief guard suggested they make their way to a tavern tucked away amongst the twisty-turny streets, where they would be provided with food and drink. "But," he cautioned, "move quickly through the streets at night, for the court, in its munificence, has thrown open its gates to all manner of residents of the Far Lands, and many are inimical to Fragile Creatures. They reside not only in the low town."

Following his directions, they set out along the rain-slicked cobbled streets, carefully watching the numerous dark alleys and shadowed doorways along the route.

"Was it just me," Mahalia said, "or did it seem as if they'd have been just as happy slitting our throats and tossing us over the walls?"

"They're cautious," Crowther said. "They don't want to come down on the wrong side."

"You know more than you're saying." There was a combative note in Matt's voice.

"He learned it all in his little college in Glastonbury," Mahalia chided sarcastically.

"You ought to share it," Matt said. "We're all in this together. Any information that might help us work out what's going on . . ."

"All right," Crowther snapped. "There's no need to harangue me." He was clearly less able to resist Matt than he was Caitlin, Mahalia, and Carlton. "I was taught by someone who had visited this place. The information he brought back, the knowledge he amassed during the period of the Fall, formed a significant part of the teachings."

A man, or what they took to be a man, rushed out of one of the side streets and was so intent on staring fearfully over his shoulder that he almost crashed into them. He was unnaturally tall and thin and was wearing a large floppy-brimmed hat that hid his face. "Have you heard the news?" he said, nonplussed by their presence. "The Lord of Vengeance has been sighted roaming the Marches of Gisbourg beyond the Wish-Lakes to the east. Truth. I was told." He made a snipping-scissor motion with both his hands. "It's an omen. Everything's coming to an end." He shifted his head and the torchlight caught his face. They all shrank back when they saw that his eyes had been sewn shut.

Somehow he loped away on his needle-thin legs in a straight line into the next dark alley.

"For God's sake, let's get somewhere a little safer." Crowther nodded at a spot further down the street where they saw the tavern. Unlike many of the surrounding buildings, a welcoming light flooded out of the bottle-glass windows. A sign depicting a stylised sun with a smiling face swung heavily in the wind. By the time they had taken all this in, Crowther was already halfway to the door.

The tavern was filled with a hubbub of low, conspiratorial voices and a heady atmosphere of beer, sawdust, woodsmoke, and spiced meat. But then they saw the clientele and once more they were struck dumb. There were more of the small, intense men and a few women, but the others were bizarre beyond imagining. Some were tall with insectile eyes, others swathed in fluttering rags that moved as if they were alive; some had wings, others horns; it was as though they had stepped into a scene from a child's fairy tale.

"Bloody hell," Crowther said under his breath.

The tavern's occupants stopped what they were doing to survey the new arrivals curiously, but their attention only remained for the briefest moments before they returned to talk of broken treaties, armies being amassed, subterfuge and deceit.

At the bar, the landlord, a stout beer-bellied man with ferocious eyebrows, offered them food and drink without asking for any recompense. He watched them suspiciously while pouring tankards of a deep black porter for the men and Carlton, and glasses of red wine for the women.

"You're too young to drink," Matt said to Mahalia as she took the pewter goblet.

"I've killed people," she said, and it was answer enough. Yet Mahalia still cautioned Carlton against drinking the beer and insisted on water for him instead.

They took a table next to one of the windows where they could look out into the deserted street, as the noise and warmth of the tavern wrapped itself seductively around them.

"It's time to talk," Matt said to Crowther. It was clear to the others that Matt was highly suspicious of the professor and was not about to let him get away with anything.

"Who is Lugh?" Caitlin asked. She knew the question had come from Brigid inside her; strangely, the old woman appeared to know more than she did.

"Lugh was one of the gods of the Celts." Crowther sipped his beer with an oddly self-satisfied air. "When these beings, the Golden Ones as they were known, crossed over into our world millennia ago, the ancient Celts named this one Lugh and defined him as a sun god. The gods had a falling out with another group called the Fomorii, who were the basis for our myths of devils, I suppose. The gods retreated to the Far Lands—here, the Otherworld—and the loss of that battle diminished them in our eyes. They grew physically smaller, less powerful —though still imposing—and ended up walking into our stories as fairies."

"How could the loss diminish them?" Matt said with keen interest.

"You will notice," Crowther said patronisingly, "that nothing here is as it seems. This land is *fluid*, and to a degree perception, and belief, shape Existence."

"So because we were less scared of them, they became less powerful," Mahalia chipped in.

"You're quite a clever girl behind that front." Crowther gave her a smile, but she didn't return it.

"Tell me about this war—that's the important thing," Matt said impatiently.

"Of course it is," Crowther said blithely. "Things don't get any more important. We're at a cusp, all of us, and it could go any way from here on in."

Carlton surprised them by leaning across the table and resting one hand on Crowther's arm. Most of the time he was invisible and for all but Mahalia it was easy to forget he was there, but sometimes Caitlin would catch him watching them all intently, and at those times she could see how much was going on inside his head. This time, his expression was grave. He exchanged a long intense glance with Crowther, and whatever passed between them made the professor grow more serious.

"The Fall was a crucible for humanity, though none of us could see it at the time. *The seasons have turned*, that was how it was put to me. Mankind now has the opportunity to move on from the position we've occupied ever since we came down from the trees. If we seize our chances, we can move on to the next level, the next stage of evolution. We can become . . ." He tried to pluck the right word from the air, failed. ". . . gods, I suppose."

Matt eyed him with disbelief, but there was a glimmer of awe in his eyes. "Gods?"

"We have the potential inside us—we were made that way. Now is our time. But—"

"But some of the other *gods* don't want us getting in their club," Mahalia interjected.

"That's right." Crowther took a long, deep draught of his beer. "Some of them don't. Some of them accept that this is the way of Existence—always rising higher, attempting to reach . . . nirvana. And that is why they're on the brink of a civil war."

"Is this for real?" Matt's voice was hushed, incredulous. "What do we have to do?"

"Who knows?" Crowther made a dismissive gesture, but Caitlin saw his gaze fall briefly on Carlton. "It has something to do with the Blue Fire, the earth energy. After being dormant for many years, it's now alive in the land again. I have no idea what that means, how it will affect us. It may be happening now; we may have to wait a millennium. The cycles of Existence don't operate on our timescale."

"But if we could hurry it along . . ." Matt said breathlessly.

"If, if, if." Crowther waved him silent. "Strategically, this will work in our favour. Normally, our chances of making any headway at all through the Far Lands would be close to nil. But with the Golden Ones divided . . . some of them supporting humanity and others undecided and not wishing to do anything to offend us, you at least stand a chance of making some progress."

"You?" Caitlin said.

"I'm not coming with you. I've done my bit, getting you here."

They all looked at him in surprise. "But I thought—" Caitlin began.

"No," Crowther said firmly. "You won't convince me."

"We need you!" Caitlin protested.

"No, you don't."

"Why did you bother coming at all?" Matt said.

"I have my reasons."

"Who cares?" Mahalia said. "Do we need him? I don't think so."

"But you know so much," Caitlin said directly to him.

"I don't know much at all." Crowther concentrated on his beer, uncomfortable now.

"But what you do know could be the difference between life and death for us," she persisted.

He looked into Caitlin's face briefly but couldn't bear what he saw there. He stared into the depths of his tankard and then said, "I'll give you one piece of information to send you on your way, Sister of Dragons." He looked at her from under his heavy brows.

"What does that mean?"

"Dragons are the symbol of the Blue Fire, the earth energy, that vital spiritual power that fills everything. Yet these Fabulous Beasts are more than symbol—they're reality. They are the key. The spirit-power is the key." He took another long draught. "The distinction between belief systems we saw in modern times is false. The Dragon Power underpins every single religion, however disparate, from ancient Chinese spirituality to Christianity. Medieval Christian art made the connection explicit, with paintings of Christ the Dragon. It makes you think a little differently about those old biblical stories, eh? The serpent in the Garden of Eden. Decode them and the truth emerges."

"What truth?" Caitlin said. "You're being deliberately oblique, as usual."

"Well, let me be direct, then. The Dragon Power flows directly to the God-head, and certain people are infused with it, to act as . . . champions, I suppose. Gallant knights who will fight for all that's right in the universe, regardless of creed or culture or political belief. A universal rightness."

"Me?" Caitlin said in disbelief, but the prophecy Mary had made now fell into sharp relief.

"The Pendragon Spirit is in you. It was the reason I was sent straight to your friend's door."

"I'm no champion."

"Yes, I know. Difficult to believe, isn't it?"

"What is it, Carlton?" Mahalia had noticed that the boy was growing anxious. He kept looking round as if he expected someone to attack them, but all the drinkers continued their quiet, intense conversations, seemingly oblivious. A few seconds later, the door burst open and a fat man in a half-squashed hat was blown in by a gust of rain. He was in a state of high anxiety. "The Lament-Brood!" he called out. The entire tavern fell silent. "They are here, beyond the walls!"

The hanging moment broke in a burst of agitated voices and activity. Some ran out of the tavern, others huddled closer to the fire, clutching their drinks tightly against their chests.

"They've followed us here?" Caitlin said. Inside, Amy was sobbing.

"I think we should go and see." Matt stood up. Beyond the window, they could see people running down the street.

"I think I'll stay here, if you don't mind," Crowther said, looking to the bar for another beer. "Keep me informed if it's anything to be concerned about."

Matt and Caitlin made it to the door, then Caitlin turned back and beckoned for Mahalia and Carlton to follow.

"I thought you were going to leave us with that prat," Mahalia said, though her face showed no gratitude.

Flitting shapes moved down the steeply sloping streets toward the walls, searching for some vantage point. They acted like people tasting the uncertain edge of fear for the first time.

"In here." Matt caught Caitlin's arm and pulled her into the entrance to a tall tower. The door was open, and they quickly made their way up spiral steps worn by what must have been thousands of years of feet. At times the steps were so precarious that they threatened to plunge any climber back down to their deaths. At the top, the steps opened out onto a small balcony running around the circumference of the tower, far above the confusion of slate roofs. The rain had abated and there was a clear view to the plains beyond the walls.

They knew instantly what was there before seeing any detail. "Oh, no," Caitlin said dismally.

Mahalia came up beside her, and when Caitlin looked into her face the hardness had dissipated, and for the first time she saw the desperate, innocent girl trapped within. "They're never going to leave us alone, are they?"

The girl's small voice was caught by the wind and whisked out toward the battlements beyond which a purple mist coalesced, filled with despair and the end of all hope.

Mary's head throbbed and her throat felt as dry as the dusty road along which she walked. Delirium tremens made her feel like an invalid, or fifteen years older than her true age, and although she'd washed profusely in a stream, she still couldn't get rid of the occasional whiff of vomit. She'd got through the bottle of whiskey and cleaned out all the other alcohol she could find in the house—some cider, a couple of bottles of beer brewed by one of the villagers, some sloe wine (no alcohol lasted for long and she was lucky she had that amount)—but she still yearned for more, while at the same time hating herself for the desire.

It's not a problem, she said with the alcoholic's deranged conviction, while the real her that lived at the back of her head looked on with impotent despair.

She hadn't wanted to leave her cosy cottage and carefully structured life to venture out into the chaos of the world—it was too dangerous, filled with night-terrors even in the midday glare—and for a while she had almost convinced herself that it wasn't her responsibility to try to find some way to help Caitlin, that there was nothing she could do anyway, so what was the point. That had been the way she had lived for so many years, existing with a fear that had grown out of self-loathing; what had happened to her at the end of the sixties had contaminated the rest of her life. In some people's eyes, her transgression might have been only a small thing. To her, it was a blinding revelation of who she really was, and that terrible disappointment was something she thought she would never get over. Even now she couldn't think about that single moment; it remained, unconsidered, like toxic waste polluting her subconscious.

And so her thoughts had naturally turned to Caitlin, unable to say good-bye to the husband and son she loved, and Mary had felt the heat rise within her: Caitlin would never suffer as she had suffered; Caitlin would not see her life dribble away in might-have-beens. Mary was more determined than she ever had been about anything else before.

She would never be able to live with herself if anything happened to Caitlin that she could have prevented. And so she had steeled herself with the alcohol—while knowing that *steeling* was just an excuse—and when she was too drunk to consider the fear she took the old rucksack she had packed, with Arthur Lee poking his head out of one side, and set out on the road.

It was going to be a long journey, certainly the first leg, and she guessed there would probably be more after that—these kinds of things never went simply—so she'd also secreted several weapons about her person. Food would be a problem, but she knew enough about wild herbs and plants to find herself some sustenance, but she would really need protein and the chances of her catching a rabbit or a bird were, she guessed, slim.

She paused on the brow of a hill and surveyed the green fields stretching out into the glare of the morning sun. It had taken her a long time to decide on her destination, involving much pondering, more attempts at communing with the powers that be, many of them failed. It quickly became apparent that she would need to seek guidance from something more potent.

And that was only really available in the old places, the sites that had been marked out by the ancient people in the dim dawn of mankind, when humans were more sensitive to what was around them, not dulled by civilisation's many drugs. She considered Stonehenge and Avebury, wondered about venturing even further afield, but she decided she needed something specific to her predicament. She needed to talk to a god. Not one of the gods rumoured to have returned with the Fall, but something higher. An old, old archetype; a power from the very beginning of it all.

Further down the road, there was a crossroads. From a distance it had appeared as deserted as the majority of the surrounding countryside, but as she approached, a figure had mysteriously become visible, standing next to the old wooden signpost that marked the crossing of the ways. She squinted and blinked; it was as though she was viewing the scene through a rippling heat haze. But after a few more steps, her vision cleared and she realised it was a man in old tattered clothes, leaning on a strangely incongruous staff that had some kind of worked shape to it. His grey hair was wild and wispy around his head and as she neared she saw his skin was filthy with the mud of the fields.

She slipped her hand into her pocket to grasp the handle of the already open penknife. At the same time, she felt a ringing in her teeth and a dull ache at the back of her head that reminded her of the unnerving sensations she had experienced when the stranger had visited to set her on this path. She still hadn't come to terms with who he was, or more precisely *what*, but she knew without a doubt that his kind scared her on some fundamental level.

As she neared the crossroads, her senses screamed at her to run. Whatever it was that she sensed about the man made her stomach turn and her thoughts skitter frantically; it felt like two magnets of opposing polarity being forced together. It was clear that he was waiting for her.

Even when she was a few feet away she said nothing, even tried to slip by, but his eyes widened with a hideous warning, forcing her to a sharp halt.

"Are you here to help me?" she asked, queasily.

Those filthy lips moved, but there was an unnerving second-long dislocation before the sound actually emerged. "You must beware. You have been noticed."

"Who's noticed me?" Mary thought she was really about to vomit; she desperately fought back the bile.

"The . . . Void."

Mary had the impression that the stranger wasn't used to speaking English, wasn't used to any kind of language she could comprehend. "The Void? What's that?"

His eyes grew wide once more and she backed away a step, unable to look him in the face. Fear engulfed her and she thought she might faint. But when he spoke again, his words were measured. "Each day, your lives play out in rhythms, *lat-dat*, *lat-dat*, *lat-dat*, without change, without significance. And then, one day, a break . . . awareness . . . direction. Import."

"I've been noticed . . . because I'm doing something important. And something's going to try to stop me." Her fear changed, became deeper, colder. What was the stranger hinting at? Who had noticed her? Who was after her?

She suddenly felt tiny, manipulated by powers beyond her understanding, and from that came the question to which she dreaded the answer. "Where do you come from?"

There was a long, trenchant pause, and then, "I come from above . . ."

"Above?"

". . . behind, beneath, beside . . ."

His words made her shiver, and reminded her explicitly of something she had heard when she was learning the Craft: "There are beings around us all the time. We can't see them, but they can see us. They can see what we've done. And what we will do."

"Go!" The word boomed out, and Mary almost fell to her knees. There was a terrible rage in the stranger's face. "Go . . . and beware!"

She turned and ran down the road, tears burning her eyes. She had the awful feeling that her death was virtually decided. When she did finally recover enough feeble courage to look back, the crossroads was empty.

Beyond the walls, the Whisperers waited, a haunting vision that transfixed Caitlin, Matt, Mahalia, and Carlton at the top of the tower. After a while, Mahalia left Caitlin and Matt, irritated by what she saw was an obvious attraction between the two; though how anyone could contemplate affection for someone as clearly insane as that mad bitch was beyond her. Out on the cobbles, she turned to Carlton and felt instantly calmed by his warm, beatific smile. "What are we doing here, mate?" she asked gently.

He gave a *Who knows?* shrug, but Mahalia didn't believe it for a second, and then he nodded back toward the grim palace.

"OK, we'll go back," she said. "We could both do with a good sleep." She was overcome with a wave of affection and gave him a big hug. "I'm really glad you're with me, matey."

He hugged her back and then broke free, grabbing her hand to drag her up the street.

"I wish you could talk," she said, gradually slipping into the familiar state where she used Carlton as a sounding board for her own thoughts and insecurities. "Don't get me wrong, I don't doubt you—I couldn't, not after what I've seen. But I'd really like to hear exactly what you know about what's going on . . . it's so hard to keep at it without knowing what we're doing or where we're going."

He turned and looked at her seriously. In his big, dark eyes, she thought she could see the universe turning. "I do trust you, Carlton," she stressed.

They continued the rest of the journey in silence, but Mahalia's thoughts occasionally turned to the question that troubled her: not what Carlton knew, but how he knew it.

In the palace, she was afraid she'd never remember the mazey route back to their rooms, but Carlton did not hesitate. Yet when they weren't far from their chambers, Carlton stopped sharply and then propelled Mahalia into a shadowy alcove, pressing his finger to his lips to silence her. She could only guess that he'd heard something beyond her range.

A clanking sound slowly came into her hearing, followed shortly after by two of the short bearded guards, who were herding a tall youth along the corridor. Mahalia could tell he was quite young from his frame, but beyond that it was impossible to know anything more about him—a thick black hood covered his head, with only two eyelets so that he could see where he was going. His upper body was wrapped in so many heavy iron chains that Mahalia was astonished he could move at all. His progress was unbearably slow as he coped with their weight, but he still held himself erect.

As he passed the alcove, a strange thing happened. Though Mahalia and Carlton were hidden deep in the shadows, his eyes flickered toward them as if they were in plain view. Those eyes were a startling grey-blue and filled with a pleading desperation that made Mahalia shiver.

Mahalia and Carlton waited until the prisoner and his guards were long gone before continuing on their way. It was just another strange thing in a very strange world, yet as she lay in her bed she couldn't shake the look the prisoner had given her, and sleep did not come for a long time.

chapter six

BETWEEN THE VIADUCTS OF DREAMS

> *"Oh, for the time when I shall sleep*
> *Without identity."*
>
> Emily Brontë

"Don't go near the walls—they'll get you!" Briony's whining voice rose above the keening wind that cut like a knife across the Ice-Field.

"I'm not about to go near them!" Caitlin snapped back. She hugged her knees and looked out over the desolate landscape that appeared to go on forever beneath the night sky; a black-and-white world. It was unbearably harsh, yet at times it still felt preferable to the place inhabited by her body.

"They're after you, you know," Brigid cackled. "They don't care about the others."

"Why would they be after me?" Caitlin replied sourly. "Why should anyone be interested in me? I'm no use to anyone. I can't heal people. I couldn't save . . . couldn't save . . ."

"Don't talk about them!" Amy shouted, her eyes wide with fear.

"They know you're special," Brigid continued. "They know you're a Sister of Dragons."

Caitlin spun round. "What does that mean? I don't know! It's just words . . ."

The old woman tapped her scrawny hand against her chest. "It's in the heart, it's in the blood . . ."

"It doesn't matter," Briony interjected, "because you'll never get past those Whisperers. They're waiting outside the walls. They can't come in, but if you try to go out . . ."

Brigid began to laugh hysterically, her phlegmy whoops soaring higher and higher until Caitlin wanted to scream at her to shut up.

"Let me out!" The harsh, rustling voice crept out from the shadows at the back of their tiny sheltered spot. Caitlin's blood ran cold. "LET ME OUT!"

Amy began to cry and Briony fell to her knees and covered her face, but Brigid just laughed and laughed and laughed . . .

"Caitlin?"

She woke to find Matt leaning over her, his blue eyes searching her face. Once he saw that it was her and not one of the others, he smiled. "You're a deep sleeper."

"Something like that." She sat up and scrubbed at her hair, which she was sure must look like a haystack.

"They're still out there. I just checked from the tower . . . it's been three days now. That weird purple mist keeps moving all around the walls."

"They're not going to go away. They want me."

"What have you done to attract that kind of attention?"

He felt unbearably close, so she swung herself out of bed and walked to the other side of the room. "All I know is we have to find that cure. And nothing's going to stop us."

"I wish I had your positivity."

"Have you been able to convince the professor to come with us?"

"I haven't been able to find him. I think he's avoiding me . . . or just soaking up the beer in some dive."

"I can't understand it. He seemed so desperate to get here." She splashed her face with icy water from a pewter bowl next to the bed. "What's the point in crossing over and then just hiding out in this godforsaken place?"

"I haven't been able to keep track of Mahalia or Carlton, either. They're roaming all over this place, night and day. They'll disappear for hours into the corridors, as if they're searching for something. And you know what a maze it is."

"No great loss. Well, Mahalia, anyway. Carlton's a different story."

"What do you mean?"

"I don't know exactly. There's something about him . . . I can't help feeling as if he's the key to what's happening."

"Can you explain it?"

She sat back down on the bed, but left a gap between them. "I don't know . . . it's in here." She tapped her heart and her head. "Instinct. I just think there's something locked away inside him, something important, if we could only get at it. He knows things . . ."

Matt clearly knew what she meant, judging by the expression on his face.

"We can't afford to sit around any longer, whatever Lugh said about time being strange in this place." She stood defiantly and waited for Matt to join her. "We need to get whatever information we can from this place and get back on the road. And," she added flintily, "Crowther is coming with us. We need him."

Caitlin and Matt decided to split up to search for the professor, and soon after Caitlin found herself in a maze of mews that had a faintly menacing air. She was the only one walking the cobbles, but occasionally she would catch a glimpse of someone standing in a darkened doorway. They would beckon to her, whispering promises of something or other—magic, escape, things she didn't understand but which sounded threatening or perverse—and she hurried on, knowing it would be dangerous to get too close.

The mews grew thinner and darker the further she progressed into the heart of that quarter, so that eventually she could touch both walls at the same time if she reached out. The sky had almost disappeared behind the overhanging upper storeys. The oppressive atmosphere at that point became more than she could bear; she couldn't shake the feeling that someone, or something, was waiting behind the doors to grab her and drag her in, never to be seen again.

It was at the moment when she decided to turn back that she heard her name. It sounded like the buzz of an insect, almost lost beneath the echoes off the cobbles.

She stopped sharply. "Who's there?"

No immediate reply came, but her instincts were sharp enough to make her move quickly away. Yet after a few yards, the sound of her name made her glance back again. At the end of that section of mews was the knight with the boar's-head helmet who had pursued her at the Rollrights, his gleaming black armour almost lost in the shadows.

Caitlin didn't wait to see any more. She ran as fast as she could through the labyrinthine streets, not even pausing to see if the knight was in pursuit. Yet in her keenness to escape, she missed her turning and found herself in an area she didn't recognise, and soon after that she came up sharp against the end of a twisting cul-de-sac.

Her hopes that she would have time to retrace her steps were dashed when she heard the clatter of the knight's approach. He appeared around a bend and stood in the centre of the street, arms at his sides.

"What do you want?" Caitlin said defiantly.

"Caitlin Shepherd." The same fizzing voice, distorted, like high-tension wires. "None of this is real, Caitlin Shepherd." There was an awkwardness to his intonation, as if he wasn't used to speaking.

"What do you want?" Caitlin repeated.

"You." The word chilled her. "I want you."

A nearby door opened with a loud creak and a short man with wild white hair emerged carrying a box of empty bottles. Caitlin saw her moment and dashed through the gap, almost knocking the man over. His curses rose up behind her as she scrambled through a dark, dusty back room into what appeared to be an apothecary's shop. Bottles and jars of herbs and coloured liquids filled shelves on every wall.

She burst out of the front door onto a main thoroughfare and continued to run for several minutes, only resting when she was sure the knight had not followed her. The experience troubled her immensely. It wasn't only the Whisperers who were tracking her incessantly. Who was the knight? What did he want? And why did she feel so scared by his presence?

Caitlin finally found Crowther sitting at the back of the Sun tavern. The place was deserted, but he looked happy enough. She'd spent most of the morning scouring the rain-swept backstreets, ignoring the uncertain glances of the strange, gloomy residents, poking into bakeries where the scent of fresh bread almost turned her head, or strange emporia filled with disturbing and magical objects that appeared to have been lost from the pages of a fairy tale.

"Hail and well met," Crowther said tipsily, raising a foaming mug.

"You're in a good mood." Caitlin sat opposite him on a rickety stool.

"And why not? Food whenever I call for it, good beer—and all for free. What more could a man want?"

"How about survival for his fellow man?"

He made a flamboyant gesture of weariness. "Please, don't get on that moral high horse. I've done my bit. I got you here."

"We need you, Professor. Wherever we have to go, it's not going to be easy, and the more help we can have on the road, the better."

"That may very well be the case, but I'm not your man."

"Why? Are you afraid?"

"Of course I'm afraid. At my age you're afraid of everything . . . afraid of dying from some hideous illness, afraid of spending your last days eking out a miserable existence, afraid of . . . of . . . loneliness." He stared into his beer for a long moment, then flapped the thought away with a hand.

"You don't need to be afraid . . ."

"Really? And I should be taking life advice from someone who hasn't crossed thirty, why exactly?"

"You don't gain wisdom just through years. You get it from experience, and tragedy . . ."

"And I've had my fair share of that, believe me." He slammed his pint down so hard beer slopped across the table. "Listen to me. We move from innocence, hope, and joy to compromise, disillusion, and misery," Crowther said. "Why do you think no one wants to grow up?"

"I don't believe you," Caitlin said.

"Of course. Because you haven't grown up yet. It's waiting for you, make no mistake."

The happiness had drained from his face once again, and in the harsh lines that remained, Caitlin saw hints of what lay behind his posturing. "What tragedy, Professor Crowther?"

His eyes misted, the repressed emotion released by the alcohol. "Just the usual. Wife taken in the Fall. Children missing and grandchildren . . ." His shoulders loosened and sagged so that he appeared to diminish in stature. "You're never happy with what you've got until what you've got has gone. I had no time for them, no time for anything apart from myself. The whole family taken, and I couldn't do a thing about it. Useless, you see. All my life being an academic . . . wasted time. It didn't help me one jot. My whole ethos has been pointless."

"That's not true—"

"It is true."

Caitlin leaned across the table and grabbed his wrist supportively. He flinched as if he'd been burned. "You don't have to feel this way. I've suffered loss too and I—"

"Ah, but then you're stronger than me, you see." He pulled himself free of her and took up his drink.

"You were brave enough to come here."

"Brave enough?" he laughed bitterly. "This is my refuge, my escape from the world of tears. Here I don't have to face up to anything. I can live forever, or near enough, free of fear. I can just . . . be." He looked deep into her eyes and forced a smile. "I needed you to help me cross over here. Most people can't activate the transition unless they have the untrammelled force of the Blue Fire in them. And you're one of them, one of the few. I went to the college in Glastonbury with the explicit aim of gaining the abilities to seek you out. And once I'd done that, I left, taking with me all I needed to find you."

Caitlin pulled back as his meaning slowly dawned on her. "Then you lied to me—I wasn't some *chosen one* destined to cure the plague. You just needed me to get you here . . ."

"See what a horrible person I am. You really don't need me around you anymore." He sucked in a breath of air. "That's not true. You are the one. I simply saw a confluence between what I wanted and what was expected of you."

Caitlin stood up, but it was Amy who surfaced to speak their mind. "I really am disappointed in you, Professor Crowther."

He thought he would be inured to her words, but that little-girl voice from Caitlin's place of innocence hit to the very heart of him. Caitlin/Amy saw it in his face, but made no attempt to comfort him. She left the tavern as quickly as she could.

Mahalia and Carlton had spent hours trawling along the twisting, dark corridors of the palace. They had seen many secret places and overheard whispers of great importance, but still hadn't found the object of their quest.

"Maybe they executed him," Mahalia said. "That could have been why he'd got the hood on, and the chains . . ."

Carlton shook his head and pressed ahead.

"Haven't we been down here already?" But the words caught in her throat when she noticed an unfamiliar tapestry hanging on the wall between two sizzling torches. It showed five people—humans by the stylised design—joined by the sinuous coils of what appeared to be a serpent. Other illustrations surrounding the central motif appeared to tell a story that, at first glance, ended in some great disaster, but before she could examine it closer, a voice called out clearly, "Who's there?"

Mahalia dragged Carlton into her protective grip. He fought free and advanced quickly along the corridor with Mahalia at his heels until they came to a heavy oaken door with a small barred window set into it.

"I know you're there. There's no point hiding."

Cautiously, Mahalia approached the window and peered into a small, dank cell. Straw was scattered on the stone flags, and pinned to the far wall by chains was the hooded prisoner. Surely, Mahalia thought, he must be a real danger to be secured so forcefully. She ducked away when she saw those brilliant eyes fixed on her through the holes in the hood.

"Don't go."

His voice, though clear, was faintly pitiful and she couldn't help coming back to the window and that hypnotic gaze. "You're not one of them," she said.

"No. I'm one of you." He rattled the chains for her attention. "Can you get me out of here?" Though he was clearly human, there was an awkwardness to his speech as if he wasn't used to talking.

"Right. Free the psycho imprisoned in the bowels of the palace. That's a good idea."

"I'm not a psycho. They're just . . . scared of me."

She laughed. "Why would they be scared of you? You look as if you'd snap in two in a strong wind."

He didn't reply for a few seconds as he sorted his thoughts, then he said, unconvincingly, "They just are."

"I don't waste time talking to people who lie to me . . ."

She made as if to go and he called her back with a desperate urging. "I'm sorry. I'm not lying! I just . . . it's hard to talk, with you out there and me hanging here . . ."

Mahalia gripped the bars. "Well, if you think I'm coming within arm's reach of you, you've got another think coming." She eyed the large padlock below the handle. "Besides, there's no way I'd get through this thing."

"You could find some way," he said hopefully.

"How'd you get here, anyway?"

"They stole me."

"What?"

"From my mother, when I was a baby. That's what they do . . . what they've always done—steal infants so they can experiment on them."

"I don't believe you." Empathy fanned up inside Mahalia. Then: "You've been a prisoner all your life?"

"Since I was a baby. I escaped from them once, but now they've recaptured me and they're going to send me back to the place where they carry out the experiments—the Court of the Final Word."

Mahalia couldn't decide whether she should believe him or not. She hoped Carlton would give her some sign, but the boy's face was impassive. "What's your name?"

"Jack."

"How old are you?"

A pause. "I don't know." He sensed he was making some headway with her, so he continued to talk in the hope of winning her over. "There are two factions amongst these people—"

"I know all about that."

"Well, this lot are neutral. They don't want to offend either side till they've decided who they're supporting, so they're not going to risk having me here as a point of contention. They're sending me back as soon as they can. I need your help. I couldn't bear to go back there again. The things they do . . ." He swallowed heavily. "If I went back there'd be no point in me living."

"Don't say that."

"If you were in my place you'd feel the same."

Mahalia chewed on a knuckle. She felt for him greatly, but there was also a part of what he was saying that didn't add up. She'd grown adept at recognising risk and the last thing she wanted to do was to make their situation worse.

"I need to think about this." She grabbed Carlton and pulled him away from the door.

"Don't go!" Jack pleaded.

"I'll be back."

"Don't go!" This time it was a yell of desperation, and she could still hear his agonised calls when she had put many, many lengths of corridor between them.

Matt was lost in a maze of narrow mews when frantic cries came to him on the wind. He followed the sound out of the oppressively dark backstreets until he came up against a force of heavily armoured soldiers rushing in the direction of the walls. The silvery metal of their helmets and breastplates transformed them into a river of light washing down the dismal streets in the drizzle that had fallen ever since the group's arrival.

The urgency of their actions made Matt uneasy, and he grabbed at a woman hurrying away from the source of the disturbance. "What's going on?" he asked.

"They attack," she said breathlessly. "They have found a way past the defences." She broke away from Matt and continued on her way before turning to point an accusing finger at him. "Your fault," she hissed bitterly before disappearing into the throng.

Matt fought his way through the citizens swarming away from the walls until he had a clear view of the activity. That sickening purple light was everywhere, drifting like the smoke of a battlefield, and through it came hideously misshapen figures, transformed by the Whisperers like the poor hermit from the Motor Museum who had attacked them at the Rollrights. Bones protruded from limbs, skulls shone through flesh, and weapons—swords, spears, axes—had been embedded in their frames as if they were natural parts of the body. They lurched with the relentlessness of zombies from some horror movie, the purple illumination leaking out of them.

Even at that distance, Matt could sense the paralysing despair they carried with them. As the soldiers approached, they stopped in their tracks, their swords falling hopelessly to their sides. Some simply lay down on the cobbles, offering themselves up to the sweeps of the Whisperer weapons, demanding to be released from the pain of life.

The Whisperers, Matt guessed, had caught some poor travellers making their way across the plain to the court and were using them to breach whatever magical defences kept the court secure. Somehow they had clambered up the vertiginous walls to gain access to the city. The ones within were now forcing their way down the road toward the gates, to throw them open for the leaders who waited without.

There were only twelve of them, but the horde of soldiers seemed incapable of stopping them. Thirty or more of the little men already lay dead, their blood running down the stones in a claret stream, and now the others were starting to hold back, realising the futility of their attack.

Without a second thought, he turned and bounded up the steep streets until he found the shop he had noticed earlier. It was a fletcher's, the interior hung with more bows of all description than he had seen in his life. The owner eyed him suspiciously, but did nothing to stop him as Matt selected one he thought he could handle, along with a quiver full of arrows, and then he was hurtling back down toward the mêlèe.

He clambered precariously onto a water butt, steadied himself, and fitted an arrow to the bowstring. His experience instantly came into play, mechanical, cool. The bow flexed easily and he loosed the arrow straight at one of the Whisperers. It smashed into one side of his head and tore straight out of the other. The Whisperer tottered for a few seconds, as if coming to terms with the fact that his life was over, and then he crashed facedown onto the stone.

The heads of the soldiers turned as one toward Matt, and then they set off for the fletcher's shop. Matt got another Whisperer, but by that time the remaining interlopers were well on the way to the gates and his view had been obscured by the jumble of rooftops pressed up tightly against the walls. Jumping from the butt, he joined the soldiers, who parted with a little grudging respect to allow him into their midst, and then they all set off in pursuit.

One Whisperer went down like a pincushion with fifteen arrows sticking out of him. Others followed, but the soldiers found it difficult to make progress over the bodies of their comrades who had paid the price for venturing too close to the pervasive, toxic emotions the Whisperers radiated.

Frustrated, Matt pushed his way back through the soldiers and ran up the street, taking a right turn through an alley until he located another route down toward the gates. The thoroughfare was completely empty, but he had to temper his run for fear of slipping and breaking his neck on the precipitous street. Finally the gates loomed up ahead of him and he fitted an arrow as he moved.

He turned a corner, ready to fire, and came straight up against a Whisperer.

The shock paralysed Matt for a second. Spears protruded from each of the Whisperer's shoulders, and the thing used them by pivoting at the waist to knock the bow from Matt's hands. The lethal tip of one of the spears narrowly missed taking one of Matt's eyes out as he threw himself backward onto the ground.

As the Whisperer loomed over him, its shimmering purple eyes aglow, Matt felt the slow, damp creep of despair. His muscles ached; tiredness inched along his bones. He didn't have the energy to do anything but lie down and give up. The soldiers were too far away to help him. There was no point, in anything.

Yet even with his abilities shutting down, his instinct remained a powerful force. As his fingers closed on the fallen arrow, he was almost amazed to see it rising up in his hand, up and up, until it was driven into the eye of the stooping Whisperer. Matt rammed it deep into its brain then fell back wearily, but he had done enough. The despair ebbed away quickly and his strength and purpose returned.

The last remaining Whisperer was already at the gates, ready to open the intricate locking system. He was beyond the reach of the soldiers' arrows.

Matt jumped to his feet, put one foot between the shoulder blades of the fallen Whisperer, and wrenched out one of the spears. In a fluid motion, he turned and hurled it. It smashed into the last Whisperer's hand, pinning it against the wood of the gate. A few seconds later, the whistle of arrows signalled an ending.

As the adrenalin seeped away, Matt sagged against a wall. He could hear the heavy trundle of the other Whisperers' mounts just beyond the gates.

His thoughts were echoed by the captain of the soldiers, who marched up to Matt holding the head of one of the Whisperers. He brandished the grisly trophy in Matt's face and said, "This will not be the end of it." And then he returned to his troops, the accusation hanging in the air with the hint of future menace.

A plan was already forming in Caitlin's mind as she left the Sun, but she had no time to act on it before the captain of the guard and three others came sweeping up to her from one of the many side streets.

"Our Lord requests your presence," the captain said in a manner that suggested it was not a request at all.

Caitlin was led briskly back to the palace and then along the miserable corridors to the same darkened room where Lugh sat in the same chair, staring into the blazing fire as if he had not moved since the last time she had seen him. As the guards retreated, Lugh acknowledged her with a morose glance and then returned his attention to the flames.

"There has been trouble at the walls," he said. "A breach by those who wait without."

"Oh."

"They come for you, Sister of Dragons. Your presence here compromises the security of the Court of Soul's Ease. This degree of threat is more than we can tolerate."

"You're scared of them. I understand."

He glared at her so suddenly and murderously that she backed away a step. But then he relented and waved her toward a chair on the other side of the fire. "My race is above all, as always, forever. Yet what these things represent is not to be taken lightly."

Despite his words, his tone suggested deep fear kept tightly in check.

Caitlin sat. "What do they represent?"

"You do not know?"

"No."

"You do not know why they pursue you?"

She shook her head.

He held out his hands to the fire. Despite the stifling heat it radiated, he couldn't seem to get warm. "Then it is not for me to say, Sister of Dragons."

"But you could help—"

Lugh allowed himself a bitter laugh. "The Extinction Shears are the only thing that could fend off what is coming, but their whereabouts is unknown." He examined her intently.

"What is it?" she asked.

"It is intriguing to meet you, Sister of Dragons. You are known to us, from the old stories. The Broken Woman, one of the last generation of Brothers and Sisters of Dragons before your kind . . . *become*."

"Become what?"

"Greater. One Fragile Creature exists who can bring everything together—the Far Lands and the Fixed Lands, Fragile Creatures and gods . . ." He slipped once more into a daze, so hypnotised by the fire that she couldn't tell if he thought this a good or bad thing. "His destiny is unknown even to him. And it is the destiny of the Brothers and Sisters of Dragons to bring him to the point where Existence turns."

Caitlin recalled what Crowther had told her about the hope for the human race, and the war the gods were fighting over that ascension. "There's someone who can help us achieve our potential?"

"Only one. His aid is essential."

"Then we won't do it without him." Her mind was racing; she had taken in so much since she had left her home; it all felt like a dream—fantastical things she could never have imagined, unknown worlds, and now schemes of such incredible import that it was almost impossible to take on board exactly what was at stake. "Who is it?" she asked. "If you know, please tell me."

He gave a small, cruel smile, relishing what little power he had. "That is not for me to say, either. But he will be drawn to the Brothers and Sisters of Dragons. Existence will see to that."

"He?" Caitlin mused. She jumped as something separated from Lugh's belt, where she had thought there was a buckle. It sprouted long spiderlike legs and scurried into the shadows beneath his chair. "Ugh. What is that?"

"The Caraprix?" He thought for a long moment, as if he wasn't wholly sure of the answer himself. "They are with us at all times. Sometimes they are almost . . . a comfort."

Some kind of pet, Caitlin presumed. She returned her attention to Lugh; he wasn't going to answer questions about the mysterious saviour, but there was more pressing information that she needed. "Answer one question, at least," she said.

He gestured magnanimously.

"Where is the House of Pain?"

Her query surprised him, for he sat forward in his chair and peered at her. "You are searching for that place?" An unsettling note caught at his voice, and if Caitlin didn't know better she would have said it was fear.

"Where is it?"

"Far, far from the Court of Soul's Ease," he said. "North. Across the Forest of the Night, beyond the great river, past the Plain of Cairns. It lies on the very edge of the Far Lands, where all worlds meet—where, if you look correctly, you can see forever."

Caitlin nodded thoughtfully. "I'm sorry we've brought the . . . Lament-Brood to your home. We don't intend to stay long—"

"You cannot stay any longer."

"All right. Then we'll leave now, if we can find a way past the Lament-Brood."

Lugh shook his head. "We cannot risk the Lament-Brood punishing us. We shall present you to them."

His meaning dawned on Caitlin slowly, and with horror.

"Make your peace with your fellow Fragile Creatures, Sister of Dragons. You will be delivered to the Lament-Brood shortly."

Caitlin related everything she had learned from Lugh to Matt, Mahalia, and Carlton in the privacy of her room.

"The bastards," Matt said. "They invite us in, give us hospitality, and then toss us to the wolves."

"They can't be trusted," Caitlin replied. "That was one of the big lessons in the old myths and legends I remember."

"We definitely can't get out the front," Matt said. "The Whisperers look as if they're busy expanding their forces. They took over some people like they did with that hermit and tried to storm the walls. They're probably transforming everyone who comes up the road to the main gate."

"They're not the only problem," Caitlin said. She told them about the knight with the boar's-head helmet. "I don't know if he's with them or what, but he's definitely after me, and he's here, inside the walls already." She massaged her forehead; her skull throbbed fit to burst. "Why is everyone after me? What's going on?"

Matt gave her shoulder a squeeze. "Are you going to be OK?"

She shook her head, glad of his support. "We've just got to find a way out of here."

Mahalia had been cleaning under her fingernails with a knife. "I think I know somebody who might be able to help."

"This way! This way! You're back!" Jack's excited calls unnerved Mahalia, for their approach had been uncommonly quiet to avoid detection, yet he had known the four of them were on their way long before they came anywhere near his door. When Mahalia peered between the bars, he was straining at the chains in anticipation. "Who's with you?"

"Friends." Mahalia found herself excited by Jack's thrill, and that puzzled her.

"You're going to get me out?"

"Depends. Do you know another way out of this place?"

Thoughts flickered across his crystal eyes. "You can't go through the gates," he surmised. "Then yes, there is another way. An escape tunnel under the mountainside."

"You're not just making this up so we'll set you free?" Mahalia said threateningly.

"No, I swear. I always make sure I know another way out of a situation. I didn't want to go back, but they caught me before I made it to the tunnel."

Mahalia turned to Caitlin and Matt. "What do you think?"

"It's not as if we've got any other options," Matt said. He examined the padlock. It was old and rusted; the cell didn't appear to have had much use in recent times. He advised the others to stand back, then gave it kick after kick until the metal catch eventually disintegrated.

Matt led the way in. "We'd better not hang around," he said. Matt pulled the black hood off Jack's head, revealing the strong, honest face of a youth of about seventeen. His blond hair only emphasised the eerie intensity of his eyes.

"Thank you," he said.

"You're not free yet." Matt examined the many chains that swathed his upper body before dismissing them with a curse. "We'll have to work on those later. But we should be able to get you off the wall—those fixings look as weak as the padlock." Matt set about straining to pull them free, with Jack offering his own weight to assist. After much sweating and pulling, both wall-chains shattered.

"They really kidnapped you from our world?" Caitlin asked.

"I don't know who my father was, but my mother travelled around the country in a group of old vehicles with several others. She's dead now."

"I'm sorry—" Caitlin began.

But Mahalia interjected, "If you were taken as a baby, how do you know about your mother?"

"When I was on the run, I found myself at a watchtower that hangs between the worlds. I thought it might be the safest place to hide, which it was for a while. But it's a very strange place where you can see all that has happened, and probably all that will, and that's where I saw my mother. I wasn't taken long ago by your terms—three or four years—but this place does strange things to you."

"You look like a teenager," Mahalia noted curiously.

"I feel much older."

Cautiously, they ventured back out into the corridor. "Which way?" Matt asked.

"I think, if you agree, that we should collect some weapons for you," Jack said hesitantly. "There's a store not far from here, and we should be able to get rid of the rest of these chains there."

They agreed, and Jack led the way deeper into the bowels of the building. Just as they came to the arms store, a strangely neglected open door to a vaulted chamber that stretched as far as the eye could see, they heard activity some distance away in the palace.

"I think they're looking for us," Caitlin said.

"You'd have thought," Matt said, "that once Lugh told you he was going to hand you over to the Whisperers, they'd have imprisoned you straightaway."

"I wondered about that, but I think he's crippled by arrogance," Caitlin said. "They're all so convinced that nothing is a threat to their superiority that they never bother to act until the last moment."

"Look at these." Mahalia was dazzled by the array of weapons, not just swords and bows and spears, but also eccentric oddities such as portable brass cannon and blades that formed a fan.

"You should just take something simple that's easy to carry," Jack suggested. "Some of these things are too dangerous to take with us."

"You seem to know a lot," Matt said suspiciously.

"I do." Jack turned to him deferentially. "I've always kept my eyes and ears open. I wanted to learn as much as I could—anything that might help me get out of this place."

"You could be of great use to us, Jack," Caitlin said.

"I'd rather just go home," he replied wistfully.

She shook her head, and the sadness she revealed was honest. "I'm sorry, I can't allow that. Not until we've found a cure for the plague that's loose in our world. You wouldn't want to return if you could help save us all, would you?"

"I suppose not." He flashed a glance at Mahalia, who met his eyes for a moment before looking away.

"Well, well." Matt was grinning, arms crossed.

"What?" Caitlin said.

"I see leadership potential. You're clearly getting better. What next—you're going to be ordering us into battle?"

"Don't be sarcastic."

"I'm not. We need someone to take charge, and I'm a sucker for that dominatrix thing." He winked at her, then turned before she could respond, moving amongst the stacks of weapons, testing axes for weight and crossbows for portability, before opting for a bow and arrows, a scimitar in a scabbard, and two short daggers that he secreted about his person. Caitlin immediately chose a longbow and a double-quiver of arrows, which she slung easily over her shoulder.

"You know how to use that?" Matt asked.

"I was very good at archery when I was at university," she said. "Not Robin Hood standard, but I can hit a target."

Matt looked impressed. "There you go again. Lights and bushels and all that."

"How about you?" Caitlin asked.

Matt shrugged. "I did some historical battle reenactments at university. See—the Halls of Academe still have their uses."

Mahalia found a box of rusted, bloodstained weapons and removed a short sword that looked sickeningly brutal, one edge razor sharp and the other serrated; two curling prongs arced from the tip. She made a few gentle sweeps and was pleased with the feel of it.

"That's a Fomorii Glakshi," Jack cautioned. "It's designed to leave the opponent with lethal wounds, not kill them outright."

"That's good," Mahalia said, missing his point entirely. It came with a simple leather scabbard, which she strapped onto a belt around her slim waist.

With disgust, Carlton refused all Mahalia's attempts to press a weapon on him. When she suggested that Jack arm himself, he shrugged and said mysteriously, "I don't need one."

As Caitlin watched Carlton's innocence manifest itself in his refusal to take a weapon, she felt a deep tide of affection that had been growing in her ever since she had first laid eyes on him. Here was all she had lost, and in him Caitlin also saw hope—for herself, as much as anything.

She knelt before him and rested her hands on his shoulders so that she could look deeply into his mysterious eyes. "You're a very special boy, Carlton," she said gently.

He smiled. Nearby, Mahalia's attention was drawn to the scene with a cold intensity.

In that instant, Caitlin was hit with a flash of insight.

Mahalia saw the shocked expression on Caitlin's face. "What is it?"

Caitlin continued to stare into Carlton's eyes. "Lugh told me there was someone very important, someone who could bring together all the different sides to . . . I don't know . . . save us all, make us better." She stood up to address Matt and Mahalia. "I think it's Carlton. Lugh wasn't giving anything away—just teasing me with bits of information—but he said this person would be drawn to the Brothers and Sisters of Dragons."

"You, in other words," Matt said.

"Or one of the others like you," Mahalia pointed out. "The professor didn't say you were special or anything. Just that you were a champion . . . not *the* champion."

"I know," Caitlin said, "but . . ."

"He is special," Mahalia said with a grin.

"Then we'd better make sure we look after him." Matt scrubbed Carlton's hair. "Right, kid?"

Carlton's strange smile did nothing to disavow any of them of the notion.

"I'm already doing that," Mahalia said. Her voice was hard, but her eyes looked strangely worried.

"And we're all going to help out," Caitlin said.

They made their way out of the palace as quickly as possible, and were relieved not to meet anyone en route. But outside, Caitlin turned to them and said firmly, "I want to stop off at the Sun."

"To get Crowther?" Matt said. "That's insane. You know he's adamant he doesn't want to come." He glanced back in the direction of the palace, where the outcry was now growing. There was more activity near the walls, and he guessed that the Whisperers had embarked on another assault. It was time to go, whichever way they looked at it.

"I need to ask him one thing. Don't worry—it won't hold us up long."

Matt could see that she would not be moved. They moved quickly off through the drizzle, keeping their heads down, staying close to the walls.

Crowther was still in the same place, a little tipsy, but still not completely in his cups despite the amount of ale he must have consumed since Caitlin had left him. She motioned for the others to wait at the door while she went over to his table.

"You're not about to have another go at convincing me to leave, are you?" he said wearily.

"No. I can see that wouldn't do any good." Relief tinged his smile. "I just want one more piece of advice," she continued.

He gave a drunken theatrical gesture for her to continue.

"What you said when we first came here," Caitlin began, "about this place being the first staging post of the dead . . . You meant it?"

"Absolutely. To the Celts, this was Otherworld, the Land of Always Summer . . . heaven."

"And is it?"

The question was too big, too taxing; his shoulders sagged a little. "Look around you . . . does it look like heaven?" He saw the flicker of sadness cross her face and softened his tone. "There is some evidence to suggest that whatever remains of us after we die passes through here, en route to . . . somewhere else."

"Go on."

He looked surprised at her questioning. "The Grey Lands . . . the Land of Mists. And from there on to the next place, whatever that might be . . . on forever, for all I know. Learning a little bit more as we pass through each place. Then coming back here to close the circle, hopefully a little wiser, a few more steps down the road to nirvana. Why the sudden interest in metaphysics, Caitlin?"

"You say the dead pass through here," she pressed on. "How long do they stay in this place?"

"I don't know that . . ."

"But it's possible Liam could still be here . . . and Grant. That I could get to them before they move on."

He blanched. "I don't think that would be a good idea, Caitlin—"

"Bring them back with me."

"Don't go down that road—"

"Answer me!" Her voice was low, but her eyes blazed.

"Yes, it's possible—"

"Where would they be?" she demanded, feverishly talking over him.

He sat back in his chair, folding his arms defensively. "A long, long way from here, probably on the very edges of this land. The true nature of reality is clearer here. Nothing is fixed. Lands, dimensions—whatever you want to call them—are fluid, merging and mixing at the fringes. At least according to my limited knowledge."

"And the dead . . . ?"

"Would probably be at the point of greatest flux—the liminal zone between this world and what lies beyond—where energy exists in its purest form."

The smile that crept onto her lips troubled him immensely. "Do you believe in coincidence, Professor?"

"Why do you ask?"

"Because that's the place I'm supposed to go to find the cure to the plague. Perhaps this is happening for a reason. Perhaps I'm being led there for my true task . . . to bring Liam and Grant home."

"Oh, Caitlin, please don't do this to yourself." Deep sympathy wiped the drunkenness from his brain.

"We need you, Professor. We need your knowledge. We can't do this on our own." In her eyes, strange spirits danced; not Caitlin.

Crowther felt a chill run through him. "What are you—?"

The flagon came from nowhere; he hadn't even seen it clutched in her right hand. It smashed into the side of his head with a force that belied her size. In the brief instant before unconsciousness, a single thought flared: how sweet and innocent she looked, what darkness lay within . . .

"I don't think that was fair," Jack protested as he led them through the myriad backstreets, so high up the mountainside that the court beneath them was swathed in cloud.

"She did what had to be done," Matt grunted, hauling Crowther's heavy, limp frame as quickly as he could.

"She'd better not look down her nose at me again." Mahalia chuckled coldly. "She's the Queen Bitch round here. The poor old idiot only wanted a few drinks and an easy life. Now we're taking him to the ends of the world."

Jack stopped at a simple oak door set into a sheer face of rock that rose up from the street for twenty feet.

"Is this it?" Matt asked. "Shouldn't it be guarded or something?"

"I don't think they ever expected anyone to use it," Jack said.

The only thing that held it shut was another rusty padlock, which Matt demolished with a single kick. "Looks like we're out of here," he said.

Caitlin pushed by him, her jaw set. "Let's hope we're not going from bad to worse."

chapter seven
ENCHANTED

"So many gods, so many creeds,
So many paths that wind and wind."
Ella Wheeler Wilcox

For three hours they trudged along the tunnel hewn through the rock, choking on the smoke from torches fixed intermittently along the walls. The mood was sombre and for the most part no one spoke.

Crowther came round a short way into the journey. Once he understood what had happened, he ranted and raged and attempted to force his way back up the tunnel, but Matt blocked his way and the brutal look on Caitlin's face forced the professor to accept the futility of his situation.

"So I'm a prisoner now," he said bitterly, before joining their march, refusing to look at any of them.

The tunnel emerged at the back of a deep cave at the very edge of the foothills. They fought their way past a wall of wild rose obscuring the cave entrance and then picked a path through a sea of nettles and tangled brambles filling a small gully. Brilliant sunlight stunned them after the constant greyness of the Court of Soul's Ease. There was summer birdsong, and clouds of small flying insects buzzed back and forth in search of patches of shade.

Velvety green grassland rolled gently, patchworked by lazy cloud shadows, reminding Caitlin of the South Downs and happier times. Behind them, the snow-capped peaks looked down impressively. Caitlin took in the whole vista, then said, "This is just like the book I was reading to . . . reading to . . ." The name choked in her throat.

"That's hardly surprising," Crowther said sullenly. "Nothing here is really how it appears."

"That's life," Matt said whimsically. "Everything's a front and nobody is how they seem."

"We're dull and stupid beings, trapped by the limitations of our senses," the professor continued, ignoring him. "The human brain continually reshapes the signals it receives, making everything more acceptable to our poor, weak minds. It's like a short-sighted man thinking the world is really blurred and indistinct."

"So what's it really like?" Caitlin asked dreamily.

"The Eastern religions had it right." Crowther rested on his staff, depression overcoming him as he came to terms with the fact that there was no escape for him. "Reality, at least at this level, is shaped by will. The strongest wills create what lies around us. And not just here. We *make* this world, and we make our own world as well."

"We make our world?" Matt laughed.

"Well, I wouldn't expect *you* to understand. Shallow thinkers always accept things as they see them. Don't you understand—nothing is ever how it appears. Everything is a metaphor! Everything a symbol! Realising that is all part of our journey to the next level."

Crowther stalked away, leaving Caitlin and Matt to ponder his words.

They marched as quickly as they could for the next hour in case any of Lugh's men were in pursuit. Once the foothills were behind them, the going was easy through meadows of thigh-high grass waving in the gentle breeze. Psychedelically coloured butterflies the size of Caitlin's hand fluttered lazily around them. The lowlands eased in gently, with copses suddenly breaking the tranquil scenery, the grass becoming shorter and greener. Then, as they came over a rise, they saw a thick, dark forest stretching out almost as far as the eye could see. It was oddly menacing, and they all stopped and surveyed it for a long moment. In the middle of the forest, the steely, mirrored glint of a river caught the sunshine.

Caitlin brought them to a halt on the edge of a copse of ash, with the wood still some three miles away. "Lugh told me where the House of Pain lay." She waved toward the north. "But I want to be sure there are no major obstacles in the way."

"What are you going to do? Call the RAC?" Crowther sneered. He took off his hat and mopped the sweat from his brow.

"No," Caitlin replied, "you're going to find out for us—and any other information that might be of use."

"Really. And how do you propose I do that?" Crowther slumped against the base of a tree.

The others waited for Caitlin to reply, but instead her eyes rolled back eerily until only the whites were visible. "Don't try to trick us." It was Brigid's voice, punctuated by a cackling laugh.

"I wish she wouldn't *do* that," Mahalia hissed.

"It's in your pocketssss . . ." Brigid said, teasing him.

Crowther blanched. "What are you talking about?"

"In your pocketssss." Another cackle. "The secret one, in the lining of your coat."

Crowther shook his head uncomfortably.

"The mask. We need the mask," Caitlin/Brigid hissed.

"Go away." Crowther looked spooked now.

Matt pulled the professor to his feet. "What are you hiding?"

"Get away from me!" Crowther brandished his staff, his fear plain to see.

"We needssss it," Caitlin/Brigid keened.

Crowther held his threatening pose for a moment and then sagged. From the voluminous depths of his overcoat, he pulled an object that glinted like sunlight. It was indeed a mask, but fashioned of the purest silver. The male face shaped on the front was perfect—the wide, empty eyes just the right distance apart, the nose straight and small, the lips full, the cheekbones beautiful—so much so that they all found it attractive. Yet its effect was even greater than that: the simple appearance was so powerful that it moved them to tears, sucking swelling emotions from places that had never been touched before.

"What is that?" Mahalia whispered in awe.

Jack made a strange sound in the depth of his throat. "The Immaterius. The Mask of Maponus."

"You know it?" Crowther said, surprised.

"I've heard whispers . . . in the Court of the Final Word." Jack couldn't take his eyes off it. "They say you can look into the very depths of Existence with it, understand the reasons behind everything, but it was tied into the mind of one of the gods . . . and when he went mad, something happened to the mask, too."

"If you look through it in the right way you can see God," Crowther said dully. "And if you look in the wrong way you see hell—you go mad, like Maponus."

"That was how you found me," Caitlin said. "You looked through that and saw me, and you came."

Crowther nodded. His hands were shaking as he held the mask. "You don't understand . . ." He attempted to put the mask away, but appeared unable. "Every time I use it, it takes a part of me, a little sliver of my soul. It's killing me a bit at a time. That's the price I pay for getting its knowledge."

"Do you think I care?" Caitlin said coldly. "This is about more than you, or me, or any of us. It's about saving the human race—all those poor people dying for something that has nothing to do with them—and if sacrifices are needed, that's what we have to do."

"I didn't sign up for that," Crowther replied dully.

"No, you thought you were getting an easy ride to an easy life. Tough. You made the wrong choice. You were better off where you were."

Crowther stared at her unwaveringly for a moment, seeing her with new eyes. "I don't know whether you're quite hateful, or simply deluded," he said eventually. "Well, you can't make me."

Caitlin's icy smile made him uneasy. "Don't tempt me."

The sun was setting in a flame of deepest red when Crowther finally felt ready to use the mask. Odd, discomfiting shadows crept from the base of the sprawling forest and strange hungry bird-sounds echoed from its depths. The incarnadine glow gave a hellish tint to the mask's sheen as Crowther searched for a location for his ritual. He eventually settled on a spot near a sprawling rowan bush, its flowers emanating a sickly sweet perfume.

While Caitlin and Matt helped Crowther to settle, the younger ones sat several yards away, watching the scene. "You know all about this," Mahalia said to Jack. "Who's Maponus?"

"He's one of the Golden Ones," Jack replied. "They called him the Good Son and he had a special place amongst the gods. Really powerful, you know, but they all loved him, too. And then he became trapped on your . . . our . . . world and that drove him mad. Now the Golden Ones keep him locked up somewhere in the Court of the Final Word, trying to cure him. Even they don't dare let him loose. He could destroy everything—and probably would, given half the chance."

"And this mask is really powerful?" Her eyes glimmered.

"Very powerful." He gave her a sideways glance. "Too powerful for you or I. Best not to get involved in things like that."

As Crowther sat cross-legged, Matt wandered off to the place fifty feet away from where he and Caitlin had decided to monitor the proceedings. Caitlin was about to follow him when Crowther spoke.

"Making sure you don't get too close, I see," Crowther said savagely. "The risks appear to be all on my shoulders."

"You chose it," Caitlin said. "Do you know what you're doing?"

"No. I know what I'm trying to do, but these things never go smoothly. Especially with this." He looked at the mask with naked hatred.

"Brigid tells me you can't get rid of it," Caitlin said.

"It's like a damn drug," Crowther replied. "I wish I'd never picked it up."

"How did you come across it?"

He shifted uncomfortably. "I stole it . . . from the college in Glastonbury. That'll teach me, won't it? It came from some treasure trove of magical items the miserable old fool in charge of the college had been guarding for God knows how long. I don't think they really knew the value of it."

"But you did."

"I had an inkling. These artefacts of power often insinuate their way into plain sight, waiting for the right person to come along." He laughed bitterly. "Or the wrong person."

"You're talking as if they're alive," Caitlin said.

"You don't know how right you are." Crowther weighed the mask in his hands before saying, "I should have known there was no running away. After everything I've done in my life, I wouldn't be allowed to get off so easily. You'd better go back to your friend. And whatever happens, don't come near me until I've removed the mask."

Caitlin returned to the sheltered spot with Matt, all thoughts of Crowther now obliterated by the screaming monkey noises emanating from the back of her head; her other selves were scared—apart from the one who resided at the very back, in the shadows. Emboldened, she was continuing her slow creep into the light.

They watched and waited for almost half an hour until the sun was a bloodred incision on the horizon and the cacophony of bird-sounds in the forest had died away, leaving an eerie silence. Only then did Crowther lift the silver mask to his face.

He paused when it was just an inch away, as if overcome with second thoughts, and then the strangest struggle began; from the others' viewpoint the mask appeared to be fighting Crowther, or perhaps it was his subconscious fighting himself. But then, when the silver was just half an inch from his skin, bolts unfurled from the side of the mask where previously they had been invisible, rose out, and rammed themselves into the sides of Crowther's head.

He screamed. There was a whirring noise as the bolts screwed themselves into bone and then the mask levered itself into position and clamped on tight. Crowther went rigid.

"Do you feel that?" Matt whispered.

Caitlin did; the air was heavy and infused with a steely sheen like the atmospherics before an electrical storm. Everything was so still and quiet it was as though all sound had been sucked out of the vicinity.

"Something bad's going to happen," Caitlin/Amy whimpered.

Entranced by Crowther's display, Mahalia wasn't aware that Carlton had wandered away until she saw him just feet from the professor. She attempted to run to him, but Jack grabbed her wrist and dragged her back.

"Don't," he hissed. "It's too dangerous."

"I don't care!" She wrenched her hand free. "Carlton!"

But by then it was too late. Carlton was by Crowther's side, reaching out, his fingers skimming the surface of the mask.

There was a sound like the swash and backwash of water or the beat of a heart in an echo chamber, rising slowly from somewhere near the horizon, but rushing closer, until it was all around them. *Sh-ssh, sh-ssh, sh-ssh.*

Light leaked from the ground, as if the illusion of reality was breaking apart to reveal what lay behind it. A few seconds later there was no forest or country-side, no sky, just a strange wan light with no up or down.

The six of them were suspended in nothing, Crowther still sitting cross-legged. Vertigo brought them to the point of sickness, until they suddenly adjusted as if it were the most natural thing in the world.

"What the hell's going on?" Matt said. "This wasn't supposed to involve us."

And then Carlton spoke, except his lips didn't move, his face bright with a broad smile. "There's time enough for rest later. We have a job to do now."

He pointed, and as they turned to see what he was indicating, the whole of Otherworld was suddenly spread out before them.

"Oh, God," Mahalia gulped. "We're standing in the air!"

"We *think* we're standing in the air," Carlton said. "We think a lot of things that aren't true. But this is the important thing now. Look."

Ahead of them, the primal forest swarmed with darkness, but slicing through it was a ribbon of silver: the river. It meandered past a swamp, where a brilliant blue something lay partially hidden. The river continued through fields of green and gold and more clustering forest until it swung around on the edge of a small desert. On the rolling sands, they could make out strange piles of rocks—cairns—as if they were next to it. And beyond the desolate plain, the land itself appeared to fall away.

There was mist, and colours fragmenting, before the inky-blue void of space scattered with a million stars. And right on the edge between what was solid and what was forever stood an indistinct black shape: the House of Pain.

"You will find the cure for the plague in the heart of that place," Carlton said. "It's a dangerous journey. It takes us from the hard here-and-now through the changing climes to a place where everything we know starts to fall apart. There, on the edge, we will face true darkness; and we will look deep into ourselves. We will face death." He took Caitlin's arm. "If you want to find your son, that's where he'll be. The dead pass through that place, to the Grim Lands or other places."

"My husband?"

"Already gone. I'm sorry."

Caitlin's heart fell, but it rose again quickly when she thought of Liam and the chance that she might be able to bring him back.

"How can you speak?" Mahalia asked Carlton with tears in her eyes, yet as she said it, she was troubled that this wasn't how Carlton should sound. His words and tone made him appear much older, wiser; not a boy at all.

"Look over there." The grim note in Matt's voice made them turn.

The purple haze brought an instant frisson of anxiety to them all. Bigger than they would have anticipated, it billowed close to the Court of Soul's Ease, but was unmistakably moving in their direction. Through gaps in the mist they could just make out the Lament-Brood, driving forward on their reptilian mounts, their numbers swelled.

"If we hesitate for a minute, they'll catch us," Matt said.

"We're not going to waste any time." Caitlin was defiant.

"Be brave," Carlton said genially. "Be true. The best of us can defeat the worst."

"Wait," Caitlin said, suddenly tense. "Something's happening . . ."

They returned their attention to the House of Pain, and now they could sense in it a presence, skittering like an insect running from the light. It wasn't afraid; rather, it had seen them and was now sizing them up, moving this way, then that, looking at them from all angles.

In a twinkling the benign atmosphere changed. A ripple moved out through the scenery, gentle at first, but building until it was a tidal wave of destruction, distorting everything they could see. Finally it hit them and they were thrown off their feet, spinning through a world of broken shards and flickering colours, spinning round and round uncontrollably until . . .

The storm crashed overhead as Caitlin swam through liquid clay. She was in a deep hole and as she rolled onto her back she saw an oblong of night sky, immeasurably distant and desolate. She knew where she was before the hands erupted from the earth on either side of her and folded across her waist in a mockery of a love-hug.

"You made me die," the husky voice whispered through a mouthful of clay into her ear. "If you'd been there to care for me, and love me, I wouldn't have suffered. The disease wouldn't have eaten its way through me and my final hours wouldn't have been filled with pain . . . and your son wouldn't have died. But you didn't love us. You only loved yourself. Your fault . . . all your fault . . ."

And the hands slowly began to pull Caitlin down into the slurping clay. She didn't resist, because the voice was right.

In the confines of a sweltering attic, with only a thin shaft of sunlight for illumination, Mahalia huddled on an old sack, knees tucked into her chest, and stared into the blue face of a dead baby. Its voice sounded like pebbles on stone. "No one will ever love you. This is a world where mothers give up their children to save their own lives, where everybody looks after themselves. Don't expect comfort, or security, or sacrifice, or tenderness. The only rule is to survive at any cost. You're on your own. You'll always be on your own."

And though Mahalia cried and plugged her fingers in her ears, the rattling, sickening baby voice never stopped.

✳

Matt stood alone. A cold wind blew across a landscape devoid of all humanity.

Every fibre of Jack's being was alive with pain as the inhuman surgeons of the Court of the Final Word cut and peeled and flayed and took him apart down to the smallest atom, and then built him back up again, in their image. Seeing how he worked. Seeing how he could work. And he had no memories of his mother to protect him, apart from what he had glimpsed from the watchtower, and he had no connection with anything soft and human at all. He was completely and devastatingly alone.

And he knew what plans they had for him, coded into the very structure of his genes.

In the oppressive darkness behind the mask, Crowther saw all that was happening to his fellow travellers, felt what they were feeling, succumbed to the same terrors and suffered his own magnified fourfold: the self-loathing, the loss of his family, the loneliness. The emotions were so acute, so sickening, it felt as if his mind was being ripped away.

And behind all of them was the chaotic buzzing of the mad god Maponus. His powerful consciousness extended out from the Court of the Final Word, through the medium of the mask, to taint them all, to show them the despair and the dread and the hideous confusion of his own fractured existence.

There was no escape for any of them. Insanity and suffering prevailed.

And then the strangest thing happened, just as the clay began to flow into Caitlin's mouth, as Mahalia brought blood to her ears in an attempt to shut out the sound. Carlton was there, with all of them, at the same time, and in the same way that Maponus had been. He said, simply, "This is what it means to be human."

His words unfolded in their minds to reveal a hidden message of universal support: they weren't alone. And as soon as they accepted that unmistakable concept, the suffering and madness fell away. Caitlin gulped and choked and found herself sucking in fresh night air, grass beneath her back. The others were scattered around, dazed and shaking, propelled back into reality but with their suffering still close.

The Mask of Maponus lay in Crowther's hands. He stared at it blankly, chest juddering with a silent sob, thin trickles of blood running from the holes in the sides of his head; he looked like an old, old man. Caitlin felt a wave of guilt at what she had put him through, but she could say nothing to comfort him, for she knew she might have to ask the same of him again.

Carlton stood nearby, smiling benignly, and Caitlin shakily went over to give him a hug. "Thank you," she whispered. She knelt down so she was on a level with him. "You are the special one."

Carlton continued to smile and gave nothing away.

Mahalia roughly shoved Caitlin aside. "Can't speak again, mate?" Carlton shook his head. She put a protective arm around Carlton's shoulder and led him away.

"He's a weird kid," Matt said. "The things he was saying, the way he was acting . . . he seemed—"

"More than us?" Caitlin finished. "I think Carlton's going to be more help getting us through this than we thought." She grew sad. "He's a lovely boy."

"He reminds you of your son."

Caitlin was surprised by Matt's empathy, and the fact that he had noticed something she had only been vaguely aware of herself made her warm to him even more. "He's nothing like Liam in so many ways, but there's a quality . . . a calmness . . . that is so Liam. We have to look after him, Matt. Life's so cruel these days . . ."

"I'll keep an eye on him, don't worry. Besides, it looks as though he's got his own personal minder." He nodded toward Mahalia, who sat with her arm around Carlton, talking gently about what they had just experienced.

"Do you trust her?" Caitlin asked.

"God, no," he replied, without a second thought.

As Mary continued her journey eastward across the South Downs, she felt herself growing fitter. Her craving for alcohol was driven out of her by the simple fact that there was none to be had, although it never completely disappeared. She travelled by day, keeping to the high ground, as far removed as she could manage from human habitation. First and foremost, she didn't want to risk coming in contact with any centres of the plague, but she was also aware that a woman travelling alone was a tempting target for some of the forces of anarchy that had risen up since the collapse of the country's governance.

Her thoughts were never far from Caitlin. What worried Mary the most were the marks of subtle machinations and sinister manipulation on everything that had happened since the plague had appeared.

For the first few days, she grew increasingly hungry and even the herbs and edible plants she foraged from the bursting spring countryside did little to assuage her pangs. While Arthur Lee foraged for himself, catching shrews and birds, Mary experimented with a discarded piece of netting and some sticks, and one night managed to catch a rabbit, which kept her going for a couple of days. Over time she perfected her technique and even managed to net a few of the game birds now thriving along the south coast since the Fall.

Most astonishingly, each morning that she woke—secure in an abandoned ruin or camouflaged in the depths of a ditch—she felt as if another year or two had fallen from her. She had anticipated that the travails of the journey would make her feel old and weak, but her limbs were stronger than they had been in a long time and her mind was clear. The breathtaking views from the Downs across to the sea made her feel even more alive. Every aspect of the countryside exhilarated her, from the overgrown fields to the leafing trees, from the morning mist and the glorious spring sunshine to the afternoon drizzle, the birds and rabbits and squirrels.

Part of that sense of wonder was her realisation that she walked in the footprints of history. She was following the South Downs Way, an age-old track that ran from Winchester to Eastbourne, and in more ancient times was linked to other paths that ran to Stonehenge. She felt herself to be a part of something great, and strange, and wonderful.

And on the second week she realised something had started to follow her.

At first she only glimpsed it from the corner of her eye, a flicker that could have been a dust mote on an eyelash, but the more she saw it, the more real it became, as if the act of noticing it had given it substance. In those early times it kept its distance, tracking her along the lowlands but holding back a mile or two, sometimes lost in the greenery and ruined buildings.

Gradually it became more solid, though still too distant for her to define its form. Yet it scared her, as if she was sensing something on another level that spoke darkly of its true nature, and so she hurried her step, afraid to pause even to sleep. The pace began to take its toll; sooner or later she would have to lose it, or face up to it.

At the close of the third day after she had noticed her pursuer, with exhaustion threatening to overwhelm her, she came to a large village. It was in the early stages of the plague. As night fell she watched sobbing relatives gathering in the flickering light of candles and saw village elders struggling to make sense of what was happening, anticipating what lay ahead, but never for a minute grasping the true horror.

It was as good a place as any to make a stand. Her knowledge of the Craft, while not as deep or wide ranging as some, was still enough to afford her use of some simple trickery that she hoped would be enough to throw her pursuer off the scent.

Wearily, she made her way along the dark high street, a plan slowly taking shape in her mind. The charnel house was a large four-bedroom executive property. Its new occupants were laid out with respect in the lounge, old bedsheets thrown over them, the hint of body shapes in the fold-shadows somehow worse than if what was covered had been laid bare.

But it didn't scare her—death never had, and that was one of the things that had convinced her to accept the Craft, where the dead are as much a part of Existence as the living. Old friends, fondly remembered family; sometimes, a little more worryingly, old enemies.

Mary remembered the first time she had seen a dead body. It was in the clinical care wing of the hospital where she had just started her career as a psychiatric nurse. Some poor girl, arms like bones, disproportionately large head giving her the distended doll-form of the bulimic, had gone missing. They found her in the grounds, on a hard winter's night, frozen like a fallen bird amongst the chiaroscuro trees. Her eyes were wide, staring at the spray of stars visible through the branches, her expression oddly optimistic. Mary found it sad, but not scary. Worse things were out there, and she'd come across a few of them in her life.

She made her way up the stairs and chose one of the smaller bedrooms—bare boards, Winnie the Pooh wallpaper, the smell of abandonment, not yet tainted by the corruption rising from the lounge. Moonshadows fell across the floor; the house was silent. In her pack, Arthur Lee lay still, remarkably calm.

After half an hour, she wondered if her pursuer would come, but then she heard the click of the front door opening with secretive care and she knew her instincts had been correct.

With the wind rustling around the outside of the house, she closed her eyes and instantly slipped into her practised trance state. The sigil she required formed against the velvet of her imagination; the words came to her lips without any conscious thought. When she stood up, she knew she was a ghost, no longer visible to any prying eyes. Whoever was there would hear the whisper of her breath, feel a breeze at her passing, but that was all.

She had left the bedroom door ajar so she could slip out easily. If she had timed it right, her pursuer would still be exploring the lower level. She moved to the top of the stairs and waited. No sound came from below. He was good, she thought; a ghost, like her.

Arthur Lee's warning hiss came just as movement flickered at the corner of her eye. It came straight out of the master bedroom, moving faster than she had ever anticipated. A blur of speed, then a few seconds of eerie, awkward slow motion, then another burst of movement.

It had the shape of a man, but it looked as if it had been built from discarded pieces randomly stitched together. The pelvis was twisted so one side pointed forward, while the legs were almost in one line, one in front of the other, mystifying her further at its incredible speed. The arms appeared deformed because the joints had been attached irregularly. It was naked, its distended penis permanently erect. Yet the most disturbing thing was the head, which was on backward. There was something in that image—human yet not human, living but should-be-dead—that horrified her much more than if it had been alien in appearance. A Jigsaw Man.

Mary was rooted in shock for just a second too long. Even though its eyes faced away, it knew exactly where she was and within an instant was upon her. Her misdirection spell worked just well enough to prevent it from killing her outright. Hands that appeared weak and flailing gripped with preternatural strength, broken, dirty nails puncturing her flesh easily.

Mary yelled in fear, lashing out with the knife she had been carrying for defence, but the thing's powerful hold prevented her from striking home. "Get off me, you ugly bastard!" She brought up her knee toward its groin, forgetting its deformed shape. Her knee crashed against the twisted pelvis and made her yelp in pain.

The Jigsaw Man forced her down with increasing pressure until she felt sure her bones would break. She was too weak, too scared. Rough hands worked their way inexorably up her arms toward her throat.

Finally she collapsed to the floor at the top of the steps, the full weight of the creature crushing against her chest. She felt the erect penis dig into her leg and somehow that gave her the impetus to move when she saw her opening.

As the Jigsaw Man shifted its balance, Mary brought her knee up into a position of leverage. The creature teetered. With one jerk that brought stabbing pains up from the small of her back, she launched it toward her head.

The action was enough to break its grip and send it over, though it tore flesh from her arms in passing. With its limbs flapping awkwardly, it crashed down the stairs, hitting the bottom with a sound like dry wood snapping.

With tears in her eyes, Mary hauled herself upright using the banister. Her back was in agony, and the pain from her muscles and ligaments, aged and never used to such a degree, made her feel sick.

"You bastard!" she said with a stifled sob that contained all her anger and fear.

It was still writhing at the foot of the stairs, and as it forced itself up on its twisted arms, Mary could see that its neck was broken. The lolling head scared her even more, and for the first time she wondered if it was even possible to kill it.

She hobbled down the stairs as quickly as her back would allow, and just as the Jigsaw Man was pulling itself up from its knees she kicked out sharply at the base of the skull. The bone shattered under the force.

Mary scrambled by it and out of the front door. She was already muttering under her breath and painting the sigils in the air with her hands as it hauled itself up and launched itself at her. The barrier came up just in time. The Jigsaw Man bounced back impotently, still lurching, still grasping.

Mary allowed herself a moment's satisfaction. She'd done better than she had anticipated; perhaps she wasn't as weak and ineffective as she had thought. "You see, you bastard, you can't get me. That should hold you there for . . ." Her mood deflated a little. ". . . five minutes." It wasn't long; but that wasn't the end of her plan.

She stepped back, closed her eyes; more mutterings, more sigils. When she looked again, she had a sudden spurt of fear that it wasn't going to work. Finally the flames flickered across the floor of the hall, just a glow of light at first, but within seconds an inferno raged within. There was a noise like metal being twisted and broken, and Mary realised queasily that it was the Jigsaw Man's cries; of pain, fear, or anger, she didn't know. Though the conflagration engulfed it, the thing still tried to get through the door, still fought wildly, wouldn't lie down and die as she'd hoped.

With a sinking feeling, Mary realised she couldn't wait any longer. She turned and hurried back along the main street, glancing behind only once with a quiet, desperate hope that she had done enough.

chapter eight
WILDWOOD

"Why was I always suffering, always browbeaten,
always accused, forever condemned?"

Charlotte Brontë

The dark wood loomed before them, vast and low, breathing the slow, measured breath of the predatory animal. Beneath the thick canopy, only shadows lay; sometimes they moved of their own accord. Nettles, brambles, and emerald ferns clustered around the forest's edge, the only easy access along the thin path that wound into the heart of it.

Midges danced in the uncomfortably hot morning sun while birds fluttered here and there but never appeared to enter the trees.

Caitlin wiped a thin slick of sweat from her forehead and thought of the book she had been reading to Liam. The echoes still reverberated through her mind and she mulled over Crowther's suggestion that the impression of this world was created by the people who viewed it. Was she plucking this wood from her memory? Was she remaking the entire place as fractured and desperate as her own deep subconscious? If that was the case, what chance did they have?

"This place has haunted us since we crawled out of caves." Crowther was at her side, drawn and weary, but at least he was finally talking to her again. Unsettlingly, he appeared to be reading her mind, or perhaps the troubled expression she wore whenever she glanced at the deep dark forest. "It's the Wildwood," he continued, "the primeval forest of our deepest, darkest memory, where all the real terrors lay. This Otherworld is a land of archetypes, and the wood is one of the most affecting. Do you feel it?"

She nodded, thinking oddly of *The Wind in the Willows*, of Robin Hood and his green men, of the place where Laurence Talbot loped amongst the trees. "Have you forgiven me?"

There was a long pause before he replied, "No. I'm simply good at making accommodations with life—always have been."

Matt came up, swatting away the flies that buzzed around him. "Better get a move on," he said cheerily. "With the Whisperers on our trail, we can't be sitting around."

"Has anyone told you that your continually perky and upbeat attitude is monumentally irritating?" Crowther said sourly before stalking away.

134

"You'd think he'd take off his hat and overcoat in this heat," Caitlin said.

"He thinks it makes him look like Gandalf," Matt replied caustically, "when actually it makes him look like a fat old git in a hat and an overcoat."

She laughed. "You can be very unkind."

Caitlin was aware of Matt standing so close that their shoulders almost brushed. It gave her a strange flush of excitement, and that made her unconscionably guilty; how could she even begin to have such thoughts so soon after Grant's death?

"I'm sorry we haven't had time to search for your daughter," she said, bringing the conversation firmly back to family.

"There'll be time. I didn't bring it up because I didn't want you clubbing me round the head and dragging me off."

"The professor was different—" she began to protest until she saw that he was joking. His teasing grin brought another unnecessary flush of *something*.

"I think about Rosetta all the time," he said, "but I understand our responsibilities to the people back home. If we don't find a cure for the plague, there won't be any human race left for me to take Rosetta back to."

"I promise you, once we've delivered the cure, I'll come back here to help you search . . . however long it takes."

"I appreciate that."

A moment of mutual support and tenderness swelled between them. Matt saw her dismayed confusion and moved to ease it. "This place looks like it might be dangerous. We need to have somebody at the front and back on guard, and I think weapons should be drawn until we're sure of how it's going to play out."

Her mood changed as she turned to practical matters. She organised the others into a group at the entrance to the wood, despite disruption from Mahalia, who had plainly taken it on herself to challenge Caitlin's authority at every turn.

"Keep Carlton at the centre of the group," Caitlin said. "We have to protect him at all costs."

Though she undoubtedly agreed with the sentiment, this comment appeared to annoy Mahalia immensely, for her knuckles grew white around the Fomorii sword.

After the blazing heat of the day, the air was cool and sweet beneath the thick canopy of leaves that cast the world in emerald and grey. Where the branches were at their thickest, the forest floor was almost bare, but in the areas where the sun came through in gleaming shards, thick vegetation rising high above them reduced the path to a ribbon so narrow that they could only walk single file. At those points where visibility was limited, they most feared an attack. Constant movement in the undergrowth kept them permanently on edge.

They broke for food after a couple of hours' hard trekking. Matt had brought some of the food regularly left for them in their chambers at the Court of Soul's Ease—fruit, dry bread, cured meat. They refreshed themselves with rainwater collected in the cups of exotic blooms that occasionally spread across their way; it tasted sweeter than any water they had drunk before, and its effect was potent: weariness was flushed from their limbs.

"Look at this," Jack said curiously. He cupped in his pale palm the head of one of the flowers. The petals were black and withered, dripping the liquid of rot.

Mahalia made a disgusted face. "You're getting it all over you. Put it down!"

He tossed it away and flashed her a smile. Her response, blunt and challenging but secretly teasing, was lost beneath a low rumble that rose to a high-pitched shriek, somewhere deep in the woods. It was clearly a large animal, though it was impossible to tell if it was hunting or in pain.

They all jumped to their feet. The cry affected them on some primeval level, where the race memories of prehistory were fossilised.

"What the hell was that?" Matt said.

Crowther remained rigid. "What would be here, in the Forest of the Night?" he mused to himself. "That wasn't the Wild Hunt. What other dark myths, what other archetypes . . . ?" His words turned to muttering and retreated inside him.

"Let's move," Caitlin said.

They set off quickly, the animal call still echoing in their heads.

"Could any of you estimate the size of the forest from the view we had when we were wrapped up in the mask?" Matt called.

"Vast." Crowther wheezed as he levered himself along on his staff. "But that doesn't matter in a place where time and space are meaningless. We might be through it this afternoon or a hundred years hence."

"Thanks for the boost," Matt said.

"We'll be all right as long as we don't stray from the path."

Mahalia tried to read Crowther's face, saw his subtle mischief, and couldn't resist a smile. He was surprised how warm the connection made him feel, and he responded with a smile of his own. Strangely, she didn't scowl or glare, but held his expression briefly.

Not even the jagged rocks could keep out the brutal winds of the Ice-Field. Caitlin huddled in a nook, watching the others. Brigid sat cross-legged, cackling to herself like some caricature of a witch from a child's fairy story, while Briony paced back and forth, chain-smoking and bitching to herself. Amy hugged her arms around her, scared as she always seemed to be. Occasionally, though, the little girl would wander over to Caitlin to check that her other self was all right.

The figure in the shadows at the back of their feeble shelter, the one who scared them all, had moved forward enough that Caitlin could just make out her shape against the deeper darkness. She was angular and predatory, her hair wild, and at times she resembled a giant bird more than a woman. Her influence was growing stronger. Sometimes she would call to Caitlin with an insidious whisper, luring, cajoling; at other times she would bellow with a terrifying rage, and on those occasions the others would back away to the very edge of the shelter where the glacial sheets encroached. Although she didn't know why, Caitlin dreaded what would happen when the woman finally emerged into the light.

Amy sat next to Caitlin and slipped an arm around her. "There's a lot of upset ahead. But whatever happens, don't ever, ever give in to despair. It's easy to slip into that . . . and once you do, everything goes wrong." Her voice had taken on a dark tone.

"Despair doesn't just come from the inside," Brigid said. Her cackling had gone; her face was grave. "Events conspire, people conspire. You've got to watch out for . . . anything that might drive you toward despair. Because that's what they want."

"What who want?" Caitlin's nerves were prickling. This wasn't just part of the conversation; Brigid was imparting something important.

"All the forces lined up against life. The things that want to destroy anything that's good. And behind them all is one thing, one force."

Caitlin moved away from Amy's comforting arm. She felt cold, colder than she ever had before. "What do you know?"

"Things are falling into place. You have to be on your guard." Brigid sighed. "But it's not all down to you. Sometimes despair is like a spike and others drive it into your heart. They haven't decided yet . . . they're still thinking. Is the one too precious to them? That's what they think. It could go either way . . ."

"You're not making any sense!" Caitlin said desperately.

"In the end, it's all down to people," Amy said sadly. "Good people and bad people—and sometimes there's nothing you can do but pick up the pieces. If it goes wrong, it won't be your fault, Caitlin. Remember that. Just try . . . try not to let despair poison your heart."

"It depends," Brigid mused, "on how they drive the spike. She might not have a choice."

"So sad," Amy said. "So sad."

Caitlin was overwhelmed with a desperate sense that things were falling away from her. "Stop talking in riddles! If something bad's going to happen, tell me so I can stop it!"

Brigid shook her head. "I can't tell you any more. I'm not allowed."

"Not allowed by whom?" Caitlin demanded.

There was a long pause while Brigid turned the question over. In the end, she simply said, "Not allowed."

She returned to her detached cackling and Amy got up and wandered away. Caitlin stared out to the bleak horizon where the black sky merged with the white Ice-Field, terribly afraid of what lay ahead.

An hour passed, two, and then they started to lose all sense of time. There was just the greenwood, dense and never-ending, like green static hissing at the back of their heads. Oak, ash, elder, hawthorn, rowan, thick banks of creeper, fern, nettle, gorse, long grass. Sometimes they would chop the path clear with Mahalia's rusted sword, only to see it mysteriously close up behind them. Yet it was hypnotic in its monotony, lulling them into a somnambulistic state.

Perhaps they even slept as they walked—none of them could be wholly sure —but it was a while before Caitlin's conscious mind accepted that it was seeing movement under the trees on either side. "Did you see that?" she asked lazily.

No one responded; the only sound was the rhythmic plod of their feet.

She glanced back and forth, seeing nothing unusual, but when she looked ahead, the flickerings on the edge of her vision disturbed her once again. "What is that?" she muttered with irritation, plucking at her eyelashes to see if dust was distorting her vision.

A breeze; her skin turned gooseflesh. Or was it wind, for despite the heat of the day it was cold and it was here and gone in a fraction of a second; it felt like a breath.

As she continued to walk she became more receptive to movement, on both sides. At first it looked like the flashes of shadow and light that appear outside a fast-moving car on a summer's day, but the more she concentrated, the more they fell into relief. Shapes. Figures! Insubstantial, like mist forming the essence of a person. They moved quickly, flickering amongst the boles of the trees, some near, some far away.

Now she had realised what it was, the spectacle was mesmerising. She was in a dream, sitting on the lawn on a summer's eve as the curious moths came from all over to investigate the lamp.

In this half-detached state, it took her a while to realise that one of the shapes had stopped and was allowing itself—if that was the right way to consider it— to stand in full view. She looked directly at it and was surprised to see a man with long white hair and a pleasant, smiling face beckoning to her. Still insubstantial, he had a Regency look, wearing a frock coat and pantaloons, and his mood was one of cheery optimism, as if he had just spotted a long-lost friend.

Behind him, the other shapes continued to flit hypnotically amongst the trees, scores of them, perhaps hundreds.

Caitlin smiled and the ghost smiled back. He beckoned again. He had something he wanted to show her, or hospitality he wished to offer.

She wondered briefly why a man in Regency costume would be haunting a forest in the middle of another world, but the thought came and went as quickly as his brethren. She was fascinated: by him, by the way the light broke through the leaves, by the constant movement, but she barely considered the fact that all sound had disappeared from the world.

"Come," he appeared to be saying in his silent way, "we shall have such fun together."

Something large thundered through the trees deeper into the wood; an enormous oak cracked and fell, jarring the ground so forcefully that she almost stumbled. Whatever had crashed into it continued on its way, but the disruption broke the spell.

The ghost looked over his shoulder in shock and in an instant his appearance changed. Caitlin had a fleeting impression of something old and twisted, not human at all, and then it was gone into the trees, screaming silently.

Caitlin shook her head as if surfacing from the depths of a swimming pool. There was a pop and sound returned: the rustle of leaves and the creak of branches, bird calls high above the canopy, and somewhere far away, people calling her name.

She looked around. The others were nowhere to be seen. The path was gone. And all around the ghosts flitted like angry wasps, preparing to move closer.

Her heart pounded. How could she have been so stupid as to fall under such a spell? Why hadn't the others noticed? Now she had no idea which way the path lay, and the trees distorted the calls of her companions so that it was impossible to tell their origin.

Her first instinct was to fit an arrow and draw her bow, though she knew instinctively it would be of no use. Now that her head was clear she could sense the ghosts' predatory nature; she had the impression that they hated her, wanted not only to destroy her but to torment her in the process.

She caught a glimpse of another face, eyes too big and dark, mouth wide. Not human at all.

She ran, hoping she was heading toward the others. Branches tore at her face. And then she thundered straight into a long, low object that winded her. She was shocked to see it was a casket, standing on its own with no sign of why it would be there, in such a lonely, inhospitable place. It was constructed from gold and ivory, and the lid was made of a heavy, frosted glass. On the side was a legend: *Here lies Jack Churchill, Brother of Dragons—His final battle fought.*

Before Caitlin could work out what it meant, the ghosts-that-were-something-more flitted all around, hurrying to close the circle. There was still an opening, but before she could break through it, she was knocked to the soft peat-mold. Though winded once more, she fought wildly until powerful hands clamped her down and a gentle voice said, "Do not struggle, Fragile Creature. I am a friend of you and all your kind."

She looked up into an incredibly beautiful face: golden skin, high cheekbones, almond eyes, long hair—everything about him was filled with a lustre. More than that, he exuded a tremendous power that invigorated and excited her.

But as he looked into her face, his expression grew curious. "A Sister of Dragons? Can this be?"

"My . . . my name is Caitlin."

He rose, offering an exquisite hand to pull her gently to her feet. As he looked her up and down, with a surprising awe that mirrored her own, he nodded and said, "Yes, it is so. And here, in the Forest of Glimmering Hope." He gave a formal bow. "My name is Triathus. I am one of the Golden Ones, the people your tribes once called the Tuatha Dé Danann."

Caitlin was briefly puzzled—he looked nothing like the short, stout residents of the Court of Soul's Ease. But before she could question him, he became aware of his surroundings and quickly took her hand once again. "Come. We must reach the path before the Gehennis decide to attack."

The circling ghosts had drawn back at Triathus's appearance, but were now confident enough to move closer once again.

"What are they?" Caitlin asked. Some quality in his nature made her trust him instantly. She allowed herself to be led by the hand as he loped gracefully through the trees. The ghosts buzzed with increasing annoyance, unsure what to do.

"They are the dreams of dying Fragile Creatures," he replied. "Bitterness and hatred for what has been lost consumes them, for they know they can never be dreamed again. They prey on all who stray from the path, but Fragile Creatures are always their choicest meat."

"They eat us?"

He glanced at her with a puzzled expression, as if she were speaking a foreign language, yet his English was impeccable. "Not in the manner that you mean. They have no interest in your corporeal form. But who you are, what you think, what you *dream* . . . that is what feeds them."

"My soul?"

He nodded, satisfied. "The Gehennis are soul-eaters."

The calls of Matt and Crowther were now much clearer, and through the foliage Caitlin could glimpse them ranging back and forth. "There are my friends," she said.

"The Gehennis chose you because your essence, your *soul*, is stronger. Otherwise your friends would be long gone."

The Gehennis made one last move as the path came into view. They streamed from several directions, their true appearance growing more horrific with each passing second. Triathus faced them and made a strange gesture with his hand that resulted in a blaze of golden light. When Caitlin's eyes cleared, there were no Gehennis to be seen anywhere.

"We must hurry. They will return," Triathus said.

They came to a halt on the path where Matt and Crowther's astonishment quickly turned to suspicion.

"It's OK," Caitlin said. "He helped me."

Jack hung back, his face dark with fear and hatred. Triathus noticed him and held out both his hands, palms upward. "I see in you the mark of the Court of the Final Word," he said. "I can only apologise for the atrocities of my people. I stand with Fragile Creatures, as do all members of my court."

"Which court is that?" Jack asked darkly.

"The Court of Peaceful Days."

This appeared to placate Jack, but he continued to keep his distance from Triathus.

"What were you doing out there, alone?" Caitlin asked.

At this, Triathus grew sombre. "My people are at war—"

"We were told—by Lugh."

"Then know this: the first skirmish has already taken place. The horns of war have called forth and the Golden Ones are split asunder, perhaps for evermore." There was a desperate sadness to his voice. "My comrades and I were travelling the Endless River, bound for the Court of Soul's Ease to persuade Lugh to join our cause, for if Lugh agreed, other neutral courts would quickly follow. But as we moored, we were attacked—unwarned, at our backs, against all the long traditions of my people—by a group from the Court of the Yearning Heart. My comrades were slaughtered where they stood! Golden Ones, eternal, part of Existence itself . . . lost for all time! How could this happen? How could one of my people commit such a crime against another?"

"We've been asking that question for a long time," Matt said.

"I still do not know if this is the first strike in the greater battle, or simply a minor altercation, prefiguring what is to come," Triathus continued. "My people are patient—we have eternity at our disposal—but if it is the beginning, those who fight for the future are ill prepared. We will be slaughtered." He added coldly, with disbelief, "Perhaps that is what the other side wants."

"A fight between those who want to hang on to the past, and those willing to grab hold of the future," Matt said thoughtfully.

"Between consistency and change," Triathus said. "My people, of all the peoples, should know that change is the lifeblood of Existence. But we have remained stagnant for too long, and we have grown arrogant in our superiority. We do not want to be supplanted."

"Then why do you fight for us?" Caitlin asked.

"Because my side do not believe we will be supplanted. There is no reason why the Golden Ones and Fragile Creatures—no longer fragile!—cannot go shoulder to shoulder into the future, equals in an unstable realm."

Triathus's sadness and shock were affecting. But it was Carlton who came from the back and took Triathus's hand. He looked up at the god with his beaming, innocent face and a sparkle came to Triathus's eyes.

"Intriguing," Triathus mused as he examined Carlton, without giving any further explanation.

Crowther, who had been listening with an expression of deep concentration, rudely pushed his way past Caitlin and said, "You've got a boat?"

Triathus indicated along the path. "Moored on the Endless River—"

"Is it damaged?"

"No."

"Will you allow us to use it? We are on a very important quest for the survival of . . . Fragile Creatures."

"Of course," Triathus replied without a second thought. "I will accompany you. I must return to the Court of Peaceful Days to recount what has occurred."

"Let's get moving," Matt said. "I don't like all that movement in the trees . . . and that wild animal we heard earlier . . ."

They set off quickly, with Triathus leading the way.

The path ran straight as a die for what must have been ten miles, through forest clearings where they enjoyed the sun on their faces after the chill beneath the branches, through patches of briars that they had to hack their way through, across crystal streams, and by brackish pools, where strange bubbles rose occasionally to the surface of the oily water.

When they were less than half a mile from the river, according to Triathus's estimations, they realised they could smell it, fresh and invigorating after the oppressive aromas of sun-heated vegetation.

Mahalia was unusually drawn to Triathus. Throughout the course of the journey, the others all saw her eyes repeatedly pulled toward the god, and a mixture of awe and wonder light her often sullen face. At those moments she no longer resembled the hardened, brutal young woman they had come to know, and there was a hint of the child she might have been in easier times.

Finally they could glimpse the river through the trees, ablaze with the reds, oranges, and golds of the setting sun. After the gloom of the forest it was an uplifting sight, and their step quickened despite their exhaustion.

Jack was keen to rush ahead to the water, but Matt caught his shoulder before he could run off. "Wait. I can hear something."

chapter nine
FOLLOWING THE RIVER
TO ITS SOURCE

*"I do not wish them to have power over men;
but over themselves."*

Mary Wollstonecraft

Caitlin washed her hair by moonlight in crystal-cold river water pulled up from their wake by a silver bucket. As the grease and dirt came out, she felt a little better, but the exhilaration of the new world and the feeling of passing through a fascinating dream was gone for good. It had all felt so fantastic: a trip to a mystical realm to find a magical cure for something so devastatingly human as illness. Now questions were beginning to pile up. Why was the Lament-Brood hunting her? Why were the Whisperers so desperate to get her that it seemed they would never give up? Why did she feel she was playing an important role in some vast, unknowable scheme? She hoped it was all part of her fragmented state of mind—paranoia and megalomania building—and that everything really was as pure and simple as she had originally imagined. But things were never that simple, were they?

It didn't help that Brigid was chattering incessantly in the back of her head. Caitlin had stopped listening to her a while ago—it was the only way Caitlin could go about her life—but the old woman was certainly concerned about something.

While fumbling for the cloth she was using as a towel, it was pressed into her hand. Carlton was there.

"Hello," Caitlin said, as she dried herself off. "Aren't you on lookout with Mahalia?"

He smiled and nodded to the prow, where Mahalia sat with Jack.

"Ah, she's got a boyfriend," Caitlin noted. Carlton laughed silently. "Well, sit with me a while."

They settled into a bench seat set against the rail, where the warm evening breeze would dry her hair. Caitlin was surprised when Carlton rested his head against her shoulder; she put one arm around him.

"I wish I knew exactly what was going on inside your head, Carlton," she said. "Were you always like this, or did something happen to you?"

He didn't look up, didn't acknowledge that he had heard her at all.

The warmth of his body next to hers brought a sudden swell of emotion, surprising in its intensity after the numbness she had felt for so long. She fought back the tears, somehow managing to control her voice. "I used to have a little boy—his name was Liam. He used to like books and computer games and music, and his skateboard. I don't know if you like any of those things, but . . . you're like him in a different way. Quiet, thoughtful . . . I think he was a good person, and I think you are too, Carlton. There aren't enough good people in this world." She gave him a squeeze, trying not to sound too maudlin, nor to swamp him with adult emotion. "I'm going to look after you," she added softly.

In the quiet that followed her words, there were only the gentle river noises, until somewhere in the distance an owl hooted.

A while later, Caitlin made her way to Triathus, who stood at the stern looking out over the moonlit water, deep in thought.

"We appreciate your help," she said.

"These are difficult times," he replied. "We should stand shoulder to shoulder as allies. Perhaps more than that. We are all Children of Existence."

"If only your people agreed on that."

"I fear there will be much suffering before the Golden Ones are united once more," he said sadly. "That it has come to this fills me with despair."

"Are the other side likely to attack us here on the boat?"

"Perhaps. I keep watch for any sign."

"But you never saw them coming before?"

"No." A shadow crossed his face as he watched the white wake spread out in a V.

"Can you see something?"

"No, but still . . . Something troubles me, if only I could identify it."

Caitlin followed his gaze, but could see nothing out of the ordinary.

"I feel . . . a presence. But I see nothing." He turned to her and smiled gently. "And my eyes are keener than yours."

"When I heard about the old gods returning, I never imagined them to be quite like you, Triathus. You're gentler than I expected. Where are all the flashing lights and displays of power that terrified the Celts?"

"Though we like to think of ourselves as immutable, we—some of us—were different in the days of which you speak, Sister of Dragons."

He placed one hand on each side of her head. She flinched at first, but his gentle nature calmed her. His fingers felt cool, but deep within them something crackled like electricity. "You have suffered greatly," he began. "High tragedy. Yet you continue to strive for the good of others." Caitlin felt a soft movement in the back of her head, as if his fingers were probing there. "The Broken Woman," he mused. "Shattered, yet still whole." His expression changed. "Something else lies there . . . hiding." He snatched his hands away; Caitlin felt a sucking sensation inside her head.

"What is it?"

"I do not know. I sensed . . ." He pondered, then made a dismissive gesture. "Perhaps it is nothing."

"I don't envy you probing around in my mind. I know . . . I know I'm not well."

"You make a misjudgment common to your kind," Triathus said. "There is no one way of *being*, no singular way of seeing the world. Your spirit has made your . . . mind how you need to be for this moment, to survive, to win."

"That's nice of you to say, but it still doesn't feel right."

"In the old tribes, the Fragile Creatures who first welcomed us to your world, their wise men and magicians often had an altered perception of Existence—"

"They were all mad, too."

"Words . . . meaningless. Everything without you is a mystery and everything within, too. Worlds upon worlds upon worlds—no view is the same."

Caitlin peered into the depths of Triathus's shimmering face. He appeared to be trying to tell her something important, but she couldn't quite grasp the essence of it. "Anyway, I'm learning to deal with it. Carlton's the saving of me. I feel a bond with him. If he hadn't been around, I don't know what . . ." She became aware of Mahalia standing in the shadows nearby, listening. Caitlin turned to tell the girl not to eavesdrop, but Mahalia had already melted away into the moonshadows washing across the deck.

Strange white faces appeared amongst the trees when the boat drifted close to either shore. It was not the Gehennis, but other, even more disturbing denizens of the Otherworld, stirring from their alien dreams to see what unusual beings had been washed up at their homes. They came and went before their true appearances became clear, leaving their motivations undivined. No one could bring themselves to look at them for too long.

It was deep in the middle of the night when Caitlin stirred from a shallow sleep. A silent calling ushered her to the rail; there was some activity on the riverbank that she had to see.

For the first time the forest was still, and briefly she wondered if she was just acting out a dream. But then there was a sudden burst of blue lightning and a smell of electrical generators. Sparks fizzed out into the water, and within the display Caitlin saw a figure. It was the knight with the boar's-head helmet, watching her passage.

Her heart fell. Surely he should have been left far behind. How could he be there?

The light display continued until the boat had passed, and then winked out. The knight was either gone or lost to the dark.

Caitlin had started to think that the knight was her burden alone; certainly she had a sense that he had no interest at all in the others. With that notion came another more disturbing impression. She had thought that she was on a journey to save humanity; a glorious mission. Perhaps it wasn't that at all. Perhaps she was on a road to hell and the knight was there to ensure that she reached her destination.

Sleep proved elusive on the heels of such morbid thoughts.

Sunlight dappled the deck, shimmering through dancing shadows cast by branches and leaves. Triathus stood at the helm, proud and erect, as if he had not moved all night.

Caitlin stretched and yawned, driving out her disturbing thoughts of the previous night. Matt slept nearby, his face untroubled. It left Caitlin with a deep yearning; she couldn't remember the last time she had been like that. Mahalia, too, looked at ease with her head resting on Jack's shoulder. She had her arms tightly around Carlton as though afraid someone would steal him in the night. Crowther was nowhere to be seen.

Caitlin made her way to Triathus, who nodded politely when he saw her. "Where's the professor?" she asked huskily.

"Making breakfast for you in the galley. He did not sleep well. There is much that troubles him."

"Hardly surprising. He thought he could run and hide from all the world's problems, and his own. Now he's discovered you can't do that."

"He should be content. He has taken another step along the path of wisdom."

Caitlin surveyed the river. It had grown narrower during the night and now the banks were only an arrow's flight apart. On either side, the trees rose up for almost forty feet in an impenetrable wall of twisted branch and gnarled, protruding root. Occasionally, spaces would appear, allowing her a glimpse of green hills and, in the distance, misty purple mountains. It was an epic landscape of awe and wonder.

In one of those gaps, her attention was caught by crumbling stone ruins on a distant hilltop. Though distant, she could tell that they were incredibly ancient, the stone shattered by the years, festooned with ivy. "What is that?" she asked Triathus.

"A memory. This is an ancient land, older than the Fixed Lands, almost as old as Existence. My people like to think of themselves as a pure part of Everything— the first and last and only. But in truth we know there were others before us. We are simply the last generation of gods. Before us came the builders of great stone cities, erected in such a way that they resembled mighty cliffs, part of nature itself—in the tops of trees, beneath the waters, in the dark crevices beneath the earth. Before us came the fighters of great battles that laid waste to the Far Lands, so that no green thing grew and only smoke drifted across the burned and blackened realm. Before us came the great monsters, the devils, the avatars of the Void. There are even tales sung by the *filid* of Fragile Creatures who once had a great civilisation here in the times before time. The echoes of all those races still ring out across the Far Lands, in stories, mysterious ruins, artefacts of great power, wisdom—to which my people have laid claim, but which come from long before us. Only one thing has remained unchanged, throughout all the ages: the Fabulous Beasts—not beasts at all, but messengers of Existence."

"What happened to those people?"

Triathus looked thoughtful. "They moved on." His gesture suggested that they still existed, somewhere.

"And so my people came here to take their place, from four wondrous cities of the Northland—Falias, Gorias, Finias, and Murias. Forced to wander, always searching, never finding. Yet we always carry with us memories of that happy home, when we were part of Existence and all was right. And the twenty great courts were established, and our reign of power began. And the Far Lands were shaped to our thinking, and everything became as you see around you."

Caitlin rested on the rail, enjoying the fresh, cold scent of the river and the way the sunlight flashed across her face. "It's a beautiful place—but dangerous, too."

"Like my people." He brought his hand sharply to his forehead as if afflicted by a sudden pain, but the mood quickly passed. "We know from our observations of Existence that there is a season to everything. Death in winter. New shoots in spring. The cycles continue eternally, but nothing lasts forever. The Golden Ones *will* be supplanted . . . and Fragile Creatures will take our place. That is clear, yet the other side refuse to accept it, as if the sound of their voices could drive Existence back. There is an arrogance to my people, an arrogance that afflicts all who remain in power for too long. But the truth will emerge, in time, and the seasons will continue to change." There was a sadness to his voice that affected Caitlin deeply. He could see the good times fading, yet somehow he accepted it with equanimity.

Matt was enjoying the peaceful morning at the rail when Mahalia eased her way out from between the sleeping Jack and Carlton and came over. This attempt at sociability was suspicious enough, but her fresh features couldn't contain her uneasiness.

"Can I ask you something?" she asked.

Matt surveyed her, and in that unguarded moment he could see all her innocent fears. "Sure. What's up?"

"You and Caitlin get on all right. I mean, I've seen you both. I know you fancy her, and I reckon she fancies you as well."

"You don't know what you're talking about."

She made a dismissive gesture. "Whatever. I just need to know what's going through her head." Matt saw her furtive glance back at Carlton.

"What exactly do you need to know?"

"What's the deal with her and Carlton? She's always crawling round him. What does she want with him?"

Matt chose his words carefully. "Caitlin's suffered a great tragedy. She's lost her only son—"

"And she wants Carlton to take his place?" The edge to Mahalia's voice suggested Matt had touched a nerve.

"In a way. He's a surrogate, I suppose . . . filling that hole she's got inside her."

Mahalia's jaw set. "She's not going to take him away from me."

"You shouldn't think of it like that—"

"You don't understand. Carlton's all I've got. Everybody else walked out on me, but he's stuck by me through all the shit we've come up against. He's family. She's not going to have him."

"You've got to be reasonable here, Mahalia. You don't own Carlton—"

Mahalia glared at him. "I never said I did. So what do you think she's going to do? Be, like, his mother?"

"Maybe. It would be good for him. You've got to think of that, Mahalia."

She had the jittery look of a frightened animal. "She won't take him from me," she repeated. "I'll do whatever I have to to keep him."

Matt watched her stalk away. He realised, for the first time, that Mahalia was truly capable of *anything*.

Crowther had spent a good hour familiarising himself with the contents of the galley. It came as a welcome relief after a long night of struggling and failing to sleep. Events weighed heavily on him, and food was always one of his favourite diversions. He found a selection of the ubiquitous dried, spiced meats and several loaves of the nutty bread that never appeared to lose its softness; an abundance of fruit, too, none of it blemished, even though it must have been on the boat for a while.

He munched heartily while he set about preparing breakfast dishes for the others, and eventually the tactile and olfactory ritual allowed him to shuffle some of his black thoughts to one side. He had almost reached a state of blank bliss as he bit into a ripe peach that sent juices spraying across his face when he was jolted by an electric voice.

"Put me on."

He whirled, not knowing whom to expect, but the galley was empty. The steps led up to a sun-drenched and deserted quarter of the deck. An odd cold-hot flush swept over him. The voice had a crackling, otherworldly power.

"Put me on!"

The force of the command physically threw him back against the wall. Now he knew its source, and the realisation filled him with dread.

With trembling fingers, he hesitantly withdrew the Mask of Maponus from his overcoat. It felt hot to the touch, the silver flashing like lightning in the sun.

"Put me on."

Crowther dropped the mask with a jerk. It clattered onto the floor, blank, inhuman eyes fixing a gaze of terrible gravity upon him. The lips had moved when it spoke; they had moved as if the thing were alive.

Crowther clutched at the work surface with sweaty, itchy hands. "I'm not putting you on," he said in a low, tremulous voice.

"You must. You have opened yourself up to the infinite vision of the Good Son. Bonds have already been forged; they cannot be shattered. You have partaken of the wonders that spring from my eternal joy and now you must pay the price."

"No. I know what'll happen if I keep putting you on—"

"The things you shall see! The knowledge you shall gain, the wisdom! Worlds shall be spread before you, all Existence under your will. Nevermore to be afraid . . . of anything . . ."

"No!" Crowther kicked the mask furiously so that it spun across the floor. It was all he could manage, and he knew his hands were already reaching down for it as his foot lashed out. "I know what will happen!" he shouted. "There won't be any 'me' left. You'll suck me in, swallow me up in your madness . . ."

"What are you doing?" Matt stood at the top of the steps, surveying Crowther curiously.

The professor blinked slowly and stupidly, the echoes of Maponus's voice still fizzing around inside his head.

"You were talking to yourself," Matt pressed. "Don't tell me you've developed a few extra personalities in your cranium as well."

"Don't be so stupid," Crowther snapped. He snatched up the mask, slipping it effortlessly into his hidden pocket, despite the way it tugged at his fingers. "Talking to myself, you say?" He tried to read Matt's attitude and decided the mask had not spoken aloud; perhaps it only spoke to him inside his head. Perhaps it didn't speak to him at all. Perhaps he *was* going mad. Maybe that was the price any human paid for venturing into the Otherworld.

"Look, we haven't got time for you to play silly buggers," Matt said with exasperation. "Caitlin's having another of her turns."

"And that should concern me why, exactly?"

"Just come and listen." With irritation, Matt spun round and marched back on deck.

"*I am the eggman, they are the eggmen,*" Crowther said after him, with a dismissive gesture. "*Goo goo goo joob.*"

"They're there, I tell you!"

Crowther found Caitlin marching back and forth along the aft rail, glaring menacingly at the white wake. Her voice belonged to the irritating, neurotic Briony.

"I've tried to explain to her that we know the Whisperers are behind us," Matt said, "but they can't be close because there's no way they could move quickly through the forest. And if they *were* there we'd see the disturbance they make . . . or at least hear that God-awful whispering."

"This personality is a construct to provide a voice for her inherent paranoia," Crowther replied quietly. "After what's happened to her, she feels the whole world is against her and something bad is just around the corner."

"So we can safely ignore her?" Matt asked.

"I wouldn't say that," Crowther replied.

"See, shithead." Caitlin/Briony gave Matt the V-sign.

"These constructs come from the primal mind," Crowther said. "If Jung's theory of the collective unconscious is correct, they may have access to information denied to the rest of us."

Matt looked suspicious of this intellectualising.

Crowther wasn't deterred. "And in quantum theory we are all connected. Some have said that consciousness isn't confined by the brain. At the quantum level, consciousness—perhaps an analogue for the soul—can move beyond the form, explaining how some seers can see events at a distance . . . telepathy . . . magic . . ."

"You're just doing this to make me feel like an idiot, aren't you?" Matt said.

"Yes. Is it working?"

"Will you two stop having a wank," Caitlin/Briony snapped. "You'd better listen to me or it's all over."

Crowther pushed past her and surveyed the tree line. "No sign of anything moving in there," he said after a moment. He listened. "Can't hear anything either."

"That's what I said." Matt shook his head with exasperation.

But despite their words, both Crowther and Matt could feel *something*. An oppressive atmosphere had settled over the area.

"I think we should take it in turns to keep watch," Crowther suggested.

On a warm spring evening with the sun only just turning orange and the midges alive with excitement, Mary crested the final rise to see the object of her search in all its majesty. The Long Man of Wilmington was etched in white along more than two hundred and twenty feet of hillside, gripping his twin staffs proudly. She had broken away from the South Downs Way to follow a path to Dragon Hill for just such a view. It seemed right to process toward it in that way, a part of the ritual that lay ahead.

The Long Man's size surprised her—bigger than the pictures suggested—and she was also surprised to see that the chalk outlines were still sharp and clear. She guessed the locals must have continued to look after the figure as their ancestors had done for hundreds of years. Did they sense something more potent than a simple illustration; a race memory of hill figures as signals to the gods? Or even as the gods' presence on earth?

She hurried down the slope toward Windover Hill, the birdsong loud and melodious, the scents of the English countryside uplifting. This was how she always thought of England—on the brink of summer, with the elements conspiring to conjure up that unique mystical energy that coursed through the land.

Only one thing cast a shadow across her thoughts: Caitlin. So many days had passed since Mary had set off on the long, trudging march from her home that anything could have happened to the young doctor. Perhaps the whole quest and its many privations had been for nothing. Caitlin could already be dead at the hands of whatever dark force had set the plague upon the population.

In the end, it all came down to hope, and faith, as so many things did in life. Mary had to do the best she could and place her trust in the Universe to make everything all right.

She eventually found a quiet spot that had the right vibrations for what she had planned. It afforded a perfect view of the Long Man's ancient form; she could already hear the beyond calling to her.

The Long Man had been carefully crafted by the ancients. Viewed from the ground, the proportions had been drawn just right to make the figure appear as if it were standing upright; a remarkable feat of engineering, or perception. And from her vantage point she could also see something else clearly. The Long Man was not supporting himself on two staffs, he was holding open a gateway. To where? She had already guessed the answer.

She removed from her bag all the doings she had brought with her for this moment—the tiny packets of herbs, the mortar and pestle, the cream that would provide the base for the alchemical ointment. She hadn't brought her broomstick—too cumbersome for the long road journey—but she had another ritual applicator carved from smooth soapstone.

Stripping off her clothes, she briefly enjoyed the heat of the sun on her skin. The breeze made her nipples hard and there was a familiar flurry of excitement deep in her belly that was almost sexual; it always felt like this, that moment of heady anticipation on the verge of the ride of her life.

The herbs and cream were prepared with a ritualistic attention to detail, the right words muttered, the correct movements followed, and finally, as the sun eased toward the west, she was ready.

She applied the ointment to the applicator and then lay with her legs apart, facing the Long Man. Already moist from the sexual tension, it was easy to slip the applicator inside her. An electric thrill ran into her belly. This was how her sisters had done it, in times long gone, when the Old Religion was the only religion. The true night-flight, the real broomstick ride, for sexuality and spirituality were always inextricably linked, part of the great worship of life.

The psychoactive elements of the herbs rapidly entered her bloodstream through the porous walls of her vagina. It felt like heat, like energy, engorging her clitoris, rushing up through her body to her brain where it tripped the right switches and threw open doors to secret rooms. And then she was falling back, back, through darkness, the hidden door at the back of her head. She emerged through it, and the rush was as astonishing as it had been the first time she had embarked on the spirit-flight, sucking her up high into the sky where the sheer wonder of it all made her head spin. Far below, her prone, naked body looked so fragile; here she was glorious.

As the light of the setting sun made her spirit-form sparkle with an inner warmth, she soared even higher until the landscape was a mass of green with the Long Man standing out in stark white. It was only then that she realised the figure had been designed for viewing from above as well as horizontally. Yet it had been constructed at a time when man was supposed to have been rooted to the earth. Perhaps everyone in those times indulged in spirit-flight, an era of true freedom that made a mockery of the claims of the leaden modern age, trapped in materialism, a fixed worldview. Everywhere she looked, the marks of ancient mysteries, forgotten mysticism, lay across England's green and pleasant land. Gateways to old knowledge, hidden powers, secret stories, forgotten tales. They'd tried to concrete over it, trap it under roads and pylons, but it was still there, dreaming, just beneath the surface.

She was shocked to see she was not alone. Ghostly figures were dotted all around Dragon Hill, glistening like patches of mist, their heads raised to look at her. Mary drifted down, unsure if there was danger present, and found herself drawn to one particular figure, a man, tall and imposing, his hair long, his face strong-jawed and high-cheekboned.

"We greet you, sister." His words came to her, though his mouth did not move.

"Who are you?" Mary asked suspiciously. She had seen many strange things since the Fall, but nothing like these people.

"Old souls. Guardians and guides. We move along the lines of Blue Fire, shepherding mortals who need us at the points of power, offering wisdom to those who seek answers to questions of the spirit. For centuries, the ley system lay in ruins, fragmented by those who had lost their link to the world-mind, and our influence was restrained. But now the Fiery Network is active once again, and so we are free to move and guide. And our presence is needed more than ever at this time, when the seasons have changed, great events fall into alignment, and mortals prepare for the great step into the unknown. We are the Elysium, and I am Sharish."

Mary wondered if these beings were responsible for stories of angels, for there was certainly something angelic about them, more in their nature than their appearance. They almost appeared to glow with the faintest blue light, but their features were not benign; indeed, they had an unsettling subtle quality that made Mary quite afraid.

"My name's Mary," she replied. "Are you here to help me? Or stop me?"

"We are guides, helpers. We do not interfere, whatever path you choose."

"I want to petition the Higher Powers," Mary began. "I'm very concerned about a friend who has gone off into a dangerous situation."

Sharish's gaze fell on her powerfully, drove straight into her. "Your desire to help is good, but sometimes desire is not enough, and events must unfold as Existence requires. Are you prepared for what you have to do?"

"Yes. I'll do anything. Can you help?"

Sharish motioned to the Long Man, and as she looked Mary was aware of a subtle change in the landscape. Now thin veins of blue light ran just beneath the turf like the pulmonary system of an enormous living being; she could feel the energy pumping through them. One line, stronger than others, ran through Dragon Hill to Windover Hill, illuminating the feet of the tall, old god, and then beyond. She had a vision of the network crisscrossing the globe, linking points of great spiritual power.

"There is more at stake here than you think," Sharish said.

"What do you mean?"

"The smallest things are always part of something bigger. What may seem random events become part of a structure when viewed from a greater perspective."

"You're telling me to take care? Are you being my guardian angel now?"

He smiled and in an instant everything about him softened. "When you step into a dark room, it is good to have a helping hand to bring you back to the light. That is why we are here."

Mary looked up at the Long Man, his hands pressed against the symbolic gateway. "I want to open the door," she said.

"Then know that you will contact something very old, and very high. He is beyond all you will find in the Fixed Lands, and in the Far Lands—even those who think themselves above all else. He was here when this place was first made, and he shall be here at its end."

"God, then?" Mary asked. "The highest?"

"There is always something higher." Sharish moved to her side, and Mary felt every fibre of her being prickle with a strange anticipation. "Ask him what you will, seek his aid, but know that the direction comes from you, and you may be wrong."

"That wouldn't be a surprise."

"Would you like to know more of what is at stake?" He was looking at her in a way that suggested she should seize this opportunity. She nodded, and he pointed to Hindover Hill in the dying light beyond Windover Hill. "His companion stood there, once—the Goddess. Twin gateways to the powers that make up all Existence. She was the night to his day, the moon to his sun. Many old things have been torn asunder under the mistaken rule of mortals, and some have been put right in recent times, but this still remains. The Goddess is lost to him and he mourns."

"You want me to find her?"

"She will return, when she is called. But the call must be loud and clear." His spectral, shimmering hand touched her spirit-form and she jolted. "Four million women died across your world, burned at the stake or hanged by fearful men afraid that the Goddess power would manifest within them."

His cold, hard rage was frightening to feel. Mary knew what he was talking about—the persecution of witches carried out by religious zealots throughout the Counter-Reformation. "And I would have been one of them if I'd lived back then," she said.

"And that is why you are here, whatever you might think. Some men do not want the Goddess ascendant—they have grown comfortable with their own rule, with their wars and their money and their science and their logic. Fearful men have driven the Goddess away, but there must be a balance if mortals are to advance."

"I still don't see what I can do—"

"You will be guided. The seasons are still changing. You know these words: *'Also a damsel shall be sent from the city of the forest of Canute, to administer a cure. Once she has practised her oracular arts, she shall dry up the noxious fountains by breathing upon them. Afterward, as soon as she shall refresh herself with the wholesome liquor, she shall bear in her right hand the wood of Caledon, and in her left the buttressed forts of London.'*"

Mary clearly recalled the potency of the image. "Yes. It's from the prophecies of Merlin. I've read them." She paused, thoughtfully. "You're saying it's all about women?"

"England's gateways are closed. They must all be opened again. Bear this in mind as you go about your business."

He stepped back, and Mary realised it was finally time. She had prepared some minor ritual to try to open the way, but it was clear that it would not be necessary. Some other members of the Elysium had congregated on the vein of blue, and now it was growing brighter, pulsing. The vibrancy moved quickly through the ground toward Windover Hill and then rushed directly into the Long Man. At first, Mary thought it a trick of the fading light, but in the blue glow the figure came alive; his hands pressed the gateway wider and a sapphire light shone out across the landscape.

"The door is open," Sharish said.

"I don't like her." Mahalia sat in the crook of Jack's arm, watching Caitlin balefully. Carlton was now staring up at the doctor with puppy-dog eyes.

"Why?" Jack was surprised at Mahalia's vehemence.

"She's manipulative. She's a nutcase. And she can't be trusted."

Jack peered at Caitlin as if trying to see through a disguise. "I don't understand." He shook his head. "If you'd spent all your life stuck in this place without any other humans, any family or friends, you wouldn't be so quick to judge."

Mahalia's expression changed quickly. "I'm sorry. Don't think badly of me. I can be a bitch sometimes, when I'm not thinking."

He tightened his arm to hug her closer. "I couldn't think badly of you." There was a tension in his muscles that puzzled her. After a moment it manifested in his voice. "I like you."

She looked up into eyes that sparkled, his intention clear. "I like you, too," she said.

"You don't understand. During all my time in the Court of the Final Word, I never thought I'd ever get close to another person, never thought I'd . . ." He gently reached out and touched her face with his fingertips as if he were committing some terrible indiscretion. He snatched them back, as if burned by the contact with her. "And I never, ever dreamed the first person I found would be someone like you. You're so good, in your heart. You care deeply about things . . . and . . . and you're afraid that people are going to hurt you . . . emotionally . . . so you pretend you're someone else."

Mahalia was taken aback. "You really see me like that?"

"They gave me lots of abilities in the Court of the Final Word. I can see right into the heart of you. You're a good person, Mahalia."

His words overwhelmed her. She moved her face, inviting a kiss. He was just as innocent, didn't really know what to do, but her intent and his desire were clear. They somehow found each other's lips, hesitantly and with embarrassment, but the purity of what they felt drove out all else. Mahalia, never before kissed, felt something profound happen to her, though she still didn't know enough to understand exactly what it was.

When they broke off, they held each other, hearts racing, trying to comprehend what had just occurred. And only once did Mahalia's thoughts grow cold and divert her eyes to Caitlin, who now had one hand on Carlton's shoulder.

The journey upriver continued, the banks getting closer with each mile that passed. The day had been hot and the insects that clouded over the water had long been a nuisance, so the travellers had spent most of their time beneath gauzy makeshift shelters or below deck.

They had increasingly noticed a fruity odour of corruption, growing stronger the further they advanced; in the heat it was florid and overpowering and occasionally so strong that they had to cover their noses and mouths.

It was not long before sunset that they came upon another boat travelling downstream. Triathus saw it with his acute eyesight long before any of them had any idea it was there.

"There is danger ahead," he said, turning to them. "A skiff approaches. It bears the sigil of the Court of Glimmering Hope."

Matt stood at the prow and peered ahead beneath a shielding hand. "How the bloody hell can you see that?"

"They're the enemy?" Caitlin asked.

"Five courts stand firm alongside the advancement of Fragile Creatures. Five are opposed. Ten remain unaligned. The balance has been held with tension in recent times, but our side believe preemptive strikes by the others . . . the enemy . . . could drive more into their alliance."

"So, it's all about to go pear-shaped." Crowther emerged from below deck with a canister of water. "A civil war amongst the gods."

"Leave them to it," Jack said passionately. "We don't need them. We should locate the cure and then return to our world."

"We can't bury our heads in the sand." Caitlin tried to see the approaching boat, but the sun on the water was too bright. "That's what the Golden Ones have often done. We'll have to deal with the repercussions sooner or later . . . they won't leave us alone, whoever wins."

"Are they going to attack?" Matt picked up his bow from the rail where it had been leaning.

"They will strike if they see me aboard," Triathus replied.

"Then we hide you below deck," Caitlin said. "And we hope they leave us alone."

"You think they're going to be scared off by us?" Crowther sneered. "Have you looked around recently?"

"Speak for yourself." Mahalia stood on the rail, one hand clutching the rigging, the other holding the Fomorii sword.

"She's right," Caitlin said. "We're not going to give up easily now. We've got something to fight for—they haven't."

"What an absolutely wonderful speech," Crowther said sourly. "I'm sure they will be quaking in their boots."

"Nobody's going to take me again," Jack said defiantly, though fear lay clear beneath the surface.

"Do not forget," Triathus said, "though their forms are changed, they are still Golden Ones. They cannot be slain—"

"We'll see," Caitlin said. "Now you go below."

Triathus hesitated, then did as she requested.

"You can go, too," Caitlin suggested to Crowther.

"I might as well die here on deck as down below." His sweating hands moved beneath his coat before he snatched them out suddenly. "I'll find a weapon . . . do my part. Don't worry."

"Thank you," Caitlin said affectionately. Crowther harrumphed, and then went in search of something he could use.

They gathered along the port rail, tense with weapons at the ready, knowing there was nowhere they could run. Eventually the skiff came out of the low sun, its sail bearing a stylised star insignia. Six people stood on board, shorter even than the low men of the Court of Soul's Ease. There was something primal about their swarthy skin and thick black hair, and the unusual agility they exhibited as they moved across the deck to gain a better view of the approaching boat. They wore body armour made of leather and black steel, and carried short, cruel-looking knives, like roadside bandits. As the skiff drew nearer, everyone could see their eyes glittering coldly.

One of them wore a scarlet kerchief, which marked him out as the leader. He leaped onto the prow as the skiff drew alongside thirty feet away and eyed them slyly. "Ho, Fragile Creatures!" he hailed. "Who speaks for you?"

Caitlin stepped forward, bow in hand. "I do."

Puzzlement, then uneasiness crossed his face as he scanned her. "A Sister of Dragons? Here, in the Far Lands?" A tremor ran through his comrades, and he silenced them with a sharp cutting motion. "What business do you have on the Endless River?"

"We seek a cure to a plague that has devastated our homeland. We hope to find it upriver."

"Upriver? You know what lies upriver?" The leader laughed, then looked to his crew, who joined him in the mockery.

"We're not afraid," Caitlin said defiantly.

This made them laugh even more. But as the laughter died away, the group of strange little men grew more menacing. Caitlin noticed the barely perceptible shift of their expressions, the way they clutched their knives tighter, and moved close against the rail. Unbidden, the skiff began to drift toward *Sunchaser*.

"It was nice to meet you," Caitlin said to them. She glanced at Matt, who was watching her carefully for any sign. Without drawing attention to himself, he notched an arrow. "But we have to be on our way now."

"Stay a while, Sister of Dragons. Let us talk some more." The skiff continued to drift toward them. "We so rarely have the chance to talk with Fragile Creatures. Tell us news of the Fixed Lands. We miss our old home."

One of the crew at the back surreptitiously lifted his knife, ready to throw. Instantly, the air whistled as Matt's arrow rammed into the centre of the little man's forehead. The crew member squealed as he was thrown backward wearing an expression of shock.

His comrades erupted in fury. "At them!" the leader roared. A knife embedded itself in the mast just to the side of Caitlin's head. The skiff picked up speed.

Caitlin loosed an arrow, spiking the leader in the throat. There was no blood. She notched another arrow with a speed that surprised her and fired again. Matt was firing too, while Mahalia yelled a stream of four-letter obscenities and brandished her blade ferociously. Caitlin couldn't comprehend what was happening. Her body appeared to be moving of its own accord, her hands rapidly notching and loosing as if she were an expert archer; a part of her observed what she was doing with a detached amazement.

The arrows tore into the little men, but still they stood, like pincushions.

"He's right—we can't kill them!" Matt yelled.

The leader snapped off the shafts of the arrows penetrating him, his face contorted with rage. The words that streamed from his mouth were now incomprehensible, but clearly filled with venom. The skiff raced toward *Sunchaser*, and when it came within a few feet, the little men leaped the gap. Caitlin fell back, wishing she had a sword. But Mahalia was there before her, slashing back and forth like a veteran with her Fomorii blade. It raked open the face of one of the little men and knocked another back against the rail.

Even Crowther stepped forward, brandishing his staff, which was tipped with iron. He rammed it into the stomach of the leader and tried to lever him over the side.

But it quickly became clear that the little men would overwhelm the travellers in no time. Though their bloodless injuries mounted, nothing hurt them. They were an unstoppable wave of wild activity. Matt's forearm was opened up by one of the knives. Crowther went down with one of the attackers straddling him, arm raised, knife ready to plunge into the professor's throat.

Caitlin backed against the starboard rail, her mind racing. Her only option was to make Triathus ram *Sunchaser* into the shore in the hope that it would unseat the little men and give the rest of them—whoever survived—a chance to escape into the forest.

But before she could move, she smelled charred metal on the breeze and an intense white glow burned on the periphery of her vision. She turned to see Jack pressed against the rail, distraught, tearing at his hair as tears flowed down his cheeks. The burning light was emanating from his stomach. It was as if it had opened up to reveal a furnace, but the illumination moved out from him in waves that had the glassy appearance of a heat haze.

He howled, in physical or emotional pain, and the molten light erupted from him in a blast. It hit each of the little men full on, sending them flying through the air, over the rail, and cascading into the river. The light slowed, twisted into tendrils, and hung for a second, before lashing out in a second wave. It smashed into the skiff and tore it into matchwood.

And just as quickly, the bizarre display sucked back into Jack's stomach and winked out.

Jack collapsed to his knees in dismay, stifling sobs. Mahalia, confused and troubled by his state, rushed to comfort him, but he forced her away. He looked broken.

Triathus rushed up from below deck, while the others scrambled to their feet, dazed, trying to comprehend what had happened. The remains of the skiff disappeared beneath the slow-moving water.

Appearing oddly elated, Crowther staggered to the rail, gasping for breath. "If they can't be killed, they should be surfacing any minute. We need to get this old tug moving."

Triathus took his position at the prow and *Sunchaser* obeyed his silent command to move ahead quickly.

The water astern remained placid. "They're not coming," Crowther said. He turned back to Jack. "What has he done to them?"

Once they were sure the little men would not be surfacing, Caitlin, Matt, and Crowther gathered round Jack, who sat with his head pressed against his knees.

"Leave him alone," Mahalia snapped. "Can't you see he's upset?" She was upset herself, though hiding it as well as she could.

"What happened, Jack?" Caitlin asked softly.

Jack looked up at her with tearful eyes. "They did it to me . . . in the Court of the Final Word."

"What did they do?" Matt asked.

"They took me apart and put me back together, trying to find out how I work. That's what they do with all humans." Jack choked back the words. "Only they didn't leave it there. They turned me into a weapon. They put something inside me. Not . . . not physically inside me, but bonded to me somehow, on some level."

"Do you know what it is?" Crowther asked gravely.

"A Wish-Hex." Jack bowed his head again.

Crowther blanched.

"What is it?" Mahalia said with a desperate voice.

"The Wish-Hex is the ultimate weapon," Crowther replied. He dropped a comforting hand onto Jack's shoulder, and that simple act from someone so undemonstrative underlined the gravity of his words. "As the atomic bomb is to us, so the Wish-Hex is to the gods. It can destroy all reality."

"But why did they put it in this . . . this *lad*?" Matt said.

"I'm a secret weapon," Jack said bleakly.

"Because no one would suspect you, you could get right into the heart of the enemy," Matt said. "And then they'd . . . detonate you."

"All right." Mahalia looked as if she was about to burst into tears. "There's no need to go on about it."

"Who were they planning to use it on?" Caitlin asked. "Surely not their own kind?"

"I don't think so," Jack said. "It was for some time in the future, for some big threat, a last resort . . ."

"A doomsday bomb," Crowther explained, "that would take all of Existence out with them, because they couldn't conceive of anything carrying on if they were ever defeated."

Matt glanced back to where the skiff had been. "That didn't look so bad."

"I only used a tiny fraction of the power," Jack said with dismay. "Only a tiny, tiny fraction. But it still shouldn't have killed them. I can't understand it. Where are they?"

They all moved aft to stand at the rail. There was definitely no sign of the little men. The sun had almost disappeared behind the tree line and the bats were now loosing themselves from branches to skim across the water, scooping up the flurrying insects.

"Something's wrong here," Crowther said.

chapter ten

A SMALL DEATH

> *"Because I could not stop for Death,*
> *He kindly stopped for me,*
> *The carriage held but just ourselves,*
> *And Immortality."*
>
> Emily Dickinson

The moon glinted off the water like glass. *Sunchaser* rocked soothingly on the currents, moored for the night in midstream. Ahead lay a steep-sided gorge where the river turned white and turbulent as it gushed through rapids so dangerous Triathus would only navigate them in the light of day.

For the first watch, Caitlin had taken a position aft on a carved wooden chair. The tranquillity of the night did not move her, for she could not escape the feeling that something was amiss. She watched like a hawk, shifting her gaze from one bank to the other, paying attention to every splash and gurgle, every movement of branch and leaf.

At the same time, her mind worked overtime trying to understand her mysterious skill at archery. She had trained at it before, but her display during the attack had been that of a master, her reactions instinctive. All she could think was that it had something to do with her heritage as a Sister of Dragons, whatever that really meant. And then she recalled the casket she had come across in the Wildwood. The plaque said it belonged to a Brother of Dragons. Coincidence? Or was it a warning to her about what happened to all the mysterious champions of life?

Her constant companions didn't help the growing apprehension she felt. Amy, Briony, and Brigid had all slipped into a troubled silence as they watched the figure in the shadows preparing to emerge. And what would happen when she did?

Before Caitlin could consider an answer, an arm clamped around her chest, another around her shoulders. A knife pricked her throat. She tried to throw off the assailant who had come up as silently as a ghost, but the jabbed response of the blade stilled her movement.

"I hate you, you bitch." It was Mahalia. Her hissed words carried the weight of desperation and fear and loneliness.

"I'm not your enemy," Caitlin said. "I don't know what—" The stabbing pain grew more intense; blood tricked down to her clavicle.

"I've seen what you're doing, how you're manipulating everyone, trying to get Carlton on your side. No one does that to me. No one!"

Caitlin felt the subtle tensing of Mahalia's muscles and knew in that instant that the girl intended to carry out her murderous threat. The revelation came like a douse of cold water. Despite all she had seen, Caitlin had never thought that the teenager would really hurt those who had been her friends.

As Mahalia prepared to slice, Caitlin smashed the back of her head into Mahalia's face. Mahalia howled and the knife slipped from her fingers.

Caitlin's action threw her wildly off balance. Unable to control her momentum, she rolled over the top of the rail and plummeted the short drop into the water. The currents in that part of the river were strong and she was sucked under before she had time to grab a mouthful of air or call for help. Adrenalin and the shock of the cold water gave her a tremendous surge of energy. Battling her way to the surface, she managed to fill her lungs before going down again.

This time, though, she caught sight of something in the depths that made everything else recede: colour, several splashes of it, visible in the beams of brilliant moonlight that penetrated to the reedy bottom.

The current whisked her away and once again she was fighting for air. With an effort, she clawed her way to the surface, sucked in more breaths, and then fought her way to the slow, steady movement on the periphery of the flow. In the shallows, fallen trees and branches lay half submerged where she could anchor herself to recover.

She couldn't be sure; she had to see again.

Steeling herself, Caitlin took another gulp of air and plunged beneath the surface. In the ghostly underwater world of shadows broken by moonlight beams, she once again glimpsed the colours: drifting gently above the swaying vegetation like oil paints spilled in the water. She struck out toward it. Not colours, but one colour in various shades. One colour. Purple.

Her heart began to thump wildly. In the back of her head, Amy came alive, her searching questioning—*"What is it? What is it?"*—gradually turning into a frightened keening. Desperately, Caitlin fought to keep the little girl contained. She couldn't afford to give herself up to Amy, not there; the girl would panic and they would both drown. Even if she did survive the river, Amy couldn't be allowed to take over with what lay ahead. She'd never escape.

Still not quite believing her eyes, Caitlin swam on, hoping to prove herself wrong. Gradually, indistinct grey shapes emerged from the surrounding murk like spectres.

Marching laboriously along the river bed toward the boat were the Lament-Brood, their ranks now swollen by others who had fallen to their corrupt influence. They ranged across a portion of the river bed as wide as a football pitch, and more ranks were emerging from the depths behind them. All of them were twisted and broken, shambling, the purple light leaking from their eyes. At the front were the little men who had attacked *Sunchaser*—the reason why they had not surfaced now clear—and in the centre Caitlin could just make out the leaders, riding their lizard-horses.

The silence of the approaching army was eerie, but then Caitlin began to hear their incessant whispering filtering through the water like the susurrations of malignant phantoms, spreading their message of despair and pain and death.

They saw her, but they didn't increase their pace. They would not be deterred; they would reach their prey sooner or later.

Amy surged to the front of Caitlin's head and her childlike terror brought a brief convulsion before Caitlin forced her back. *Not now*, she prayed, before turning in the water and striking out for the shore. Anxiety turned to panic; her lungs burned.

She broke water in the shallows and instantly yelled out. At first she couldn't make out the boat, but then she saw its silhouette a little further ahead; they had a few minutes before the Lament-Brood would reach them.

"Wake up!" she screamed. "For God . . . for God's sake! Danger!" Amy scrabbled again at her defences; pressing, pressing.

There was movement on deck. It looked like Triathus at first, followed by Matt and Crowther.

"Caitlin?" Matt called.

"I'm here, on shore! Get the boat moving upriver. Quick! The Whisperers are in the water . . . coming up on you fast!"

"Where are you?"

"Just move!"

With relief, she saw the boat start up. Cloudy purple light began to drift up from the water, like an early morning mist. She would have to head into the trees and do her best to keep pace with the boat, if Amy let her. But just as she clambered out onto the muddy bank, she glanced back to see *Sunchaser* moving toward her, and picking up speed.

"No!" she screamed. "Forget about me! There's no time—"

"Don't worry," Matt shouted. "We'll be with you in a second."

The heads of the Lament-Brood began to break through the surface of the water as they moved into the shallows. The violet light was everywhere now, like licking flames of marsh gas, or as if someone had lit scores of candles and set them adrift. The whispering rose up into the still night air and Caitlin felt her heart sink the moment she heard it.

The boat continued to head toward her. Couldn't they see the danger? Now she could clearly make out everyone on deck, apart from Mahalia. Where was she?

Caitlin began to splash back out into the river, wondering if she could help them by getting to the boat first, but Whisperers were already coming up between her and *Sunchaser*. She waded back to the water's edge. She would have to run soon or they would have her.

A grinding noise tore through the dark and the boat started to list heavily. The Lament-Brood were beneath it, using their bodies to try to capsize it. Others came up, driving spears and swords toward the hull, trying to hole it beneath the water line.

"Don't do that!" Caitlin/Amy cried.

There was more grinding and the boat was raised further. Those on deck rolled and hit the rail hard. Another heave and they went over with loud splashes; only Triathus clung on.

Frantic activity exploded in the water along the tree line. Caitlin couldn't tell what was happening, but it looked as if most of her companions had made it into the trees.

Sunchaser began to move backward, tearing itself free from the attack of the Lament-Brood. It righted itself with a loud splash and moved more quickly back toward midstream with Triathus now back in position at the helm, controlling it by the force of his will.

"The Court of the Dreaming Song is near here." His voice carried crystal clear across the water. "Follow the paths. I will meet you on the other side of the gorge, at the Gethil March, Port of a Thousand Paths. Ask at the court—they will show you the way."

Sunchaser turned into the stream and headed off toward the gorge. The Lament-Brood made no attempt to follow.

"It's me they want!" Caitlin/Amy sobbed. She threw herself into the trees, forcing her way through the thick vegetation, tripping over bushes and roots in the dark, banging her head, bruising her ribs, crying, crying, not knowing what she was doing.

The whispering was always following her, and when she looked back, the purple light floated amongst the trees, like moths, always moving, a hundred of them; a hundred or more.

The forest grew even more dense and it became harder and harder to force her way through it. The roar of the river diminished to be replaced by the creak of branches and the rustle of leaves, and the pounding of her feet on the dry forest floor. Tears stung her eyes as Amy's desperate thoughts were pushed aside by the chaotic jumble of panic.

In the dark, she came up on a steep hollow without seeing it. Her foot caught in a bramble at the top of the bank and she went headfirst down the slope, the thorns tearing at her flesh. She landed in a sea of bracken at the bottom, winded and stunned. As she levered herself up above the swaying fronds, she could just make out a small figure huddled in the centre of the hollow. It was Carlton.

And in that moment of realisation, Amy scurried back to her place in the shadows and Caitlin snapped back to the fore.

"Carlton? It's me, Caitlin," she whispered as she crawled out of the bracken. The boy had his arms wrapped around his knees, terrified and tearful. Caitlin hugged him tightly. "Don't be frightened," she said. "I'm here now. I'll look after you."

She couldn't hear any sounds of the Lament-Brood, but she knew they couldn't be far behind. "We have to move, Carlton," she whispered. "Triathus said to follow the paths to a court. We'll be safe if we can get there."

Caitlin stood up, but Carlton remained rigid at her feet. "Come on, honey," she urged. "You're the important one. We need to look after you." *Carlton is the key*, she told herself. *If I have to die to save him, then that's the way it's going to be.* She pulled him to his feet and he relented, looking into her face with such trust that her heart melted. She kissed him gently on the head. "Don't worry—it'll be OK."

They ran and hid for hours, until the shadows began to turn grey and the first light filtered through the thick canopy. Occasionally they accidentally turned back on themselves in the dense, confusing forest and caught sight of flickering purple light in the distance, accompanied by the stirring of ghostly whispers. But mostly they kept going in the right direction.

They never saw any of the others, but every now and then they'd hear movement in the dark nearby, though they were always too afraid to call out for fear of attracting unwanted attention. Caitlin's memories of the Gehennis were still too raw.

They came across a path in the thin hour after dawn. It was hard-packed with white stone, a gleaming trail in the permanent penumbra of the forest. It wasn't just a physical path, for the instant Caitlin stepped on it she felt her mood lift and her weariness dissipate as if she'd been given a shot of some drug. Carlton smiled for the first time that night and gave her a hug, which raised her spirits even more.

For the next hour they made good progress until Caitlin was distracted by movement amongst the trees away to her left. She caught at Carlton's shoulder to make him stop. "I think I just saw Jack." She peered through the trunks. Someone was definitely there. She took a chance and called Jack's name.

There was a brief pause before the reply floated back. "Caitlin? Where are you?"

She pinpointed his position from his voice and then replied, "Stay where you are. I'll come and get you." She turned and knelt before Carlton so she could look deep into his serious face. "Stay here. I'll only be gone a few minutes. You should be safe enough on the path, but I think it's much more dangerous off it, so this is the place to be. Listen to me—don't wander off the path, whatever happens. Even if you hear me calling to you. It might not be me. There are things out there that like to trick. If you stay right here, you'll be safe," she stressed. "Got it?"

He nodded.

"OK. I'll fetch Jack." She steeled herself and then stepped off the path.

In the hot summer sun, the house glowed with warm browns and oranges beneath a brilliant blue sky. The garden was lush, the roses in bloom in reds and yellows, the shade beneath the apple tree inviting. It had the kind of colours and warm, lazy feel that only come from a memory. Reality always seems much harsher while it's happening.

Mary hesitated before the heat-blistered blue door at the back, struggling to find her position in time and place. It was the sixties, she was in her mid-twenties, and this . . . this was home.

The familiar smells hit her the moment she stepped over the threshold: fried bacon from lunch, the old skillet still cooling on the side, faint sulphury smoke from the recently stoked boiler to her left, the pristine tang of cleaning fluids—her mother had been hard at work as usual. The pang of yearning she felt was acute: if only she could go back. Why did we always want to go back? What did that say about life, about what was lost on the journey from child to adult?

Her mother, hair dyed black and permed in that sixties mother-style, looked up from polishing the sideboard. Kip, the mongrel her father had brought back one day from a chance meeting at the pub, kicked on the hearth in the throes of some dog-dream. In the front room, Mary could hear the rustle of a newspaper, her father relaxing after lunch. She so desperately wanted to see him again, one final time, and she knew she would cry if she did.

Her mother smiled warmly. "This is a surprise."

A thousand thoughts and emotions rushed into her head, so fast Mary thought she would fall apart in a panic; she dampened everything down, refused even to consider what was tugging at her.

Mary expected some words, quiet disappointment; the life she had chosen had not been the one expected. Too wild, too exciting, fun and hedonism, a break from the working-class tradition of diligence and labour. Parents sacrificed for children and children sacrificed for their children, but Mary had accepted the sacrifice and used it for enjoyment instead of carving out a place in the world. Yet her mother was there, welcoming her as if Mary had just been to the shops instead of away for weeks without writing or calling. Mary wanted to rush over and hug her and say how sorry she was, for everything, but more urgent matters were tugging at her mind.

"He's upstairs." Her mother's smile grew sad. "I'm glad you could get back to see him, you know . . . before he's gone."

Another pang. She hadn't made it back, had she? She'd even missed the funeral—too busy having fun, tripping in a field, listening to music with some boy or other; she couldn't even remember which one. How many times had she been so thoughtless and uncaring?

Mary nodded sadly and turned to the stairs; the door was ajar, the interior dark as it always had been, even on a summer's day. She climbed slowly, remembering every creak, the steps she had to avoid when she sneaked down while her parents slept. We try to be good children, but never hard enough; are they always disappointed with us?

Sunlight streamed through the front bedroom window, illuminating the floating dust like tiny flakes of silver, something so mundane yet so wonderful. Her grandfather sat in the sun by the window, looking out at the quiet street. He turned and smiled at her, just like her mother had done, with no disappointment, no subtle accusations, and Mary felt the emotions inside her cut like a razor. His white hair was aglow in the sun, his eyes keen and bright at the sight of his favourite granddaughter. The only time he'd ever cried in public was when she'd been born. His skin had blue blemishes here and there, coal dust impacted too deep in the pores to be removed, the legacy of a pit collapse that had also taken two fingers. He looked too alive to have only a week left.

"Hello, Grandad." She couldn't think of what else to say, was afraid of saying anything for fear of crying.

"Hello, Mary." He beckoned for her to come closer.

She sat on the end of the bed. "You look so much like him."

"I am your grandfather . . . and I'm not." He smiled enigmatically.

"You've never been happy since Grandma went. I always felt you were just waiting to die to be with her again." She caught herself. "I'm sorry, all this . . . it's confusing me."

"Don't worry. It's understandable, lass. But there's a reason for it, like there's a reason for everything."

"I'm here for help, and guidance."

"I know. And I'll do everything I can. These are difficult times for everybody." He looked back out of the window. A car drove lazily up to the roundabout at the top of the road.

"The angels . . . the Elysium . . . they said the Goddess had to be called back."

"She has to be called back, for the sake of everything."

"Is that my job? Is that the price I have to pay for your help?"

"No. There is no price for my help."

"I thought there was always a price to pay?" Mary said curiously.

"Not here. There is never a price here." His lazy smile reminded her of even sunnier days as a child, when things had been uncomplicated and she'd even probably liked herself. Next to him she felt even more wanting, whether it was her grandfather who'd struggled hard all his life for the sake of others or the true form that lay behind his face.

"You make me feel at ease," she said.

"That's the idea. Your kind are so trapped in your own bodies, Mary. No idea of what things are really like beyond your five senses. No idea of what powers lie within you. You construct everything you see with the power of your will, and the strongest can change it all by wishing, lass. Just by wishing. You don't know any of the true rules. The rules you do have are just there to keep you safe, like the bars on that cot I made for you when your mother was in hospital. But you're all so important, and one day, maybe sooner than you think, you're going to break out and see what the universe is really like. And then you'll be in for a fine old time."

"Sounds like . . . magic."

"Aye. Magic. That's just what it is. And it can't come soon enough in my book. Things were going right for a while, and then the wrong sort took over. The ones who only thought about money and power, who'd do anything for it without thinking about the bigger picture and where they fitted into it. The ones who made a mess of the planet . . . drilling and burning and poisoning, all for money. All for bloody money. They're the ones who drove the Goddess away."

Mary heard her mother turn on the radio downstairs, then begin to hum away to some golden oldie by Johnny Ray. "But will she come back again? Can she?"

He examined the stump of one of his missing fingers thoughtfully before pulling a white paper bag of barley sugars from his pocket. He offered her one, and when she unwrapped the cellophane and slipped it into her mouth, she experienced a rush of overwhelming sensation that made stars flash behind her eyes.

"What is this?" she gasped.

"Just a taste of what's out there—if you get up off your bums." He unwrapped one of the barley sugars himself and sucked on it thoughtfully. "Can she come back? That's where it's up to you lot to make a change . . . a big change. In the end, I think it'll probably come down to her daughters. They've been getting back on their feet for a few years now, getting back to their old place, shoulder to shoulder with the blokes." He leaned forward and gave Mary's knee a squeeze. "See, lass, you can make a difference."

Mary shivered. It was almost as if he had seen into her and peeled back all her fears about her weaknesses and her many, many failures. One wasted life; was it too late to put it right? The lump in her throat was hard. "That's what I'm trying to do."

"I know."

"But I wonder if I should have just stayed at home. I don't know if I'm up to it."

"No one really does. And the few who think they do are usually wrong."

"I've got a friend, Caitlin Shepherd. She's a good girl, bit of a misery-goat, worrying about everything instead of enjoying life like all good folk should . . ." She smiled tightly. "But I suppose we've all got our flaws. Anyway, I want to help her."

Her grandfather nodded knowingly, waiting for her to continue, but Mary sensed he already knew much of what she had to say.

"She's gone in search of a cure for a plague that's come down hard on our world. Only it's not just a plague—it's something magical. I don't know for sure, but I think she's being tricked . . . I think, maybe, the whole *point* of it was to get her to cross over to the Otherworld, where she's going to be killed. And I had this vision that she's important. I mean, she's always been important to me, but I think she's important to the world, too—maybe even important in bringing the Goddess back."

"She's a Sister of Dragons," her grandfather interjected, and now he looked a little less like her grandfather, though she couldn't quite put her finger on what had changed.

"That's right, dragons! That's what my vision said. And dragons are symbolic of the Earth Spirit, earth energy . . ."

"Which is the same energy that flows through humans, too—the *spirit* that flows through everything."

"Dragons, snakes, serpents, it's all symbolic. When you think about it like that, the Bible reads very differently—the Garden of Eden, St. Michael killing the dragon, St. Brendan driving the snakes out of Ireland . . . and Caitlin is connected to this big, big thing . . ." The notions came thick and fast, surprising her with their intensity. "I've got to bring her back. I'll do anything for her. It doesn't matter about me—I'm not important."

The words ended on an interrogative note and she eyed her grandfather hopefully, but he shook his head slowly. "I give no guidance here. This is one of those times when your choices are important."

Mary rubbed a hand through her wiry, grey hair. "I don't know! How can I know? I'm just going on my gut instinct . . . and I want to bring her back."

"Are you sure?" Blue light flickered behind his eyes.

Mary steeled herself. "Yes. I want to bring her back. Can you do that?"

"Yes. It is done."

Mary sat back, relieved, and then stood up to go. The radio downstairs was playing "Alone Again Or" by Love. Her song; how coincidental, although she knew it wasn't a coincidence at all. She leaned forward and kissed her grandfather on the forehead, unbelievably sad that she was leaving him and would never see him again, that she was leaving the family home where she'd been happy for so long; perhaps the last time she had been truly happy. "Thank you," she whispered.

But as she pulled back, she caught a change in the cast of his face, and saw concern there, and in that moment she knew she had made the wrong decision. "No," she whispered. "I take it back."

But she was already moving back through the house, the walls elastic, the light distended, and in her ears were his words: "We stand or fall by our choices, Mary. That's the important thing."

The trees were even more dense in that part of the forest: oaks that even six men linking hands couldn't encircle; hawthorn, thick and lethally spiky; yew, sprawling and twisted like sour old men. Caitlin pressed between the trunks, picking her way over the mass of root material that obscured most of the forest floor. It was so dark it could well have been night.

"Jack?" It was more of a whisper than a call, but it rustled out through the still air beneath the branches. She didn't sense the growing army of the Lament-Brood anywhere near at hand, but other threats lurked in the shadowy depths of the Forest of the Night and she didn't want to draw attention to herself.

There was no longer any sign of movement, but it was possible that Jack, if it had been him, had already slipped by her in the confusion of tree and branch. She stopped and listened; the crunch of a foot on dry twigs echoed, but the mass of trees distorted the sound and made it impossible to pinpoint the location.

As she pressed by one tree, she thought she heard a barely audible voice issuing from deep within the wood; to her ears it struck a warning note, but she dismissed it as her overworked imagination responding to her anxiety.

The trees were like a maze and Caitlin began to worry that she wouldn't be able to find her way back to the path and Carlton. Perhaps it would be better to wait there. If the others had heard Triathus, they would all be trying to find the path anyway.

Carefully, she retraced her steps. When she did finally get a view of the path, it was much further away than she had anticipated. She could just make out Carlton, tiny and alone and in desperate need of her. She resisted the urge to call out to reassure him.

A movement sounded in the trees nearby. Her senses tingled. Perhaps it wasn't Jack at all. Just like the Gehennis, something could have tried to lure her off the safety of the path. Carefully, she unslung her bow. Another twig cracking. Near or far? Was it stalking her? Waiting for a chance to attack when her defences were lowered?

She dropped low, moved cautiously at first, then speeded up, dodging lithely amongst the trees, heading for the path. And then she had the strangest buzzing sensation in the tips of her fingers, before it moved up her forearms with a feeling of deep warmth. She felt oddly out of sorts, as if she'd spun round on the spot too many times. A bolt of light shot across her vision.

She fought the disorientation and tried to focus on any signs of whoever was nearby. Carlton appeared in a space between two trees. He looked frightened. She had to get to him, to protect him.

Another bolt of light arced across her vision, and she felt as if she were unravelling, the cords that bound her together peeling back from fingertips to toes. An uncomfortable feeling of detachment descended on her. She felt as if she was watching the surroundings through a bubble of glass.

The other, near or far, near or far? She looked, looked, and saw, but not near at all. The shape flitted through the trees near the path with lethal purpose. It wasn't after her at all.

Desperation and horror burst in her mind. Carlton was turning; he'd heard a noise.

Caitlin threw herself forward with wild urgency, struggling with her bow, trying to notch an arrow. But her reactions were too slow, and she was all over the place, as though drunk. She felt herself slipping away and the figure, indistinct but quick and dangerous, was almost on Carlton now. The boy was looking up into a face, smiling.

And Caitlin thought, "If this wasn't happening to me, I would be there by now, protecting him, doing my job, saving Liam."

She leaped over a fallen tree, almost fell, tried to aim the arrow, but her hands looked as if they were made of water and felt as if they were made of light. And she fell, rose up, and looked at the world as if though the bottom of a bottle. She couldn't see the figure, but she could see Carlton, see him smiling, his expression changing.

And she thought, "No, he's the important one. Everything depends on him. He can't—"

And she saw the flash of the blade, and the blood, and Carlton falling, reaching out to her.

And she thought, "I could have saved him. I should have saved him. Just like Liam . . ."

The figure jumped over the boy's twitching body and was away, and she couldn't tell if it was man or woman, young or old, but she knew the truth in her gut, and she couldn't understand why.

"I could have saved him."

Her last chance for salvation was gone.

And then there was only the world rushing away, and her screams, and the terrible, terrible night falling in all around.

chapter eleven
BIRMINGHAM

"Does such a thing as 'the fatal flaw,' that showy dark crack
running down the middle of a life, exist outside literature?
I used to think it didn't. Now I think it does."

Donna Tartt

Eight lanes of dirty Tarmac stretched out before her, now camouflaged by tufts of yellow grass bursting through cracks, and nettles and thistles and wind-blown rubbish. Caitlin stood against the central reservation, watching the road sweep down between high walls, other roads crossing overhead so that it felt as if she was looking into a tunnel. And beyond were the towers and office blocks against a slate grey sky slowly turning toward night.

Not so long ago, the Aston Expressway would have thundered with traffic making its way to and from the M6, and the air would have been filled with the cacophony of the city, engines, voices, music, one never-ending drone. Now there was nothing but bird-song and the wind against the concrete. A fox roamed across the lanes, searching for prey. Rabbits quickly ran back to their burrows beneath Spaghetti Junction. Birmingham had been reborn into the new age.

Caitlin would have recognised the city, but Caitlin was shivering in the heart of the Ice-Field, thrown free of her shelter and the others, alone, dispirited, barely surviving. Caitlin's body knew very little at all. She chose a direction at random and trudged blankly down the Expressway into the heart of the city.

Darkness clung tightly to the high buildings that lined New Street, but further ahead on the pedestrian precinct a bonfire blazed. The light drew Caitlin like a moth, the thick, acrid smoke obscuring the sickening stink that hung heavily in the air.

On her journey through Colmore Circus she hadn't seen a soul, but now men flitted from shadowed doorways, scarves tied across their faces. They were young, carried knives openly, communicating with high-pitched calls and guttural growls resembling nothing more than the rats that she had seen swarming along the gutters of the business district in sickening numbers.

She stood staring into the bonfire, the heat bringing a bloom to her face, hypnotised by the flickering flames as they consumed the ripped-out fittings of a clothes shop. A young girl barely more than nine, also with a scarf across her face,

174

hurried up and warmed her hands briefly before flashing a murderous glance at Caitlin and disappearing back into the dark.

"Hey."

Caitlin didn't hear the voice, though it was directed at her.

"Hey!" More urgent this time. A man in his late twenties with short black hair and eyes that were just as dark emerged from an alley, glancing up and down the street nervously. A red silk scarf was tied across his mouth. "You. You shouldn't be here."

"Thackeray, you twat! Leave her alone. They'll be here in a minute." The other voice came from further down the alley.

Thackeray paused, unsure, then cursed under his breath and hurried up to Caitlin. He gripped her arm and she looked at him blankly. "What's wrong with you? Don't you know—" The blank look in her eyes brought him up sharp. He waved one hand in front of her face, then snapped his fingers twice.

"Thackeray!"

"She's fucked in the head."

"Well, leave her, then! Christ, at a time like this you're trying to pick up women."

Thackeray looked deep into Caitlin's face, searching the beauty of her big eyes, taking in the shape of her lips and her cheek bones and her nose, but it was something much deeper and more indefinable that stirred him. He pulled on her arm. "Come on."

Caitlin stared back, blinked once, twice, lazily, saw nothing.

From the piazza at the end of New Street near the town hall came the dim sound of motorbikes, roaring like mythic beasts. Thackeray cursed again. "Come on!" He dragged Caitlin sharply toward the alley and after a few feet she began to walk of her own volition.

Just as they stepped out of sight, ten bikes rolled up to the perimeter of orange light cast by the bonfire. The riders wore leathers sprayed with a white cross dissecting a red circle and they carried an array of weaponry: shotguns, handguns, souped-up air rifles, even a crossbow. They moved slowly, searching all around like predatory animals. Occasionally they'd shine a torch into a doorway, but as they neared the bonfire they came to a halt before what had once been a shop and was now clearly some kind of squat. Dirty curtains were draped over the picture windows to provide some privacy, but they were thin enough to reveal the flickering of candles within.

The lead rider got off his bike and marched up to the door. He had long greasy hair and a thick beard, while his huge belly, the result of too much day-time drinking, was barely contained by the fading "Altamont Heaven" T-shirt.

He hammered on the door with a meaty fist. "Plague warden. Open up." The candles inside were blown out, but no one came to answer. "If you don't open the door," he roared, "we'll just burn the place down. You know we will."

Rapid scuttling echoed from inside. The door was flung open by a frail-looking man in his late fifties with a bushy moustache and florid wind-licked cheeks. "What's wrong?" he asked in a shaky local accent.

"We had information one of your family had the black spots," the plague warden said.

The man blanched. "No. Not here."

"Get 'em out, then."

"What?"

"Get 'em out here!" the warden shouted. The man quaked. The warden checked a small, dirty notebook. "Five of you. You, the missus, her sister, mum, daughter."

The man started to stutter, but was silenced as the warden waved a shotgun near his face. Broken shouldered, the man went back inside and emerged a few seconds later with three others.

"Where's the old lady?" the warden bellowed. "Are you fucking around with me?"

"No, no!" The man held up his hands to try to fend off the shotgun, which cracked him on the jaw.

"Get her!"

After a moment, the man led out his mother, a lady in her seventies with wild white hair. She bore the black marks of the plague on her skin.

"You idiot," the warden said. "You know the rules. First sign—very first fucking sign—you hand 'em over so we can deal with 'em."

"We were just going to look after her at home," the man said weakly. "She's me mam . . ."

The warden raised his gun and shot the old lady in the face. Blood and bone sprayed over the man, who was frozen in shock. "Now look," the warden said. "You're contaminated."

He nodded to his men, and before the family could flee they were all taken out in a volley of shots. One of the riders at the back came forward; he was wearing big biker gloves and a contamination mask.

"There's a drop-off point round the way," he said, muffled.

"Nah, stick 'em back inside," the warden replied. "It'll be a warning."

The one with the mask dragged the bodies back into the family home, shut the door, and then took out two cans of spray paint before proceeding to mark the door with the circle and cross.

"Shit. There goes another load," Thackeray whispered to himself. He looked at Caitlin. "You don't know how much you have to thank me."

He pulled her up the steeply climbing alley where another man around Thackeray's age waited anxiously, shifting from foot to foot. He had a thin acne-scarred face and long hair, and wore an old greatcoat and motorcycle boots.

"You're a stupid fucker, Thackeray," he hissed. "If they catch us now because of her—"

"I couldn't just leave her out there, could I?" Thackeray protested. He turned to Caitlin again. "This is Harvey. Not a six-foot invisible white rabbit, but just as much fucking use."

The bikers reached the end of the alley. A flashlight shone up and Harvey threw himself into a doorway. Thackeray pressed himself against Caitlin and her against the wall. His nose was only a centimetre from hers. He stared deeply into her eyes, which were seemingly untroubled by the threat below. Whatever he saw there brought a smile to his face.

One bike turned into the alley, paused briefly while the engine gunned, and then began to move slowly up. Thackeray dragged Caitlin into the doorway where Harvey cowered. They exchanged a nervous look and then Thackeray nodded to the door. Harvey wrenched at the handle, but just as it came open the light shifted enough to reveal a white cross on a red circle.

"Fuck. Charnel house," Harvey whispered.

"No choice." Thackeray propelled him through, then thrust Caitlin in with him and eased the door shut. "Don't hang around near the door in case he checks inside," he hissed.

"I can't see anything!" Harvey whined. "And shit, it reeks!" He coughed. "I can't breathe! I'm going to choke to death in here!"

Thackeray gagged and pulled his scarf tighter. "She's not moaning so you can't either, you big fucking girl. We haven't got a choice. Get a move on."

"Bastard."

The sound of Harvey shuffling through the dark filtered back to them, and then Thackeray followed suit, holding Caitlin's hand tightly.

"Look, I'm going to use my flint," Harvey said. "They won't see the light through the door."

He struck it three times and then a light flared. The shadows swooped back to reveal a scene so terrible Thackeray and Harvey recoiled, but there was nowhere to avert their eyes. Bodies bearing the unmistakable signs of the plague were stacked against the walls in various stages of decomposition, men, women, young, old. The floor around their boots was puddled with juices.

But that wasn't the worst thing. Several pairs of eyes followed the light, and then the moans started. Some were barely human, a whine on the edge of death, a hum of madness inflicted by the situation. Others whimpered. And a few called out in frail, pitiful voices: "Help me. Please help me."

"Shit!" Thackeray said in horror. "The bastards have dumped some in here while they're still conscious."

"There's nothing we can do about it." Harvey tried to sound hard, but he couldn't keep the desperate humanity out of the end of the sentence. "Bastards," he said under his breath, keeping his eyes straight ahead.

"What kind of person are you to do something like that?" Thackeray guided Caitlin ahead of him until they reached an area where there were only corpses.

"I don't know how many times I've see this, but it still makes me sick." Harvey picked his way through the cadavers to the back of the room where the flickering light revealed a door. "I hope you're right and we are immune."

"We'd be dead by now if we weren't." Thackeray glanced back to the area where the barely living still moaned, wondering if there was anything he could do.

"There must be, what? . . . thousands gone by now . . ."

"Tens of thousands."

"Smacker says there's whole areas where they haven't cleared them— Erdington, Bearwood . . . They're just lying in the streets, what's left of 'em now, in their homes . . . He said there's like, plagues of rats and clouds of flies as big as your fist, and the stink—"

"All right, I don't need you to paint me a picture. Let's just get out of here."

They made their way through the door and into the back of the building where there were even more bodies. A section had been set aside where corpses could be prepared for disposal, but neither Thackeray nor Harvey paid any attention to it.

They eventually made their way out through a window onto a flat roof and then a fire escape. The roar of the bikes had now moved down toward Digbeth.

They moved through the still city, the smell of corruption never far from their noses. Occasionally they'd glimpse frightened people scavenging amongst the cavernous buildings, masked with scarves or hooded to keep the stink out or in a feeble attempt to stop the spread of infection. A medieval air now lay across a city that had been thriving and modern only months earlier.

Thackeray and Harvey had their base in the Mailbox, a once-upmarket shopping mall now reduced by looters to a maze of empty rooms. They lived in the barricaded back offices of a former shoe shop, with dwindling supplies stolen from a supermarket lorry in the early days of the Fall. Their food cache had once been secured in an entire shop—bottled water, trays of cans, sacks of pasta and rice—safe behind a steel security gate that could only be opened by a key Thackeray had taken from a security guard killed in the first rash of riots. Now it filled barely a tenth of that space. They still didn't know what they were going to do when it was all gone.

Once safe inside they relaxed. They had a couple of armchairs, sleeping bags under rickety tents of designer sheets to make it more homely, the food for the day in one corner, a £1500 Arabian rug on the floor, scatter cushions all around, and a poster of *FHM*'s cover girls on the wall.

"It might look like a seedy smackhead's squat, but we like to call it home," Thackeray said, sitting Caitlin down on one of the cushions.

"So what's the deal with the bow and arrows?" Harvey said, nodding toward the weapon that was still strapped across her back.

"I don't know. Maybe she uses it to hunt animals. Nothing like a bit of roast squirrel." He went to remove the bow, but Caitlin's hand went up unconsciously to block him. "OK. She wants to keep it on. Might be uncomfortable sleeping in it, but that's her call."

Harvey threw Thackeray a can of sardines and opened one himself, eating with his fingers. Thackeray took out one sardine steak dripping with thick tomato sauce and offered it to Caitlin. She looked straight past it, past him, so he put it to her mouth, rubbing it gently back and forth on her lower lip. Eventually her tongue flicked out to taste it, then she took a bite, and then took the whole piece into her mouth hungrily.

"I don't know where you came from," Thackeray said softly, "but you can't have been walking round this city long in this state." He fed her another piece of sardine. "And it looks like it's been a while since you ate. So how did you get here? Couldn't have wandered in from the outside. Getting past all the check-points . . . it was bad enough before the plague. Muzzy in the west isn't letting anybody pass through his turf. Siegler in the east has bolted everything down— and those bastards down south, you wouldn't be in this good a condition if you'd passed through there." A look of distaste crossed his face.

"You don't really reckon she can hear you?" Harvey peered into Caitlin's blank eyes, then shook his head and returned to his can of sardines.

"It's trauma—hardly surprising in this place. She's probably locked up deep inside, understanding everything I'm saying. A fugue state . . ."

"You've had too much of a bloody education, you have." Harvey finished his can and tossed it into a shiny dustbin in the corner. "I have to ask you, mate— isn't it going to hamper us a bit carting a zombie-bird around? We've had enough close calls as it is."

"We couldn't just leave her out there, Harvey, for all those other bastards to pick off. How humane would that be?"

"You just fancy her."

Thackeray didn't answer.

✳

Thackeray and Harvey cared for Caitlin for the next week. After the first day she was able to feed herself, silently, laboriously, and she was capable of coping with her other bodily functions once they showed her the toilet. When her period started on the third day, Harvey went out and located a large cardboard box of sanitary towels from the storeroom of the Queen Elizabeth Hospital.

Thackeray slept on the cushions while Caitlin had his sleeping bag, and during the day they gave her plenty of exercise walking around the roof of the Mailbox. Though she didn't realise it, from that vantage point the true state of the city could be seen.

Parts of Balsall Heath were burning and a thick cloud of smoke hovered over the area. There were gaps in the urban sprawl in other areas where similar con- flagrations had been allowed to run their course. Abandoned cars and buses were everywhere. Some roofs had caved in due to more localised fires or disrepair, and there were few windows that hadn't been smashed. Barricades had been set up in many streets while bonfires blazed all over the place, pockets of hellish reds and oranges in the grim spread of browns and greys. Few people were visible on the roads, but occasionally white faces briefly passed gaping windows.

Yet there were flocks of birds all over, starlings swooping with evil eye and sharp beak, crows roosting on the rooftops of offices or nesting in the dark, empty interiors of broken-windowed tower blocks. There was greenery in unusual places, self-set elders in guttering, weeds on rooftops, out-of-control ivy swarming over entire terraces. Nature was reclaiming its own.

"It's a real mess, isn't it?" Thackeray said. He took Caitlin's hand when she ventured too close to the edge. "I used to love this city. They'd turned it round from that horrible industrial past . . . lots of culture sprouting all over the place, galleries, clubs, restaurants, places you actually fancied going out to for a drink. I went to university here and decided to make it my home." He laughed bitterly. "Good choice."

Harvey came up behind them. "Don't get too close to the edge. We don't want Buckland's goons knowing we're hiding out here."

"Ah, yeah, good old Buckland. The King of Central Birmingham," Thack- eray said sarcastically to Caitlin. "He came up fast after the Fall, some local crook with plenty of thugs on tap to enforce his ways. There was too much chaos to get any opposition going, and once he was established, that was it."

"That's not just it," Harvey interjected. "It's the thing he picked up at the Fall . . . the devil . . ."

"Superstition," Thackeray sneered. "You'd believe any old bollocks, you would. That's the kind of stupid stuff they put out to keep people like you in line."

"It's true! Smacker saw it."

"He did, did he?"

"Well, not exactly . . ."

"Buckland's just a hard man who'll go that extra mile to stay in power. And none of us are inhumane enough to match him. So we just hide out, and live a life in the shadows." His voice was filled with self-loathing, but he turned to Caitlin and forced a smile. "You know what they say, you're either part of the cure or you're part of the disease. So that's us done for."

"I wish we could get out of here," Harvey said wistfully. "Maybe go down to Worcester. I had some good times there, in the Lamb and Flag. They're mellow down there."

"Forget it. We're never getting out," Thackeray said. "Look at it—they've got it bolted down tight with their little principalities and banana republics, living off the leftovers of society and doing over everyone else who comes into view." He scanned the skyline thoughtfully, then added sourly, "This city is a metaphor. Everybody has their own Birmingham—it's a state of mind. You never get away from it."

"Bloody ex-student," Harvey muttered.

Mary erupted into a twilight sky high over Wilmington, filled with an over-whelming sense of failure, but not really knowing why. Below her, on Windover Hill, the god was slowly closing the door with a fizz of blue fire.

Her confusion and dismay were quickly supplanted by a burst of unfocused anxiety. She trusted her instinct in the spirit-form, where every thought and sensation was heightened, and quickly looked around for the source. What she saw made all the ecstasy of her current state quickly drain away. Her body was not where she had left it. It had been dragged twenty feet across Dragon Hill. The culprit stood nearby: the twisted dead man she was sure had died in the fire, looking completely untouched by the conflagration that had engulfed him.

It was being tormented by the Elysium, but in their spectral state they clearly had no true ability to physically stop him. They swooped and soared around him, their faces transformed by howls of pain. For a moment, Mary was locked in panic. How could she have been so stupid as to leave her body in such an exposed position? She knew the risks: if her body died while she was in spirit-form, she would drift like a ghost before she finally broke up and blew away.

The Jigsaw Man lashed out at the Elysium, somehow clearly able to see them. Sharish broke off from the battle and rushed up to Mary like a beam of light reflected off glass.

"You must come quickly," he said. "We cannot hold him off much longer."

But Mary was already moving before the final word had been uttered. She re-entered her body with force, desperate not to accept the usual period of lazy read-justment, tinged with sadness, her limbs feeling as heavy as lead, her head stuffed

181

with cotton wool. She attempted to get to her feet, but her legs buckled beneath her. It felt as if a rock pressed on her shoulders.

The Jigsaw Man noticed her sudden movement and instantly ignored the Elysium. Its gait was as fast as it had been in the abandoned house, slow for a split second, then speeded-up and jerky. Dead hands clasped around Mary's throat before she had barely registered that the Jigsaw Man had moved.

"You must fight him!" Sharish said. "We can do nothing."

The fingers clamped tighter and tighter. Mary couldn't breathe; the pressure in her head grew intense.

"Use the Blue Fire!" Sharish pressed. "Your kind have always been able to manipulate it."

As the oxygen disappeared, a strange clarity came over Mary and she knew exactly what Sharish was telling her. She recalled the lines of earth energy rushing from Dragon Hill to the Long Man, and with one grasping hand reached down to the scrubby grass. Her fingers clutched at the air, missed, clutched again, and somehow she was able to extend herself enough to scrape the ground.

The Jigsaw Man helped by pressing her down toward it, but her life was fading fast under his rigid grip. The back of its head faced her, but she could just glimpse the eyes, turned away, rolling wildly.

In her mind, she formed the image, but she had no idea how to activate it. And then Sharish was beside her, whispering a word in her ear that she had never heard before and which made her slightly queasy. Without thinking, she repeated it.

All she saw was blue, across her field of vision, deep in her head. Sapphire flames ran from her fingertips through her body and into the Jigsaw Man, exploding in a cascade of sparks twenty feet above her head.

When her vision cleared, her attacker spasmed on the ground several yards away, smoke rising from his joints.

"You must hurry," Sharish said. "The thing will not stay down long."

"Goddess, what is it?" Mary gasped, rubbing at her sore throat as she scrambled for her clothes.

"Its power comes from you." Sharish floated at her side while she bundled up her possessions and hurried down the hillside, Arthur Lee bounding at her heels from wherever he had been hiding. "Despair. Self-hatred. Failure. It will not stop attempting to destroy you until all those things are gone from within you."

"Then it'll never stop," Mary said bitterly. "Never."

By the time she reached the foot of the hill her head had cleared. The blue fire rushing through her had a strange effect on her system: she felt positive for the first time in years. "There must be something I can do to put things right," she said to herself. She turned to Sharish. "OK, if I failed with the god, then I want to find the Goddess."

He shook his head slowly. "It—"

"Don't tell me how dangerous it is. Don't tell me how I'm going to fail. Just tell me where I can find her. I've got to do one good deed before I die . . . before that thing gets me."

He stared into her face. "You are stronger than you think."

"Don't give me flannel. I just want to help Caitlin. I've messed up again, as usual, but I can't give up now—she's depending on me."

"Then you must be prepared for a long journey," he said. "And a terrible trial. You may not survive."

Time passed for Caitlin in a haze of food and rest and as much comfort as could be conjured from the makeshift premises. She was not aware of anything, least of all herself, but a part of her knew that she was cared for, and beneath the dull, flat line of her existence, that felt good. In her head, she still wandered the bleak, frozen plains of the Ice-Field, but it had become more of a Zen meditation than a desperate search for a way out. In time, perhaps she could even accept it.

Thackeray never left her alone for fear she might accidentally harm herself. When they crept through the darkened streets in search of premises to ransack, he held her hand, guiding her carefully past dangers, always watching out for her. Occasionally he would take her off with Harvey for what he laughingly called a "road trip," sitting by the canals throwing stones while Harvey attempted to fish, or breaking into the council chamber to lie on the floor and examine the majestic architecture of the sweeping ceiling.

"Even in the middle of all this you've got to seek out anything that might give you a laugh, make you feel as if you're alive," he said one warm day on the edge of summer. "Otherwise, what's the point?"

That night, Thackeray laid out a dinner for the three of them with a white cotton tablecloth on the floor, silver cutlery, and crystal glasses for one of their very rare bottles of wine. As they sat around, with the candlelight flickering, he thought Caitlin looked more beautiful than ever and told Harvey so.

"You know, matey, I have to say this, but all this is a bit, you know . . . sick," Harvey replied uneasily. "She's, like, disabled or something. Or, you know . . ." He tapped his temple.

"I'm not going to take advantage of her," Thackeray replied. "But I can still see the person she was, or is—maybe will be again. It's there in her face, just beneath the surface. A good person . . ."

"You think she's going to get better?"

Thackeray shrugged. "I can't help myself."

"I think you should get over her, mate, for your own good."

Thackeray raised his glass to both of them and took a sip of the Zinfandel.

"Let me tell you something, Harvey. You're going to say I'm a complete wanker, but like I care what you think, right? Loving, and having someone who loves you, is addictive. Your whole being comes alive and suddenly it feels as if the life you had before was just floating in treacle. And the clichés, they're all true, like you're living some *Woman's Weekly* life. You can't eat, you can't sleep, you can't get her face out of your head, or the moments you spent together, and the things you did, and the words you said, and some stupid song that fixes it in melody and moment, constantly replaying, turning over, as if you were hoping you'd be able to step back into them and live them all again, just like the first time."

Harvey smiled, but in a nice way, sipping his own wine with one self-mocking little finger extended.

"And all these other clichés," Thackeray continued. "Connections . . . gut instincts that transcend rational thought. Love at first sight, if you will. How stupid is that? You think to yourself, stay away from this person, they're bad for me, I'm settled, survival routines in place, my life would be a real mess if I threw in with them, and your subconscious, or your heart, says do it, this is right. The person in the back of your head just *knows*. And you can't help yourself. You're lost to it. That person—the real you in your deep, deep subconscious—he always knows what's right for you, at that particular time, what you need. And he or she recognises links that transcend physical space. You see a face, he sees a soul mate, something so deep it's rooted in both your genes. And when that connection happens, you know it's going to be high passion, that you're going to blaze like a star, and that you'll probably crash and burn soon after. And you don't care, you don't care." He stared into the deep red depths of his wine with a faint, troubled smile.

"It's going to end in tears, Thackeray," Harvey said softly.

"Yeah. 'Course it is."

They ate a long, varied meal, determined to enjoy themselves in spite of everything. Thackeray fed Caitlin the first mouthful of every dish so she could acquire the taste before continuing herself. After they had finished, Harvey strummed them romantic songs on his acoustic guitar, tongue in cheek at first, but by the end they were all lost in a haze of plangent emotions.

Finally they sat in silence, thoughtful, enjoying a faint alcohol mood. And that was when they heard a tremendous crash.

Thackeray and Harvey instantly scrambled to the front of the shop to peer out into the concourse. The strengthened-glass security doors had been smashed off their hinges by a flat-bed truck that had reversed into them at speed. There was movement all over the shadowy first floor of the mall. Eventually torches burst into light and the burly leather-clad forms of the plague wardens fell into relief.

Thackeray glanced at Harvey, who was shaking and looked as if he were going to be sick. "We can't pull down the security shutters—it'll make too much noise," Thackeray hissed. "We'll have to hide in the back and hope it's just coincidence they're here and that they're not looking for us."

Harvey was rigid and fixated on the swarming figures until Thackeray gave his shoulder a squeeze. Then they both slipped back to the living area.

"Oh, God, they know we're here!" Harvey whined, scrubbing a hand through his greasy hair. "Someone must have seen us on the roof. I knew it was a mistake to go near the edge!"

"No point moaning about it now—it's done." Thackeray took Caitlin's hand and pulled her to her feet.

"Aren't you scared?" Harvey asked.

"Yes," Thackeray replied tersely.

"You know what Buckland will do to us if he gets us."

"Maybe he'll just be happy with our supplies to add to his vast warehouse of looted consumer goods."

"Right. After he's hung us out to dry." Harvey hugged his arms around himself; tears of fear sprang to the corners of his eyes.

Thackeray gave him a rough shove and followed it up with a smile. "Come on—into the hiding places. And good luck."

Harvey forced a smile. "You're a bastard, Thackeray, but we've had some good times."

He made to go toward a packing crate, but Thackeray caught his arm and said, "No, the good one. And take her with you."

Harvey searched his friend's face for a moment and could see no point in arguing. Reluctantly, he went to a wall panel like any other and slipped a penknife into the join to prise it open. Behind was a dusty, claustrophobic space in the dry wall. Briefly, Thackeray hugged Caitlin to him, smelling her hair, wishing things were different. Then he hurriedly pressed her into the hidey-hole first, motioned her to remain silent with a finger to his lips, then let Harvey slip in after her before replacing the wall panel.

The sound of the plague wardens violently searching the concourse drew rapidly closer. Thackeray threw himself behind a packing crate and burrowed under a pile of filthy, mildewed rags. They fell in just such a way that he had a very limited view into the room.

The plague wardens entered seconds later, whooping the minute they saw the remnants of the meal. "Here it is! Bastards have been having a party!" someone exclaimed.

"Search the place—they're here somewhere," a gruff, authoritative voice ordered.

Thackeray remained tense, his breath a lead weight in his throat. He watched as the tablecloth was ripped up, the crystal smashed, the sleeping quarters torn and stamped. He knew they'd get him sooner or later; Harvey had known it, too, but one being caught might allow the other to escape, and they both accepted Thackeray was the least likely to fold under pressure. At least until the torture started.

Seconds later they approached the crate. Thackeray steeled himself. The rags were torn off and the room filled with jeers and abuse. Threatening hands yanked him to his feet before a fist smashed forcefully into his face. Blood splattered from a burst lip and he saw stars for a second.

"Where are the others?" The authoritative voice came from the plague warden who had shot the woman in the face on the night he had met Caitlin.

"Fuck off."

Someone hit him again and this time he did black out for a while. When he came to, he was supported between two thugs and the leader hovered inches from his face. "I'll ask you again," the leader said. "And this time we'll cut off your ear if you get smart."

"All right," Thackeray said with mock weakness. "They got out . . . across the roof and down the back. We had an escape route planned. I was supposed to lock up the base, but there wasn't time . . ."

He let his head droop. The leader grabbed him by the hair and yanked it back up. "How many?"

"Two others." The leader nodded, satisfied. Thackeray knew he would have seen the places set on the tablecloth.

"So, you thought you'd disobey all Mr. Buckland's rules, hoarding your own stuff while the community starves. You selfish bastard."

Thackeray wanted to laugh at the idea of Buckland being a provider for the poor and oppressed, but he managed to control himself by feigning almost losing consciousness again.

The leader backed off and waved his hand in a circle in the air. "Clean this place out. Make sure you get all their stores. The bulk's probably in some other place. And get this bastard out of here."

Thackeray knew his fate, but he was surprised that his first thought was not regret or fear, but of a woman he hadn't even heard speak, who had given him no sign of who she was.

Harvey and Caitlin emerged from their hiding place into darkness an hour later when it was clear that the plague wardens had definitely gone, and all the supplies had been removed. Harvey was sobbing silently, smearing his tears across his blotchy face.

"Sorry," he said to her without really talking to her. "I'm pathetic." With an effort, he composed himself. "Look, they're not going to be back here, so you wait . . . I need to find another place for us to hide out. Somewhere safe." He chewed a knuckle, looked queasy, then gave her as much of a reassuring smile as he could muster before pressing her down to sit next to the wall. He lit a candle. "Don't be frightened," he whispered. "I'll be back for you."

And then he was out of the door and running, his footsteps echoing like gunshots in the dark vault of the concourse.

Caitlin sat and watched the shadows flicker on the far wall. Deep in the bleak chambers of her head, something stirred.

"Where am I?" Her voice shrieked above the howling wind, her throat raw from her anguished screams. The fierce gale buffeted her back and forth, whipping snow into her face like hot pins so she couldn't see where she'd been or where she was going. Even wrapping her arms tightly around her couldn't stop the terrible cold from penetrating deep into the core of her being.

There was only the whiteness of frozen nothing all around as she staggered across the Ice-Field. No warmth, no hope. It would be better if she simply lay down to die, let the snow cover her over, let the permafrost build up, crush her down, make her a part of the ice itself.

Electricity crackled around the room, sending incandescent sparks fizzing from the metal fittings. Thunder boomed off the walls and there was ozone in the air. In one corner stood the black knight in the boar mask, his hands on the broadsword balanced on its tip between his astride legs.

"Caitlin Shepherd!" His voice sounded like bees swarming from a hive.

Caitlin stirred; light flickered in the lanterns of her eyes. In the Ice-Field, the snowstorm shifted briefly, and the hard rocks of the shelter emerged in grey from the white.

"Caitlin Shepherd!" the knight said again, in his detached, alien voice.

Caitlin blinked; the white gave way to the shifting shadows of the room. More electricity flashed around her so that it felt as if they were in some glass jar cut off from the real world.

"Are you my guardian angel?" she whispered, dazed. "Or just some other devil sent to lead me on to damnation?"

"None of this is real—I told you that," the knight said sonorously. His voice was clearer than it had been the last time. "We make our own reality. It is fluid. The truth lies behind what your senses tell you. If enough people believe the world is a certain way, that is the way it shall be. But some people have the power to change all reality. The world does not have to be this way, Caitlin. It is in the process of being rebuilt. Humanity is moving on, moving up. The seasons are changing."

Gradually, her consciousness pieced together where she was and what had been happening. She remembered Thackeray and Harvey and the plague wardens; and she recalled Carlton and his brutal and unnecessary death, and the pain hit her so hard she cried out, "Who killed him?"

"Paths have been chosen. Events are no longer in your hands," the knight replied. "Only blood can turn things around—blood and vengeance." He paused while the lightning flashed across the room in coruscating streaks, and when he spoke again his words were barely audible above the thunder. "The time has come to let her out, Caitlin."

Caitlin staggered from the restless ocean of the Ice-Field into the small rocky shelter. Briony eyed her hatefully, while Brigid rocked backward and forward, cackling to herself nervously and glancing to the shadows at the back.

"We thought you were never coming back," Amy said dismally.

Caitlin walked past them without a glance. Could she do it?

"Don't be stupid, bitch," Briony said with a mixture of fury and fear.

Caitlin stood before the figure half-cloaked in the shadows and said uneasily, "Come forward. I need you."

Brigid's laughter became an anguished howl and Amy began to sob uncontrollably. The figure stepped forward, slowly at first but then with pride, and the shadows sloughed off her like silk.

Caitlin thought she would be struck blind with pure terror. Though her eyes saw the form, her mind couldn't latch on to the slippery alien essence of the creature that emerged, and every aspect of Caitlin's being rebelled at what she perceived. At first it appeared as though she were seeing crows flying madly, and then fluttering black rags from which a ghastly white face stared horribly.

Finally a beautiful and terrible woman stood before her, with lustrous black hair like a storm, flashing green eyes, and ruby red lips. She wore a black velvet gown that appeared to run like oil, with a belt of bloodred, and she carried two wicked silver knives with sinuous blades. Carrion birds flew all around her, and at times appeared to be part of her.

"You have released me!" Though the woman barely moved her lips the words thundered so loud Caitlin had to clutch her ears.

"What are you?" Caitlin asked weakly.

"I am the beginning and the end," the woman replied. "Fertility and destruction. Love and war. I am the messenger of death. I am the true power of all women."

"The Morrigan!" Brigid cried, beating her chest and tearing at her hair. "War goddess of my Celtic people, treat your daughter well! Oh, fearsome *Badhbh Chatha*, Raven of Battle."

Caitlin recalled the eerie hooded crow she had seen the night she first encountered the Lament-Brood, and then again, barely recognised, on her chest as she lay on the edge of madness at Liam and Grant's graves. Somehow, Caitlin knew, this terrifying being had seen some connection inside her, had entered her and bonded with her very soul. All she had needed was Caitlin's word to come out into the open. But Caitlin was afraid of what would now happen; that the cure would be much, much worse than the disease.

"Weep for those who stand before us!" the Morrigan said, her eyes blazing. "There will be no more suffering, Sister of Dragons. We stand as one!"

The Morrigan opened her arms and Caitlin was sucked into the infinite darkness of flapping wings.

Harvey slipped quietly through the concourse, desperately afraid. He was sure they could hole up in one of the warrenlike office buildings on Colmore Row, but it would only be a temporary measure. After that, he had no idea. He wasn't a thinker like Thackeray and he really couldn't see himself surviving on his own, especially now he had the added responsibility of the girl. But he couldn't abandon her. How could he?

He slipped into their former home, expecting to see Caitlin still sitting where he had left her. Instead she stood in the centre of the room. He could see instantly that there was something different about her. She stood erect, her body taut, ready for action, and for the first time there was fire in her eyes and intensity in her face.

"Oh, you're up," he ventured. "I'm going to take you to—"

"You're going to take me to Thackeray."

He jumped back in shock at the sound of her voice. "You . . . you're all right now?"

Caitlin fingered the ornate carvings on her bow, looking past Harvey into the darkened concourse. "We're going to get Thackeray back."

Harvey held up his hands. "OK, I'm glad you're feeling better, and Thackeray was right that you were paying attention while you were . . . you know . . . doolally. Sorry. But you don't know what you're asking. We can't—"

Caitlin stepped forward quickly and gripped his shoulders with fingers that felt like iron. "We're going to get him out—"

"He's probably already dead!"

"—and you're going to show me the way." She spun him round and shoved him toward the exit, lost to the thunder of blood in her head.

chapter twelve

DIFFERENT PATHS

"I know I have the body of a weak and feeble woman,
but I have the heart and stomach of a king."

Elizabeth I

After what seemed like hours, Crowther emerged from the trees onto a shim-mering path. Relief flooded through him. In the timeless Forest of the Night, he had begun to think he might be wandering in the green world forever, lulled into a dream state by its peculiar haunting qualities. He had even lost consciousness for a while, he was sure, and was worried that he might have put on the mask. Was it controlling him so easily now?

Many things moved through the trees just out of sight, but they didn't scare him, and he had come to accept that he was no longer afraid of death; more and more it felt like a way out. There had been no sign of the Gehennis, but at one point curiously he had heard horses and baying hounds, a hunt pursuing its prey. However, on occasion he had glimpsed the drifting purple light that signified the Lament-Brood and that did frighten him: to become part of that zombie army, to think and feel inside, perhaps, but to be controlled by another intelligence was his greatest nightmare.

Resting on his staff to catch his breath, he was surprised to feel his weariness easing the longer he stood on the path. As he scraped his fingers along its surface, they tingled and an easy feeling of well-being rose through him. The Blue Fire really was the fuel that drove everything, just as everyone had been taught at the college in Glastonbury.

Might he actually have found peace if he'd stayed there and devoted himself to studying? The search for knowledge had always been the thing that had made him feel complete in the old days. Without finding an answer, he set off along the path.

It wasn't long before he spotted a small dark figure sitting cross-legged. It was Mahalia, unmoving, head bowed so that her black hair covered her face like a hood. She didn't even stir when he came within three feet of her.

"You got out, then," he said.

"Looks like it." She didn't look up at him.

"Have you seen any of the others?"

She began to shake her head, then caught herself.

"What is it?"

This time she did look up and Crowther was shocked by the devastation he saw in her face.

"Carlton's dead," she said bluntly.

"Dead? The boy?"

"I . . . I saw the body." She motioned further along the path. Every fibre of her being was directed toward suppressing her emotions. "His throat's been cut. He's lying across the path . . ."

Crowther tried to make sense of what he was hearing. "Across the path? That can't be. The dangerous things that live in this forest shouldn't be able to touch us on here."

"Well, he is dead," she said sharply. "No mistaking that."

"Show me," Crowther said with irritated disbelief. Realisation of what he was asking came a second later and tenderness crept into his voice. "I am sorry. That was very . . . thoughtless of me. I know how close you two were." He rested one comforting hand on her head, but she felt as rigid as stone beneath his fingers and he withdrew it quickly. "I'll check."

He hurried along the path and found the boy's body round a bend, as she had described. The cut had been made skillfully. This was no attack by wild beast or some haunted forest thing.

For a moment he was honestly overwhelmed with emotion. He had seen a lot of brutally upsetting things in recent times, but he couldn't understand how anyone could kill a young boy.

He shed a few tears before another thought struck. Caitlin had been convinced that the boy was vitally important to the great scheme that was being played out around them. What did his death mean for that?

After taking a moment to recover, he picked up Carlton and carried him a few feet into the forest. The loam was soft and he managed to clear enough of it to make a shallow grave in which he laid the body. It wasn't enough, but it would have to do. He scooped up handfuls of the loam to cover it, and then picked up as many fallen branches as he could to rest along the surface, so that in the end it resembled a wooden tomb. He forced one of the branches into the ground at the head as a marker.

Then he returned to Mahalia and brought her back to show her his work. "I think we should say a few words," he said.

"No point. He's gone."

Crowther winced. "Even if you don't believe in anything spiritual, the ritual would be good, to help you adjust to his passing."

"I don't need to adjust. I can see he's gone. Come on, let's get out of this creepy forest." She set off along the path before he had time to reply.

Her state troubled Crowther immensely. He had seen how angry and upset she had been when anyone had tried, however innocently, to come between her and Carlton. The boy appeared to mean more to her than life itself. And now she was acting as if she didn't care at all.

"Look at this, Matt." Jack motioned to an area off to the right of the path. The trees seeped an oily black ichor and all the leaves were shrivelled and mottled with black spots. It had affected at least twenty trees that Jack could see and was spreading to the ground vegetation.

Matt examined it from the path, then moved closer. "It's the same thing that was on that flower you found earlier."

"I wouldn't get too near to it," Jack warned.

"Wait." Matt held out an arm, his attention gripped by something on the ground among the affected trees. Cautiously, he motioned for Jack to join him.

Jack had to blink a few times until he was sure of what he was seeing. Where the forest floor should have been, there was what he could only describe as a rip, as if he were looking at a painting and the canvas had been torn to reveal what lay behind it. In the centre of the rip was a deep black emptiness, like space, with the same endless quality. It made him feel queasy staring into it, for there was no sense that it was a hole in the ground. He felt that he could fall through it and into . . . nothing. "What is it?" he asked in a hushed, uneasy voice.

"I don't know." Matt stared at it for a moment and then guided Jack back to the path.

"You know what it looked like?" Jack said as they continued on their way. "It looked like whatever was attacking the trees had eaten that hole away, too . . . but a hole right through everything." He thought for a moment, and then grew uneasy. "What could do that?"

"I have no idea. You know more about this place than I do. As far as I can tell, anything can happen here. It's like a dream . . . or a nightmare. No point getting concerned about it." He clapped a hand across Jack's shoulders. "If we're going to start worrying, we've got more important things to worry about."

"I hope the others got out."

"You hope Mahalia got out."

Jack blushed.

"I've seen the way you've been with her."

"She's nice. I like her."

Matt shrugged. "Personally I think you've got a tiger by the tail, but it's your life. Just be careful." He shook his head with mock weariness. "What is wrong with me? I sound like a dad."

Jack laughed. "I never knew my father. You'll do for the moment."

"Don't you go putting that on me. I've got quite enough on my plate without getting all paternal too." He stretched aching shoulder muscles and adjusted the bow and quiver. "I feel like we've been walking for weeks."

"Perhaps we have. You can never quite tell here. I still think we should have waited—"

"We talked about this." Matt stood in front of him and put his hands on the boy's shoulders. "We all got turned around in the dark. It was blind luck that I ran into you. The others, if they did get out, could be way ahead of us. The best thing we can do is get to that place Triathus mentioned and wait for the others there."

They set back off on their way, but it wasn't long before the boy was talking again. "You know, I like this."

"What? Getting lost in a forest with no provisions and no idea if you're going to get slaughtered when you go round the next bend?"

"No. Being with you . . . with people. I've never known humans all my life. Just the Golden Ones." Anger rose but was quickly suppressed. "Can you understand what it's like? Not to be with any of your own kind, just to hear stories about them, or sometimes see them across the barrier between the worlds, but never talk to them. Never *be* with them."

"Yeah, and look at what your first experience of it was—us lot. Of all the people in all the world you ended up palling around with a bunch of psychos, liars, and losers."

"No, that's not true!" Jack said. "I can see a lot more than you think—*because* I've been apart." Matt eyed him curiously. "I can tell what people are really like," Jack continued. "Everyone puts up barriers, and some people put up thicker walls than others. Take Professor Crowther. He can act very unpleasantly to everyone, but he's scared . . . of everything. He pretends he can cope, but he really can't cope at all."

"So, you're a part-time psychoanalyst, too." Matt laughed.

"And Mahalia, she's scared, too, but trying to appear strong. In fact, everybody's scared, but nobody wants to appear weak."

"What about Caitlin? I bet you'd have a field day there."

"I can tell you like her."

Matt looked away. "All right. Let's not have any of that."

"And you . . ."

"Wait!" Matt silenced him with a raised hand. "Can you hear that?"

Dimly, through the rustling of the leaves, a dull roaring was audible. "Water," Jack said. "That must be the gorge."

They hurried along the path until the heavy greenery of the trees gave way sharply to brilliant blue sky. An instant of rushing vertigo hit both of them, for they stood on the lip of a dizzying drop down a sheer granite face to rushing white water far below. The ravine was barely wider than the length of a football pitch, the Forest of the Night pressing up against the very edge so that ancient oaks and twisted yews overhung the chasm. Anyone not following the path would come out of the trees and over the lip with no warning.

"That," Matt said, gripping a branch tightly, "is a long way down."

The path went down a flight of rough-hewn steps to a ledge ten feet below the edge and continued hugging the wall of the ravine until it disappeared around a bend. Barely two feet wide, there was nothing between whoever was walking the path and the sickening drop.

"We could wait here," Jack said hopefully.

"I think the least we should do is see what's round the corner," Matt replied. He winked at Jack. "Don't forget—it's not the fall that kills you."

"Huh?" Jack said, but Matt was already edging his way down the steps.

In the gorge, the crashing water was deafening. They made their way slowly, gripping on to cracks and crevices in the cliff face for protection against the eddying wind that threatened to pluck them off if their guard dropped. At times, Jack grew rigid with fear and had to stop. Matt urged him on, yelling to be heard above the water and the wind. And then they rounded the bend, and what they saw took away all thoughts of the drop.

Set into the cliff face was a city, stretching almost from the water's edge to the very top. Monolithic blocks of stone formed the basis of the structure, protruding in balconies and terraces, buttresses and gargoyles, so that it was impossible even to begin to guess how it had been constructed in such a precarious position.

Set against it was a different style of architecture, more graceful and delicate, with glass, silver, and bronze, designed in sweeping arcs, with huge multi-panelled windows that would allow sunlight deep into the heart of the construction, which, it appeared, burrowed deep into the cliff.

The two styles, brutalist and cultured, worked strangely well together so that the overall appearance was quite stunning; both welcoming and a little frightening in its magnitude.

"Is that it?" Matt asked, trying to take in the full sweep of the magnificent city.

"Yes." Even Jack was awed. "The Court of the Dreaming Song."

As Thackeray descended the frozen escalator steps into New Street Station, the light of a hundred torches came up out of the gloom. They burned along the length of the huge concourse, where travellers had once stared up at the rows of electronic timetables, filling the lofty roof with acrid smoke. Behind it lay the familiar smell of engine oil, hanging around like the ghost of better times. At that moment it felt as if he was entering the jungle compound of some Stone Age tribe, where brutality and ritual still ruled, and in a way he was right.

The plague wardens flanked him, their heavy boots clanking on the metal steps. He was desperately aware of the guns and knives and axes they carried, but it was their fists that had put the pain into his ribs, arms, and jaw. He could almost feel the bruises forcing their way to the surface.

Approaching the ticket gates, he saw that they had been all but obscured by a wall of razor wire. One heavily fortified gate lay in the centre. The lead plague warden hammered on it three times and then stepped back so that it could swing out to reveal two shaven-headed bruisers nursing shotguns. One wore a St. George flag on his T-shirt. The other had a cheap leather jacket pulled tightly across his beer belly. Thackeray's heart fell even more at the realisation that the people he would leave a pub to avoid had now taken over the world.

They ushered him in, past more burning torches and a flaming oil drum stoked for heat in the chill station. Finally he was presented at a suite of offices, packed with incongruously plush furniture, antiques, and works of art. The lead plague warden took him into an office that had once belonged to a faceless executive and was now a sumptuous testament to bad taste, thuggery, and greed. To Thackeray, the first was probably the greater crime.

Buckland sat in a leather armchair, feet up on a table, drinking whiskey from a crystal glass. He had a look of Boris Karloff about him, with sunken eyes, an icy pallor, and silver hair swept back over his shoulders, but was probably only in his midforties. He glanced over at Thackeray with cold contempt and then returned to contemplating his porn magazine. The lead plague warden whispered a few words in his ear before Buckland threw the magazine to one side and came over.

"What is it with you people?" Buckland said, irritated that his reading had been disrupted. He was educated but not clever, Thackeray could see from his eyes; he survived on cunning and an ability to be one degree harder, one notch more brutal than anyone else. "You know the rules," Buckland continued. "Everyone on my patch knows them. They were designed for the benefit of the people living here. Are you antisocial or something?"

Thackeray almost laughed, but a very basic fear helped him maintain a straight face.

"Rule number one: no one hoards anything. All supplies have to be held centrally for the good of the people. You know that?" Thackeray nodded; there was no point in lying. "Rule number two: any sign of the plague has to be reported so we can take steps to deal with it."

"I don't know anyone with signs of the plague."

Buckland pushed his face close to Thackeray's; he smelled of meat. "No, but you hoard!"

"It was a mistake—"

"You're right there. Do you know how hard it is to keep order in this fucking world? Do you, you little toe rag? Everyone's trying to look after themselves . . . no one's thinking about the common good. Except me. And what thanks do I get? No bloody respect." Buckland finished his whiskey and went to pour himself another from a decanter on an antique table in one corner.

Thackeray couldn't quite tell if Buckland had spouted his crazed fantasy so many times that he was starting to believe it himself. But Thackeray knew all the stories of how Buckland had come to power. How he'd used to run the drugs and prostitution rackets in Sparkhill with his gang of local thugs, earning his reputation with the judicious use of a double-bladed Stanley knife to carve up the faces of his enemies because it was impossible to stitch the two parallel cuts at Accident and Emergency. There were so many people walking around Sparkhill with his mark that it acquired the nickname Razor Town. And then, once the Fall began, and communications broke down, and all the weird rumours about what was happening outside the city took off, Buckland was ready to start the looting and the rioting.

In a moment of lucid slyness, he had realised that Sparkhill was too small for him and had moved straight into the city centre, adding to his band of thugs as he progressed. No Stanley knives for him then; he'd graduated to proper weapons. They say he personally killed three hundred people on the first day of his rule. Who could fight something like that? Who had the time or the energy or the inclination when personal survival was paramount? It was somebody else's problem. So here he was: unassailable. The Butcher King of Birmingham. And Thackeray was about to become a lesson for all the other poor bastards living in fear in his Kingdom of the Damned.

Buckland returned with his whiskey. "You know I'm going to have to make an example of you?"

"You could let me go. I wouldn't say anything."

"You see, it doesn't work like that. People always say they won't say anything. Then they go out and have a drink, or start trying to impress someone . . . some woman . . . and suddenly it's, 'Mr. Buckland couldn't touch me. I'm *better* than him. I'm smarter. I'm harder.' And some people are stupid—they think that kind of stuff might be true. And then we have problems. You see, problems breed problems. So I always try to sort things out early. It's simpler that way." He sipped his whiskey while staring deep into Thackeray's eyes. A faint smile came to his lips. "You're scared."

"Who wouldn't be?"

"That's true." Buckland took a long swig and flashed a glance at the plague warden, who moved toward a door at the back. "You're a smart bloke," Buckland continued. "I can see that. I'm a good judge of character. You know things are different now." He sucked on his lip while he searched for words to rephrase. "You know there's things out there you wouldn't even have dreamed of a couple of years ago."

"I've heard stories."

"Not stories, friend. The truth. They're . . . supernatural." He nodded with pride at his choice of word. "And you know how hard I am? I'm so hard I caught one of them. I'm so hard that now it does everything I say, like a Staffordshire bull terrier, because it's scared of me. Can you believe that?"

Thackeray grew even more nauseous. Harvey had been right. He'd expected to be taken out and shot, maybe even beaten to death. But now his imagination was racing at what his fate would be. If Buckland had preserved this particular horror for teaching lessons, there was no doubt it would be even worse than anything he could imagine.

"I think you're going to have to meet him." Buckland motioned to the door at the back where the plague warden waited.

Thackeray thought of Caitlin.

All the guttersnipes and lowlifes were out on the street at night, slipping through the gloom, avoiding the areas where the occasional torch burned. Everywhere smelled of shit and urine and rot. In one area, women turned tricks for food, thinking there was safety in numbers. Children threw rocks at the rats, whose undulating movements created an eerie optical illusion in some streets where it looked as if the dark was rippling with water.

And the plague wardens came and went, scores of them on circuit after circuit, seeking out the latest poor afflicted, shooting some, herding others ahead of their bikes to the houses of the dead.

Caitlin passed through it all like a ghost. Blood thundered in her head, her heart, colouring her vision. Blood everywhere; inside, from the last surge of her period. Harvey kept a few paces ahead as he led the way, occasionally glancing back, unsure and a little scared of the woman who only hours earlier had appeared so weak and unthreatening.

Caitlin's skull echoed with the constant hard-edged whispers of the Morrigan, telling her terrible secrets, relating horrific stories of battlefields and slaughter, hinting at things to come. Caitlin's own inner voice felt insignificant next to it, but they were both there, side by side, sisters-in-blood.

"New Street Station's just up there," Harvey hissed, then jumped when he saw that Caitlin already had an arrow notched. "But I tell you, it's pointless.

You'll never get past his guards. There's millions of them! Besides . . ." His voice grew sad. ". . . Thackeray'll be long gone by now."

"You like him." Caitlin scanned the approach to the station. Nothing moved.

"He's a good mate, the best. There aren't many that would have stuck with me." He turned away from her. "I'm not much good, really. Bit of a liability. Thackeray would have been better off on his own. He's got what it takes to survive. But he stuck by me. I'll never forget that."

"When I go in, you stay far enough behind so you won't get hurt in any crossfire."

"Don't worry about that—I'll be a speck on the horizon. You're mad, you know." He took a step away in case she lashed out.

"That's what they say." One hand went to her quiver to check her supply. "I'm going to have to reclaim arrows as I go . . . don't have many left."

"Right, right. You're sure you don't want to try to get a gun first? It would be—"

"Let's go." She pushed past him toward the entrance.

A firm hand between the shoulder blades propelled Thackeray into the room and the door closed behind him. At first, all he was aware of was the thunder of his heart in his head and the shortness of his breath. Then he became aware of the most foul stink, like rotting meat.

The room appeared pitch black until his eyes grew used to a thin light coming through small holes punched in the walls. It was just enough for him to see where the occupant of the room lay. Initially it looked like a shadow denser than any of the surrounding gloom, as though it were sucking the light into it like a mini–black hole. But then it began to move, rising up in the corner where it had been gnawing on something, and its skin glinted like oil. There were eyes, bestial and lethal, and a mouth, and mandibles, and a carapace of interlocking plates, and bony ridges, but every time he focused on a detail it changed before his eyes, so that all he had was a perception of something monstrous and deadly.

"They called themselves Fomorii," Buckland had told him before he entered the room. "The Fall came after a war between them and some others . . . some kind of gods. The Fomorii lost, and then they were gone, just like that. Except this one. This one couldn't get away because I had him."

Thackeray had no idea how Buckland knew all this, or if he was just making it all up. He couldn't understand how Buckland could keep something like that constrained, working to his will. It didn't matter.

The Fomor rose up nine feet or more, its shape flowing, becoming more terrifying with each incarnation until Thackeray thought he might go mad simply from looking at it.

He backed slowly into a corner.

Caitlin came down the escalator so stealthily her feet never made a sound. The contrast between the blazing torches and the heavy darkness all around would have been distracting for some people, but Caitlin's vision now operated on a different level. It was as if she was staring through a scarlet filter. Every thing hidden in the shadows was available to her, and distance fell away so that she could pick out the finest detail across the length of the concourse.

She saw the razor-wire wall across the ticket barrier and the door in the centre of it. There was a slot halfway up the door.

Caitlin coughed loudly. The slot slid back and she saw a pair of piggy eyes glinting inside it. Raising the bow and loosing the arrow was a fluid blur. It sped across the concourse, slipped perfectly through the slot, and rammed dead centre between the eyes with a sticky thud. A cry of shock rose up from her victim's colleague.

She only expected stupidity and she was easily rewarded. Another pair of eyes appeared at the slot, only this time she didn't loose an arrow. She was already standing a foot away from it, smiling innocently, her bow out of sight. She could almost hear the slow turning of the guard's mind.

"Quick," she said breathlessly, "let me in . . . before he gets me."

The guard acted on instinct; the door eased open a little. Caitlin was through it in an instant. The guard was stunned by her speed, but only had a second to register surprise before her stiffened hand rammed into his throat, bursting through his windpipe. She curled her fingers and ripped, tearing across until she ruptured his carotid artery. Blood sprayed all over, gouting up the door, across the floor. The guard fell down, clutching at his throat, still not quite believing what had happened. It was a woman; only a woman.

After reclaiming her first arrow, Caitlin continued down the corridor, turning briefly when she heard Harvey exclaim behind her. For a second she was caught in the glare of a torch, stained red, droplets falling from her nose, her eyelashes, the ends of her hair.

"Jesus Christ!" Harvey said. "It's like . . . Carrie!"

Plague wardens and other guards began to emerge from rooms on every side. Caitlin, her eyes wide, emotionless, turned to meet them. Inside, the Morrigan's whispering reached a crescendo, laced with glee and threat. Caitlin raised her bow.

The arrows swept along the corridor. Four men fell before the others even realised Caitlin was armed. Even though she was a woman, one of them was taking no chances. He pulled up a shotgun and fired. The blast echoed down the corridor, the shot passing through the spot where Caitlin had been. By then she had yanked the shotgun from his hands and brought the butt up hard to shatter his jaw. As he went down, she yanked the gun above her head and brought it down three times in quick succession, smashing his skull into pieces and bursting his brain across the grimy floor.

The rest were caught in disarray. They were burly men, used to casual brutality, but they had no response to the woman who moved like mercury amongst them, savage and relentless as a storm. She appeared next to one, using the shotgun like a club, and before he had fallen she had taken his machete and slashed open the guts of another. Three more fell before the machete was knocked from her hands, and then she launched herself at another's throat to rend and tear with her teeth. She came up from him, spitting meat, blood, and skin, to find herself alone.

The Fomor was taking its time toying with its prey like a lion in the veld. Thackeray had managed to duck under two of its lunges and dart to another corner, but he knew he was only delaying the inevitable. And he had discovered what the inevitable was: bones, gnawed clean, lay in a pile in one corner and they were all clearly human.

Despite its size and power, the beast moved sinuously across the room while the array of changes to its form continued with a near-poetic grace, armour plates giving way to rows of cruel spikes, shifting to mighty bat wings, all gleaming black.

Thackeray ducked beneath its sweeping hand, only for the hooked fingers to extend with razor-tipped talons, tearing through the back of his jacket to raise blood. As he rolled out of the way, cursing with the pain, a spike burst from the creature's thigh to miss his head by an inch and punch a hole in the wall.

You might as well give up, he told himself. But he couldn't.

A glancing blow almost took his head from his shoulders. He could taste blood in his mouth, feel it trickling down his back and into his eyes. The Fomor was tiring of its sport, growing faster, more vicious.

Thackeray jumped out of the way as a fist smashed down at him, raising a cloud of concrete dust from the floor. But in his rush to escape, he slammed his head against the wall, and slid down, dazed. His time was up.

Light flooded into the room. In his stunned state, it took him a second to realise that the door had been thrown open. Someone was standing there, silhouetted against the torchlight beyond, and as the figure shifted he saw that it was some hideous apparition, stained with blood from head to toe, white eyes staring furiously from the scarlet. It was armed with a machete, but Thackeray only had a second to take that in before the figure launched into action.

It threw itself at the Fomor, the blade a whirl, sparks flying in golden showers where it crashed off the armour. The beast made an inhuman howling noise that set Thackeray's teeth on edge, and then it became a whirlwind of mutating activity. It was impossible for Thackeray to get a handle on what was happening, so furious was the movement. All he could capture were brief snapshots of a struggle that was apocalyptic in its intensity.

Somehow the darting figure always managed to stay a fraction of an inch beneath the claws, spikes, and fangs, thrusting with the machete in search of some chink in the creature's defences. Thackeray couldn't believe there was one— it was too much of a killing machine—but then a gout of black liquid burst across the room and splattered next to him, sizzling as it burned through the floor. The bass rumbles of the beast became a deafening high-pitched whine that made Thackeray want to vomit.

The black liquid spouted from somewhere beneath its head. It stumbled back, but the scarlet figure didn't relent, hacking and chopping and thrusting in a crazed bloodlust, taking advantage of the Fomor's increasing inability to armour itself. Chunks of quivering black flesh fell to the floor, followed by wriggling digits and then limbs.

Even when the beast lay trembling on the floor, the figure continued to chop, and finally there was nothing left but unidentifiable lumps. Thackeray had to look away.

A moment later he realised the figure was standing over him, and he wondered if it was now his turn. With surprise, he saw a woman behind the blood-stained exterior. Gradually recognition dawned. It was too much of a shock, leaving him grasping for comprehension.

Finally she reached out a sticky hand and helped him to his feet. "My name's Caitlin," she said.

Despite everything he had seen, hearing her voice sent a shiver through him. "What are you?" he asked.

She tossed the machete to one side and for a second he thought he saw tears in her eyes. Then she threw herself at him with the same passion with which she had attacked the Fomor, forcing her lips onto his, kissing so hard he saw stars, giving every fibre of her being.

The force of the kiss, and the crackling energy that lay behind it, drove him back down. He was too weak to resist, nor did he want to. She continued to kiss, and then bite at his face and neck, her hands feverishly running over his body, before she broke off and started to tear first at his clothes then her own. Her breasts and belly were white against the crimson stain of her face and hands. Her hair lashed the air as she ground her groin against his, showering droplets of blood onto his face, his chest. Her nails raked his skin, but she was oblivious to the occasional bursts of pain that she caused him, so lost was she to her sexual frenzy.

Thackeray was dragged along by her fire and gave himself up to her fully. She was like a drug; his blood thundered, his head spinning with hallucinogenic desire, transformative, sacramental. Connections blazed with energy, blue, blue fire that lay beyond the physical. She was all he could ever have wanted.

When she'd dragged his trousers down, she used her hands and her mouth to ensure he was fully erect, and then she raised herself to slide him inside her. She rode him furiously, ducking to kiss and bite, and there was blood everywhere, on his skin, in his vision.

When he came in a blazing burst of euphoria she refused to let him withdraw, her own orgasm coming a second or so later. Only then did she collapse on his chest, breathing hard, her heart pounding. It felt as if she had given him everything within her.

"I think I love you," he said, stroking her sticky hair; and he meant it.

They dressed and ventured out into Buckland's office. The thug lay in one corner, moaning gently to himself. Both his kneecaps were shattered. He began to curse loudly when he saw Caitlin and Thackeray.

Harvey loitered in the doorway, both scared and overjoyed. "Thought you were a dead dog," he said to Thackeray obliquely.

"Nearly . . . a couple more minutes."

"Glad you pulled through."

"Yep. Looks like you're stuck with me for a bit longer." They shuffled round for a moment, unable to face their emotions, and then Thackeray nodded at Caitlin. "What about her, then?"

"Yeah. Who'da thought it?" Harvey eyed her warily. "Like somebody out of *The Matrix*."

"Red Sonja, more like. You remember Conan? The She-Devil with a Sword. Or in this case a machete."

"They're all dead, you know." Harvey jerked a thumb in the direction of the corridor leading to the concourse. "All that bastard's men."

Thackeray looked Caitlin in the eye; he couldn't quite understand what he was glimpsing there, though it certainly wasn't the blankness he had seen in the woman with whom he had first fallen in love. "I'm not going to be able to take you back to mother, am I?"

"But why didn't you kill him?" Harvey nodded toward Buckland, who was increasingly delirious with the pain.

"He's facing his own punishment." The new vision Caitlin had gained since the Morrigan had come to the fore was proving a revelation. As Caitlin watched Buckland, she could see the devils dancing over his form, teasing the plague along the meridians of his body where the chi flowed. She knew what it was now: a spirit-plague, a corruption of the soul that attacked the life-giving essence of reality. It wasn't just designed to kill people; it was there to destroy everything. The Blue Fire would be attacked first, and then physical matter would follow.

And while it could be a natural infestation, the presence of the devils and the malignant and modulated way in which they went about their terrible business made Caitlin sure there was an intelligence behind it. Something had loosed such an awful thing; something wanted Existence destroyed. And that made her think that it was all connected—the plague, the Lament-Brood, the attempt to eradicate her. But who or what could possibly want to wipe out everything that ever was?

"So, we getting out of here?" Thackeray said. "Buckland's not going to be much of a threat anymore. In a world with the flimsiest of health services, what you've done to him is pretty much a death sentence."

"For what it's worth," Caitlin said.

"Maybe we could take over from him," Harvey mused. "With an enforcer like her, nobody would mess with us."

"Nah," Thackeray said. "Too much responsibility. I'd rather go on holiday."

He looked at Caitlin hopefully, but her face told him all he needed to know.

They stood on one of the station platforms, the intense darkness thrown back in one small arc by a lone torch held by Harvey.

Thackeray had his arms around Caitlin's waist, pulling her close so he could feel her tenderness. "You've really got to go?"

"Yes. People are counting on me."

His sigh was supposed to be theatrical, but it carried the full weight of his feeling. "It's understandable. You're getting out of Birmingham. Who wouldn't?"

"You could leave, too."

"You'd think, wouldn't you?" He looked deep into her eyes and tried to appear blasé. "I'd go with you."

She shook her head. "I don't think I'll be coming back, Thackeray. What I've got to do . . . well . . . my instinct tells me the price is going to be my life. These things always end badly."

"Yeah. You see, responsibility . . . I don't really get that word."

She leaned forward and kissed him gently on the lips. It was subtle but as potent as the passion he had experienced from her earlier. A shiver ran down his spine. He knew in his heart that he would never find another who meant as much to him. Their time together could be counted in days, yet the connection he felt with her was as deep and abiding as the ocean. He wanted to tell her how much he needed her, how he could see, even though she hadn't examined it herself, that she loved him, too. But he could also tell it was pointless. She couldn't stay; obligation lay on her shoulders like a millstone.

"In this world we've ended up with," he said, "things are just too, too tragic."

She smiled and electricity jumped between them, but the poignancy was almost too painful for him to bear. She pulled back and his hands fell from her waist. "Bye, Harvey," she said with a wave.

There was a hint of relief in his smile. "You want to get some shampoo for that hair, Red Sonja."

She laughed and dropped from the platform onto the tracks. They watched her as she moved along the lines, and only once did she look back before the darkness swallowed her up. At that moment Thackeray thought he was going to die.

Harvey slapped a hand on his shoulder. "I'm sorry, mate. But look on the bright side . . . you'd never have been able to argue with her."

Thackeray tried to pierce the gloom, imagining her wending her way out into the night, fierce and beautiful and wild, like nature. "I'd have jumped through fire for her, Harv. I'd have crossed the world."

"You're a stupid romantic, Thackeray, and it's a wonder you've got any friends." Harvey turned away and waved the torch toward the exit. "Come on . . . let's nick Buckland's whiskey stash."

chapter thirteen

IN THE COURT OF
THE DREAMING SONG

"O Liberty! What crimes are committed in thy name!"
Madame Roland

Crowther was hot and irritable and the path appeared to go on forever. The still air beneath the trees had grown oppressively muggy and even long drinks from the numerous cool streams that cut through the forest did little to ease his discomfort.

Mahalia, dealing with her grief, spoke little, but what worried him was that when she did talk, she was polite, thoughtful, almost good-natured. He was concerned that Carlton's death was an unbearable stress that could eventually destroy her.

"It might help to talk about him," he said as he watched her kicking small stones into the thick undergrowth. "The boy . . . uh, Carlton . . ."

"There's nothing to talk about."

"You could tell me how you met him."

She thought about this for a moment, then said, "It was after I'd escaped . . . from the attic. I'd been living rough, trying to get food anywhere I could . . ." She grimaced. "I ate some disgusting things, just to stay alive. That showed me you'd do anything to survive—anything." She continued walking, not looking at him. "I expect you can guess what it was like—a young girl on the street, easy target. One morning four men, four *bastards* . . ." She spat the word. ". . . tried to rape me. Broad daylight, on the footpath, in one of the main shopping areas. People were nearby. Nobody cared, however much I screamed. They just wanted to get on with their business. My problems were my problems."

Crowther watched the back of her head, reading the unspoken emotions amongst her words.

"Carlton came out of nowhere," she continued. "Somehow he rounded up some of those people walking by—I don't know how he did it, he couldn't talk, but, you know, he had a *way* about him—people liked him, people followed him . . ." She stifled a sob in her throat, took a moment to wipe her eye, but still remained in control, still diamond-hard. "They drove the men off . . . saved me. Carlton saved me. And when he came over and held out his hand to help me up, and just smiled, that way he always did, I knew I'd found a friend—someone who'd help me, someone I could help."

Crowther watched her shoulders grow taut and her head bow. Awkwardly, he reached out a hand and laid it on her shoulders. He felt uncomfortable at making such a connection, but it did the job, for she flashed him a brief, sad smile. It made her look like a different person.

"Now we're never going to find out who he really was . . . or what he could do," she said.

"Perhaps he was simply a good person," Crowther said. "No more, no less. Perhaps he had already done the job intended for him, and nothing more was planned for him. His work was over."

Mahalia eyed him curiously. "Do you believe in God, Professor?"

"I did, then I didn't, and now . . . I'm open to arguments." The question unnerved him and he quickly moved the conversation away. "So where do you come from, young Mahalia? You've been a little bit of a dark horse since we met. You've clearly had the benefit of a good education and there's an air of the well-to-do about you." He kicked himself mentally for sounding so false, but trying to be nice didn't come easily to him. It felt as if they were two blind people groping round in the dark, trying to discover if the other was animal, mineral, or vegetable.

She sighed and for a second he thought she was not going to answer. But the openness they had both displayed had worked a spell on her. "I don't really like talking about the past," she said. "It's gone, dead. But . . . OK . . . I went to Cheltenham Ladies' College. A boarder. My dad and mum lived in Hampshire. He ran a financial services company. Mum did charity work, that sort of stuff. It wasn't easy to be black in those sorts of circles, but they did OK. They seemed to like it. When the Fall came and everything started going mad, I tried to get back to them. I stole a car with a couple of friends, and when it ran out of petrol I walked. Got back to the house just over a week later. There was no sign of them."

"Do you have any idea what might have happened?"

She shook her head, but had a strange faraway look on her face, as if remembering long-forgotten facts. "There was some food on the table, half eaten, but they were gone—like they'd been snatched away. Who knows? Whatever . . . you know, the things they did . . . they didn't give them any sort of skills to survive in the world we've got now. In their world, they were big shots, but now . . . what use are people who only know how to make money?"

He raised his voice as a strong breeze rustled the undergrowth. "You're very keen on this survival thing."

She shrugged. "When it comes down to it, you've only got yourself. No one else is going to look after you."

He couldn't argue with that. Mopping his brow, he realised something curious: there was no cooling breeze, so how could the undergrowth continue to rustle? The answer came at him like a wolf, and he turned with dread.

Purple light floated amongst the trees as far as his eye could see. The Lament-Brood's advance had been as silent as death, hidden behind the conversation and the background noise of the forest. He cursed himself for not being more on guard.

His shock was compounded when he saw that the army had at least doubled in size from the number that had emerged from the river. Could the Whisperers have altered some of the Gehennis, perhaps other of the forest's mysterious inhabitants? A virus, infecting, transforming, spreading exponentially.

Crowther urged Mahalia to run just as the insidious whispering grew louder. He imagined the virulent sound as snakes slithering through the vegetation, preparing to rise up once near them.

Mahalia was lighter on her feet and quickly moved ahead while the professor lumbered on behind, lungs burning, face red. Further back, but not much, the thunder of the Lament-Brood's mounts shook the ground.

Mahalia slowed when she realised he wasn't at her heels.

"Don't wait for me," he said.

She hesitated.

"I said, don't wait for me!"

She broke ahead and he did his best to keep up, the whispering growing more intense, insinuating into Crowther's head. Black thoughts bloomed, their florid misery spreading through his mind. His legs grew leaden.

Give up. Lie down. Die.

With a rapid flick of his wrist, he smacked his staff against his forehead, and then even harder against his nose. He howled a stream of four-letter words and blood splattered onto his lips, but it earned him some respite.

Ahead, he saw Mahalia veer into the trees. She'd seen something—probably a short cut, for the path was curling round upon itself. Against his better judgment, Crowther followed. Through the trees, there was blue sky; the forest's edge. Mahalia suddenly came up sharp, wobbling back and forth and trying to balance herself with flailing arms.

"Wait—!" she cried.

Crowther couldn't stop. He ploughed into the back of her, propelling her forward, over the edge of a cliff. He yelled out in shock, catching a branch to stop himself from following her and then lashing out with his other arm. He was too late. With a scream, she went plummeting down.

Crowther could hear rushing water and glimpse the white of the rapids far, far below to his right, where the view over the lip was clear.

Panic exploded in him. He'd killed her! Ignoring the rapidly approaching Whisperers, he dropped to his knees and peered over the lip. Ten feet below, a thin ledge wound its way along the cliff face. There was no sign of Mahalia. A cry caught his attention, and away to his right he saw Matt and Jack edging their way as quickly as possible along the path toward him.

Dazed, Crowther lowered himself over the lip. He took one last glance at the purple mist drifting dreamily amongst the trees, and then he let go, not really caring if he overbalanced and was smashed on the rocks far below.

Jack yelled at him. He read the words on the boy's lips before the sound came to him: "She's still alive!"

Perplexed, he leaned over the edge to find Mahalia clinging to a crevice not far below the edge of the path, her face bloody from a gash on her forehead. Overcome with a sweeping joy, Crowther tried to get to her, but Jack and Matt barged him to one side so that this time he almost did overbalance. Jack and Matt knelt down, reaching for Mahalia's hands, but the path was so narrow that they could barely gain any purchase.

Mahalia's arms trembled with the strain, and her face had the desperate fear of someone who knew their life was numbered in minutes. Then her wild, white eyes rolled to the right and the fear became more avid.

Crowther glanced back along the path to see one of the Gehennis, its horrific form twisted, the purple mist running through it like capillaries of smoke.

Aware of the approaching danger, Matt and Jack worked frantically, but still couldn't get leverage. Crowther stood up, braced his back against the rock, and gripped both their belts. There was a brief moment of anxiety, and then they gave their trust to him, pushing themselves out over the edge and allowing him to take their weight, in the certain knowledge that if he faltered they would all go.

Crowther knew it, too, but he was determined in a way he had never been before to live up to what was expected of him. Matt and Jack lunged down to grab Mahalia's arms.

Behind the Gehennis, more of the Lament-Brood followed. The whispering even began to drown out the thunder of the water.

"I'm not listening!" Crowther roared.

With a heave, Mahalia came up. For a second they all feared they were going over, but Crowther held firm until Mahalia was on the path.

"No time to rest!" Crowther yelled. "Move!"

Jack helped Mahalia along, though she looked fit to fall again, and Matt followed. The vividness of the experience gave Crowther a moment of startling clarity as he realised that he didn't want to die after all.

The Lament-Brood pressed hard at their backs as they edged along the precipitous ledge. Finally, the Court of the Dreaming Song came into view. They clambered up a flight of stone steps to a large flagged courtyard suspended over the gorge. An arched oak door twenty feet high led into the interior of the court. But as they hurried toward it, Matt held out his arms to stop them. "This is a defensible position. We have to destroy the path to stop them getting in here."

"How can we do that?" Crowther snapped. Nervously, he glanced back to see a column of Lament-Brood barely two minutes away from the steps. "Come on," Crowther said. "Inside."

"No." Matt grabbed Jack's shoulders. "You've got to use that thing inside you. Like you did on the boat."

Dismay seeped into Jack's face. "I can't!"

Matt shook him hard. "You have to."

"Leave him alone." Mahalia tried to pull Matt's hands free, but she was still weak from the shock.

"I can't control it," Jack pleaded. "I'm afraid . . . I could set off the whole Wish-Hex! I could destroy everything!"

Matt thrust Jack in the direction of the path. "Just do it. You controlled it before—"

"That was by chance!"

"—you can do it again."

Jack hovered, looked to Mahalia for support, and then with shoulders sagging, he ran to the top of the flight of stone steps.

"What if he does take us out?" Crowther yelled above the roar of the water.

"He won't," Matt said. "They wouldn't have put the bomb in him if it could be randomly detonated. They're not stupid—they must have some kind of military mind to do a thing like that. There has to be a fail-safe."

"You could have told him that!" Mahalia said.

"I want him upset and angry so he'll blow that path to kingdom come."

Jack looked small and forlorn against the stone rail that ran around the edge of the courtyard. He bowed his head, then pivoted at the waist. When he rose up, a sheet of silvery light ballooned out from him. All the sound was sucked out of the vicinity until, with a pop, the bubble of light burst.

Matt, Crowther, and Mahalia were knocked flat on their backs by a wall of pressure. A sonic boom made their ears ache and when they looked up Jack was clutching on to the rail for support. Beyond him a cloud of dust rose up from where the path had been, and mingling with it were the last few strands of purple mist.

Matt nodded with satisfaction. "That did the trick."

"There is another way of looking at it," Crowther said. "Let's hope we get a warm welcome, because there's no going back."

"Somebody's having fun." Matt nudged Crowther as they examined the large, impressive doors. Jack and Mahalia sat on the rail overlooking the gorge. They were locked in a deep embrace. There was more desperation than passion in their kiss, the recognition of kindred loneliness and a hunger to fill that void.

"Good for them," Crowther said. "At least someone is finding something worthwhile out of this whole miserable experience."

"I don't know what to do about Caitlin," Matt said.

"Yes, perhaps you should have thought of that before you blew up her one route into this place."

"You know I had no choice."

"Then she'll have to find another route . . . or not. There's nothing we can do about it."

Crowther could see that Matt was obviously trying to distract himself from his anxiety by focusing on the matter at hand, but his fellow traveller was deeply affected.

Matt scanned the door for some way of opening it. "I can't understand why no one has been out to greet us. Surely they must know we're here."

"Triathus certainly implied they'd be eager to help us." Crowther leaned on his staff. His back ached from the tingling insistence of the mask; its influence was growing more intense, so that sometimes it felt as though fiery fingers were digging into his spine.

"There seem to be two different forms of architecture," Matt said, pointing to the monolithic blocks and the delicate, surrealistic detail that overlaid them.

"That's because it's the work of two different races." Jack stood behind them, his arm around Mahalia's shoulders. "The Golden Ones like to pretend they're the only people who ever ruled here, but there were others." He walked over and patted one of the huge stone blocks. "This comes from the Age of Warriors. The Drakusa were a hard, violent race—at least, that's what I heard. Not much is known about those who came before. Though *before* isn't really the right word in this place . . . you know, time doesn't have any real meaning. I suppose they still do exist, somewhere. The Golden Ones just aren't interested in finding out any more about them."

"Did they influence humanity?" Crowther asked.

"I don't know . . . I suppose. It's said they had the power to shape rock, to pull up whole structures from the earth itself and mold it with the power of their minds. When I was in the Court of the Final Word, I made friends—although that isn't really the right word—with Math, the Keeper of Records. I think more than anything he was just keeping an eye on me once they'd done their *work*. But it gave me the chance to get into the library. They've got so many secrets hidden away in that place."

"Sounds like you might be even more valuable to us," Matt noted.

"More valuable than just a weapon?" Jack's tone suggested the hurt he felt at Matt forcing him to act against the Lament-Brood.

"Can we just get inside?" Mahalia snapped. "After nearly dying I could do with a sit down. And don't for a minute think I've forgotten who almost sent me flying to my death." She fixed an eye on Crowther, who studiously ignored her.

"Most of the great courts have doors that can be opened by anyone, if you know the right way," Jack said. "The Golden Ones aren't afraid of anything, so they never think anyone would be stupid enough to attack them."

Matt eyed the professor slyly.

"What are you thinking?" Crowther said defensively.

"You could use the mask—"

"No! Absolutely not!"

"You could—"

"You saw what happened last time! Are you an idiot?" Crowther presented his denial forcefully, but he felt a feverish desire tingling throughout his entire body. The mask responded to his yearning with a gentle tug at his emotions.

"You're a smart bloke. You can control it . . . or you can learn to."

"And in the meantime I risk destroying everything."

"You're doing to him what you did to me!" Jack protested.

"I'm not trying to make anybody's life miserable, or to risk anything." Matt sighed. "But we're in a difficult situation with a lot at stake. Everyone has to do what they can to further our mission, even if there's a personal price involved."

"I don't see *you* paying any price." Crowther pushed past Matt and sat cross-legged in front of the door. His hands were sweating as he tugged the mask from the hidden pocket in his coat. "You have a very unpleasant way of manipulating people to your ends. Do you like seeing everyone suffer?"

Matt dismissed the comment with a shake of his head, and went to watch the proceedings from the rail. Crowther held the mask for a second, but he was shaking with excitement and couldn't delay the gratification any longer. He held it up, and once it was near his face, the spider-leg protrusions burst from the sides and slammed into the holes in his head. There was a faint buzzing as it fixed itself to his skull.

"This time will be like honey." The seductive voice of Maponus lapped around Crowther's mind. *"There will be no shocks . . . no fear. It will be like floating on your back downstream, watching the clouds pass by above you, feeling the warmth of the sun on your face, knowing you could sleep if you wanted. You will be at peace in a way that you never have been. And you will want this peace again. You will always want it, for the rest of your days. After this moment, you will desire to wear the mask . . . to connect with the greatness and wild wonder of my mind . . . forever."*

And it was just as the mask said. Detached from everything that was happening, Crowther drifted in a state of pure joy and comfort, vaguely aware of the faint veins of blue that stretched across the door into a focal point three feet up from the ground and two feet in from the right outside edge. It glowed and shimmered before moving sinuously in a circle, round and round. It was a dragon eating its own tail.

Languorously, he rose, walked toward the door, and placed his palm in the centre of the circling dragon. There was a fizz of blue sparks from his fingertips and the door swung open.

"See, mate, I told you there wouldn't be a problem." Matt clapped Crowther across the shoulders.

The professor stared intently at the mask lying flat in the palms of his hands where it had dropped after it had removed itself from his head. He had tried to keep it clamped there, but it had refused his urgings. Maponus's faint, tinkling laughter echoed around his skull.

"Are you all right?" Matt asked.

"Of course. I'm absolutely hunky-dory." Crowther walked away through the doorway so that Matt couldn't see the tears in his eyes.

An enormous hall soared up into a vaulted roof filled with shadows. The main walls were constructed from the monolithic blocks of the Drakusa, but everything else, every pillar, balustrade, arch, column, buttress, ridge, rail, and shelf, was carved in such an intricately detailed manner that it was almost hallucinogenic. It was impossible to take in the level of detail, for the longer they looked at something, the more that would emerge, and continually so. The symbolism was heavy and portentous, and while not obvious to them, it worked its magic in their deep subconscious. Strange, troubling thoughts blossomed, as if someone were whispering hidden information into their ears.

Mahalia caught Jack's arm. "Can you see it? I thought it was an optical illusion—the light making the shadows shift . . ."

Yet the light source remained constant, the shadows sharp and hard.

"It's the carvings . . . they're moving," Jack replied uneasily.

And they were, barely perceptibly but enough to trouble the companions. The strange beasts and alien figures continually shifted slightly as if they were alive; plants and trees moved in a faint breeze that didn't exist; birds adjusted their flight patterns. The effect was of the carvings shifting their perception as the four of them walked by, to get a better view of the strangers in their midst.

"I don't like it," Mahalia whispered, and hated herself for sounding so pathetic. She knew she could cope with hard, physical things that would bend to her will or her blades, but this was beyond her control.

"Why is it so dark here?" Matt said with irritation. "If there's a whole court full of Triathus's people here, you'd have thought they'd have invested in good lighting. You know, nipped down to Ikea for some of those nifty little lamps on wires you can slide around." He cursed under his breath. "The window let the light in, but there must have been some kind of mechanism to transmit it into the depths of this place."

Mahalia unconsciously moved closer to Jack so that he could slide an arm around her. The four of them stood huddled together in the centre of the vast hall for a long moment, drinking in an atmosphere of claustrophobia and incipient dread.

"It feels to me," Jack began hesitantly, "as if something happened here. I don't know what . . ."

Crowther had finally gained enough control over himself to return the mask to its pocket. "Well, we can't go back," he said, with an edge of bitterness. "So we'd better hope there's another way out of here."

Matt ventured toward one of the walls, wincing as the carvings shifted to watch him. Plucking a torch from a metal bracket, he struck his flint and ignited it, so that the shadows swept away; it only added to the eerie movement across the walls.

Matt walked slowly toward the darkness at the far end of the hall. The others fell into line behind him, glancing behind at the comforting sunlight that broke through the open door.

The hall gave way to a maze of corridors and chambers, everywhere decorated with the disturbing carvings. They would glance up to see a horned figure watching them from above an arch, or something sinuous slither around a door-jamb and into a room.

They began to think they could hear the carvings talking. What sounded like sibilant voices came and went in phased patterns. It was only after a while that they realised it came from small globes fixed high up on the walls, with holes of varying sizes bored into them. As the four of them moved, they set off air currents that passed through the holes to create the constant sounds.

Once they understood the source of the noise they decided it didn't really sound like voices at all. There was timbre and rhythm and cadence; it was music, but of a kind they had never experienced before.

Crowther theorised that many people moving through the corridors and rooms would create louder, more vibrant tones so that it would appear that the entire court was always filled with soothing music. But with only the four of them there, the effect was creepy and unsettling.

In one large hall, they made out paintings on the walls, so heavily faded that only by holding the torch close could they see the design. Parts of the paintings were obscured by the carvings, making it clear that they came from the earlier age of the court, when the Drakusa occupied more spartan surroundings. There were mountains and fire and vast plains, epic forests and gushing rivers. But one section made them all pause. Here were strange silver objects like eggs with legs.

"Clearly they are the Caraprix," Crowther mused as he examined the silver shapes. "They are symbiotes. All the Golden Ones carry them."

"Caitlin mentioned Lugh had one," Matt said.

"Yet here they are huge, dominating the scenery." Crowther was puzzled. "Then, the Drakusa knew of the Caraprix too. Yet the way they are drawn . . . it's almost as if they were deified."

He wanted to consider the issue more, for he was convinced it was of deep importance, but the others were keen to hurry along in search of daylight.

The court appeared to stretch for miles, from the cliff face deep into the bowels of the earth. Flaring up in the shifting torchlight were grand columned halls with designs of brass and glass, drapes of scarlet velvet and floors of shining marble, sweeping staircases that could have taken fifty people walking side by side. There was a room where the walls were entirely made of mirrors, giving an unsettling sense of the four of them striving throughout infinity, seeking survival in endless dimensions.

The chambers cried out for a throng of people devoted to art and beauty, continually accompanied by the music of their movement. But nowhere was there any sign of life. The scuttling, chattering, whispering sound that followed them wherever they went only added to the abiding sense of loneliness.

Finally, when weariness had turned their legs to lead, they opted to rest in a smaller room where they didn't feel so exposed. Matt fixed the torch in a bracket on one wall, but its faint light did little to dispel the feeling of a sea of darkness all around, waiting to submerge them.

"Ever get the feeling we've taken a wrong turn?" Matt said as he settled down at the foot of a wall. The oppressive atmosphere had crushed all the humour out of him.

"I can't understand this at all," Crowther muttered. "Everything suggests this place was clearly occupied very recently. Triathus gave no sign that it was deserted. So where could they possibly have all gone?"

It was a rhetorical question, and no one even began to answer it, though it had been troubling all their minds since they had first stepped into the court.

Both Matt and Mahalia fell into sleep quickly. Crowther, who had spent much of their trek through the court struggling with his desire to wear the mask, forced himself to sit down beside Jack. Even in the grip of his addiction, other concerns were at play in his mind. He watched the boy preparing to put his head down and then said, "So, you and young Mahalia are . . . stepping out, as we used to say in my day."

Jack's brow furrowed. "Stepping out?"

"An item. A couple. Romantically intertwined. You really have led the ultimate sheltered life, haven't you?"

"I love her." Jack's eyes sparkled in the semi-gloom.

"Really. Sorry to burst your bubble, but it's only infatuation. You're awash with hormones. It's a genetic process designed to facilitate speedy bonding for continued propagation of the species."

Jack stared at him blankly. "I know what I feel."

"No, you *think* you know what you feel. That's what all this mess is about—everything is an illusion and the truth lies somewhere behind it. Tell me about love when you've been with someone for years, cared for them when they're ill, put up with them when they're miserable or grumpy, taken the sharp side of their tongue and still come back." He looked away into the dark, and added quietly, "Tell me about love when you've acted quite appallingly, and the other person has still accepted you."

"Why are you so concerned about us, Professor Crowther?"

Crowther snorted. "I'm not concerned. Ridiculous."

Jack eyed the gentle rise and fall of Mahalia's chest. Occasionally, she would twitch and half-heard words would spring to her lips. His attention was caught by Crowther fumbling inside his coat, and for a second Jack thought the professor was after the mask again. Instead, he pulled out a dog-eared picture.

"What's that?" Jack asked as he shuffled closer to peer at the snap. "A painting?"

"A photograph." Crowther's voice was strained.

The picture showed two teenage girls, long, blonde hair, wide smiles, sparkling eyes. Anyone other than Jack would have recognised the fashions of the early nineties.

"Who are they?" Jack asked.

"My daughters." Crowther's face was shrouded by shadows.

"What are their names?"

"Sophie. And Stacia."

"Where are they now?"

"You ask a lot of questions," Crowther said grumpily. He tapped the photo gently with the tip of his index finger. "I have no idea where they are. They left home. Never really got in touch much."

"That's not very nice."

"No, it's not their fault," Crowther said firmly. "I wasn't the best of fathers. Quietly obsessed with my own life, you see. Children were a distraction." He fell silent for a moment, then added quietly, "It seems to be true what they say—you never really know what you've got till it's gone." He tucked the photo away.

"Well, I know what I've got with Mahalia," Jack said adamantly.

Crowther pulled his hat low over his face and shuffled deeper into his overcoat, ready to sleep. His mumbled words issued quietly into the dark. "Be careful how you treat her, boy."

"I wouldn't do anything to hurt her, ever." Jack tried to pierce the shadows beneath the brim of the hat, but Crowther's face was lost to him. "You care about her, don't you?"

But all that came back was a long, low snore.

They woke together, and realised some sound must have disturbed them. Matt instantly took charge, keeping them silent with a cutting motion of his hand while they listened intently. From a distance, a scraping noise came to them, faint, but in the tomblike quietness it might as well have been an alarm.

Matt grabbed the torch from the wall and they all crept out of the chamber.

The noise was intermittent and indistinct and they would often have to wait for long periods until it emerged again to guide them in the right direction. They moved along a broad corridor and eventually came to a large hall that could well have been some place of worship, for there was a strange air of sanctity present. Exquisite paintings of fantastical scenes lined the walls and in the centre of the floor was something resembling an altar—a large stone table set with objects of reverence. In that room the motion-tones took on a different texture, sombre, haunting, prickling the hairs on the backs of their necks.

The scratching sound came from the foot of the altar. As they moved closer, the torchlight set shadows dancing across the hall. The darkness unfurled to reveal a shape crumpled on the floor, and an odd fluttering movement above it.

"Don't go any closer," Mahalia said in a weak, strained voice, tugging at Matt's sleeve. He threw her off, curious and unnerved at the same time. He had to see.

The shape fell into relief. It was one of the Golden Ones, a male, resembling Triathus with his beautiful features, faintly shimmering skin and long hair. He was twisted half on his back, occasionally clutching feebly at the altar to try to pull himself up.

Mahalia exclaimed quietly, a note of sadness in her words, for they could tell he was dying. They hurried to his side and though his throat had been slit and there were numerous other wounds in his torso, there was no blood. Instead, his body was breaking up into tiny pieces that transformed into something like moths, glowing and golden as they fluttered up to the shadows that swamped the vaulted roof. Inside him, it appeared as though he were made of nothing more than light.

Crowther pushed Matt to one side and knelt beside the dying god. At first the professor attempted to staunch the fragmenting of the body, but when it became apparent that the process was irreversible, he leaned forward and said, "Who did this?"

The god's lids snapped open to reveal shimmering eyes that ranged back and forth until they fell on Crowther's face. Then, with the last of his strength, the god reached up to grab Crowther's coat to pull him closer. His voice was a thin husk. "They come," he said. "They come."

No sooner were the words out of his mouth than his hand fell back and his eyelids fluttered shut. The deterioration of his corporeal form suddenly became intense; a cloud of fluttering golden moths soared skyward, blinding all those who watched, and when they finally cleared there was nothing left.

"That's why there's no one here," Crowther said with horror as he stared at the space where the god had lain. "They've all been murdered. All of them . . . the entire court."

"Over here!" Jack's voice carried from the edge of the penumbra.

The others ventured over, distracted and disturbed by what they'd seen. A powerful feeling of dread crept up on them. They found Jack looking up at a standard that had been rammed into the floor with such unnatural force that cracks radiated out across the marble from the base of the metal spur. At the top hung a flag made of some kind of shimmering but ultralight metal featuring a stylised drawing of a seashell.

In the thin torchlight, Jack's face appeared to have drained of all blood. "It's the standard of the Court of the Yearning Heart," he said weakly.

Matt grabbed him by the shoulders. "What do you know?"

Jack wiped his hand across a suddenly snotty nose. "They're one of the worst of the courts. They don't care about humans . . . they don't care about anything." He looked around, eyes blinking stupidly. "They killed them all. Their own people!"

"We need to get out of here," Crowther said. "That poor soul gave us a warning—"

A deep, sonorous tolling echoed somewhere in the depths of the court, moving slowly through the thick stone walls, spreading its warning until every room and corridor was filled with the dim pounding.

"They know we're here," Mahalia said, wide-eyed. "How do they know?"

Matt cursed. "Someone obviously just killed that Golden One . . . a mopping-up exercise. They were probably just leaving when we arrived." He looked around with uncertainty. "I can't tell if the alarm is coming from ahead of us or behind."

Their moment of paralysis was broken when they heard what appeared to be the skittering of insects. It took a second for them to grasp that it was the sound of many feet approaching from a great distance.

"An army!" Crowther said with horror. "Bloody hell fire, there's an army of them!"

Matt propelled the other three in the direction of a large arched opening leading to an annex dominated by a rectangular shallow pool of water. The torch sent rippling patterns of light and shade moving across the wall as they passed. Beyond lay a processional corridor lined with lush heavily patterned drapes that led on to what may have been a ballroom or a concert hall, the disturbing carvings giving way to gleaming white columns and swirling confections moving along pink walls; a raised dais lay at one end.

The pattering footsteps were louder now, coming from all sides. "It sounds like children," Mahalia gasped. She had drawn the Fomorii sword, ready to lash out as she ran.

They emerged through an open gilded gate into an enormous indoor garden of trees and well-clipped hedges, wrought-iron fences and pergolas covered with flowering creepers, beds of alien blooms of red and blue and purple that released an intoxicating perfume, sheltering boulders and gravelled areas filled with tall grasses. It was designed in such a way that the paths led through it like a maze, revealing each new section only at the last moment. The most startling thing lay at the focal point: a well of sunlight streaming down through a hole in the roof, dazzling in contrast to the gloom that lay all around. A system of mirrors were fixed here and there, so that at certain times they could be turned to give light to the whole garden.

It was only when they'd ventured deep into the complex maze that they realised their mistake. The design made it impossible for them to see the approach of attackers from any direction until they would be upon the companions.

"Let's make it to the sun. It'll be lighter there and we can make a stand," Matt said fatalistically.

It wasn't long before they realised they were surrounded. Running feet pattered by on every side in the dark, crunching on gravel, rustling past bushes, or disturbing wind chimes. The sound became intense, like rain on the window in a heavy winter storm. They could just make out bodies, flashing past gaps in the vegetation and garden architecture, not human, small, smaller even than the people of the Court of Soul's Ease.

Words from a poem kept repeating in Crowther's head: *For fear of little men . . . for fear of little men*. And he did feel fear, and revulsion, and he could see it in the faces of the others. There was something in the size, and the way they scurried rapidly, that suggested rats, bringing up feelings buried since the earliest development of the human mind.

Their pursuers closed in rapidly, waiting for the moment when the four were completely surrounded. And that point came when the companions finally reached the column of sunlight, which centred on a raised platform of white marble. They thrust themselves into it, relishing the warmth on their faces, but all detail beyond the pillar of illumination disappeared into the dark and, reluctantly, they had to step back out of the column of light to see what awaited them.

From their vantage point, they had a view across a larger part of the garden. Small, scurrying figures were everywhere, stretching back into the deep dark, a writhing, squirming sea of rodent life. The nearest ones revealed the previously hidden forms: pale skin, long limbs, squat bodies, nasty eyes, and brutish brows.

Crowther couldn't believe that these people had once appeared as the stately, graceful Golden Ones. They had regressed to some point far, far back on their path of evolution, a state that spoke of viciousness and bestial urges, scratching out an existence in the dark places beneath the earth, only emerging at night with murder on their breath and hatred in their hearts.

And as he looked, with the fear swelling like an ocean inside him, he thought he understood why. They appeared to his perception as they truly were, no longer the aloof godlike Golden Ones, but the scrabbling creatures of humanity's darkest nightmares, broken by defeat and bitterness, desperate to prevent men from reaching the next stage of spiritual evolution, filled with all the basest urges. The more they gave in to hatred and murder, the more devolved they became.

They were all carrying tiny knives that glinted in the light. Crowther guessed they could gut and dress a body in minutes, seconds if they fell on a victim in numbers. This was it, then. Mahalia, Matt, and Jack braced themselves for any attack, weapons at the ready. Half-heartedly, Crowther raised his staff.

The seething throng parted as a figure moved forward from the darkness at the back. As he neared, they could see that he stood more erect than the others, though he was just as small. He had a long grey beard, but his eyes had the same black, hateful essence as his fellows'. Once he reached the front of the throng, he eyed them with cold malice. "Fragile Creatures," he said contemptuously. "What do you want here in the Far Lands?"

Matt stepped forward. "We're not concerned with whatever war you've got going on amongst your people. We're not going to interfere. We just want to get on our way, and to deal with our own business."

"Interfere?" The little man laughed hollowly. "My name is Melliflor, first lieutenant to the Queen of the Court of the Yearning Heart," he added, regarding them slyly. "And we do not like Fragile Creatures here in the Far Lands. You have your own home, Son of Adam, and now you have ventured far beyond the fields you know."

The crowd of little men behind him was like a tidal wave, waiting to break upon the four standing near the light. They surged and pressed, but Melliflor held them back by the force of his charisma while his cunning weighed the situation. He removed his own little knife from his belt and proceeded to clean his long, dirty fingernails in an ostentatiously threatening manner.

One of his army couldn't hold back any longer and darted forward, grasping toward Mahalia's foot. She lashed out savagely with the Fomorii sword and took his arm off at the elbow. He howled in pain, rolling backward across the floor. A hiss whistled through the assembled army and they rose up as one, ready to strike. Matt, Mahalia, and Jack steeled themselves.

"No more sunlight for you," Melliflor said with false sadness. He raised one arm; the little men prepared to move.

The constant itching that assailed Crowther's back became at that moment a full-scale rush of molten iron in his veins. Even if he had fought he wouldn't have been able to prevent his hands from darting to the secret pocket and removing the mask. If he was about to die, he wanted to do it in the luxurious, stimulating, cocooning world of the mask, the only place he had ever known true pleasure and true acceptance.

But the moment he brought out the mask, the sunlight gleaming off its silvered surface, the little men drew back as one, as if they were about to be burned, their nasty little eyes grown wide with fear. Matt saw their response and clutched at Crowther's arm. "Don't put it on—just hold it out," he hissed.

With trembling hand, Crowther just about resisted, though it edged slowly toward his face.

Melliflor recovered first, his eyes filled with a hungry gleam that Crowther knew only too well. "Give me the mask. It is too dangerous for Fragile Creatures. Give it to me and you shall be allowed to leave here."

"How can we trust you?" Matt shouted.

"You have my word—on the weft and weave."

"A promise?"

"A promise. And we do not give our word lightly, Fragile Creature." Melliflor appeared hypnotised by the light dancing off the mask, desperately yearning and fearful at the same time.

"Give it to him," Matt whispered to Crowther. "We don't have any choice. Even if we can't trust him, it might cause enough of a diversion for us to get out of here if you throw it right into the heart of them."

"No." The word was quietly spoken and steely hard.

"Don't be stupid!" Matt dug his fingers into Crowther's arm. "What's wrong with you?"

"Do you have any idea what they could do with this mask?"

Matt searched Crowther's face. "That's not the real reason. What's going on?" Matt didn't wait for an answer, instead lunging for the mask. Crowther elbowed him sharply in the face and stepped away so he could turn defiantly and clamp the mask onto himself.

An exclamation of terror rushed through the army of little men like a wind on a stormy night. At the back there was frantic movement as some of them turned and fled; others scurried for cover, while the ones near the front were paralysed with fear.

Melliflor looked ghastly pale in the light coming off the mask. "Good Son, forgive us," he said in hushed, desperate tones.

The second the mask had attached itself to Crowther's face, Matt, Mahalia, and Jack noticed a change in the atmosphere. A terrible weight bore down on all of them; sound became muffled and light, what little there was, became distorted.

Behind the mask, Crowther cried out. His hands rushed toward his face to tear the mask off, but then they suddenly fell limply to his sides, and he turned to face the little men. Melliflor was already backing away into the crowd. The little men scrambled and attacked each other in their desperation to escape, but their numbers were too great.

The mask fixed its attention on Melliflor with those cold, unseeing eyes. He dropped to his knees beneath the weight of the stare and clutched at his face, his nails biting deeply into his sallow skin. There was a slight nod from Crowther, and in the blink of an eye, Melliflor turned inside out. His organs and musculature appeared outside his body in a sticky mess. His eyes, still staring, registered an instant of surprised horror, and then his body disappeared in a frantic cloud of moths. This time, however, they were of the deepest black.

The atmosphere of tension broke as the frantic little men scrambled hither and thither, hunting for ways back into the dark places where they could hide. A route opened up toward the other side of the garden.

"You can take the mask off now!" Matt yelled, but Crowther was lost to the surging power. The air around him shimmered and became like glass, ballooning out across the garden. Escaping figures were thrown into the air wherever it passed, limbs falling away as if they had been severed by surgical knives, organs pulled free and dismantled with a lazy curiosity by invisible hands. Soon the air was thick with black moths.

"He's lost it!" Mahalia said.

"Let's get him out of here!" Matt ordered. He grabbed one arm and Jack took the other, both of them fearful that the powers the mask was exhibiting would soon be turned on them. As they hurried out of the garden, the devastating attack by the mask continued in full force, lashing backward at the fleeing little men, plucking up the stragglers, disappearing into passages, drains, and culverts where some hid.

But once the three of them led Crowther into the rooms beyond, the power became less aggressive, though still potent. Psychedelic colours painted the walls or surged in fountains in the air. Briefly, Mahalia's hand became like crystal. The motion-music burst from the walls with the force of a hundred orchestras, beautiful melodies and wild, percussive rhythms fighting for space, so loud they could barely hear themselves think, the compositions brilliance and madness in equal measure.

And wherever they went, the air appeared to peel back to give views over alien landscapes, or into deepest space where cold stars glimmered, into other worlds, other dimensions. People came and went in a flash, faces that appeared vaguely familiar, some old friends, others strangers, but behind it all was an unnerving sense of meaning, as if they were seeing the structures of reality laid bare.

Jack saw a Fabulous Beast soaring high over London, its jewelled scales glinting in the burst of fire that erupted from its mouth onto some dark tower. Mahalia glimpsed a desperate man who'd done desperate things shoot himself in the head, dead, dead as a doornail, and then later running with a sword through what appeared to be a cathedral, though the order of the visions made little sense to her. And Matt, he saw generals and spies and dead-eyed men sitting around a table plotting some big lie to deceive a population, only for that lie to become reality. And they all saw someone reading a book, painting mind-pictures from the words, creating more realities with every thought, making them hard and fast and real. Existence was fluid, everything was changing.

They rushed onward, dragging Crowther between them, while the chaos and the madness of the warp surged all around, so that after a while their minds began to rebel, not knowing where they were or what they were doing.

The court was a vast maze, and in the heavy darkness it was impossible to tell if they were doubling back on themselves. They began to feel as if they would be in there forever, trapped in an awful purgatory.

But then they discovered that Crowther was beginning to lead them, at first subtly suggesting changes in direction with a shift of his body weight, then increasingly pulling them along with him. They hurried down extravagantly decorated corridors, through vast, ringing halls, until they came to an arch big enough for three buses to pass through side by side. Over the top was a carving of a coiled, bewinged Fabulous Beast with sapphires for eyes, and beyond lay steep steps winding down into darkness.

"This looks like the way out," Jack gasped breathlessly. He let go of Crowther's arm; the professor stood quietly, the mask now silent. "Why's he suddenly calmed down?"

"Don't hang around talking," Mahalia pressed. "I just want to get out of this creepy place." She headed through the arch without giving the others a chance to debate.

The stairs were broader and more grand than the secret way out of the Court of Soul's Ease. Celtic spiral patterns in mosaic lined the walls, suggesting that the route was perhaps ceremonial. After fifteen minutes, they opened into an enormous cave with a small beach and the river lapping against it. Through the cave mouth they could see the late-afternoon sun on the slow-moving water and, beyond, the thick forest pressing heavily against the far bank.

"Looks like we bypassed the gorge and the rapids," Matt said, with definite relief. "I don't want to tempt fate, but we may be able to pick up Triathus."

"Blind luck," Mahalia said. "It's about time something worked out in our favour."

They helped Crowther as they picked their way over the slick rocks around the cave mouth, and after splashing through the shallows with the refreshing sun on their faces, they eventually pulled up onto the bank and lay amongst the trees at the river's edge.

"I thought we were dead in there," Mahalia said, one arm across her eyes, the rise and fall of her chest gradually calming.

Jack sat next to her, unable to resist gently stroking her hair. "Professor Crowther saved us. If he didn't have the mask . . ."

"I don't reckon it's as simple as that," Matt interjected.

Mahalia looked up at the dark tone in Matt's voice. He was watching the professor uneasily, who sat against the base of a tree, unmoving, the mask still clamped to his face.

"Why doesn't he take it off?" Mahalia asked.

Matt grimaced. "I don't think he can."

Caitlin marched through the night, the world red and black. Birmingham was far behind her. Lightning surged through her arteries, blazed across her mind; she was supercharged, glorious, almost floating above the land as she walked.

At times her own mind was present, though hyperaware, with none of the doubts that had torn her apart before. The clarity and confidence only added to her sense of ultimate well-being. At other times, the Morrigan's dark presence wove its way through her consciousness, like the thrashing of a murder of crows, and then there was only chaos and fragmented thoughts, like glimpses of a terrible battle through the drifting smoke of destruction.

Caitlin had covered miles in her energised state; she had no idea where she was going, but the Morrigan certainly did. The Midlands landscape had rolled under her feet. She neither tired nor paused for rest over a day and a night, gaining sustenance only from the fruit and wild vegetables she found on her route. Now she was passing through the lush Leicestershire countryside, a place of overgrown fields and a rampant, once well-tended forest that had spread almost magically across the area.

She came to a village called Griffydam, so named, according to myth, because its water supply had once been guarded by a griffin, the legendary half-eagle, half-lion creature. Crowther could have told her that such ancient stories were a code, denoting places where the barrier with the Otherworld was thin and where strange things often crossed over. But Caitlin knew this instinctively.

As she approached an old stone-lined well beside the road, thin lines of blue slowly rose to the surface of the ground beneath her feet, growing brighter and stronger as they rushed toward the well, casting a sapphire glow across the hedgerows and walls in that dark time just before dawn.

At the base of the well, cold blue fire blazed up higher, then formed lines of coruscating energy that rose up and up, crossing over, building a structure like a church with the well at its heart, as visible as a beacon across the surrounding countryside.

A burst of thunder shook the ground and continued to roll out all around as blue sparks fizzed and crackled in the ionised air. Caitlin stopped and stared in a moment of clarity brought on by the awe and the wonder, but then the familiar, urgent cawing of the Morrigan rose up once more.

Standing nearby, though he hadn't been there before, was the knight in the boar's-head mask. In her detached state, Caitlin half-made to speak to him, still not sure if he was there to help her or torment her. But all he would do was guide her toward the crackling blue light with his pointed sword.

She cast one last, wary look at him, and then the Morrigan propelled her into the blue.

chapter fourteen
LONG MEMORIES

"Women must come off the pedestal.
Men put us up there to get us out of the way."
Viscountess Rhondda

A ll day long, carrion crows swept in clouds so vast they brought a nocturnal gloom down on the fields, even in the middle of the day. Rats, too, swarmed everywhere, bigger, more daring, and more vicious than any Mary had ever known. She tried not to get too biblical, but the symbolism of portents and omens was vivid for anyone who wished to see them.

Her winding journey through England's heartland had followed ancient trackways away from the centres of population, but signs of the plague tightening its grip were evident in even the smallest hamlet. Plumes of smoke rose up like markers of despair, sometimes whole villages burning. The stink of decomposition tainted the wind, ever-present behind the sweet aromas of summer countryside.

Mary knew her history. During the Middle Ages, the Black Death wiped out twenty million people across Europe and killed a third of the population in its first onslaught, with even more dying subsequently. Questions haunted her. How many were dying now? Thousands? Millions? How many people were needed to create a viable population? Once that defining line had been crossed, humanity would just wither away, another extinction in a long, long line.

She had spent many an evening next to the campfire considering the nature of those malign imps she had seen tormenting the infected and spreading the plague with their touch. In her contemplation, she had sensed subtle strands coming together into a grand scheme, and as she examined them she realised that something didn't make sense.

And so she broke her journey at Stonehenge. As she entered its circle, the energy in the ground was so potent it made her entire body tingle. She found she could follow the flow by sense alone, making her way to the focal point. She wouldn't even need to spirit-fly to achieve connection.

She sat cross-legged with her eyes closed and visualised the Blue Fire. Instantly, she felt the force rise through her chakras, the Kundalini snake of the Eastern mystics. The site was like an enormous battery! The flames surged up her spine to her head, rushing into the metaphorical third eye. When it opened, it felt as if her skull was unfolding to let the universe in. And when she opened her real eyes, the truth was revealed.

A cathedral of flaming blue energy soared high over Stonehenge and everything within it was alive with such a potent spirituality that Mary reeled. The Elysium stood all around.

"Sharish?" Her guardian angel came forward at her summons. He bore a faint, knowing smile. She cut straight to what was on her mind. "You weren't there randomly at Dragon Hill. You were waiting for me." With the blue light surrounding him, he appeared truly angelic for the first time.

"Why do you say that?" he asked simply.

"I was thinking about connections and coincidences, and how some things always seem to turn out the right way . . . as if they're planned."

The quality of his smile changed slightly, suggesting infinite wisdom, forever beyond Mary's reach. "There are no coincidences."

"So, there was some kind of . . . plan. And I thought I was acting on free will."

"All living creatures naturally assume themselves to be the centre of the world. It is not within human nature to consider oneself a part of something much, much larger—"

"A cog in some machine—"

"—an essential part of a grand plan."

Mary hardened. "That Jigsaw Man—he wasn't sent after me by whoever's causing the plague. You put him on my tail."

"Not us—"

"Then whoever you're working for. It was obvious when you think about it. The thing that created the plague, those little imps, could have destroyed me in an instant. It didn't need to set that thing hunting me across five counties. What's going on?"

Sharish nodded benignly. Mary had feared the worst—that somehow the Elysium were working with the one behind the plague—but her instinct told her otherwise. "If you had not been pushed to the limits, you would have failed in your search," he said.

"So it was for my own good?" she said tartly.

Sharish pressed the fingertips of both hands together and thought for a long moment, as if deciding how much he could tell her. "Growth and development only take place through . . . trials. Not just for individuals, but for entire races. Trials bring about change within. Those who wish to achieve the next stage must embark on a spirit-quest. They must overcome obstacles, plumb the very depths of their resilience, develop new skills. *Become* . . ." He gave the final word added weight.

226

"Then the Jigsaw Man can't really kill me."

"Oh, yes, it can. And it will. If it were not a true threat, it would not serve its purpose."

"And is that what this plague is? A trial for the human race? Millions might die, but don't worry about them because the ones who survive will come out of it better?"

"It is a trial, but not of our making. All of life is a trial on the road to . . ." He caught himself. ". . . somewhere else. It is a school, if you will. A school for the spirit."

"And we don't get to graduate until we pass all the exams." She laughed without humour. "Excuse me if I don't cheer. I'm too busy concentrating on all the pain and suffering."

"I understand your reaction. From your perspective . . ."

"Oh, bollocks to it!" She flapped a hand at him. "I suppose it's too much to ask that you just leave me alone so I can get on with what I have to do?"

"There are schemes, grand schemes, great powers beyond your wildest imaginings. From your perspective, it is impossible to see what part you play, great or small. Or what is at stake."

"You could tell me."

For the briefest second, his face became frightening and filled with awe; she thought she saw whole universes reflected within it. "Your part must remain closed to you or your development will be tainted. But as to what is at stake? Everything is at stake. All of human existence has been leading to this point. We stand on the cusp of Everything . . . and Nothing. Of Life and the Void. Humanity must ascend if the seasons are to continue to turn."

Sharish saw her puzzlement, and in response reached out to touch her in the middle of her forehead. An image flashed into her mind: a figure wrapped in what looked like a shroud, the one Mary had come across at the crossroads.

"The gods who came here with the Fall are not the only ones. There are greater gods above them, older gods," Sharish said. "They are the ones who have been guiding you. In your world, they are now seen as spirits of place, *genii loci*, at crossroads and lakes and rivers and mountains, but their appearances belie their true nature."

"And the god of Wilmington and the missing Goddess are part of them?"

"They exist beyond your frame of reference," Sharish continued obliquely. "The scope of Existence is too vast to understand even a part of it, and it encompasses many things, in a scheme of bewildering complexity. For any living thing to see even the smallest aspect is too much."

"You serve the Older Gods," Mary said.

"I am one of their agents." Sharish began to lead her back to the beckoning warmth of the blue. "Now, I have answered your questions. So take this advice, too: you are important. All things are important. Everything plays a part. No one dies without a reason. None suffer unnecessarily.

"There is an abiding structure. There is meaning."

Mary gained a tremendous comfort from his words. It made her feel part of something important, so that her own troubles were diminished next to it.

"You could turn back," Sharish said. "The one following you would likely fade away in those circumstances."

Mary laughed at his transparency. "You're testing me. No, I'm not going to turn back. I'm not doing this for myself. It's for Caitlin, somebody extremely valuable to me, and it's for the Goddess. I spent all my early years betraying those closest to me. Not in any big way . . . not selling them out to the cops or robbing them blind. But betraying them in a way that felt like I'd punched a hole in my heart. I'm not going to do that again. Perhaps this is my chance to make amends."

Sharish's smile was astonishingly warm. He reached out to touch her on the forehead once again.

Sometime later, Mary found herself alone in the shadow of one of the megaliths. Sharish had gone; the cathedral of blue fire had flickered out. Her first thought was clear: of all the people who could have been chosen, why her? She wasn't deserving. Was this really leading to the punishment she had expected for the last thirty-five years? A grand scheme to pay her back for wasting her life?

Sunchaser was moored a few hundred yards down the river in a deserted port, its fantastic buildings disappearing into the depths of the forest. The final light of the fading sun had brought the midges out to dance above the water in clouds and there was a hot and sticky tropical feel to the air. It had taken Mahalia, Matt, and Jack a while to pick their way through the thick tree cover while steering Crowther along with them. It was as if he were sleepwalking; he never responded to their words, never looked to right or left, but somehow managed to put one foot in front of the other.

When they reached a jetty opposite the boat, Matt hailed the Golden One. Though Triathus didn't appear on deck, his response came back sharp and clear. *Sunchaser* drifted slowly toward them. When it was close enough, they splashed into the shallows and clambered up a rope ladder hanging over the side, hauling the professor behind them.

"Where's Triathus?" Mahalia asked warily. The boat moved away from the shore to midstream, ready to make its way upriver. After their experience in the Court of the Dreaming Song, none of them moved from the rail.

Triathus eased their worries when his voice floated up from below deck. "Down here."

Eager to see a friendly face, they hurried to the hatch, but when they peered down into the galley they were stunned into silence. Triathus sat on the floor against one of the storage units, his golden skin covered in black lines as if he had been tattooed. His breathing was shallow, and he barely had the energy to look up at them.

"God," Mahalia gasped. "He's got the plague."

Matt, Mahalia, and Jack left Crowther on deck and hurried down to the god's side. "The first signs appeared shortly after you left." Triathus's voice was clear despite his state.

Matt feebly checked the god's forehead for a temperature, then gave up. "I wouldn't know where to start—"

"Do not concern yourself." Triathus gave a faint smile. "There is nothing you can do."

"There must be something!" Mahalia protested.

Triathus shook his head sadly. "I am being removed from Existence."

"Dying," Jack said with quiet amazement. Sympathy surfaced through his inherent fear of the race that had tormented him for so long.

"I didn't think your kind would be able to catch the plague," Matt said.

Triathus's eyes moved along his limbs, seeing things that were invisible to the rest of them. "The plague is not a disease as you would perceive it. It attacks the force that binds things together . . . the energising spirit of all Existence."

"We've seen things," Matt recalled. "Flowers, plants, all being attacked by something like the plague. And there was something else." He attempted to describe the hole in space that he and Jack had seen shortly before entering the Court of the Dreaming Song.

"The Far Lands themselves are in danger of being destroyed," Triathus replied. His voice had grown a little weaker.

"We brought it here, didn't we?" Mahalia said.

"You must not blame yourselves." His eyelids fluttered and he slipped to one side. "I am sorry. I grow weak."

"Come on, let's get him to a bunk," Matt said, "make him comfortable."

"No. Take me on deck, where I can watch the sun set." There was a terrible note of finality in his request.

Jack and Matt carried the god up the steps and found a pleasant spot. He felt unnervingly light, as though there was nothing to him.

Mahalia stood at the rail, watching the darkness slowly coalesce amongst the trees. She didn't look up when Matt came to stand beside her. "You know, there's a definite feeling of *what's the point* about all this," she said.

"Of course there's a point," Matt chided. "People are dying like flies back home, you know that."

"I haven't forgotten. But do you really think we can do anything? Carlton's dead." The words caught briefly in her throat, but her expression didn't change. "Caitlin might as well be. Triathus is on his way out. The professor is a zombie. There's just you, me, and Jack. We don't know where we're going. We don't know what the cure is, or what to do when we find out. And everything is falling apart around our ears."

Matt stared into the darkening trees. "I was wondering if we should go back, try to find Caitlin."

"Good idea. You'll be able to navigate this tug through the rapids, right? We'll be able to scour the forest, dodge all those Whisperers—"

"All right." It was the first time she had heard real anger in his voice and it frightened her.

"Look, I know how you feel about her, but she's the kind of person who's going to survive if she can survive. We could always search on the way back . . ." Her words dried up; they sounded hollow even to her.

She turned her attention to Crowther, who stood, swaying, with the red light of the setting sun gleaming off the eerie mask. Mahalia pushed herself away from the rail and marched over to him. Dragging on his overcoat, she forced him to sit on the deck, and then she pulled out a knife.

Matt started in shock, and rushed over. As she brought the knife to the side of Crowther's face, Matt knocked her hand away, the knife clattering to the deck. "What do you think you're doing?"

"It's the mask—it's got a life of its own. You remember what he told us—"

"What are you doing?" he repeated. The coldness he saw in her eyes unnerved him, and it was very rare that anything upset his equilibrium.

She picked up the knife and held it easily. "I'm going to get the point into the side of his head and prise out those bolts. And if it's attached in any other way I'm going to cut it off his face."

Matt tried to decide whether she was joking or just trying to annoy him, which she seemed to try to do to everyone at one time or another—a control thing—but her face was impossible to divine. "You'd cut his face?"

"Well, let's look at it this way: what's more important to him—a career on the catwalk or being stuck forever behind that thing, with it sucking the life out of him?"

"You don't know that's what's happening. The process might just be taking longer this time. It might drop off of its own accord."

"*Might.* You like that word, don't you?" She read Matt's eyes carefully and saw that there was no point in pursuing the matter. "You've got no idea what he's like."

"And you do?"

"Actually, yes. He doesn't like being controlled—"

"Nobody does."

"He *really* doesn't. He feels he's not up to much and he tries to hide away, but all he's really doing is hiding away from the things that he believes control him. He's a free spirit." She sheathed the knife.

"You really think you're smart, don't you? And tough. But you're a kid. That's all you are. So don't ever forget it."

Mahalia watched him walk away, the ice in her face gradually giving way to a dull heat beneath.

Shortly after, the mask began acting up again. The first sign was beautiful colours shifting in psychedelic patterns over the river, their reflection making it appear as though vast and astonishing alien creatures swam back and forth just beneath the surface. For a while it was entrancing and Matt, Mahalia, and Jack watched it from different points around the deck. Then came the sounds, bass rumbles and high-pitched shrieks, invisible fireworks, music fading in and out, some almost familiar, some intriguingly otherworldly; a mystical *son et lumière*.

Slowly it became more intense and disturbing. Mahalia sought solace with Jack under a blanket near the aft-rail, kissing and groping, but he came at the touch of her hand with a young teenager's desperation. She didn't know whether to be upset or thankful for the sudden stickiness. She would have made love to him, her first time and not out of love at all, but out of a desperate need for closeness and comfort and some stability in a mad, mad world.

Sometime in the small hours, Mahalia and Jack were woken by Matt's exclamation. A tremendous surge of golden light rushed over the boat and exploded with silent but furious illumination beyond the other bank. At first, Mahalia thought it was another of the mask's creations, but when a second blast came over she realised it was too regular.

She went over to the rail and saw that some kind of battle was taking place amongst the trees on both sides of the river. Fleeting figures, some golden, some dark and squat, moved swiftly back and forth, attacking each other. Occasionally, strange sounds retorted and someone would fall before a fluttering cloud, either golden or black, moved up into the branches; or there would be a burst of light, white or multicoloured, or a surging blast of red heat.

She jumped as a plaintive keening came from behind her. Delirious, yet on some level aware of what was happening along the banks, Triathus was either crying with grief or singing, she couldn't quite be sure, but the alien sound churned up a heaving swell of emotion inside her.

Something bumped against the hull and she hurried to see if the boat itself was under attack. Numerous logs floated in the dark water—the remains of blasted trees, she thought at first, yet the shifting shadows gave the illusion of movement. Another explosion of light directly overhead revealed the truth, and Mahalia recoiled in shock. The objects *were* moving. They were not the remnants of trees, but the little, dark men, all on the verge of death, their bodies so torn and tattered that some were impossible to see as having been human-shaped at all.

Every now and then the spark in one would expire and the corpse would explode in a mass of frantic fluttering, gone in a second. Mahalia was sickened but transfixed. The flow of bodies appeared to be never-ending, the hull now sounding a relentless beat of war drums. Triathus's keening reached another level.

"This is madness." Matt was at her side, watching the water with a grim expression. "They're just slaughtering each other. What's it supposed to achieve?"

The mask's incessant hallucinogenic effects only added to their sense of dislocation. Yet in the occasional flash, they saw similar warping effects occurring far off along the horizon.

"What *is* that?" Mahalia was no longer sure of anything anymore.

Jack's hand wormed its way into hers. "It's the edge of the world."

"Where reality starts to break up and leak into the Great Beyond," Matt said, recalling what they had learned in the Court of Soul's Ease. He took a deep breath. "We're nearly there."

An hour later, with the cataclysmic battle barely diminishing, they realised Triathus's time was nearly gone. The course of the plague had been rapid. His breathing was thin, his eyes fixed. The golden light that made his skin glimmer had faded to a dull washed-out yellow and the black lines now ran the length of his body.

Matt, Mahalia, and Jack knew instinctively that it was a time for silence. Of all of them, Mahalia watched the most intently. She noted every tremor that crossed his face and it was in that intensity of observation that she saw the rarest of sights: that fleeting instant when life finally goes. It was barely perceptible, as if the slightest breeze moved from his head to his toes. A fugitive tear surprised her, but she wiped it away before the others noticed.

The golden moths came forth with a gleaming force that surprised them after the dull shadows of his passing, twirling around in a fascinating dance of grief and hope. They wound their way up in a column, finally disappearing into the heavy clouds overhead, like stars winking out.

They stood with heads bowed, and then drifted to the rail. Now the signs of the plague were unmissable on the flora: wilting leaves or blackened night blooms, black lines visible on trunks. And every now and then they would see the unsettling rips in the air that Matt and Jack had witnessed previously. The gashes were only small but growing wider, as though the entire land was a tapestry coming apart at the seams.

"Can you see—everything's getting worse the further upriver we get?" Mahalia swathed her hands in the dirty, sweaty cloth of her T-shirt.

"And it's bad enough round here," Matt said.

After the blue, there was only the unending golden sand and a sky of heat-bleached whiteness. Behind Caitlin, the energy still crackled amongst a millennia-old circle of vitrified stones. She didn't look back.

Stepping out into the wastes, she felt the sand run away from her boots. In her head, her thoughts were carried off in a whirl of black feathers. Somewhere, Amy may well have whimpered, but it wasn't heard. The pounding of Caitlin's heart was the rhythm of war drums; her vision gleamed with blood. The world lay before her, holding nothing that she feared. The path ahead drove on toward destiny.

She walked.

The mist came in with the dawn. The fighting had died away sometime during the small hours, and everything was now still and smothered beneath the blanket of grey. Beyond the muffled lapping of the river, the Wildwood exuded an intense quiet that was just as unsettling as the chaos of the previous night. As if in response, the mask had slipped into one of its calm phases.

Matt had slept in the galley to avoid the disturbances crackling all around, but Mahalia and Jack had opted to rest under their blanket on deck, dropping in and out of sleep so often that after a while it became difficult to tell what were dreams and what was reality.

It was Mahalia who woke first, confused by the stillness. The mist was dense enough to obscure both banks; they could have been adrift at sea. She went to the rail, her spirits reflecting the damp, grey weather, and listened. The lull couldn't be trusted.

She wrapped her arms around herself and watched Jack, who still slept deeply. Memories of Carlton surfaced and she shed a few tears, and after a while they were accompanied by a wash of guilt that the terrible loneliness she had feared had already partly been assuaged by Jack, whom she was convinced she loved, and was loving more with each passing day. That purity of feeling was contaminated by the desperate knowledge that she couldn't face losing him; any more loss in her life, she thought, would destroy her.

They had worried that *Sunchaser* wouldn't work for them after Triathus's death, but whatever instructions he had given to it still appeared to be in effect. It responded to their needs, going faster when they considered it necessary, or adjusting its position in the flow of the river. At that moment, Mahalia could tell from the shifting patterns in the water that the boat was drifting in toward the port bank. She told herself that couldn't be true, but then ghostly trees started to appear from the mist.

She ran to rouse Matt and Jack, and when they returned to the port rail, *Sunchaser* had come to a halt next to the bank. They were surprised to see that the Forest of the Night had ended. The trees Mahalia had glimpsed were intermittent in a flat, scrubby landscape that had the oppressive rotting-vegetation smell of a marsh, though how far it stretched was impossible to tell, for the mist only allowed twenty or so yards of visibility.

"Why have we stopped here?" Jack's voice was a nervous whisper.

"I don't think Triathus would have allowed *Sunchaser* to take us into danger." Matt took in every detail of the area in an instant. "Perhaps we're supposed to take on water here, or something."

"I don't think I'd like to drink that water." Mahalia indicated the brackish pools lying amongst the reeds and yellow marsh grass.

They looked back and forth uneasily as the mist shifted in a faint breeze, revealing and then hiding aspects of their surroundings. After a moment, Mahalia jolted when she saw that what she had taken for a copse were men, eight or more, standing stock-still, watching the boat.

Matt went for his bow, Mahalia for her sword, but the men made no attempt to attack. Bearded and long-haired, they were in their late forties and older, two certainly in their seventies, and they wore long grey robes, tied by a cord at the waist like some monk's habit, and a circlet of oak cuttings and ivy around their brows.

One who carried an intricately carved staff stepped forward. He was around sixty, but imposingly tall with piercing grey eyes. "Welcome," he said in a theatrically resonant voice, "to the last encampment of the Culture."

The leader's name was Matthias. It took a while for him to convince Matt, Jack, and particularly Mahalia that his group posed no threat, but eventually the three of them disembarked, leading Crowther carefully in their midst.

Matthias came to a halt when he saw the professor. "The mask!" he gasped.

"It's all right—he's not dangerous," Mahalia said hopefully. "Please . . . he'll just walk with us."

Matthias relented, but the other members of the group kept their eyes on Crowther.

"We still try to measure time in the old way, though it is nigh-on impossible here," Matthias said, "but it has been long, long years since we last met some of our fellows."

"You're human?" Matt said.

"There are a few of us here in the Far Lands, but not many. It is hard for most to adapt to the peculiar nature of this place. It can drive men mad, given time. It can make them forget everything they believed in."

"But you survived."

"We have a particular understanding of other realities. Come to our camp. We would hear news of our old home, and in return we can offer good food and drink. And here, everything is given freely and without obligation."

Mahalia and Matt both realised they were very hungry, though Jack appeared to eat hardly anything. "Can we afford the time?" Mahalia asked quietly.

"They might know something we can use," Matt replied. "At least we can actually *talk* to them on our own level."

They reached a tacit agreement and set off, with Matthias leading the way and the other members of his group taking up the rear. He picked a convoluted path through the treacherous marsh, treading carefully along ridges of turf concealed amongst the rushes. The density of the mist made it impossible for Matt and the others to remember their route; once in the depths of the marsh, they would not be able to find their way back without the Culture's help. On either side, the slimy pools bubbled and belched and the stink of rot was overpowering.

"Tread carefully," Matthias warned. "The Dismal Marsh may look shallow but it is deceptive. It will suck you down rapidly and there is an acidic quality to the liquor that will strip the skin from your bones."

Away in the mist, an unknown bird emitted a low cry of such mournful power that it instantly depressed their spirits. The place felt haunted.

"What are you doing here?" Matt asked.

"Finding sanctuary," Matthias replied, "and therein lies the irony. For what mortals could ever expect sanctuary in the Far Lands! That only goes to show the flaws of humankind, that we would feel safer here than in our own home. Our own kind are our enemies—we need no other predators. Greed, mendacity, arrogance, brutality, contempt—these things will stop us achieving our true place, not gods."

After a while they came to an island in the centre of the wastes. It was heavily wooded, but there were wide, grassy clearings amongst the trees. At its centre was a small encampment of roundhouses in the old Celtic style. Most were small living quarters, but there was one larger construction that served as a meeting place and general dining area. Sheep chewed lazily on grass in an enclosure, and another area had been given over to cultivation.

"We do things much as we did in the time when we fled our home," Matthias said, leading them into the great hall. It was easily large enough to encompass the whole group and many more besides. A fire blazed in the centre of the room, the smoke exiting through a hole in the roof. A wooden table had been erected in a horseshoe shape parallel to the curving wall.

Matthias took the lead seat, marked out by a high wooden back where carved dragons coiled. He motioned for Matt, Mahalia, and Jack to sit. Crowther stood behind them. Within minutes, the other members of the Culture brought in plates of cold lamb, vegetables, fruit, and jugs of cold water. "Eat and drink," Matthias said warmly. "It does me good to offer hospitality after all this time." Behind his seriousness, there was a decency that made them all at ease.

"There was a time when the Culture played a vastly important role—*the* most important role—in the business of humankind," he continued. "But I would think our name is no longer known, is that correct?"

Matt shrugged. "I'm sorry . . ."

Matthias looked down for a moment, then collected himself. "It was only to be expected. Then let me tell you our history. Our society has existed since the dawn of mankind. The responsibility placed upon us was to cater to the spiritual needs of the people, and as part of that role we collected knowledge, and guarded it, and taught, and tended, and we oversaw all the invisible worlds that crowd around our own. We stood as sentinels and guides between our world and the others."

The other members of the Culture had taken their places around the table, and they were nodding sagely but sadly as Matthias told his tale.

"We were priests of the grove. Our tool was the sacred sickle, our language the language of trees. The Culture originated in Britain and the true knowledge was amassed there, from the days before the stone circles were erected, and seekers of wisdom travelled from across the oceans to learn at our feet. We understood the Blue Fire and its nature as the lifeblood of all things, and we learned how to shape it, channel it. We knew the henges and the menhirs, and the sacred hills and the wells and the lakes were the places where it was strongest.

"And over time, in our learning and our wisdom, we began to see how it could be the basis of an age of peace and prosperity, guiding mankind on the next step of his journey to the stars. We had already developed our role as shepherds of humanity and guardians against the many forces that would wipe us from Existence. We helped to shape the Brothers and Sisters of Dragons from their earliest days. We hid the great weapons of power and marked the prophecies and warnings in the landscape so that future generations would come to know the truth, if they still had the eyes to see. And in time we began to pull the disparate Celtish tribes together into a dream of nationhood that would make our vision a reality."

Fire briefly blazed in his eyes as his memories played out across his mind; the others' faces grew stern. Mahalia looked around at them, remembering her school days, thinking perhaps that she understood the common name by which the Culture had passed into history.

"Those who believe in the power of the spirit over material things will always be easy targets for the power-seekers, and so it was for us. Just at the point when it seemed that our dreams would be made reality, the invasion happened. They came in their ships, at the command of Caesar, with a hunger for conquest and a contempt for other beliefs. They built their straight roads and sent out their marching legions, and killed the people in their thousands, driving the tribes to the fringes of the lands.

"And they knew of our power, for they had heard much of it in their homeland, and so they set out to persecute the Culture, to weaken us and make the people feel they had been abandoned. After the final battle at Mon when the Great Bastard Suetonius slaughtered the massed ranks of the tribes, we melted into the great forests and the mountains, and attempted to cling on. And so they hunted and harried us for the four hundred years of the great occupation, and slowly our number dwindled until there was only a handful of us left.

"We had one last chance to hold on to our dreams. Eight of us . . . this eight . . . were despatched into the ultimate hiding place: Tir n'a n'Og, the land of the gods themselves, where we could protect our knowledge and bide our time, and with the great warrior Jack, the Giant-Killer, known as *Church*, we formed our enclave, and waited. And waited. Here, in the Land of Always Summer, we never aged, but our purpose became diluted, for when you have all the time you need, why do anything? And so we are as you find us this day."

He sat back in his chair and closed his eyes, clearly sad and troubled. For a while, the only sound was the crackle of the fire. Matt looked bored by the storytelling and had long since turned his attention to eating his fill. But Mahalia had been listening intently, and the talk of Brothers and Sisters of Dragons made her feel sick. She remembered pressing the knife to Caitlin's throat, the splash as Caitlin fell into the water, the Lament-Brood.

Matthias must have seen the guilt in her face, for he asked sternly, "What is wrong?"

"There was a woman who travelled with us . . . everyone kept telling her she was a Sister of Dragons . . ."

The Culture grew animated; whispers rushed around the table. "A Sister of Dragons, here in the Far Lands?" one exclaimed.

"Yeah, we kind of heard that before," she said, trying not to give too much away. "But we're pretty sure she died."

Silence followed. Then Matthias said simply, "No."

Matt had perked up at the sudden interest in Caitlin. "What is it?"

"There are prophecies. These are the Great Times—the seasons that will lead into the Golden Age. But the Brothers and Sisters of Dragons must all be there to lead us through the darkest days or everything will fall into the Void."

Mahalia slumped back in her chair so that Matt's body obscured her from Matthias's probing gaze.

But he had forgotten her. He raised himself up and said, "Then there are important things to discuss, if you truly are the companions of a Sister of Dragons. But this is not the time, nor the place. We shall discuss this later. Now I must prepare."

With a new sense of purpose, he strode out of the hall. One of the other members of the Culture came over; he was younger but had a new air of deference about him. "Please—take your time, rest or explore our island. We are at your disposal."

Matt found a spot in one of the small roundhouses and decided to rest while the Culture hurried from house to house, talking amongst themselves in hushed voices, their faces flushed and eyes bright. It was as if they had woken from a long sleep.

Jack caught up with Mahalia as she perched on a mound of crumbling stones, the remnants of some ancient building that predated the Culture's occupation of the island. He slipped next to her, without touching or speaking, and for a while they watched the shifting mists. Their vantage point was above the cloud level, and it looked like a sea of sun-kissed gold was rolling out toward the canopy of forest in the distance.

"It's beautiful," Jack said quietly, and she had to admit to herself that it was. And then he added, "You're beautiful," and she started to cry, uncontrollably, the tears pent up for several years. He was surprised, and concerned, but he put his arm around her shoulders so she could rest her head against him, and let her cry herself out.

As night fell, the island became a magical place. Lanterns were lit amongst the trees, attracting a flurry of moths to dance around them. The Culture threw herbs on the fire in the meetinghouse, so that heady aromas drifted out across the entire island. And then they began to sing a strange kind of plainsong that was haunting and uplifting in a language Matt, Mahalia, and Jack didn't recognise.

As the subtle harmonies wove their spell, sparkles appeared amongst the higher branches, tiny figures on gossamer wings circling down to join in the music with voices that sounded like flutes and oboes.

Mahalia, Jack, Matt, and Crowther followed the Culture on a procession through the deep wood, and as they glanced beyond the confines of the island it appeared that sheets of blue light rippled in the air, like the aurora borealis brought down to earth.

For the first time that day, Mahalia felt soothed. She had honestly never experienced emotions so raw in her life and she had no real concept of where they had come from, or what was happening to her.

The procession ended in a clearing. Ancient stones were interspersed between the oak trees that formed the circle in which they all stood. Overhead, the full moon shone down upon them, the light so brilliant and white that it flung sharp shadows across the grass.

"There is magic in the air," Matthias intoned, "as there was in the old days, when we met in our sacred groves beneath a star-sprinkled sky, the winds filled with summer warmth and the echoes of the beyond all around." He smiled warmly. "I have spoken to our brother from across the Great Divide"—he indicated Matt, who had been locked in conversation with Matthias for the past two hours—"and it appears this is indeed the Great Time foretold for millennia. The time of change, of suffering and misery, but ultimately of rising and advancing to the ultimate heights, for no great thing can be achieved without great sacrifice. There is a Rule of Balance in the universe. We must not bow our heads in despair, for the Golden Age is near."

For the first time in many hours, Crowther moved of his own accord and sat down in the centre of the clearing, his masked head dropping into his hands. Mahalia wondered if he could hear Matthias's words.

Matthias turned to face the four cardinal points, slowly swinging a censer filled with a fragrant incense. It brought images to life in Mahalia's mind, so vivid she was convinced they were being played out in the centre of the clearing; and perhaps they were.

She saw Britain as she had known it, the teeming cities, the railways, the car-jammed motorways, the swarming people engaging with technology. And then the light source changed, as if the sun had quickly passed over, switching shadows from one direction to another. And with it came golden magical beings, some on horseback, some striding purposefully across the land.

"In the days of the tribes, they were known as the Tuatha Dé Danann," Matthias said. "They are the Golden Ones, who made their home here in Tir n'a n'Og but always had a desire for our world. They hated mortals, yet loved them at the same time. They wanted to deny us and wanted to be us, but in their great power and their willful contempt for all things they were a force for destruction. With them came their enemies, the monstrous Fomorii, shadows doing the bidding of their lord, Balor, the one-eyed god of death."

Mahalia saw a darkness, like oil, rush across the land as the golden Tuatha

Dé Danann did battle with the Fomorii. Cities were laid waste, hundreds of thousands died, technology failed. The country was brought to its knees. This, then, was how the Fall had happened. Why didn't anybody seem to know the true cause? Had the authorities insisted on keeping it from the people until the very bitter end?

"This great battle, this devastation, was predicted after the first such conflict between the two forces, in the time of the tribes: the second battle of Magh Tuireadh, when Balor was slain, only to be reborn." Mahalia could tell Matthias was passing on this information for their benefit. A more brutal battle played out before her across an ancient landscape. "In those long-gone times, the order of Brothers and Sisters of Dragons was founded, to prepare for the second coming of the gods and what was to follow. Indeed, the champions played a significant part in the defeat of the Tuatha Dé Danann and the Fomorii."

Now Mahalia saw five people: a man with long, dark hair, too serious by far; a tall woman, strong and proud; another woman with spiky blonde hair; an Asian man with sensitive features; a good-looking but hard-faced man whose torso was covered with tattoos. She had the feeling she knew the five, and then realised she had glimpsed them in the flickering blue light at the Rollrights just before she had crossed over to the Otherworld.

"Who are they?" she whispered to herself.

"Their leader was Jack Churchill, Jack, the Giant-Killer, known as Church, who departed across the seas of time to await the day when he would once more be needed," Matthias intoned. "The King across the Great Water. The Sleeping King. Call him back! Blow the horn loudly! For that day has come round!"

Matthias raised his arms above his head and blue sparks flashed between his hands. There was a corresponding rumble that shook the ground beneath Mahalia's feet, and a splashing of water away in the marshes. A ripple of emotion moved through the members of the Culture.

"What was that?" Mahalia asked uneasily.

Matthias looked directly at her. *"In Britain's darkest hour, a hero shall arise . . ."* The return of the gods and the war between them was only the first part of the prophecy. The struggle brought about changes in Existence . . . and humanity was noticed."

Mahalia shivered at the strange choice of words.

"On the edge of the universe, something has stirred. It moves this way . . . the Void!"

"What is the Void?" Mahalia whispered.

"It is said that in the true place of the dead—the Grey Lands—there is a temple. What do the dissolute dead worship?" Matthias nodded gravely. "It exists beyond the light of the farthest star. It has abided, in dreamless sleep. But now it has awoken, and we have been noticed. It is unfathomable, immeasurable. It is nothing . . . and everything. The greatest, and the least. Power, and the absence of power. It is the opposite of life. The absence of all that is and could ever be."

Mahalia had the impression of something as big as a galaxy rushing toward her, but her mind couldn't begin to encompass its form. She felt utter emptiness, a sensation of not having existed and never existing; nothing existing.

"Anti-life," Matt said under his breath. "Is the Void responsible for the plague back home?"

"There are things that prepare the way for the coming of the Void . . . out-riders, I suppose you could call them," Matthias said. "They will do anything to destroy the Blue Fire—and its champions."

There was movement beyond the wall of trees. Something large was circling the island; occasionally Mahalia glimpsed its bulk flashing past through gaps in the vegetation.

In her dream-state, Mahalia saw a black, misshapen monstrosity attempt to kill a man with a sword in front of a gothic cathedral. And then the Lament-Brood appeared in their purple mist, looking so real that Mahalia threw herself back involuntarily. "They are despair incarnate," Matthias continued. "They are life without hope. If the Void eats the world, humanity will never reach the answer that waits beyond the edge of the prophecy: the Golden Age, the time when we can prepare to take our place alongside the gods."

"How could anyone stop something like that?" Mahalia was crushed by what she had seen.

Matthias strode up to her so forcefully that Mahalia was sure he knew she had tried to kill Caitlin, but at the last he softened. "There are secret rules that lie behind the structure of Existence. We all know them in our hearts, but we never trust ourselves. There are universal rules—morality is embedded into the very stuff of reality. And so is love. And with those two things we can find hope. We must place our faith in the Brothers and Sisters of Dragons, as we did all those ages ago, for they represent the most wonderful, most powerful force of all. See!"

He raised his arm and gestured beyond the island. Now the thing that was circling had risen above the treetops and Mahalia could see it for the first time. It moved on heavy leathern wings, serpentine, its tail lashing the air, its jewelled scales glinting. It was like a comet blazing across the night sky, with the Blue Fire trailing behind it. To Mahalia, it appeared as if it were made completely of the spirit-energy, for she thought she could see through the skin to the bones and organs beneath, and through them, too; it was the Blue Fire given form, not a living thing at all.

"The First," Matthias said. "The closest to the Source. It came with us, to hide here, too, so that if all the other Fabulous Beasts were slain, if the Blue Fire itself was close to extinction, there would still be hope."

"But if Caitlin is dead . . ." Mahalia began desperately.

Matthias placed a loving hand on her forehead. "Failure will come if we allow despair into our hearts, if humanity once again fights against itself. What I said earlier, I say again: we are our own enemies. We have stopped ourselves from rising in the past. Shall we do it again?"

Mahalia felt sick. A prophecy as old as time. Pieces of a puzzle falling into place across millennia, leading up to the next stage of evolution of humanity; the greatest stage of all. And she had destroyed it in one instant, through her own terrible weakness. She didn't deserve to live.

Matthias watched the Fabulous Beast with a beatific expression. "The Fabulous Beast has been wakened by our ritual here tonight. He flies for the first time in millennia. We shall send him back to our world, to prepare for what is to come."

"Don't do that!" Mahalia pleaded. "What if everything goes wrong? He'll be lost. Something so wonderful will be lost!" She blinked away tears, the blue trail becoming a rainbow of glittering sapphires.

"If everything goes wrong," Matthias said, "it does not matter where he is, for all Existence will be gone."

chapter fifteen
THE PLAIN OF CAIRNS

"Dying is an art, like everything else.
I do it exceptionally well."

Sylvia Plath

After two hours beneath the blasting heat, a scrubby oasis rose up from the rolling dunes. Caitlin had come like a storm sweeping across the landscape, but now she decided to break her journey to refresh herself with water, though she felt as if she could walk without sustenance or rest forever. Beneath the cool shade of the palms, she scooped several handfuls of the clear water to her mouth, then immersed her face and soaked her lank, greasy hair, already gritty with the wind-borne sand that was insinuating its way into her nostrils and ears.

She was only minutes out of the oasis on the path the Morrigan had chosen for her when she became dimly aware that she was not alone.

As the sand shifted beneath the wind, it uncovered two mounds on either side of her that gradually revealed themselves to be figures lying buried just beneath the surface. Shaking the streaming gold from them, they stood up quickly and threateningly. They wore armour that brought to mind Japanese samurai: black enamel with delicate gold line-work of swirls and scrolls, helmets with broad cantilevered panels at the sides and back, long swords that curved into a broad blade. Yet within each helmet, the faces appeared to be nothing but sand.

Caitlin waited for it to slough off, but it didn't; it just shifted constantly into an approximation of faces, mouths yelling or pensive, eye hollows, noses long and thin or hooked.

"What are you?" she asked defiantly.

"We serve the Djazeem," they said together, their voices like the rush of granules through an egg timer. "You drank their water. It was not given freely—"

"I do what I will," Caitlin said, "and no one tells me otherwise."

"There are rules—"

"I make my own rules." Caitlin notched an arrow, but wondered how she could possibly harm the oasis guards if their forms truly were made of sand. "Don't stand in my way—I haven't got time."

The guards stepped toward her with the unnerving rhythm of mechanical men; their swords sliced the air, then poised ready to strike. "The Djazeem demand an offering in return for the theft of this most precious resource. You must pay—"

Caitlin loosed the arrow. It hit the right-hand guard in the middle of his face and punched through the back of his helmet. As she anticipated, it didn't affect him in the slightest. He continued to advance, pulling out the shaft as he did so and tossing it to one side with a gauntleted hand.

"So who are the Djazeem?" Caitlin said, attempting to buy time while she considered her options. But she had already placed the name the White Walker had mentioned when she had first entered the Far Lands.

"They are Lords of the Weeping Wastes," the guards said in unison, still advancing. "You are a visitor in their territory. You must obey their rules."

"I've already answered that one." Caitlin moved quickly to reclaim the discarded arrow.

The guards moved rapidly and balletically, spinning and striking so fast that their blades were a blur. Yet the instant they attacked, Caitlin's entire perception changed: it was as if time moved so slowly that her attackers were like statues. She projected the slow arc of their swords, considered several tactics, and then danced athletically out of their way. The blades slashed through the space where she had stood, the guards spinning in surprise that she had evaded their attack so easily.

Their dance continued for five full minutes, Caitlin weaving through their attack, the guards growing more determined, their movements more complex.

Caitlin knew she could run and would probably evade them, given time, but the Morrigan's scratching voice inside her head suggested another path.

She came to a sudden stop, no longer knowing what she was doing; the Morrigan seized full control. It felt as if a weight was forming deep in the pit of her stomach. The guards didn't slow in their attack; their swords swept fluidly to slice through Caitlin from two separate directions. The last remaining conscious part of her knew she no longer had a chance to avoid them.

The weight in her stomach twisted and turned rapidly, as if a family of rats nested there. Electricity rushed to her extremities and she was thrown backward, a black cloud erupting out of her. Crows. Born from within her, so many that they obscured the white-metal sky, the shifting sands, the two attacking guards. And still they came, pouring out of her in a constant stream of black feathers, thrashing wings, sharp talons, and darting beaks. Their deafening cawing was like the sound of a summer storm.

The cloud billowed and then drew in with hurricane force on the two guards. Caitlin couldn't see what happened in the frantic attack, but within seconds the birds were retreating inside her. It felt like being pounded by rocks.

Briefly, she lost consciousness, and when she was next aware, there wasn't a crow in sight. She lay on her back on the downward slope of a dune. Her hands went to her stomach, which was sore, as though she'd eaten a barrel of sour apples, but beyond that she was unharmed.

Pulling herself to her knees, she saw the guards' armour scattered all around, their sand bodies lost to the surrounding dunes. Movement caught her eye. A creature resembling a hairless monkey the size of her palm crawled out from beneath one of the breastplates.

Caitlin darted forward and snatched it up. It squealed in terror and pain as her fingers closed around it, the skin warm and obscene to her touch. But she held on tight and brought it up to her face.

"Do not harm me!" it said in a high-pitched whine.

"Now you listen to my rules," Caitlin said. "In return for your survival, you'll answer some questions. Do you understand?"

"I serve the Lords of the Weeping Wastes—"

"I'm not going to ask anything that goes against your obligations to your bosses. All I want is directions." The tiny creature stared up at her with its little currant eyes. Caitlin felt the rapid beat of its heart through its papery skin. "OK. How far am I from the Endless River?" she asked.

"It lies southeast of here," the guard replied curtly. "Follow the route you were taking, then turn south when you reach the edge of the Weeping Wastes. You will have to pass through the Plain of Cairns . . ." A flicker of something crossed its face, quickly stifled; Caitlin had the impression that the Plain of Cairns was not a place she should attempt to cross. "Two sunrises should see you there."

"Very good. Now, the river was taking me to a place where I could find something very important to me . . . it's called the House of Pain. Do you know it?"

The creature gave a high-pitched mewling that made it appear even more like a monkey. Its eyes ranged in its head, wide and frightened. "The House of Pain is not of the Far Lands."

"I was told it stands—"

"It stands on the Borderlands, but it is *not* of the Far Lands. It comes and goes between here and there . . . some say it even exists here *and* there. It belongs to the Great Dark."

"If I chose to go directly to the House of Pain—"

"You would not return."

"—which way would I go?"

The creature shivered, rolled its eyes, but saw no reason to try to dissuade her. Coldly, it said, "When you reach the edge of the Weeping Wastes, it will present itself to you. If it requires you, you will not be able to turn away. And there shall come an ending."

Caitlin glanced toward the horizon; her decision had already been made. It would be a waste of time to seek out her fellow travellers; besides, she had always known it would be down to her in the end. "One last thing: I don't want any more trouble from your kind, or the Djazeem. I'm just going to pass through and leave you to your own devices. Understand?"

He nodded eagerly. "And should we offer the same protection to any who follow in your wake?"

"Sure. Why not? Though I can't imagine anyone would want to follow in my footsteps." She saw the creature's fellow watching malignantly from underneath the other breastplate, and tossed the one in her hand toward him. He hit the sand with another squeal. "Now," she said, "not long ago I learned a little word to whisper to you."

Matt, Jack, and Mahalia said good-bye to the Culture on the misty banks of the river. The members of the secretive group, now eager to play some part in the events they had awaited for so long, could barely wait to get back to their camp to scheme and plot. Mahalia hardly said a word. The weight of her actions still lay heavily on her, but she was starting to see a way through it.

As the Culture trailed back through the marsh to begin the ritual that would return the First to the human world, *Sunchaser* moved back into the stream. The mists disappeared so quickly, it became apparent they were part of the peculiar defences of the Culture's home, and soon the sun was beating down hard on a savannah that reached up to a range of snow-topped mountains in the east, and disappeared toward the horizon in the west. Occasionally the yellow grass shifted violently as if large beasts were tracking the boat, but they saw no other sign of life.

"He's off again," Matt noted to Mahalia and Jack.

At the aft rail, Crowther sat rigidly while the mask began to tune into its psychedelic displays.

"It started the minute we left the mist," Matt noted.

"Perhaps we should have left him with the Culture," Jack suggested.

"No," Mahalia said firmly. "He's one of us."

"You say that now." Matt pulled his sweaty shirt away from the skin of his chest; it was growing hotter. "You saw how bad it was getting. If he spins out of control, we're in trouble."

"We'll think of something," Mahalia said.

Matt thought for a moment and then said, "You know we'll have to kill him. We can't risk failing the mission."

Mahalia fixed a cold eye on Matt that made him feel instantly uncomfortable. "This leadership thing is going to your head," she said. "You sound like some stupid army man. Or," she added as she started to walk toward the professor, "like me."

She approached Crowther cautiously. It was impossible to tell exactly how the mask would react, but the nascent light displays moved away from her enough for her to conclude that she was seen as safe.

She sat next to him and said gently, "Professor, can you hear me?" There was no reply, but she thought she saw the silver mask move a little in her direction. "I saw you in the clearing last night. Something had changed. I think you're aware in there. *Can* you hear me?"

It seemed as if he wasn't going to answer, but then his muffled voice sounded. "Yes."

She felt honest relief. "If you're yourself again, why don't you take the mask off?"

"I can't."

"Won't it let you?"

"No. I won't let me." He turned his head away.

"Professor, you know what the mask can do. You told us yourself. It's getting out of control out here." She glanced back to Matt, who was watching her, arms folded. "They won't let you stop us getting to the cure."

"I know what you're saying."

"Then take the mask off, for all our sakes."

"Go away," he said bluntly. "Don't ask me again . . . for your sake."

She waited for a moment or two to see if he would soften, but his head remained turned away and the intensity of the mask's display increased, as if responding to Crowther's emotions.

"So are we going to have to kill him?" Matt asked when she returned.

She walked straight past him to the prow. "We'll probably all be dead long before we have to make that decision."

The mood on the boat was grim, and they all settled down in separate areas, conserving their strength in the growing heat; Mahalia told Jack she needed some time to think, and while it upset him, he acceded to her wishes.

The savannah gradually gave way to a scrubby wasteland and then to an arid rock-strewn landscape that resembled the surface of Mars. The river had grown much narrower and it was apparent that they would soon have difficulty following its dwindling course. Before they had to make any decision, the boat drifted over to a wooden jetty. It was rickety and treacherous, with missing planks, some broken; it looked barely used.

"Terminus," Matt said.

They collected their things and disembarked, sorry to be leaving the relative security of *Sunchaser*.

"Which way now?" Jack asked.

Matt pointed toward the northern horizon where the sky shifted with colours like a kaleidoscope. There was an area of darkness that hinted at some kind of structure, but it made their eyes hurt to stare at it for too long.

"The House of Pain," he said redundantly.

"So all we have to do is cross this dusty old plain with all those piles of rocks," Jack said, peering from beneath a shading hand.

"Cairns," Mahalia said. "They're called cairns."

Across hills and fields she came, down long roads filled with shadows, under nights of sparkling stars, through dappled forests, across windswept plains where the echoes of ancient voices could be heard, over crystal streams and the summer-drenched meadows of wild barley and poppy. At times, Mary thought the journey would never end. It was a quest that left the path and went deep into the heart of her, where dark caverns loomed like cathedrals, unexplored throughout her long life, the terrors they contained shrinking from the lamps of her eyes.

When she finally emerged from the lanes leading out of Bradford-on-Avon on a sparkling morning of blue sky and hot sun, she was finally reborn into a new life, though she still hadn't truly understood that fact. Death continued to track her relentlessly, and it had drawn closer; on several occasions she had seen the twisted form jerking its way across the landscape and she had been forced to pick up her pace. But it no longer frightened her; it was simply there, as it always would be.

And now she had reached her final destination. Bath was spread out before her, home of her spiritual ancestors for ten thousand years, since the first Neolithic hunter-gatherers had left their simple offerings at the gushing hot springs. Mary knew her history and she knew her Craft, and everything had pointed her toward this place as the solution to the questions that gripped her.

Yet this was not the Bath she remembered. Vegetation swarmed over it, almost obscuring the grand Georgian buildings, the classical Royal Crescent, Pulteney Bridge with its echoes of the Ponte Vecchio. A wall of blackthorn the height of three men, softened by climbing honeysuckle and clematis, circled the entire city. Mature trees sprouted through the hard asphalt of the city centre's roads. Ivy draped from chimneys and gorse clustered in bushes, wild roses like small explosions of colour bloomed in every direction.

Though nature had started to reclaim many aspects of civilisation since the Fall, the density and maturity of the flora was too advanced. Magic was all around, in more ways than one: the vision of the works of humanity and nature in harmony was undeniably uplifting.

Yet the city was eerily still. No smoke drifted up from the many chimneys, nothing moved on the winding, ancient streets, neither human nor animal. Yet *something* was there; Mary could feel it, like a tremendous weight pressing outward.

Desperately hoping she had made the right decision, she set off down the slope toward the city.

She walked for almost a mile around the perimeter before she found an opening. It was barely wide enough for one person to pass through, and the vicious black-thorns were so dense and so close that one misstep would have raised blood. As she moved cautiously along the winding path, she realised it had been carefully designed to allow only one person to enter at a time, either for defence or as a processional route to some sacred inner sanctum; perhaps both.

The wall of blackthorn must have been fifty feet thick, and when she emerged once more into the sunlight, she felt as if she was being born into a new world. The city no longer had the feel of any human place; it was otherworldly, heavy with mystery and a profound sense of sanctity. As Mary moved out into the sun-kissed streets, now filled only with the rustling of leaves and the perfume of wild flowers, she felt she was on the verge of some tremendous transcendent revelation. Everything around her, even the air itself, was heavy with meaning.

Feeling humbled, she made her way through the city slowly, drinking in the incredible peace, reaching out every now and then to trail her fingers through the leaves or to caress the petals of a flower. The old tourist signs still remained to guide her way, an irony that was not lost on her.

Bath had always had a time-lost quality, with its ancient sites pressed up close against modern developments, but now it was even more affecting. And as Mary moved through it, she realised the flashes she had seen from the corners of her eyes were not simply sunlight breaking through branches. There was movement, but not life.

Ghostly men and women moved thoughtfully amongst the foliage. She saw strangely attired figures she took to be the Celts who had erected the first shrine at the city's springs in 700 BCE, and Romans who had come after, and others in the clothes of later ages, drifting in a tranquil state, barely seen but their presence felt. They weren't frightening; rather, they gave Mary an odd feeling of comfort.

Finally she came to her destination. Twin fires burned furiously in braziers on either side of the path, though there was no sign of anyone who could possibly have tended them. Beyond, the modern entrance hall to the site of the Roman baths was almost hidden beneath a thick covering of vegetation. But the doors stood open, the interior impenetrably dark.

Mary summoned up the reserves of her character. It was the time of reckoning.

"This water isn't going to last long." Mahalia moistened her lips from the canteen they had brought from *Sunchaser*.

Matt shielded his eyes from the sun to peer across the dusty plain, where only crabgrass and rocky outcroppings broke the monotony of the cairns, so regularly spaced on the sweeping uplands that they resembled some geometric design intended to be viewed from the heavens. "I don't know—it's hard to tell from this perspective, but it shouldn't be too long before we reach the other side."

"What if there's no water there, either?" Jack asked. "Not that I . . . really need it." He cast a worried look at Mahalia.

"I think that's the least of our problems," Matt replied.

Though the sun was low on the horizon, the sky was a mass of shifting colours, purple folding into gold, bubbles of red bursting into green shimmers. The sense that the Borderlands was now close was also evident in the surging eerie noises that occasionally materialised out of the wind, like the effects of some psychedelic garage band. Flavours burst on their tongues—strawberries, burned iron, cardamom, and lime. The aroma of rose petals and incense filled the air.

Crowther followed them, his own twisting of reality more muted in comparison but still disturbing, windows onto other worlds opening here and there when they least expected it.

They had been walking all day across the unrelenting landscape, the river now lost far behind them. Their clothes and hair were white with the dust that worked its way into everywhere, stinging their eyes and choking their throats.

Jack eyed one of the cairns as they passed. "What are they?"

"Just piles of rock." Weariness was evident in Matt's voice. "Someone had too much time on their hands."

"That shows how much you know," Mahalia said sullenly. "They're memorials. In some cultures, they're burial mounds."

Matt shrugged as if the distinction was unimportant, but Mahalia's words struck a chord with Jack.

He stopped and scanned the wide plain uneasily, taking in the countless cairns that stretched as far as the eye could see in every direction. "Burial mounds?" he repeated.

"That's a heck of a lot of dead bodies," Matt commented.

Mahalia saw the thoughts flickering across Jack's face; he looked ghostly in the fading light. "What is it?" she asked gently.

"I heard something," he began, struggling to pluck information from his memory's depths, "in the Court of the Final Word. About a place of the dead . . . *like an annex of the Grey Lands*, that's what they said. It had another name—"

"We don't need a history lesson," Matt snapped, with irritation born of too much trudging. "Just keep walking or we'll never get to the other side."

Jack did as he was told, but kept searching for the information niggling at him. Crowther's warping of what passed for reality was setting them all on edge; it was impossible to concentrate on anything.

Yet even through the mask's weird effects, something unusual caught Mahalia's eye. "Did you see that?" she asked. "One of the rocks rolled off that cairn over there."

"It's all that stuff the prof is causing," Matt said. He picked up his pace, eager to get through this area before dark. They could all sense something in the air, though they had been putting it down to the unusual atmosphere in the proximity of the Borderlands.

"That's just light and sound," Mahalia snapped at his dismissive attitude. "The mask isn't generating any vibrations."

A rock rolled off another cairn to her left, and another directly ahead. This time Matt saw it, too. The stones appeared to have moved of their own accord.

"See!" Mahalia said with a note of triumph.

Matt paused, then slowly turned, scanning the area. Rocks were rolling off cairns all over the place, one after the other, opening up gaps into their interiors. He glanced up at the sky. The psychedelic warping offered a deceptive illumination; the sun was almost down. On the other horizon, a full butterscotch moon was rising.

A jolt transformed Jack's face. "The Land of the Sleeping Dead!"

More rocks fell. Every cairn was coming alive. Movement was visible in the cracks splitting open the ones near at hand.

"There are things inside!" Mahalia gasped.

A ghostly white hand began to emerge from one of the openings.

"Jesus!" Matt said under his breath. He grabbed Mahalia and Jack, and yanked them forward.

"The professor!" Mahalia exclaimed.

"Leave him." Matt began to run, then looked at the innumerable cairns stretching out into the distance and realised the futility of trying to escape.

"The Baobhan Sith!" Jack said, his face as white as death.

"What are they?" Mahalia asked. She began to move forward, saw another figure begin to emerge, and turned back, only to be confronted by yet more.

"They lie in wait to suck the blood of travellers . . . you can't escape them . . ." Jack said breathlessly.

Matt noticed the cairns in the distance were unmoving. "They're waking up as the moon's rays fall on them!" he said. "If we run, we might be able to outpace them." He sprinted from a standing start.

"You can't escape them!" Jack yelled. Nonetheless, he grabbed Mahalia's hand and ran, too.

The white dust rose in clouds under their pounding feet. Across their field of vision, shimmering shapes emerged from the cairns. There would be thousands, perhaps tens of thousands; and Matt, Jack, and Mahalia were right in the centre of the vampiric creatures' homeland.

Matt's greater strength pulled him ahead, but he fell back when he saw Jack and Mahalia floundering. The Baobhan Sith drew slowly from their dark holes, hair long and wild, faces as inexpressive as dolls', dressed in tattered shrouds.

The shadows retreated before the moon's rays at a remarkable rate; there was no way Matt, Jack, and Mahalia could keep up. One night creature pulled itself out near their feet as they ran, its dumb expression flickering at their passing. Hands reached out of the cairns ahead of them. At their backs, Matt, Jack, and Mahalia could feel the weight of the massing ranks of the Baobhan Sith.

And then a terrible shriek cut through the dusty twilight air. Mahalia felt as if she'd been stabbed in the heart. It was an alarm. Matt glanced back, as more reverberating shrieks picked up the call, the look on his face revealing the horror they all felt.

And then the shrieks were all around. From the corners of her eyes, Mahalia could see masses of wretched figures sweeping toward them, a tidal wave of teeth and clutching hands. The cairns ahead were almost exploding as yet more bloodsuckers emerged rapidly in answer to the call.

And suddenly they had nowhere to run. Mahalia dropped to the ground, huddling into a ball. Jack threw himself over her to protect her. They couldn't see Matt.

All around, the Baobhan Sith rushed toward the small circle of dust where they lay; it felt like the only tiny area in the vast plain not covered by bloodthirsty bodies.

And just as they screwed their eyes shut ready for the creatures to fall on them, something very strange happened. A powerful scent of roses descended, followed by the most intense silence Mahalia had ever heard; in a fraction of a second, there was no shrieking, no wind, nothing. She opened her eyes to see a glistening bubble all around them; Matt was sprawled in the dust nearby, blood streaming from the rake-marks of talons across his forehead.

Beyond the bubble, Mahalia could see the Baobhan Sith swarming like roaches, slipping around the edge of the bubble, unable to see it or Mahalia, Jack, and Matt within.

"What's going on?" Jack asked, dazed.

Matt pointed through the bubble along the route they had come. Crowther stood there, the mask staring blankly at them. The Baobhan Sith were keeping well away from him, fearful of the power he was exhibiting.

Mahalia jumped to her feet. "See! He *is* looking out for us!"

The bubble fizzed and faded in parts before strengthening again.

"I don't think he can keep it up for long," Matt said. He looked around frantically for an option, then inspiration lighted on his face. Scrambling on his knees, he dived into one of the cairns and began to pull the rocks toward the entrance. "Come on!" he shouted to the other two.

"You're crazy!" Mahalia said. "What happens when they go back in there? We'll be trapped!"

"Any better ideas?" Matt snapped. "I'm betting they won't return until sunup. If they really are like Jack said, they probably can't stand the rays. So when this one starts coming in, we bolt out. If day's coming, they won't be able to follow us."

Mahalia wasn't convinced, but she couldn't see another option. She pushed Jack in first, then forced her way in behind. It was cramped inside. The hard rock of the cairn jabbed into backs, ribs, heads, elbows.

With Matt's help, Mahalia rebuilt the doorway, and just as the last stone slipped into place, the bubble disappeared with a faint *pooof*!

Mahalia's heart instantly sprang into her throat. Through the gaps between the rocks, she saw the Baobhan Sith surge like wild animals into the space they had just vacated. Her breath caught. Would they see them hiding there, rip the cairn open and drag them out to tear out their throats with those needle-teeth?

For a second it seemed that they might. They came right up to where the opening had been, rushing round the edge of the cairn emitting that bone-chilling shriek. Yet none of them bent down to peer into the darkened cracks, or tugged at the precariously piled rocks. She could only guess that they must be predators with minimal intelligence. The thought did nothing to ease her fear.

For the long hours of the night, she remained rigid, afraid that the slightest movement would be heard; it felt as if she hadn't even taken a breath, and by the time the darkest hours had passed her chest burned with the strain.

The shrieking died down after a while, but the Baobhan Sith continued to roam in their masses, and on several occasions one came right up to the cairn, as if it had seen something within. Jack's nails dug into her shoulder more than once, but still she maintained her motionless vigil.

And for all that time Crowther stood stock-still nearby, the mask throwing off loops and warped flashes of light. The night creatures shied away from him like whipped dogs.

Finally, the sky began to lighten. In one eerie moment, the entire seething plain of night creatures stopped moving, their noises draining away, and they turned as one to look toward the point where the sun would shortly rise. After a moment that may have been fearful or perhaps even respectful, they began to slink back to their cairns.

Mahalia felt Matt flinch against her back. Everything rested on the next few moments.

All around, the Baobhan Sith started to slip into their holes, the rocks magically rolling back into place. The night creatures passed on either side, heading home, and at last one began to stalk directly to the entrance. It paused outside, puzzling that the opening had been filled, and then began to pluck the rocks away with its unfeasibly long, thin fingers.

Matt tapped Mahalia on the shoulder and whispered, "Now."

Without thinking twice, Mahalia drove forward, sending the remaining rocks flying. Jack and Matt piled out after her.

The Baobhan Sith drew back, hissing like a cat, but it didn't attack. Instead, it cast repeated menacing glances as it passed by them, easing into the cairn and replacing the rocks behind it.

More Baobhan Sith streamed by on all sides, snarling or scraping the air with their talons, but not one of them made a move toward the companions. The three of them were frozen in the face of the preternatural terror, until finally they accepted that they weren't going to be harmed. The Baobhan Sith were driven by one primal fear: of the rising sun. Matt motioned for the other two to follow him, and they quickly picked a path, continually veering away from any of the Baobhan Sith who came too close, just in case.

Mahalia was soaked in sweat. She still couldn't believe they had got out; she had resigned herself to a quick and painful death. Glancing back hopefully, she was overjoyed to see Crowther plodding relentlessly behind them. She felt a deep and surprising connection with the professor that had crept up on her; even more surprisingly, it felt good. Once they found some way to get the mask off him, she was determined to let him know that he was a good person and that she trusted him. She felt there was no higher recommendation.

By the time the sun emerged fully above the horizon, the last of the night creatures were gone, and only then did they allow themselves the chance to celebrate. Mahalia and Jack hugged each other and then they both hugged Matt.

"I thought our number was up there!" Matt gushed. "Good old Crowther. Who'd have thought the old fool would save the day?"

Mahalia went over to thank the professor personally, but he gave no response at all. She returned to the others, undeterred.

Their survival invigorated them, wiping away the exhaustion they had felt for most of the journey. "You know what?" Mahalia said. "If we can get through that, we can get through anything."

"Don't speak too soon," Matt cautioned, but his face showed that he clearly felt the same way.

The Plain of Cairns ended in a band of lush greenery. Once they saw it, they ran as fast as they could, whooping and skipping. Just beyond, in the shade of some tall trees, lay a series of lakes. They dived in fully clothed, washing the dust from their hair and throats.

Afterward, they lay on the banks, resting and talking quietly, but they knew it was only a brief respite. The sky overhead mutated furiously with colours and sounds.

"Close," Matt mused as he looked up at it. He nodded to a steep, grassy rise beyond the lakes. "Just over there, I would say."

They steeled themselves, then set off, climbing slowly, putting off what they knew lay ahead. As they neared the top of the rise, the House of Pain loomed up in the distance. It appeared to reach right up into the sky itself, but their minds still couldn't absorb any detail. They saw it as just a black smudge on their vision, and the more they looked, the more it made their heads hurt and the queasier they felt.

Finally they reached the top of the rise. As they looked out across another massive plain of grassland and rocky outcroppings, they realised that the Baobhan Sith hadn't been the worst thing at all.

Purple haze drifted as far as the eye could see, like the smoke of some First World War battlefield. Within it and behind it lay the army of the Lament-Brood, now swelled to apocalyptic proportions. The Whisperers faced the rise, completely surrounding the House of Pain, their numbers disappearing into the misty distance.

"Jesus H. Christ," Matt said in awe.

"It looks like they've taken over everybody in the Far Lands," Jack gasped. "There must be a hundred thousand of them."

"And there's just four of us." Mahalia turned from the terrible spectacle and faced them with glittering eyes. Inside her, passion carved its way to the surface. This was it: her time. There was no backing away, no chance of survival. It was all about going out in the best way possible and she didn't care about death. She just wanted to do it right.

She smiled tightly and said, "Game on."

chapter sixteen

THE HOUSE OF PAIN

"I never said, 'I want to be alone.' I only said,
'I want to be LET alone.' There is all the difference."
Greta Garbo

Despair washed up from the grassy plain on the back of a hundred thousand whispers. Mahalia, Matt, and Jack did their best to keep its insidious flow at bay—humming, chattering, staring deep into each other's eyes—but at some level they were still tainted.

"They're not going to let us leave, are they?" Jack said dismally. He glanced back across the massed ranks as if he hoped they'd all been magicked away while his gaze was averted. "We should have known it would turn out like this. We never stood a chance."

Matt's face was filled with the realisation of their failure. He looked back at the Plain of Cairns and then over the Lament-Brood. "He's right—it's all over. We can't go back, and if we go forward we'll be wiped out in seconds . . . and any minute now they're going to come and get us." He bowed his head, attempting to come to terms with his impending death. Taking a deep breath, he looked up and forced a smile. "No point crying about it. This is it."

"Then we should go out in style," Mahalia stressed. "I don't want to be forgotten. I don't want to be some nameless loser, or if people do remember me, I don't want them calling me some selfish, spoilt little girl. I want everyone to remember me like the Culture talked about those five who stood up against the gods when they came back. They're like some myth now . . . like King Arthur and his knights or something. That's what I want." She bit her lip hard, holding back her emotions so that she could appear defiant.

Matt shrugged. "I don't think there's going to be anybody reporting back—"

"You don't know! Maybe the Void or whatever you want to call it will see us taking a stand here and think, *If all the human race is like that, I don't stand a chance. I'm going back where I came from . . .*"

Matt grinned, then shook his head dismissively.

"Don't laugh! You *don't* know. Sometimes when you do things, they take on a life of their own. Actions have energy." She waved him away and went to cross the rise to the downward slope.

Matt caught her arm. "You're right—we need to do this together. It's

Roarke's Drift time." He looked from Mahalia to Jack. "You'd better say your good-byes."

His words brought home to them the awful truth of what was about to happen. Jack and Mahalia fell into each other's arms with a desperation that brought tears to their eyes. Their kisses were just as hard and before they pulled apart they whispered into each other's ears the promise of what might have been.

Once Mahalia broke away, she instantly became unemotional, didn't even cast another look at Jack. "OK," she said. "Let's do it."

Before they began, she hurried back to Crowther. "Professor, you helped us on the Plain of Cairns and we're eternally grateful for that—you saved our lives. But we need you again. And this is even worse. If there's anything you can do . . . anything . . ." There was no response, but Mahalia was convinced that he had heard her. Against all her natural reservations, she threw her arms around his neck and hugged him, just briefly, before returning to the others.

"All set?" Matt asked, as if they were going for a stroll.

As they moved down the rise, the whispering grew more intense and the urge to lie down and give up became overwhelming. "Fight it for as long as you can," Matt said. He glanced over at Jack. "You're going to do the business?"

"As much as I can. Till I burn out—or blow the universe to kingdom come."

Facing the Lament-Brood, they were struck by the eeriness of the scene. The Whisperers stood like statues, facing the four of them, with only the rustling sound of their despairing voices to indicate that they were alive. There was a sea of them, all monsters that had once had living shapes but were now twisted and broken, with bones protruding, skulls gleaming, unnatural but perversely improved, turned into killing machines. The purple mist blew back and forth in a light breeze, leaking from the orifices and the ruptures in their bodies. And as the mist hid and revealed and hid again, Matt had the impression that there was only one beast waiting for them, a massive organism with one mind and one terrible purpose.

Mahalia saw the weapons—the swords and spears and axes—and wondered how long the four of them would last: Three minutes? One? Thirty seconds?

She expected Matt to give a signal, but he just pulled out the scimitar he had brought from the Court of Soul's Ease and charged down the slope. She followed, her Fomorii blade rusted and bloodstained, ready to take as many of them with her as she could manage.

Jack was at her side, but then he flexed himself and let out a small burst of the white light he kept coiled within him. It wasn't the full destructive force she had witnessed at the entrance to the Court of the Dreaming Song, but it was enough to blast five of the Lament-Brood into pieces. He was trying to eke his power out before he was struck down by the debilitating exhaustion it always left in its wake. The old, familiar Mahalia wished he would go for broke and take out the whole of Existence; she didn't want to think of it going on without her.

And then they were at the foot of the slope and into the first rank of Whisperers. Matt took a head off at the shoulders, then brought his sword down sharply to cleave another skull from temple to chin. The Lament-Brood didn't wait to be attacked. They surged forward, wielding their weapons like automata. The only thing that saved Matt from being overwhelmed was that the Whisperers were packed so tightly they could barely swing their swords.

Matt parried, ducked, tried to counterattack, but they already had him on the back foot. Though she fought wildly herself, Mahalia was aware of what a good fighter he was, striking and defending with all the skills of a professional.

The thought was gone in an instant as the sickening whispering rose up around her and the purple mist washed into her mouth and nostrils. All she could see was a wall of bodies pressing against her. She put her weight behind her sword and drove it into a belly; the cruelty of the Fomorii design allowed the serrated edge to rip through the skin and entrails with ease. She pulled it out, soaking herself in a spout of cold blood, and rammed it up into a bared throat.

Two were down, yet already her arms were ringing from the force of her attack and her muscles stung. She wasn't strong enough to keep it up for long. She wished she'd trained more, not been so arrogant, thought ahead, but she'd always considered that in the event of any crisis she'd be away, leaving some other sucker to stand and fight.

Her concentration slipped and one of the Lament-Brood broke through to ram a spear toward her chest. Jack came in from nowhere, deflecting the weapon with his arm before releasing a concentrated blast of his explosive power that reduced the attacker to atoms. Mahalia was half aware that Jack's eyes were smoking as if a mighty fire raged within him.

Time stretched out forever, every second packed with cut and parry, ducking and striking, feeling every ache and pain, every scratch racked up on their bodies. But they had made hardly any inroad into the ranks.

And then an enormous roaring rose up behind them, like a jet taking off. Mahalia had a half-impression of something scarlet and gold rushing past her shoulder and then a fifty-foot square of Lament-Brood exploded ahead of them, showering body parts over a wide area and smelling like a bonfire at a landfill.

The shock wave knocked her onto her back. When her head had stopped ringing, she looked back to see Crowther striding from the slope onto the plain. From her perspective, it looked as if he had grown in size, was still growing, filling with a terrible power. Walls of light shimmered off the silver mask—red, blue, green, yellow. Things formed in the air all around him, seemingly out of the very air itself. She saw a rose fold in on itself, becoming a spectral face in agony, becoming a hawk; and nearby, a lizard, more haunting faces in various stages of torment, lightning, cloud-forms, fire. The emotional aspect of the mask made him even more terrible, and it seemed that every step shook the ground.

A Whisperer who ventured too close was taken apart, the skin, muscles, organs, bones all unpeeling to scatter on the ground. And Crowther didn't even give him an instant's attention.

Mahalia rolled away to get out of his path. He strode by, another blast of energy roaring out to devastate another section of the army. The Lament-Brood were rooted, not really understanding what they were facing. For a second, Mahalia entertained the fantasy that they might win; that Crowther could just keep walking right up to the House of Pain, blasting anything that came near him, with Mahalia, Jack, and Matt hurrying in his gore-soaked wake.

But two things made her realise this would never happen. As Crowther marched on, a bolt of scarlet lightning roared from his head, twisted and crackled in the air, and then rushed toward Matt. It was only his battle-heightened reactions that allowed him to throw himself out of the way at the last instant, and even then the blast threw him head over heels, the soles of his boots smoking with heat from the explosion. Crowther could no longer control the mask.

The second thing happened at the same time. The Lament-Brood regrouped and drove forward. With the luxury of the space around her, Mahalia had a better view across the plain, and there, in the midst of it all, she was overwhelmed by the weight of numbers ranged against them. A hundred thousand didn't do it justice; it was just a number. The Lament-Brood reached to hell and back. Even Crowther, with all his elemental fury, could not get through them.

And so they battled, for fifteen minutes or more, with Crowther laying waste to vast numbers of the Lament-Brood, but with more always flooding in to take their place. Mahalia, Matt, and Jack took up the rear, preventing any of the Whisperers from coming up on Crowther's blind side, but with eerie prescience he was always aware of any attack at his back, and picked off the warriors with unceasing accuracy.

Mahalia, Matt, and Jack hacked and slashed, and occasionally danced out of the way of the mask's wild blasts. Some came too close for comfort, and they were all soon sporting burn marks on arms or face. The Lament-Brood replaced each fallen warrior almost instantly. The intense background noise of the constant whispering reached out with its infection of despair. On more than one occasion, Jack's sword arm began to drop and Mahalia had to knock it back up.

It was Matt, always on guard, never missing anything, who saw the movement along the rise. He kept glancing up as he fought, unable to give it his full attention, so he couldn't be quite sure if he was seeing what he thought he was seeing. Eventually he couldn't deny it.

"I think," he shouted breathlessly, "we've got help."

Caitlin was the first to crest the rise. With eyes that could pick out a grain of sand a mile distant, she instantly took in Mahalia, Matt, and Jack battling in the sea of swarming bodies. It was difficult to miss Crowther, who appeared, to her eyes, to be enveloped in a scarlet mist.

The vast army of the Lament-Brood had only given her a few seconds' pause—she had expected some kind of defence to prevent a frontal assault on the House of Pain, and so she had come prepared.

She felt the others appear at her back. The warriors of the Djazeem numbered no more than five hundred, but Caitlin knew the Lament-Brood would find them as difficult to fight as the desert sand. She hoped it would give them enough of an advantage.

Oddly, in that moment, her thoughts turned to Matt. She realised how close she had grown to him before she had been flung out into Birmingham and how much she had missed him. It was coupled with a dull sense of anger now that she was close to finding out who had murdered Carlton. She was convinced she knew who it was, and there would be a terrible price to pay. When she tried to picture Carlton's face, she saw only Liam's, driving the thump of blood in her head.

As if falling from a lofty peak, Caitlin plummeted into the wind-blasted Ice-Field at the back of her head and the Morrigan rushed forth. Everywhere was red. The thunder of war drums was all around. She moved forward.

She'd loosed all the arrows in her quiver in rapid fire before she was halfway down the rise. Every one had hit its target, carving out a small opening in the ranks of the Lament-Brood. They were all facing away from her, their attention focused on Crowther and the others.

As she sprinted past the first victims, Caitlin plucked up a spear and used it to pole vault over the heads of the first Whisperers. As she came down, she whipped the spear around, taking out eyes, ramming it into faces, hacking at anything in range.

Bodies fell under her. She was a blur of violence, discarding the spear and snatching up a sword when that became the best option, spraying herself with gore, moving so quickly she opened up a space around her.

And then, as the Djazeem army attacked, she drove forward, and she was terrible to behold, an engine of destruction cutting a swathe through the ranks of the Lament-Brood. Never in the history of the Far Lands had so many fallen before one Fragile Creature. Nothing could deter her. She was too quick, too brutal, darting, ducking, leaping onto shoulders and then using them as a springboard to drive forward. She turned acrobatic loops, but the sword never stopped slashing and she never tired.

260

The warriors of the Djazeem formed a phalanx, driving in behind her. As much as the Lament-Brood attacked, they could do nothing to deter the new army. Swords and spears hit hard but found nothing but sand. Occasionally one would catch a glancing blow on the tiny figure buried within the armour, but it would shift its position instantly to find a safer haven in a boot, or a leg.

They were still only few in number, but the Lament-Brood had been wrong-footed enough for Caitlin to claim a slight advantage. Her ferocity spiralled to new heights. The Morrigan ripped through the ranks, spraying body parts all around, her eyes blazing, her hair a furious mane. Crows came from nowhere and surrounded her, pecking at eyes, feeding on the bodies even before they knew they were dead.

Such was her fury that the Lament-Brood fell back from her; not because they were scared, for they had no conscious thought processes, but because they couldn't comprehend what was coming at them. It looked like a Fragile Creature, but it was destruction incarnate; nothing could stand in its way.

Mahalia was stunned when she saw Caitlin approaching. At first she didn't quite believe it, and then her guilt struck hard, but their situation was too desperate for her to dwell on it. Yet when she saw the full force of Caitlin's viciousness, she *was* scared; she couldn't understand how the gentle woman she had known previously could now act with such monstrous brutality; and what would she do when she came on Mahalia?

Matt, too, was shocked, but when he saw how quickly Caitlin was cutting through the Lament-Brood, he fought with renewed purpose. Whatever had happened to her, it meant they had a chance.

When the Morrigan reached Crowther, Caitlin surfaced.

"Professor! If you can hear me, don't attack randomly!" she yelled over the ringing cacophony of battle. "Focus the mask on blasting a tight tunnel across the plain!"

Crowther didn't appear to hear. Energy lashed back and forth, sound and fury condensed into a storm that could blow the world apart. But then the display ended with a suddenness that left an eerie silence.

Even the Lament-Brood paused, trying to comprehend what was happening. Purple mist blew back and forth. The world hung still.

And then Crowther convulsed and a beam of pure white light burst out of the mask, smashing through the Lament-Brood, shearing bodies in half, disintegrating everything in its path. It stretched right up to the gates of the House of Pain.

"Run!" Caitlin yelled.

Matt led the way along the charred path, with Mahalia and Jack following close behind and Caitlin close to them. Crowther brought up the rear, and if anyone had thought to look they would have seen that he was floating half an inch off the ground.

The path was lined by walls of burned Lament-Brood, their broken, dismembered bodies fused together. The burned-meat smell was sickening. On the far side of each wall, the Lament-Brood reeled. They struggled to comprehend what was happening, then pressed hard against the walls of their dead comrades, but they didn't have the intelligence to try to climb over.

Adrenalin drove Matt and the others on. As they ran, the House of Pain rose up before them, growing clearer and more defined the closer they got to it. It was as black as volcanic rock, but its design was like no building they had ever seen before. It loomed over the plain like a giant spider, with twisted leglike extensions reaching out through the air. There were curves and spikes, what looked like a carapace, but no straight lines. It gave the impression that it had crawled there from whatever foul place it had originated in, then settled, waiting to suck up anything that crept into its vicinity. And perhaps it had.

It was enormous. As Matt ran into its chilling shadow, he estimated it was at least five miles high. The atmosphere surrounding it was dense and sickening, infused with dread.

And as they ran closer to it, images flashed unbidden into their minds: scenes of torture, the worst acts of inhumanity, death on a universal scale, pain and suffering that never ended. Tears sprang to Mahalia's eyes. Matt thought he was going to vomit. Jack continued apace; he had been through such things all his life.

Finally, the plain gave way to black granite boulders that reached up to the foundations. Breathlessly, they clambered up them, but before they had got far, Caitlin leaped with astonishing agility, passing the others by. They couldn't understand why she was so eager to overtake them until they heard a thundering cry bouncing off the rocks all around.

It was the sound of the half-reptilian, half-horse mount carrying the leader of the Lament-Brood effortlessly across the boulders from the plain beyond the wall of bodies. Of all the Whisperers, he was the only one who bore the fire of intelligence; it flickered in his eyes and was evident in every aspect of his movement. He carried a sword in one hand and a spear in the other as he bore down on them.

As Caitlin approached, the Whisperer hurled his spear. Caitlin dodged it easily, but it would have plunged through Mahalia's chest had Jack not thrown himself to knock her out of the way. Caitlin didn't slow in her attack; wielding her sword with both hands, she flew at the enemy.

The mount reared up, its fierce jaws torn wide to reveal rows of sharp teeth, like a fish from the deep. It attempted to trample her with hooves that raised golden sparks from the granite, but Caitlin was too quick, easily evading it to try to stab at a soft spot beneath its neck.

Their dance went on for five minutes before Caitlin finally found her opening. With both hands, she rammed the sword into the beast's throat. Hot, black blood gushed out and the mount's cry became almost human, high and pained. It floundered around with the sword still protruding from it.

Its rider fought to control it for a few seconds before leaping clear just as it crashed to the boulders, thrashing in its death throes. The leader of the Lament-Brood maintained perfect poise on landing, both hands coming to the sword as he moved in to attack.

Caitlin was defenceless. Without thinking, Mahalia stepped forward and threw her Fomorii sword. Caitlin caught it with one hand without looking and instantly launched into the fight. She parried, struck, parried again. Their skill was so great, the others could barely see the movements of the swords, hearing only the reverberations of their clashes.

They battled for five minutes, but Caitlin's face remained impassive throughout, as though she were in some trance state, immersed in a work of art rather than a fight to the death. As the crows flapped around them in a black cloud, it became apparent to the others that she wouldn't be beaten; probably could never be beaten. Battle was her life, bloodshed her reason; she existed at the point between life and death, where both were experienced to their extremes.

And finally she ducked the Whisperer's strike, swung her sword with two hands, and took off his head at the neck. It bounced down the boulders as the body crashed to the ground. Purple mist swept out of it, enveloping them all before being blown away across the battlefield.

Caitlin turned to the others, drenched from head to toe in blood and looking like hell itself. She waved for them to follow her before leaping up the boulders toward a flat area in front of a door resembling a gaping mouth.

Mahalia's anguished call made Caitlin turn back. Crowther was slumped on his knees on the rocks, the Lament-Brood leader's spear rammed through his body. The front of his overcoat was already soaked in blood. The distressing sight drove the Morrigan back and brought Caitlin as close as she could be to control. Awkwardly, she clambered back down to where Mahalia, Jack, and Matt were attempting to aid the professor. His head had lolled forward onto his chest; the mask's power had retreated inside it.

Jack went to pull the spear out, but Matt cautioned him. "You might do more damage," he said.

The warriors of the Djazeem had followed the five of them along the tunnel of bodies and had now fanned out around the base of the rock on which the House of Pain stood.

"Let's get him up to the top," Caitlin said.

They lifted the professor over the boulders to the flat surface, where they propped him against a rock. Matt pulled Caitlin to one side, searching her face to see if there was still any sign of the woman he had known. Satisfied that there was, he said, "He's dying. There's nothing we can do."

After all the suffering she had seen, Caitlin felt drained of emotion. She looked back at the billowing purple mist and replied, "We can't take the risk of staying here with him."

"I know."

"I don't want to leave him to die alone."

"He's probably not aware of anything in that mask. It's pretty much taken him over."

Mahalia sensed what they were discussing and came over. "I'll stay with him."

Caitlin eyed her coldly; she could feel the Morrigan stirring at the back of her head, the frantic fluttering of black wings.

Mahalia saw what was happening in Caitlin's face and said, "I've done bad things, I know, but this isn't the time to punish me. You can do that later, after he's gone."

Without acknowledging Mahalia, Caitlin nodded to Matt and set off back over the boulders. "What's going on between you two?" Matt asked the girl. Mahalia waved him away and turned back to Crowther, the only thing on her mind now.

"I'll stay as well," Jack said when she returned.

"No. We need you." The tone in Matt's voice suggested there would be no argument.

"Go on," Mahalia said. "I'll be here when you're done." They both knew it was a lie. They hugged and kissed briefly, almost blasé, so that they could pretend it wasn't going to be the last time, and then Jack hurried off with Matt in pursuit of Caitlin.

As Caitlin approached the door, the familiar smell of burned iron drifted into her nostrils and lightning bolts crackled through the air. The knight with the boar's-head helmet stood to one side of the entrance, pointing with his sword for her to enter the House of Pain. Now Caitlin could see the truth: he belonged in some way to that awful power and everything he had done had been to draw her there. She considered attacking him, hacking open that ghoulish boar's head, but it was pointless; she should save her rage for what lay within.

"Enter, Caitlin Shepherd. Your destiny awaits you." His voice seethed with the same lightning energy.

As she passed, she pointed her sword at his throat; he didn't flinch.

"What did you do that for?" Matt asked as they moved into the shadows beneath the porch of gleaming obsidian that overhung the door.

Caitlin looked from Matt to the knight. "You can't see him?"

Matt stared at her blankly.

Her own personal demon. Without a backward glance, she plunged through the area of shadows, into the House of Pain.

Mary's footsteps echoed hollowly as she ventured across the large tiled entrance hall of the Roman Baths. The foliage that swamped the outside of the building covered the external windows and made the interior very dark, but once her eyes had adjusted she could see the ticket desks and beyond them the doors through to the baths themselves.

Mary's heart beat wildly. She knew *something* was here, but she had no idea what it was. Arthur Lee could feel it, too; the cat pressed tightly against her calves, his fur prickling.

Cautiously, she walked through the next set of doors into blazing sunshine. There was a walkway running around a square, open area. Peering over the edge, Mary could see the green water of the ancient stone-lined baths on the floor below.

The atmosphere of sanctity she had felt the moment she entered the town was even more potent here. It was almost alive, breathing. With her footsteps echoing in the still air, she moved along the walkway until she came to some steps.

They brought her out next to the pool where Romans had bathed nearly two thousand years before. The echoes were even louder there, rippling out across the water and bouncing off the stone that had been uncovered during the excavations in the earlier part of the twentieth century. Much of the original baths remained, and it wasn't difficult to imagine life going on there all those years ago.

But the Romans had only been one of many peoples who had used the naturally warm, mineral-heavy water. From the earliest days it had been a place of pilgrimage, as though the water flowed from the next world to this one, carrying with it some of the flavour of the beyond.

The tranquillity that lay across the baths was seductive. Mary knelt on the edge and dipped her fingers into the water. It was warm and oddly soothing, yet as the ripples ran out, the water appeared to take on an odd viscous quality. At first, Mary had been able to see the stone flags on the bottom, not far below the surface, but now it looked as if the water went down forever.

The change to the water was hypnotic and Mary found herself peering into the dim depths to see what was happening. There was movement. Someone was in there, immeasurably deep, swimming. Back and forth the figure went, coming up tirelessly, rolling over like a dolphin, the skin gleaming white, the hair long and grey.

Finally it stopped just a few inches beneath the surface and rolled onto its back so that it could peer up at her. Mary found herself looking into her own face. The shock made her pull back, but the swimming Mary remained at peace, her eyes big and wide.

"Who are you?" Mary asked.

The lips of the Swimming Mary moved and somehow her lilting voice sounded above the water level. "I am you."

Mary steadied herself; the sensation of looking into her own face was weird, but there was no sense of threat. She had the strangest feeling that the water wasn't water at all, rather that it was a window between two worlds.

"We are the same," the Swimming Mary continued. "All things are joined."

"Is the Goddess here?" Mary asked.

There was a long pause before her double replied. "If you wish to enter Her presence, you must first prove yourself worthy."

"How do I do that?"

"Follow the path. All will be revealed."

Her other self, whatever she really was, didn't swim away; she simply floated down and down until she disappeared into the dark green depths. Mary stood up, her knees cracking, and when she looked back into the pool the stone bottom was once again visible.

The sense of a connection with the otherworldly stayed with her as she searched around for some kind of path. As she looked around, thin blue veins rose up in the stone flags leading around the outside of the pool. It was a clear enough marker and she followed it, her cat trailing behind.

The blue veins led her into an adjoining room, another bath, this one in a more ruinous state. The room was enclosed and it was cool and dark after the warmth of the sun. It took a couple of seconds for Mary's eyes to adjust and then she was startled to realise that someone was standing as silently as a statue in the gloom in one corner.

"Hello?" she said tentatively. She tried to pierce the shadows to see who stood within.

After a moment, he or she took a step forward, not far enough for Mary to get a clear view; an overhanging light fitting, now obsolete, still cast the head in shadow.

Mary was gripped by it. In a trick of the faint light filtering through, it appeared as though its long hair was moving with a life of its own. Only when the figure prepared to take a second step did she realise that the hair *was* moving—and that in fact it wasn't hair at all, too thick, too sinuous.

Cold ran through her as tales from her childhood classrooms came rushing back, of gods and demigods, and quests and monsters. She knew she should run or feel her limbs grow as heavy as the ancient stone that lay all around, but then she would never get to the Goddess and all her travelling would have been in vain.

The figure took another step, slowly, as if testing her knowledge of its identity. Mary quickly turned her back, plucking up Arthur Lee and holding his head so that he couldn't see, either.

"You know me, then." The voice had a faint sibilance; it sounded simultaneously male and female, both and neither.

"I think . . ." Mary's voice was so shaky that she stopped speaking so as not to reveal her fear.

A faint sound, like steam escaping from a pipe, grew louder as the stranger approached. A shudder ran through Mary: the figure was now a mere foot behind her back. If she turned now . . .

"You know what will happen if you see my face?"

"Yes."

"The Greeks knew me, though I do not belong to them. Perseus saw only one aspect. The Celts knew me, thought me a man, though they were only concerned with my role as servant to Sulis. But I did not belong to them either. I am part of something greater . . . the power that resides in this place. I am the Servant. Do you understand?"

Mary nodded, terrified that the Servant would try to edge round one side or the other to catch her unawares.

"If you wish to know my being, consider this: my hair, rolling like the waves of the sea, but also stretching out like the rays of the sun. There are wings on the sides of my head. And then stone, always cold, hard stone. Water, fire, air, earth. That is what I am—a part of everything. And that is what I serve. Do you understand?" This time the Servant's voice was harder and Mary trembled at the sound of it.

"You will take my hand and I will lead you. You must close your eyes, for you know what will happen if you see my face. I could lead you to your death, to a pit down which you will fall, shattering every bone. Know that this is a trial, not a trick. Everything that seems at stake *is* at stake. If you fail, the price will be high: your death. No one will mourn. For if the trial is not extreme, success in it means nothing."

Mary forced her voice to remain calm. "I understand."

"Good. Then take my hand. Your life will belong to me completely. Live or die, it will be my choice. And you must trust me, utterly. If you pull away . . . if your eyes open even the tiniest amount to see your way . . ."

"I know, I know!" Mary clamped her eyes shut and stuck out a hand. "Go on, then."

Cool, hard fingers slid into hers; they felt almost scaly to the touch. She whispered a quiet prayer to the Goddess and then followed when gently tugged, already tripping over the minute ridges on the stone flags, her sense of balance precarious.

Mary had no idea where she was taken. She kept her eyes so tightly closed that the muscles all around them hurt and trembled. The chill hand pulled her along steadily. After the cool of the shadowy bathhouse she felt the warmth of the sun on her face and presumed that the Servant had taken her back outside, but the air smelled different, and she had the strangest sensation that she was no longer in the baths at all. That made her even more hesitant, for she couldn't begin to picture her position, or guess at what lay ahead.

At times she gasped, fearing that she was about to stumble when her foot caught against an obstacle, that her eyes would crack open instinctively on impact. And there was one terrible moment when she felt as if she was walking along the edge of an immense drop; wind currents plucked at her from the side *and* from below, and vertigo rushed up inside her dizzyingly. She had no idea how she stopped herself from tumbling, even if it was only an illusion; the Servant didn't slow down for an instant. She could only do what was asked of her: trust implicitly.

The frightening trial appeared to go on for hours, though it was probably only ten minutes, and then, eerily, she could no longer feel the fingers in hers. She grasped the air, unsure if she had accidentally let go, but could find the hand nowhere, nor could she sense the Servant in the vicinity. Her first thought was that it was another part of the trial, to tempt her to look and find the Servant there, staring into her face.

For five full minutes she waited, occasionally reaching out, and finally she decided that the Servant had indeed gone. She opened her eyes cautiously, looking at the ground first, and found with near-euphoric relief that she was standing alone near one of the tourist displays in a subterranean corridor. Nearby she could hear rushing water and there was steam in the air: the spring itself, she guessed.

She set off in the direction of the water only to find her way blocked. A wall of what appeared to be streaming water lay across the entire width of the corridor, but when Mary tried to walk through it, it felt as if she was walking into stone.

She stepped back, puzzled, and only then did she see two masks hanging on a nearby wall. One was completely featureless, though with a feminine shape. The other was a startlingly lifelike representation of her own face. It was deeply unsettling to see it there, as if her quest to Bath had been some *fait accompli* decided by the Higher Powers.

After pondering what it all meant for a moment, she decided it must be another part of the trial. She was expected to choose one of the masks, and then, perhaps, the way would be opened. It seemed so obvious as to be facile. She took down the mask of her own face, which creepily felt as if it was made of real skin.

She paused just before she pressed it into place. It *was* too easy. What was the point of it? If it was a trial, it had to call on something in her character, surely. She sat down against the foot of the wall and placed the mask facedown on the floor next to her. Arthur Lee sniffed at it curiously, then came to settle in her lap. She stroked him while she thought.

What was the meaning of the first test? she wondered. She turned it over in her mind for a little while, and decided it had to be faith. She had just put her trust, and her life, completely in the hands of the Higher Power. And she had clearly passed that test.

But this one? She eyed the blank mask, then stood up and took it down. It was cold and unlifelike to the touch. She glanced between the two masks, and remembered the Servant's warning about the price that would be paid.

Finally she thought she had it. She steeled herself and pressed the blank mask to her face. It fit perfectly, and was cool and soothing against her skin. Two things happened at once: she heard the streaming wall of water dry up and disappear, and there was a loud *pock* near her feet.

She removed the mask and looked down to see with horror two spikes protruding from the inside of the mask of her face, just where her eyes would have been if she had been wearing it. She steadied herself against the wall, dizzy at how close she had come.

The blank mask, she decided, was symbolic of her acceptance of a lack of identity, or humility in the presence of the Goddess. Faith and humility—two things she would need in the hidden sanctum.

Now extremely cautious about what other trials might lie ahead, she rehung the blank mask on the wall and moved along the corridor. It sloped downward, illustrated scenes from the history of the baths decorating the walls.

As she rounded a corner, she caught her breath when she was confronted by a figure. At first she thought it was the Servant, but this figure was short and hunched, wearing rough grey robes and a hood that plunged all its features into deepest shadow. In fact, from Mary's perspective it looked as if there was no face in the hood at all.

"Two trials have you passed," said the hooded figure, an old woman from the sound of her voice. She held up two gnarled fingers. "This third is final, and the most important. One simple question. Answer wisely and you shall pass. The wrong answer will condemn you to death, and worse, damnation: the ultimate fate. Your spirit will never pass to the Grey Lands. Here in this place you will remain, forced to live out what might have been and never can be."

Mary took a deep breath, knowing it was too late to back out. *One simple question* didn't sound like much, but Mary knew it would undoubtedly be the hardest of all the trials: the final hurdle. "Go on," she said anxiously.

"As you wish. What is the darkest secret in your heart?"

Mary brought herself up sharp, all the potential pitfalls lining up before her. Of all her secrets, how could she possibly know which was *the* darkest?

The hooded woman appeared to read her thoughts. She wagged her finger in caution. "No little secret will do. No second-darkest secret. But you know, in your heart of hearts, what is the worst—one you have never dared tell anyone else for fear they would hate you. One you have never dared admit to yourself. Choose wisely."

Mary closed her eyes and thought. Behind the panic, she realised she did know; and she had never been able to face up to it.

"Speak."

"I can't."

"Then die."

Mary gave a juddering sigh as she struggled to contain her emotion, and then, with cracking voice, she let it rise for the first time. "My mother was dying. We hadn't got on for a long while. I was a little rebel, always saying and doing things I knew would annoy her. If I had sex with a boy—even a one-night stand at a party—I'd tell her, just to shock her. Or if I took drugs. It was the sixties. We all used to do things like that back then . . . at least, that's the excuse I've always told myself. It *is* an excuse. We're all responsible for our own actions. We can never blame anyone else for anything." She was talking to herself, but it sounded as if someone else was speaking about a person she didn't know.

"I look back on myself as I was then and I hate myself. I thought I was so sophisticated, so clever . . . cleverer than my parents. They didn't know anything about this whole new world we were carving out for ourselves back then. How naïve. How fucking naïve and callous! I thought I was so smart, but I was more stupid than anyone!"

She wiped her nose with the back of her hand. Her eyes had filled with tears, but she wasn't looking at the hooded woman. Her vision was turned in on that time, sun-drenched and long buried. "I'd walked out a while before, telling my mother I didn't need her holding me back any more. The woman who raised me and sacrificed everything for me! I didn't need her! And she called . . . she told me she was dying." Her words choked in her throat; she didn't think she could continue.

"You must speak it all!" the hooded woman prompted.

Mary calmed herself, but it felt as if there was a rock in her chest. "I told her I was going away with this boy. She said it was urgent. I told her not to be so dramatic . . . she was always being a drama queen. I said I was going away and I'd call her when I got back. We went off to some free festival, took lots of drugs, had lots of sex, and then I came back and I still didn't call her. The secret? I hadn't forgotten. I just didn't want to deal with all that death stuff. A bummer. I was having too much of a good time to be brought down. And I wouldn't miss her—I mean, we didn't get on at all!"

She stared into the middle distance, watching the dreadful scene play out before her. "I remember where I was when I got the call that she had died. I was in my flat, high on acid, listening to Love play 'Alone Again Or' with some boy whose name I didn't know. And I laughed. I laughed and laughed and hung up the phone and told him I was free."

Mary covered her face for a long minute.

"What I did back then broke me. It turned me into a different person. That was the price I paid for my actions. I did miss her. I missed her more and more with each passing year, and if I could go back and make amends I'd give up everything, even my life. But I can't, so I have to live with it, knowing I'm a terrible person, knowing what I lost by being so stupid and selfish and cruel . . . and worthless. I missed a few hours with a person who loved me in a way I would never be loved again, someone who sacrificed everything, who devoted her whole life to raising me. And that's the most valuable thing in the world . . . the Holy Grail . . . and I threw it away. I deserve every terrible thing that's ever happened to me. I deserve to be lonely and unloved in my old age." She drew herself up to her full height and looked into the shadows of the old woman's hood. "That's my darkest secret. And now I've admitted it I don't care if I live or die. I don't care if you condemn me to some eternal damnation. Could it be any worse than my life now? I don't think so."

The hooded woman remained silent for a full minute, her head turned toward Mary, swaying a little from side to side. Then she said in a voice so gentle it was shocking, "Welcome, sister. You have proved yourself to be a true and good person, filled with faith and humility, able to shine the light of truth into the darkest part of her heart. You have no secrets before what lies ahead. And she loves you, as your mother loved you. And she will care for you."

Tears sprang to Mary's eyes. She felt like a child, unable to control herself, not knowing what she really wanted anymore.

"Come, sister," the hooded woman said, drifting slowly backward down the corridor without any visible contact with the floor. "You are filled with pain. Your journey has been long and your spirit is weary. Now is the time to rest. All is open to you."

She gestured down the corridor. The sound of the spring was louder now, and Mary could feel the sticky heat in the air from the hot water forced up from deep beneath the ground. As she looked ahead, she could see a faint blue light. The corridor was fading away, and a warmer and more enticing place was appearing.

Mary blinked away the tears and walked toward it.

chapter seventeen
THE QUEEN OF SINISTER

*"Trampling out the vintage where the grapes
of wrath are stored."*

Julia Ward Howe

Madness and despair leaked from the black walls of the House of Pain as Caitlin, Matt, and Jack moved cautiously along the corridor leading away from the entrance. The building was filled with an oppressive gloom and a suffocating tropical heat, without even the slightest air current to give respite.

Despite appearances, they couldn't shake the feeling that they were inside a vast, living creature. Odd vibrations ran through the floor and walls as though a vascular system was at work, and on the very edge of their hearing was a faint *lub-dub* that could have been the beating of a massive heart.

"We've got to be careful we don't get lost," Matt cautioned.

Caitlin's voice floated back to him. "I shouldn't worry. The chances of any of us getting out of here alive are pretty slim."

"Yep. Let's all look on the bright side," Matt muttered.

Jack hurried to pass Matt so that he was walking between the two of them. "This place," he began queasily, "it's even worse than the Court of the Final Word."

"Do you have any idea where we're going?" Matt asked. "This place is enormous. We could wander here all day . . . except I've got this feeling we won't be allowed to roam for long."

"Maybe there won't be any guards," Jack said hopefully. "Whoever's in charge couldn't have expected us to get past the Lament-Brood, so they might not have set up any second line of defence."

"You see, why can't you take lessons off him?" Matt called after Caitlin. "*He* always looks on the bright side."

In Caitlin's head, their voices became the buzzing of flies. Feeling herself slipping away again, she managed two last words of warning: "Something's coming." Then her vision shifted to red, the shadows sucked back, and the interior of the House of Pain fell into sharp relief.

Matt gripped Jack's shoulder to prevent him from advancing.

"What is it?" Jack said fearfully. "What can she see?"

"Look at her!" Matt said.

Caitlin's outline was hazy, as though swathed in fog. Shadows formed on her skin, slowly separated, growing fast as they flapped and swirled all round her.

"Crows!" Matt said in quiet awe. "There are crows coming out of her." The birds emerged in a frenzy of wings until Caitlin was almost obscured.

The truth dawned on Jack with horror. "The Morrigan! We have to get away from here! The Morrigan has her!"

Matt spun Jack round to peer into his face. "What are you talking about? Tell me!"

"The Morrigan is one of the gods!" Jack said. "But she's worse than all of them . . . much worse. Her thing is war, and blood . . . and . . . and other things, too! But it's the killing! They say nothing can stop her . . ."

Matt looked back at the furious murder of crows moving forcefully up the corridor with Caitlin's tiny figure the heart of them. "Then it's a good thing she's on our side." A pause for thought. "She is on our side, right?"

What Matt and Jack couldn't see, but which was as clear as daylight to Caitlin, was the thing taking shape further down the corridor. To Caitlin, it looked as if it was pushing itself out through the wall in a hideous mockery of birth, dripping with mucus and contorted by natal pangs. But as she drew closer, it became clear that it was being formed from the stuff of the wall itself. And that's when Caitlin realised that the entire House of Pain really was some kind of entity and that they were working their way into its belly.

The thing shuddered, growing larger as it added to itself, its skin the shiny black of vinyl. Finally it unfolded, rising up on two legs in the shape of a man; but it was a shape created by something that did not really know what a man was or how one worked. It staggered away from the wall, leaving a trail of dripping slime, and stepped toward Caitlin. When it looked at her, the whiteness of its eyes was piercing in contrast with its face.

Caitlin felt a shadow move across her mind as it probed her consciousness. It sickened her, but the Morrigan was unmoved. Her muscles flexed, ready to attack.

"Youuuuuu . . . drag-onnnnnnnn . . ." Though the thing's mouth didn't move, the sibilant words came into Caitlin's head like beetles swarming through her brain.

Seeing only death through the red haze, the Morrigan attacked.

"Boyyyyyyyyyy . . ."

Caitlin came to an abrupt halt. One word, but she knew what it was saying to her. And in that instant the Morrigan was gone, consigned to the desolate lands in the shadows of Caitlin's consciousness by Caitlin's love for her son, perhaps the only thing that could have defeated the Morrigan's control.

"Is he here?" Caitlin asked in a fragile voice. Her chest was so tight that she barely dared ask the question for fear that her heart would burst.

"Don't let it trick you!" Matt came running up and grabbed her, but she threw him off.

"Is he here?" Her voice cracked with anguish.

With an awkward movement, the creature gestured further down the corridor. In the shadows waited a small figure with a pale face. His features were too indistinct in the half-light, but Caitlin was convinced it was Liam. All her beaten-down emotion gushed out with such force she thought she was going mad.

"Liam?" she said in a tiny voice.

The shiny black thing reached out a hand. Caitlin knew what was expected of her, and though every fibre of her being was filled with revulsion, she could not resist. Matt knew too, and tried to drag her back.

Caitlin broke free and clutched at the monstrous hand, which felt like warm steak in her fingers. In an instant she was moving down the corridor, though her feet did not appear to be touching the ground.

"Do something!" Jack pleaded. Caitlin rapidly receded into the shadows in the grasp of the thing's unpleasantly long fingers. There was nothing they could do.

The journey was a haze. Caitlin had the impression that she was not only moving through the House of Pain, but above it and around it; and she sensed that it was accurately named. The enormous creature was filled with the darkest emotions of human suffering. Empty rooms echoed with the cries of torture. Another chamber was potent with the familiar cutting edge of all-consuming grief. A further room was bitter with abandonment, then loss, abuse, agony, hopelessness; and finally she came upon the sickening reek of despair, and she knew instantly that this was where the Lament-Brood originated. Each room could produce something real and palpable from its empty, echoing chambers and send it out into the world. In the end it proved too much and she blacked out.

She woke in a room that at first glance looked and smelled like black meat, but which quickly reshaped itself into something with which she could cope. The floor became obsidian flags, the walls gleaming black, too, the stones rising to a vaulted roof that reminded her of a cathedral, though it had no warmth or hope within it.

From an annex beyond an arch came the sound of tiny running feet. Caitlin's breath caught in her throat, the anticipation almost painful.

And then he appeared, and she knew instantly, as any mother would know, that it was him, not some construct created to tempt her; really, truly Liam, as vital and joyous as the last time she had seen him alive.

He wandered toward Caitlin as if awakening from a long sleep. Recognition came seconds after his eyes fell on her, and then his face broke with the light of an exuberant, loving smile. Her heart thundered and tears rushed to her eyes.

"Mummy!" His voice brought brilliant life to that sickening place. He ran, arms thrown wide, and she scooped him up, pressing him into her, as if she could force him back into her womb where he would be safe for evermore. His body felt so warm and wonderful; and she couldn't believe it, after all the grief and the pain, and the acceptance of his passing on. Her hope that he really would be there at the end of the quest was barely realised, a child's wish for heaven. Sobs racked her, becoming even worse when his muffled voice said, "Mummy, why are you crying?"

"I love you, Liam." She smothered him with kisses. "I love you so much. You're the only thing that matters to me."

The moment the words left her lips his body went rigid. She pulled away, terrified that this was the cruel sting in the House of Pain's scheme, and he stood there like a statue, staring blindly, still him, still real, but frozen in time. Panic burst free so hard she clawed at his clothes like an animal.

The barely human thing that was the voice of the House of Pain had crept up on them unawares. It pointed one wavering finger at Liam and said, "Chooooooooooosse . . ." in that soundless voice that made her feel sick.

One word, but as before she knew exactly what it meant. The thing made a strange, spastic movement with its hand and the wall ahead of her became transparent. In the room beyond she could see something that resembled a giant egg made of the brown meat that appeared to be the stuff of the building. From the rear of the egg, small forms were issuing with a grotesque sucking sound. They writhed on contact with the air but quickly found their feet and then scampered away. They were the plague demons she had become aware of once the Morrigan had emerged to control her consciousness, and this was the place where they were made—she refused to think "born." Hundreds of them swarmed around the egg, dancing and tormenting each other, ready to be thrust into the human world, where they would infect their corruption into the spiritual energy that infused everything.

"Anti-life," she whispered to herself. Here was the power to pave the way for the arrival of the Void. And she could stop it. All she had to do was renounce Liam, and the world and everything in it would be saved, for now.

How clever were the forces ranged against life, she thought; how could the Void know the workings of the human mind so well? If she chose Liam, the Void would win. If she rejected Liam to take the cure, she would destroy herself, she would be unable to act as a champion of the Blue Fire in the coming battle . . . and the Void would win.

Not so long ago she might have found it in her to overcome the second loss of her son for the sake of the greater good. But the death of Carlton had been the final twist in her destruction. Before that, she had fought her way through grief to see some kind of hope; but after that there was none, and never would be again, if she didn't take her chance here with Liam. Nothing else mattered. Not the cure, not the world, nothing.

In that instant, Caitlin looked at the thing and through it into the House of Pain itself and saw something of herself in the Void. They were all joined by the despair at the heart of human existence.

"No," she said. "I'm not giving him up. He's going to live. He's going to live!"

She didn't waste a second thinking about what she had done. She felt his body become warm and alive again, and she hugged him to her, and buried her face in his hair.

Her choice had been made.

Outside in the dusty, sweltering heat, Mahalia sensed a change. She looked up from tending the professor to see the warriors of the Djazeem break from their defensive position and start to drift away down the corridor through the army of the Lament-Brood.

Mahalia watched them with incomprehension, followed by mounting dismay. Soon there would be nothing to hold the Lament-Brood at bay. As she gazed over the disappearing column, she had the impression of a tiny figure or two moving in the opposite direction through the heat haze. Before she could decide if it was a trick of the light or her eyes, the professor coughed up a gout of blood.

Mahalia slipped a comforting arm around his shoulders. Anyone could see that he didn't have long left. She'd tried to stem the blood that now soaked all the way through his overcoat, but it was like trying to hold back the rain.

His head lolled onto his chest, and she thought that he had already gone, but then his hands went shakily up to the mask, and it fell limply into his palms. He tossed it to one side and looked up at her with eyes so haunted that she was truly shocked. His face looked like a skull, the skin drawn tight and as white as snow, everything vital sucked out of him.

"He doesn't want me now." Mahalia was stunned by the bitterness in his voice. "He's drained me dry and now he's ready to move on to the next victim," Crowther continued.

"How are you feeling?"

"Like death. How do you think I'm feeling?" He caught himself and forced a wan smile. "I'm sorry, Mahalia. Thank you for staying with me. I didn't expect anyone would. I've not made much good of myself."

"That's not true! You saved us—twice."

He accepted her point. "But still, I could have done so much more, couldn't I? If I hadn't been so weak. I suppose we're not all cut out to be heroes."

Honest tears burned her eyes at the self-loathing that consumed him. She didn't want him to die that way, thinking his life was without value, but every time she tried to find the words they caught in her throat and she had to fight to stop herself from crying.

He understood what she was trying to do, for his smile became more natural. "Don't worry about me, young 'un. I had my chances. I made my choices and I've got no one else to blame—I'm quite at ease with it all." A twitch around his mouth showed the lie.

"Professor," she choked, "I don't want you to die, too."

"I know, and I'm so sorry to be doing this to you. I know you've been abandoned at every turn . . . your parents . . . Carlton . . . You deserve so much more." He fumbled around as if his vision was fading and eventually caught hold of her hand. "You need to change your thinking, little girl. You're not what you think—you're a good person, a very good person. I know you're a crotchety, miserable young sociopath, but that's by the by. The only one holding you back is you. And I only wish I truly could have saved you, because I know you'll go on to better things."

Her tears blinded her. "I'm not like that, Professor—"

"You are, yes, you are." He coughed; more blood. "Fading fast now. What a way to go. I always dreamed it would be a Gary Cooper scenario, not slumped here like some drunken old tramp who's had his throat cut. Still, we're all heroes in our own minds, aren't we?" He pulled her closer. "Listen to me." His voice was so frail now. "The only thing I can give you is a lesson. It might be the only valuable thing I've ever done, my one shot at redemption, but that will be down to you . . . whether you heed it or ignore it. Not to put too much pressure on you."

She pressed her face next to his greasy hair, and smelled sweat and his own peculiar musk, not unpleasant. "I'm listening. I'll . . . I'll heed it."

"Wait until you hear what I have to say first." Even close to death there was still a snap in his voice. "I made my mistakes a long time ago. I got lost and wandered away from the path I should have been following because I indulged all my weaknesses. There's a line in *A Christmas Carol*, where Marley's ghost is telling Scrooge where he's gone wrong . . . He says, *Humanity is your business!* And that's true . . . so true. Humanity is your business, Mahalia, not looking after your own selfish interests. Helping the people who need you, helping everyone you can. I never did that. I abandoned my family . . . all the people I loved and who loved me. I did it because I thought I was weak, and if you think you're weak, you *are* weak. I still think I'm weak, and look at me now!" He gave a short, bubbling laugh.

"Don't . . ."

"No, you listen to me . . . for once in your life! Your whole future is in your own hands. You can amount to something . . . or you can carry on down the path you've set yourself on. And you'll carry on down it a little way and realise you can't go back, and all your future is mapped out for you. You'll just have to live it out, knowing how bad it's going to be . . . like waiting for a bus that you know will never come."

"I'll do what you say. I will!" She was crying openly now.

"No! Don't tell me now because it won't mean anything. You need to think about this, and turn it over, for days or weeks . . . if that time is available to you . . . if you stand a chance of getting out of this mess. And you need to remember this moment . . . look at me—look at me, damn you!—you need to remember this moment, and how pathetic I am . . . and think about what I could have been if only I'd tried. Remember that . . . think about a life wasted . . . by my own hand . . . Nobody to blame for my fate but myself. If I hadn't got myself into this state, that mask would never have been able to control me . . . and then . . ." His chin dropped down and he stared into the middle distance. ". . . maybe everything would have turned out OK."

Mahalia's attention was caught by movement. She looked up to see the last of the Djazeem warriors disappear down the corridor and then, a second or so later, the Lament-Brood began to move forward in their awkward zombie style.

Crowther saw the growing panic in her face. "What's wrong?"

"The Whisperers are coming. Can you hear them?"

He chuckled to himself. "An injection of their brand of despair would simply be overkill." Then: "Help me up."

She obeyed instantly. She didn't think he had it in him to stand, but he did, and even more, he was able to walk with faltering steps.

"Give me your sword," he said, "foul thing though it is. Yes, I know I look like I couldn't lift a feather, but trust me, I have a reserve or two. You get inside that place . . . find the others and for God's sake, save the day! Gary Cooper–style!"

"They'll take you over . . . !"

"No, they won't. I'll be dead before I start blowing out that purple mist. But at least I might be able to hold them off long enough for you to get a head start."

They made it to the doorway. Crowther steadied himself, then eased back so that the spear running through him supported him. He gave a slow exhalation of pain as it ground into his organs.

"Professor . . ."

"Go, you little idiot! I'm not doing this for the fun of it!" Briefly, he appeared to become delirious. "There's some chap here with a pig's head. What's that all about? Blue sparks everywhere. What does that bastard want? Well, he won't get it!" He brought himself back and snapped at her, "Run, damn you! Don't make me waste this last heroic gesture!"

Mahalia ducked forward and planted one last kiss on his cheek. It brought a fleeting smile to his face and then he turned toward the advancing horde. Mahalia ran into the shadows of the House of Pain, an intolerable weight on her heart.

Matt and Jack sprinted through endless corridors calling Caitlin's name, but they weren't even answered by echoes; the air was too hot and dead, the place too labyrinthine.

"We're probably just going round in circles!" Jack said dismally.

"No we're not," Matt replied. "I've got an unerring sense of direction, one of those skills you build up when you do the kind of job I do. We're going right into the heart of it."

"But what if that thing's already killed her?"

"If that was what it wanted to do, it would have done it the minute we walked in here. It's after something more . . . I don't know what, though I reckon it has something to do with her being a Sister of Dragons. Despite appearances— i.e., being as mad as a fish—she's someone who might be able to stop all this stuff going down. I think it knows that . . . it knows what she's tied into . . ."

"The Blue Fire?"

"Yeah. That's the thing that's going to win the war. She's a part of that somehow, and it wants to get at the Blue Fire through her. That's what I reckon," Matt concluded.

Jack stopped running and stared at his friend. "You know a lot you've not been telling."

Matt turned, his expression dark. "Don't tell me you can read bloody minds, too?"

"No, but . . ."

"Good. Now keep up." He ran ahead, his loping gait uncannily easy.

They rounded a corner and came up sharp. A figure was spraying dripping slime as it separated from the wall. Its fluid shape gradually settled into a bulky, muscular form that was still partly human, but with the characteristics of a bull. It moved to meet them, white eyes glaring out of its broad, black face.

"What is it?" Jack gasped.

"It's this place," Matt said, "whatever's here . . . whatever intelligence. It takes on these forms to communicate with us . . . in a manner we can understand."

"Goooooo baccckkkkkkkk . . ." The crackling words were so alien they were almost incomprehensible, but they got the gist of it from the thing's threatening posture as it positioned itself in the middle of the corridor.

"Well, that's a good sign," Matt said. "We must be getting close to some-where important if it's telling us to go away."

Jack clutched at his arm. "Aren't you scared?"

Matt gave a defiant smile that raised Jack's spirits. "Let's see if it can be hurt." He gripped his sword with both hands and rushed the beast. His first blow slammed into the middle of that broad head with a sticky crunch as if he were chopping rotten wood. The beast didn't respond in the slightest. It stood there, staring with eyes of cold maleficence, as Matt wrenched the sword free and attacked again. For ten minutes, he hacked at it until there was nothing left. And still the pieces with the eyes stared at him. They said: *You cannot harm me. You cannot defeat the House of Pain.*

Matt rested on the sword amid the gruesome remains and mopped the sweat from his brow. "Well," he said between deep breaths, "I suppose the answer is no."

Jack ventured closer, dismal once more. "What are we going to do?"

"We're not going to give up, so don't even think it."

A soft susurration crept along the corridor from behind them. Matt looked toward the sound, his mind racing. Purple mist, still thin at that point, drifted into view. "Looks like they got through," he said quietly. There was no way back.

"Mahalia," Jack said desperately. He started to move toward the mist until Matt caught his shoulder.

"Don't even think it. You won't be able to do anything. Besides, she's smarter and tougher than you. She'll be one step ahead of them. She's probably taken one of the side tunnels."

Jack looked up at the man he now trusted more than any other adult, and wanted to believe.

"Come on," Matt said. "The only way is further in."

They jogged down the corridor with Jack throwing backward glances as they ran. The further they progressed into the structure, the hotter it got, until they felt as if they were closing on some enormous furnace. A rhythmic thudding could be heard dimly through the walls, the vibrations running up through their legs and into the pits of their stomachs. It echoed the thunder of several thousand legs behind them, marching down the endless dark tunnels.

"Matt?"

"Save your breath." Sweat burned Matt's eyes, and however much he wiped it away, more flowed down.

"No, it's important. Whatever happens, don't let anyone take me prisoner again. I couldn't bear it . . . not after all that time in the Court of the Final Word."

"What do you expect me to do?"

"Whatever you have to. Will you promise me that, Matt? Will you?"

There was a silence so long that Jack thought Matt wasn't going to answer, but then he said, "Yeah. 'Course. You can count on me. Now . . . no more fatalistic talk, all right? We've got a job to do."

The darkness ahead slowly unveiled a figure. Matt came up sharp, holding out an arm to stop Jack running into it.

"Gooooooo bacckkkkkkkk . . ."

This beast was shaped like a giant spider, but still with human characteristics at the centre of its eight spindly legs. It skittered around the corridor, white eyes glaring.

"Jesus H. Christ, how many of these things am I going to have to chop to pieces before we get to where we're going?" Matt muttered bitterly.

"It can see into us, can't it?" Jack said. "Part of it's human, to communicate, but the rest of it is something it knows will scare us."

"It doesn't scare me." Matt brandished the sword again. "To answer your earlier question."

But just as he was about to attack, he sensed movement in the shadows behind the spider-thing. "What's there?" he asked himself.

The motion was at ground level, like the tide rolling in, but it was impossible to pick out detail from the darkness. Watching it approach, so chaotic, so relentless, made them shiver.

The spider-thing gestured with a human arm attached to its torso. "Disssseeeeeeeeeeeeaasssse . . ."

"Disease," Matt repeated, his mind turning rapidly.

The plague demons swarmed around the feet of the spider-thing, not slowing, but dancing, twisting, cruelty in every aspect of their tiny forms.

"Back!" Matt whispered, mesmerised by the sheer number of the approaching demons.

"What?" Jack said, dazed.

"Back!" Matt thrust the boy the way they had come. "Don't let them touch you. They're something to do with the plague."

"The Whisperers—"

"I know!" Matt snapped. "But I saw another way . . . I think."

They ran as fast as they could until Matt halted at a slit in the meaty walls.

"What is it?" Jack asked.

Matt stuck his hands into the slit and pulled back flaps to reveal a gap. Jack hesitated, but the sound of the swarming plague demons approaching rapidly concentrated his mind. He forced his way into the slit and pressed on, the meat folding around him. Matt followed.

They emerged into a chamber filled with a pale grey light emanating from a source they couldn't see. Instantly, the atmosphere in the room hit them like a wall. They both experienced a grief so deep it felt as if their hearts were being torn open. Tears welled up in their eyes unbidden, burning tracks down their hot cheeks.

In a sudden rush, Jack had an overwhelming sense of his mother, though that memory was impossible. He felt her joy at his birth, swooping, swirling, transcendent, and then the bitter, brutal comedown into devastating misery when he was stolen from her by the gods. Bereft and directionless, her death came soon after, violent and pitiless. Every negative emotion cut him like a knife. He saw it through her eyes, felt it as she did, and in some way he was convinced he was responsible for it all. The full force of the emotion came like a storm; he wanted to kill himself.

Matt gripped his arm so tightly he squealed. "Focus on me. Don't feel anything. This is why they call it the House of Pain." Matt dragged him across the room.

When they reached the other side they saw plague demons forcing their way through the meaty flaps. They weren't going to give up, ever.

"We don't stand a chance," Jack whined.

"Shut up," Matt snapped, "or, God help me, I'm going to punch your lights out."

"Don't take me into another room like this," Jack pleaded.

There was another slit nearby, but Matt ignored it. Instead, his attention was drawn by a small orifice halfway up the wall. Beyond it was a tunnel barely big enough for them to squeeze into; it pointed upward.

"There," Matt said. Before Jack could protest, Matt boosted him into the opening, then pulled his way in afterward. "Don't hang around!" Matt yelled. "Those little bastards aren't going to slow down!"

They had to force their way along the tunnel, dragging with their fingers and pressing with their toes, wriggling like snakes and driving their shoulders against the resistance. It felt like crawling through hot flesh, so tight all around that there were moments when they thought it would close in and suffocate them. It pressed hard on their backs, their heads, and every second they choked for air, terrified it would soon close in completely and they would be trapped, unable to go forward or back.

It was unbearably hot and pitch black, and they had no sense of direction. The tunnel undulated and twisted, at times so sharply they had to fold in two to get around corners. And all the time, Matt could hear the sound of frantic scrabbling behind him.

Only the desperate fear of what was coming at their backs prevented them from losing their minds in the nightmarishly claustrophobic environment. They lost all sense of time; there was only the furnace heat and the feeling that they would suffocate and die at any moment.

It could have been an hour later, or fifteen minutes, when the sound of pursuit faded away. They continued dragging themselves on for a little while longer and then the temperature eased slightly. Soon after, Jack forced his way past the final flap and emerged into a large room. He stretched his mouth wide and sucked in a huge gulp of air, not caring that it was still hot. He realised he was shaking and crying.

It was a ten-foot drop to the floor, but they were so keen to get out of the tunnel that they jumped instantly without even trying to lower themselves. At the foot of the wall, they lay on their backs, scarcely believing they had made it through the ordeal.

"Never again," Matt said. "I'll let those things give me the damn plague next time."

When they had recovered a little, they sat up and looked around. They were in a room the size of a cathedral, the roof lost in the darkness overhead. A thin green light illuminated the lower reaches.

As their eyes adjusted, they made out two figures like ghosts in the gloom; one was Caitlin, the other a boy.

The boy looked up with big, troubled eyes when they neared. "I don't know what's happened to my mummy," he said. "She won't talk to me." Caitlin sat cross-legged, her head bowed. She was rigid, her eyes wide and staring, unseeing.

"Mummy?" Jack repeated. An image of his own mother hit him hard, accompanied by the terrible grief he had felt in the last room. He wondered if it would be like that for the rest of his life, the two things now inextricably linked.

"Dammit, she really did it," Matt said in amazement. He dropped down next to Caitlin and checked her. "Pulse is fine. Looks like she's having one of her episodes."

Jack took Liam to one side. "Don't worry—your mummy will be fine. She's a great lady . . . a heroine."

"My mummy?" If Caitlin could have seen the innocent hero-worship in his face, she would have cried.

Matt held her head up so he could peer deep into her enlarged pupils, so black they almost covered the entire eye. "I wonder what's going on in there," he said.

The wind blasted across the Ice-Field with such force that Caitlin was in no doubt that a storm was coming. She shivered behind the insubstantial shelter of the rocks, peering through the gap across the gleaming white sheet to the black sky at the horizon. She was bewildered; she had spent fifteen minutes talking to Liam, and hugging him, and kissing him, and then suddenly it felt as if hooks had been driven into her flesh and she had been dragged back to this terrible place.

"You've done it now." Amy stood behind her, her singsong voice laced with judgment. "You're going to be sorry."

"I won," Caitlin said. "I got him back."

Brigid cackled bitterly. "You won? You lost it all! Can't you feel it?"

And she could; the heat was draining from her, so that she felt more acutely the biting cold. "What's happening?" she asked.

"You're a stupid bitch," Briony said. She sat on a rock, staring into the Ice-Field, smoking neurotically with the look of someone who had accepted defeat. "We counted on you . . . everyone counted on you . . . and you let us all down. Selfish. So bloody selfish."

"But—"

"Don't start making excuses! We warned you not to give in to despair. You were supposed to rise above it," Briony continued.

"But who can do that?" Caitlin said, still not understanding.

"*You* can, you idiot! That's why you were chosen. You're supposed to be better than everyone else—a champion of life. The Blue Fire was in you . . . and now it's going."

"Going?" Caitlin looked down at her hands.

"You betrayed it. You—"

"Do not treat her harshly." The voice was like a cold wind through a night forest. Briony slid off the rock and cowered behind it. Brigid stopped cackling, and Amy ran behind her, clutching at the old woman's hair.

The Morrigan emerged from the shadows at the back of the shelter, fierce and beautiful, her hair the deepest, most lustrous black, her skin pale, her lips the brightest red.

"Any mother would have done the same," Caitlin protested. "To get their son back . . . I don't care what you all say. That was the only choice I could make."

The Morrigan held out her slim hand, and though she was afraid, Caitlin took it. It was filled with a cool power that made Caitlin's head spin. The Morrigan led her to the centre of the sheltered area, and then stood facing her so that Caitlin could lose herself in those dark, unfathomable eyes.

"Women also understand sacrifice, more, much more than men." Her voice, though frightening, was also somehow soothing. "Sacrifice . . . the burning heart . . . for the sake of sisters and brothers, however much pain it causes inside. And you, Caitlin Shepherd, would have been able, when the need came, for you were a Sister of Dragons, one with the flow of Existence. But you were driven from the path . . . forced into the wilderness . . ."

"I don't understand," Caitlin said. "Who did that?"

"A man. Always a man, for since the dawn of your age only they have been capable of plumbing the depths of heartlessness, of manipulating women in the age-old struggle. The seasons have shifted, and the sisterhood is coming back to power once more. But some men will not stand for that. They cannot bear women with power. They cannot accept a sister standing shoulder to shoulder with them. And so they will play their male games of power and manipulation, of violence and unnecessary slaughter. To crush us down, sister. To make us lesser."

Caitlin's mind was racing at the Morrigan's hypnotic words. "I was manipulated . . . ?"

"Until the boy's death, you would have chosen the sacrifice to save all Fragile Creatures, despite the hurt you would have felt. His death changed everything. And it was done in the full knowledge that it would take your power away."

"I don't understand. It was done to—?"

"To stop you achieving your potential, sister. As simple as that."

Caitlin slumped to the cold, hard ground and hugged her knees. "But I got Liam back."

"Yeah, but at what price." Briony had found the nerve to speak. "All those people are going to die—horribly, their spirits infected, just so you can have a bit of happiness . . . a happiness that should never have been! Your little boy should have moved on. But the monster behind all this held him back, just so you could make this stupid move. A broken Sister of Dragons is better than a dead one. It causes despair . . . it carries on infecting . . ."

"Nobody should be asked to make that kind of decision!" Caitlin said.

"No," the Morrigan said. "Nobody should."

"I can't put it right," Caitlin said. "I can't give him up, not now I've got him back."

"It doesn't matter—it's already too late, you stupid bitch." Briony rocked backward and forward in her hiding place. "We're all going to hell in a handcart. You made the choice. The Blue Fire is leaving you. You've blown it."

Caitlin looked to the Morrigan and thought she saw a hint of sympathy in those cold features. "True," the goddess said. "You are no longer a Sister of Dragons."

Amy marched forward with the forced haughtiness of the very young. "Can't you help us?" she asked the Morrigan.

"I was sent here for a purpose, and that purpose has now passed," the Morrigan replied. "Here and now, I take my leave of you." She turned back to Caitlin and her voice softened. "You are a good sister, Caitlin Shepherd, whatever this outcome may mean for your kind."

Then she turned and disappeared into the shadows at the back of the shelter. Beyond the rocks, the howling wind grew more intense; it was getting colder.

"That's it, then," Briony said. "It's all over."

chapter eighteen
DA CAPO

"Two souls with but a single thought,
Two hearts that beat as one."

Maria Lovell

Caitlin spasmed and a large hooded crow burst from her chest. Jack bounded back in shock. Matt watched the bird circle the prone form once and then fly off into the dark.

When the beating of its wings had faded, Caitlin's eyelids fluttered and she sat up. Matt dropped down beside her to slip an arm round her shoulders.

"It's OK," she said woozily.

"A crow just came out of you. What the hell was that all about?"

"It doesn't matter now." Caitlin, still dazed, tried to assimilate the Morrigan's final words. She looked round and panic pushed all thoughts out of her mind. "Where's Liam?"

"He went over that way." Jack pointed into the dark ahead. "I think he said he'd found another room."

Caitlin jumped to her feet and ran on, Matt and Jack hurrying behind, trying to keep up. The next room was lighter and smaller, and there was an opening in the far wall that led on to another place that was brighter still.

Caitlin ran through it and stopped sharply. Liam's tiny figure was frozen in the middle of the massive chamber, staring at what lay ahead. The rear of the House of Pain was missing, and instead there was space, vast and endless, filled with galaxies and comets, seething gas giants, white dwarfs, gravity wells—a twelve-storey picture window looking out over the whole immeasurable spread of Existence. Around the edges, the warp field shimmered with psychedelic colours, where one reality merged with another.

"I never imagined it was so . . . big!" Jack gasped.

"Is that where this place crawled from?" Matt asked.

As the words left his lips, Caitlin saw movement far, far away, on the very edge of the universe, though she had no idea how she could see that far; it was as though the more she stared, the more she could see. A shadow was coming toward them. In the context of all that lay there, it appeared minuscule and slow moving. Caitlin knew that was a lie of perception: it was vast—entire galaxies disappeared behind it as it travelled—and it was hurtling toward them

286

in a manner, she knew, somehow she knew, that transcended the laws of physics.

"The Void," she mouthed.

And even though the words were soundless, the Void appeared to hear her, for she felt the full force of its intellect turned on her. It was as if it had looked at her across immeasurable light-years, looked directly into the deepest part of her where her darkest secrets lay. She staggered back, crushed by the weight of the dread and terror it elicited.

"It's coming," she said.

And in that instant the connection was gone, but she knew what waited for them, in the days, or weeks, or millions of years it would take for it to arrive.

She slipped her arm around Liam to turn him away from that awful sight, and as she did so another chill swept through her. Behind them, purple mist drifted in the dead heat. The army of the Lament-Brood had slipped in silently to fill the chamber and all the rooms beyond.

Mary basked in a feeling of utter peace. The air was warm, the sound of the spring soothing, and the sanctity of that place made her feel so secure that she never wanted to leave. More potent was the sense of *presence*; an intelligence enveloped her, at once immense yet also intimate, as if it were there just for her.

She's coming, Mary thought, and she had no idea how she knew that, but an instant later a woman appeared in the billowing steam around the hot spring. Mary didn't know what she had expected—a figure filled with lights and stars, she guessed—but what actually emerged was a woman who resembled the Virgin. Mary knew she was seeing the Goddess in a way her mind could comprehend, drawn from the once-comforting iconic images she had seen during her Catholic childhood.

"Greetings, sister," the Goddess said warmly. "You have travelled a hard road to be here. I recognise your strength; you are a true example of all that I hoped for the sisterhood."

Mary was lost for words. The Goddess sensed her awe, for she said, "Come, do not shrink from me. I serve you, as you serve me. I am a part of you, as you are a part of me. That is the message Existence has set before us."

Mary swallowed. "I don't understand what I'm supposed to do . . ."

"There are no limits to anything—worlds upon worlds, gods upon gods, no limit to the heart of Fragile Creatures, no limit to what can be achieved. Time and space are not absolute. Everything is fluid. That, too, is Existence. You must learn this if you seek to understand all that has transpired, and all that will transpire."

"Why did you leave the God? Why did you hide away from us?"

The Goddess's face grew sad. "Once, we were strong. Our ways were exalted, the way of the moon and the heart and the great, shifting oceans. But the seasons turned. You know, sister, you know. Those who seek power, the enemies of Existence, took it with an iron fist. We fell away and away. The great forests were burned, the seas filled with poisons, the grasslands torn up and buried, the hilltops devastated, the air itself filled with sulphur, and the sisterhood's voice grew small and smaller still; many accepted their lot. Too many."

"So you left," Mary said. "We let you down."

"I was still with you, in spirit. I still watched and hoped, waiting for a sign that I would be needed again. But it never came." She smiled. "Until now."

Mary bowed her head.

The Goddess stepped forward, and this time there was light, and stars; Mary couldn't look at her. "You have served me, sister, and now I shall serve you. You came to me with a request. Speak."

"My friend . . . Caitlin . . . she needs help."

"I know of whom you speak—another true sister. She, too, has awoken me."

"Then you'll help her?"

"I shall, and I already have. For as I have said, time is not absolute. What I do in your here and now will affect what you have already experienced . . ."

Mary tried to understand what the Goddess was saying. "You can alter the past?" she ventured.

"There is no past, or future. Only an endless present. It is your perception that traps you in your view, little sister. What we all do rings out across eternity."

The Goddess moved back near to the spring. A second later, a large hooded crow flew out of the steam, circling the room before alighting on the floor next to the Goddess. Strangely, Mary saw the bird but felt as if she was looking at a fierce but beautiful woman with long black hair and cold, intense eyes.

"The tribes knew her as the Morrigan," the Goddess explained.

Mary knew the name, as many in the Craft did. "She serves you?" she asked.

The Goddess smiled. "She is me. A part of me, as you are a part. All the gods are an aspect of something greater, though they think they have individual lives. Names. What are names? Here I was Sulis, and Minerva. Yes, and the Morrigan. And I am Brigid, the goddess with three faces. Three faces, sister—past, present, and future, all one, all linked, all looking out across Existence."

The crow rose up, its wings beating like the rhythm of the heart, and it flew back into the steam and disappeared.

"Gone," the Goddess said, "to a lonely lane on a stormy night, and a time of terrible heartache for one sister."

"Thank you," Mary said. Her gratitude gave way to a tremendous relief that her journey was finally over. Yet there was a strange, unsettling quality in the

Goddess's face that gave her pause. "The Morrigan will help her, won't she? That's it? It's over?"

Sadness flickered across the Goddess's features, and Mary knew the answer even before the Goddess spoke. "Caitlin will now reach the end of her quest, where she would have long fallen before. But that will not be enough. Not even the Morrigan can save her from the forces ranged against her."

There was no whispering, but the silence was even eerier. The Lament-Brood stood unmoving, as if awaiting an order.

"What are they doing?" Jack said. "Why don't they attack?"

Matt pressed Jack and Caitlin back toward the warp field, which buzzed like a high-tension wire. A sucking cold urged them to step back further, further, into that fantastic panorama where they would be drawn into the very heart of Existence.

Matt turned to Caitlin. "We made a right old mess of things, didn't we?" he said. "Don't suppose you've got any tricks up your sleeve?"

"No." She looked over at the Lament-Brood, her mind turning.

"Not ready to conjure up that Psycho-Caitlin who got us in here?"

"Why should I?" She continued to search the purple-misted ranks.

Matt put his hands on her shoulders and physically turned her toward him. "For old times' sake?" He smiled winningly. "We got close on the way here . . . very close. I saw how you felt about me, and believe me, I feel the same way. I need you to do your stuff, Caitlin . . . Jack and I both do. Don't you think you and I deserve the chance to see where things might go when we get out of here? After all we've been through, we deserve some romance in our lives—"

Her cold laugh cut him dead. "Romance?" She smiled icily, her eyes flashing. "You were so good at your manipulation, Matt."

"What are you talking about?"

"There is no missing daughter, is there? You couldn't have just forgotten her like you did. If you had a child she would have been on your mind all the time, driving every decision. But you only mentioned her when you used her to win me over . . . because you needed me to cross over to this place."

"That's ridiculous! Of course I've got a daughter. And once we're out of here—"

"You never loved me, Matt. I saw through all that, too, because I experienced real love recently, from someone who cared for me more than himself. I'd forgotten what it was like with Grant, so you could fool me for a while, but now, looking back, you were so transparent. Who are you, Matt? Really?"

He made to continue his deception and then shrugged and wandered away to stare briefly into the warp field. When he finally looked back at her, his mind made up, his pleasant features revealed a hidden arrogance.

"Before the Fall I used to be in the Special Boat Service. Where do you think I got all those martial skills? At the local pub? These days . . . well, more of the same, I suppose. I work for the government. The new government, down in Oxford. They're still keeping things pretty much under wraps, but soon everyone will know they're on the case, and then they'll be kicking the arse of all the gods and what have you. We're going to blow them out of the water."

Jack stared at Matt with mounting dismay. Matt ignored him.

"The government knows more than you might think. They're smart people, Caitlin. They understand that they need to have all the facts at their disposal before they can strike back. So they've been doing the legwork, finding out all the reasons why the Fall happened, working out who the Brothers and Sisters of Dragons are and why they exist, finding out what those gods do . . . and how we can hit back at them. They might not know everything, but you'd be surprised at what they *do* know. Like this Otherworld, for instance. They knew it was here—don't ask me how—and they'd worked out how to get to it. And that was where you came in."

"How did you know I was going to be at the Rollrights?" Caitlin asked.

"I didn't. I just struck lucky." He glanced at the Lament-Brood. "Or maybe not so lucky. Anyway, the government had one of us camped out at each of the old stone circles, and some of the other places we thought might be crossover points. Our job was to bring back a cure for the plague—yeah, they guessed it was from here, too—and any other information we could use in the fight-back. But we needed a Brother or Sister of Dragons to get us across. We gambled that sooner or later one of you would turn up. I'm sorry I had to deceive you, Caitlin, but the bottom line is, we're on the same side."

"You really think that?" she said incredulously. "After all the time you've spent with me, you know me so little?"

He sighed. "This is exactly why I didn't tell you what I was doing right from the start. Your trouble is, you're too naïve. This is war, and in war you have to do things that might not be acceptable in peacetime."

"Like killing Carlton?"

An audible gasp escaped Jack's lips. Matt looked back toward the warp field.

"How could you do that? A boy . . . an innocent boy . . ."

He shrugged, wasn't going to say anything, but she wouldn't allow him that luxury. "Go on. I'm waiting."

"He was too smart . . . maybe he even read my mind. He was going to tell you what I was doing—"

"That wasn't the only reason." She had trouble keeping her voice from trembling with the emotion she felt. "You saw how close I was getting to him . . . and you knew it was another way you could destabilise me so you could control me.

I was getting too independent on the boat, wasn't I? But I didn't make it back to you after the Lament-Brood attacked *Sunchaser*, so it was all for nothing. You killed a young boy, for nothing. How does that fit with all your lofty aims?"

Jack had tears in his eyes. "How could you do that?"

"I still don't understand . . . strategically," Caitlin said. "He was special, the key to sorting all this mess out, wasn't he?"

Matt shook his head. "He wasn't the one—that's some other kid down in Salisbury, and we've already got him in our sights. The things he can do make Carlton look like . . . some stupid child."

Caitlin visibly winced. "You're talking about military potential. The death of a child is so painful because of everything else you lose when they die. Who knows how they're going to turn out? They might become some great hero, a champion, or they might turn into you. You didn't just murder Carlton . . . you murdered his future, the possibility of what he might have become."

"I had a job to do, Caitlin—"

"Shut up." Her voice had more of the Morrigan about it than she had expected. In that instant she had the strangest feeling that Carlton knew he was going to die, that he didn't care because he realised he was part of a bigger plan, and in a way he was: if Carlton hadn't died, Caitlin would never have allowed the Morrigan to take over and perhaps Matt would then have achieved all his aims. *Something* good had come out of the whole mess; perhaps it had even been Carlton's intention all along. Mahalia had been right: he really was special. "Everything I've learned since coming here has told me you can't trust anything at face value—nothing is as it appears. You see, you believe the enemies are monsters or supernatural threats, but they're not. The real threat looks just like us, and it always has. The real threat has been amongst us since the dawn of humanity—the hard people, the ones who thought they knew better than anyone else, who could make the tough decisions about who lived or died. You think the world would be better with you and your secret government in charge, rather than all the things we've got now?"

"Of course. You think the current mess is better with all the death and the misery we've seen?"

"And next to that, the death of an innocent boy amounts to nothing, is that what you're saying?"

Again he made not to speak, but this time he couldn't resist, so sure was he that he was right. "Exactly. Anyone can see. There's no comparison."

"I used to think no life was more valuable than another, but you've taught me I was wrong."

He started to smile.

"We wouldn't miss you, Matt, you or any of your kind."

His face hardened.

Jack drifted up to Matt. In the boy, Caitlin could see the fractured response of a child whose image of his parent had been destroyed. And Matt could see too what Jack was feeling, but aside from an uncomfortable flicker across the adult's face, he didn't place any value on it. Caitlin wondered how she could ever have been fooled by him.

Then, like a snake, Matt moved. Caitlin glimpsed a face that flashed from mild indifference to steel, and in that instant his arm was around Jack's neck, the boy spun round and locked in place, a small blade pressed against his throat.

Caitlin darted forward, but Matt tipped the knife just enough to draw blood. Caitlin was in no doubt that he would kill Jack if he wanted. "Don't hurt him!" she said. "It's pointless. He's a boy—let him go."

"He's not a boy," Matt said emotionlessly, "he's a weapon. The biggest and best weapon that ever existed. If I get him back, with what's inside him, then we've got the upper hand. The other side would have to fall in line."

"What if they don't? What point is a weapon that could destroy all Existence?"

"If you can't have the world the way you want it, there's no need for the world at all."

"You'd destroy *everything*? Just because you couldn't bear not to be in charge?"

Matt began to drag Jack toward the first rank of the Lament-Brood. "It's about freedom—you wouldn't understand—"

"I know. I'm too naïve." Did humanity stand any chance of advancing when there were people like Matt around, the kind of people who always rose into positions of power? What was the point, then, in anything?

"Turn on the power, Jack," Matt said firmly. When Jack didn't respond, Matt jabbed the knife hard so that the boy howled in pain and then yelled, "Turn it on!"

The thin light of the Wish-Hex began to leak from Jack's stomach. Matt forced the boy toward the Lament-Brood, using him as a shield while keeping one eye on Caitlin; his face warned her not to make any move. "They'll let us out," he said. "They know what he can do. But more than that, they don't need us. You were the only threat. As long as they've got you, they'll be happy."

His words were shown to be true as a path opened up through the Lament-Brood. If the Morrigan had still been a part of her, Caitlin might have been able to do something, but Matt was too vicious, too cunning, for her even to get close. But more than that, she knew she wasn't up to what was expected of her, for if she were she would risk killing Jack to prevent such power being used against Existence. She couldn't do that, not even there at the end. She wasn't hard enough; not like Matt.

He gave a sickeningly triumphant smile and eased down the path toward the exit that would take him away. He still hadn't got a cure for the plague, and couldn't cross over on his own, but Caitlin was convinced that a person like Matt would find a way. He'd always win through.

Just as he reached the door to the next chamber, there was a movement a little way along the far wall. Caitlin couldn't tell what it was, but it appeared to come from one of the slits that led to the network of capillary tunnels.

Matt paused in the doorway. Caitlin didn't know if he was going to make some last arrogant comment to celebrate his escape, or simply show his contempt for her, but it never came. There was an odd moment when his face froze in puzzlement, and then a crimson shower gushed from his neck. The knife dropped from his fingers and he pitched backward, emitting a queasy gurgling noise, his body lost behind the Lament-Brood.

And there was Mahalia. The tremble in the hand that held the knife that had slit Matt's throat was visible across the chamber, and her face held the devastation of someone who had been forced to sacrifice her last chance for redemption. But she erased it in a second and grabbed Jack. "Come on," she yelled to Caitlin. "We can still get out of here."

Caitlin tried to find some remorse in her heart for Matt's death, but there was none. She pulled Liam to her side and made to hurry toward Mahalia and Jack, but she was distracted by the sucking and slurping sounds as the House of Pain birthed another representative from the floor in front of her. It emerged quickly, a spindly frame on skeletal legs. When it was finally complete, it was nearly ten feet tall with a head like a black egg, bending over Caitlin and Liam to speak.

"Cannnnooottttttt . . . leavvvvvvvve. Boyyyyyy . . . stayyyyyy. Beyonddddd . . . liesssssssssss . . . deathhhhhhhhhh."

And there it was, finally, what she had been expecting for so long: the twist in the devil's contract. Liam hadn't been returned to life—he was simply caught in limbo. If she took him out of the House of Pain, his death would once again be a reality.

"Youuuuuuuuuuu . . . staaaaayyyyyyyyyy. Beeeeeeeeee . . . Queeeeeeennnnn-nnnn . . ."

Caitlin was numb. Inside her, Amy, Briony, and Brigid howled into the storm. There was no way out. "Yes," she said. "I'll stay."

She held Liam close and walked back toward the warp field. While her back had been turned, the House of Pain had created a seat of shiny black stone, the perfect throne for the Queen of Sinister. Caitlin swallowed hard so her voice would be steady and then called to Mahalia, "Go on. I'll be OK."

Mahalia stared in disbelief, then grabbed Jack's arm and hauled him through the doorway. Caitlin felt pleased the girl had got away, and with Jack, the one who still meant there was a chance for her. That small success provided the thinnest glimmer of light in the dark existence that stretched before Caitlin.

Desolately, she walked up to the seat and sat down. It was icily cold, but soon that wouldn't matter. She looked out across the army—her army—and knew now why they waited: for their queen.

Her fate was clear. An iciness was creeping into her limbs, the legacy of the House of Pain, transforming her into something that could live in that place, revelling in the dark emotions it generated. She would sit on that cold, black throne for evermore, commanding her army of the dead, with her son standing silently at her side until the stars winked out one by one and all that was left was the Void.

Mahalia and Jack raced past the last of the Lament-Brood, through the next room, and into the network of tunnels that cut through the House of Pain.

"We could go back for Caitlin," Jack said. "We can't leave her here."

"She chose to stay—she's a grown woman." Mahalia tried to sound hard so that Jack wouldn't find a chink that would prise her back, but inside she was devastated. Not so long ago she had tried to kill her, yet now she mourned Caitlin. What was wrong with her?

Jack appeared to sense what was going through her head, for he grabbed her hand as they ran and gave it a squeeze. "I'm glad you're here," he said quietly. His honest expression of emotion brought a lump to her throat.

"You want a dirty job doing, I'm your girl."

They broke out into the main corridor that led to the entrance. Through the massive doorway, late afternoon sun glowed like a beacon.

"What are we going to do now?" Jack said.

"One more thing before we leave, then . . ." Mahalia looked across the plain to the panorama of the Land of Always Summer stretching out across the horizon. ". . . we've got a whole world to play with."

She came to an abrupt halt not far from the entrance and began to search the wall. Finally she found what she was looking for, and forced her hands into one of the nearly hidden slits that gave access to the capillary tunnel system. "Come on, give me a hand," she called.

Without understanding what he was doing, Jack thrust his hands into the slit alongside her and felt something alive inside. Before he could recoil or question, Mahalia was hauling whatever it was out into the corridor and he was helping her.

There was a sucking sound and Crowther emerged, as pale as death and covered in blood, the spear still embedded in him but now broken off on both sides. Yet he was still alive—but only just. His eyes flickered and the faintest wheeze of breath escaped his lips.

"He was planning to do something heroic, but it was so out of character I couldn't let him," Mahalia said. "So I dragged him away and stashed him in there."

"Why?" Jack could see that the professor was only a whisker away from death.

"Because I had an idea." Mahalia faced Jack, her arms on his shoulders to focus his attention on her face. "Call me stupid, but I found this thing called hope. It was something I'd not bothered with before, but when you're down to your last, you take anything you've got, right?"

He saw that same hope in her frightened eyes and felt more in love with her than he had thought possible. "What's your idea?"

"That power inside you . . . the Wish-Hex. Everybody talks about it like it's some doomsday weapon, but I've seen you use it and I thought, maybe it's not just useful for destroying things. It's a kind of energy, like that Blue Fire everyone was always wittering on about. Maybe it's one and the same thing. And . . . and . . ." She leaned forward to kiss him quickly. "I want you to try to use it to save the professor."

Jack looked down at Crowther in dismay. "I don't think I can."

"Just try, Jack. For me."

Hesitantly, he knelt down beside the prone form and cradled the professor's head in his hands. His brow knitted in concentration, and the light leaked out of his stomach and flowed into his arms and then his hands.

Mahalia watched Jack for fifteen minutes as he battled with the stream of energy, directing it, forcing it to his will. Sweat dripped from his forehead and soaked his underarms and back. For all that time, it appeared to be doing little good, for the professor continued to hover on the brink of dying; but then, gradually, colour drifted back into his cheeks and his eyes began to flicker.

Mahalia leaned forward and yanked the remaining stub of the spear from his chest. It came out with a sucking sound, but instead of a gout of blood there was only white light. As the light cleared, Mahalia could see the hole in the professor begin to close.

Five minutes later it was all over. Jack flopped back, exhausted but beaming with the wonder of what he had done. The professor moaned and then slowly opened his eyes. He looked up into Mahalia's face.

"Oh," he said. "This must be hell."

"Looks like you've got some use after all, boy," Mahalia said to Jack. Her heart swelled at the depth of feeling etched on his face; he knew now that he wasn't just a weapon, that his lifetime of suffering might have had some positive outcome after all.

But as she and Jack struggled to help Crowther to his feet, a shadow fell across them. Mahalia looked up suddenly. "Who the hell are you?" she said in astonishment.

In the hot steam of the sacred spring, Mary clasped her hands and pleaded. "I'll do whatever it takes. Please, if there's anything you can do to save her . . ."

"You will do anything?" The Goddess was serious and contemplative. "What does this sister mean to you?"

"What does she mean?" The question was curious and unsettling; there was so much to sum up. How to decide what one person meant when her impact on your life was complex and inscrutable. "She means . . . the future." Once Mary had latched on to that word, her thoughts quickly fell into place. "I've had my time—I know I've got a lot of years left, but I made such a mess of things so long ago, it's impossible to go back now. I never thought about having children. Perhaps if I had, there might have been a chance for me. If I'd made them into good people, then I'd have done *something* worthwhile. But I've not done anything that really matters. If I was wiped off the face of the earth right now, I'd leave nothing behind that anyone would remember. But Caitlin . . . she's my daughter in all but flesh. She's my hope for the future. If I save her, and she does good, then at least I've added something to life." The words were painful to express, but Mary recognised their abiding truth as they left her lips.

"I can help her, but what is required is beyond even my capabilities. There are rules of Existence that we all must follow." The Goddess raised one hand and it appeared that it was night in the spring and the moonlight was streaming all around, the world painted silver and black. "A sacrifice will be the key to unlock the door. Are you prepared to make that sacrifice?"

"Yes." Mary's throat was dry. She thought she knew what lay ahead.

"It is the greatest sacrifice . . . your life. A life for a life."

Although Mary had anticipated the Goddess's words, the enormity of what was being asked, once it had been put into words, stunned her. She was terrified, yet she knew she had no doubts. There was no alternative: Caitlin was good and decent and deserved her chance at happiness. To save her . . . that was an achievement worth dying for.

"I understand," she said. "A life for a life. I accept."

"You are brave, little sister." The Goddess raised her arms in a gesture that showed her appreciation of what Mary had overcome to make her decision. She smiled. "What lies ahead is the greatest mystery of all. But know this: death is not the end. Do not be scared, for Existence always cares for its own. Though you leave behind everything you understand, your sacrifice is recognised. Take with you the knowledge that you have committed an act of great importance and great goodness."

The moonlight became brighter, and briefly Mary thought she was in a verdant grove on a hilltop somewhere in the deepest country. "Know also, sister, that you have touched my heart. To travel here along the hard road, to overcome the three tests, to give up your life for another . . . you are all I could have hoped for in your kind. You, little sister—you alone—have turned me around."

"You're going back?"

"A new age awaits, and I shall be there to guide your people through the light of the moon. I will be there, in the forests and by the rivers, on the mountaintops and by the cool lakes. There is a struggle ahead, but if there are more sisters like you, then we have hope."

"I'm so pleased." Mary's words didn't begin to capture the magnitude of what she felt, but before she could say anything else, she sensed movement behind her. Standing in the steam was the Jigsaw Man, her nemesis.

"He is death, and when he touches you, you shall die," the Goddess said. "But there shall be no pain. You shall slide into the cool night . . . and then the moon shall rise."

Mary took a deep breath and steeled herself, yet she was surprised to find she was no longer scared. Instead, she was excited at what was to come. She knelt down, for it seemed right, and then said, "And Caitlin will be all right?"

"A life for a life, little sister," the Goddess said. The steam swirled in a gale that blew from nowhere. Blue lightning crackled all around, and as the thunder rolled out, a knight in black armour emerged from the vicinity of the stream. He wore a helmet crafted like a boar's head.

"Who is he?" Mary asked.

The Goddess merely smiled enigmatically.

The steam shifted and behind it Mary could see the storm-lashed lane leading to Caitlin's house and Caitlin hiding behind a hedge, waiting. "When is this?" Mary asked, though she thought she knew.

"The beginning," the Goddess said. "And now, another beginning."

Mary felt a cool touch on the back of her neck and her eyes fell shut, though her smile remained.

The warp field behind Caitlin came alive with crackling blue lightning, obscuring the vista across deep space. The bolts of coruscating energy sizzled like molten iron across the now-deserted chamber, the Lament-Brood long gone to who knew where. Liam danced away in shock, but Caitlin, already numb from the House of Pain's gradual transformation, only turned to stare.

From the depths of a wall of Blue Fire stepped the black knight, the fierce light transforming the boar's-head helmet into a wild beast with glittering eyes. He strode forcefully toward the throne.

"Caitlin." His voice echoed behind the grim helmet. "The time has come."

Caitlin blinked once, twice, taking in what she was seeing with the languorous abandon of someone freezing to death. Yet the knight's appearance provided a brief spark that warmed her spirit.

"You can't give in, Caitlin." His voice was clearer now than it ever had been, as if with each appearance he gained a little bit more of the person he had been.

"You've been with me right from the beginning," Caitlin said. "Why do you keep coming to me?" Curiosity brought more warmth. She shook her head, trying to remove the cotton-wool swathing her mind.

"You will have to wait a while for that answer. Just accept that someone has your best interests at heart. Now come with me." He held out a gauntleted hand.

Caitlin hesitated, then took it. Blue sparks crackled into the tips of her fingers, reminding her of some of the exhilaration she had felt as she grew into her role as a Sister of Dragons. Suddenly she missed it acutely, felt almost bereft, and another part of the iciness burned away. "Why can't you leave me alone?" she said dismally. "I've had enough of all this. I'm so tired. I just want . . ."

"What? To die? To give up everything . . . all life? That's not you, Caitlin. I heard you were a doctor once, caring for the sick and the dying. Caring for them more than yourself."

Memories of her past life surfaced, so vague and distant they seemed to belong to another person. "Yes. That's right. So what?"

"Then you still have a job to do. I've been sent here to save you, Caitlin—or rather, to show you the path so you can save yourself . . . and everyone else. Come."

He marched across the chamber, then waited for her to follow. As Caitlin watched him, she remembered what Crowther had said about the boar-king in the Forest of the Night and she suddenly understood the symbolism of the knight's strange helmet. A boar, one of the Celts' totem animals—a messenger between humanity and the gods.

"Who's that, Mummy?" Liam's voice was a pale shadow; the House of Pain was working its dark magic in him, too.

"Someone sent to haunt me, honey. Don't worry about it." She took Liam's hand and marvelled at how cold his fingers were.

The knight led the way through the deserted corridors. Caitlin expected the House of Pain to unleash one of its twisted manifestations to bar their way, but it had either decided she was no longer worthy of its attention, or the knight in some way shrouded their passing from the House of Pain's perceptions.

Eventually they came to a room closed off by a curtain formed from that sickening meat. Caitlin could hear a noise like a thousand rats on the other side.

"Steel yourself," the knight said. He threw open the curtain.

It was the room with the plague egg that Caitlin had seen before. The floor was swarming with thousands of the plague demons, while others were being birthed by the minute. As the knight strode forward, the demons attacked his ankles and then swarmed over him, but his armour kept them at bay. He drew his sword, and in the darkened room it glowed with a thin blue light. The demons surged away, shrieking in fear, scrambling over each other to disappear into the far corners of the room. The knight walked up to the egg and waited. Another demon emerged into the world and then hurtled away the instant it saw the sword.

"Here," he said, offering the weapon to Caitlin when she arrived at his side. "Destroy the egg."

"You do it—you're the good knight," she replied. "Or is this just another trick to damn me?"

"Aren't you damned already?"

His logic was impeccable. She took the sword, wavering under its weight. Not so long ago she would have wielded it as though it were nothing. Now it took all her effort just to lift it.

"This will stop any more from coming out," she said, "but it's not going to stop the ones already infecting people in my world."

"The egg births them and nurtures them," the knight said. "Without it, none of them can survive."

The last of the House of Pain's ice fell away and Caitlin felt a rush of adrenalin. Here was her chance finally to do something good. She heaved the sword up.

Despite their terror, in that instant the plague demons recognised what was about to happen. They surged forward as one, flinging themselves from every corner, screeching and squealing, their glittering eyes filled with murderous intent.

The knight became a blur of destruction, battering away the first wave. Still dogged by their basic fear of what the sword represented, the imps hadn't yet unleashed the true depths of their fury, but it would come.

"Do it now!" the knight yelled as Caitlin wavered in the face of the storm of activity around her.

She brought the sword down with all her strength.

It cut through the egg as if slicing through a giant mushroom. Around the room the shrieking of the plague demons became so intense that Caitlin dropped the sword and clutched at her ears; Liam ran from the room crying. As the creatures hurtled around the room in their death throes, the knight picked up his sword and forced Caitlin out of the chamber.

They didn't stop running until the egg room was far behind them, and they could no longer hear the awful cries of the dying plague demons. "Is that it?" Caitlin asked breathlessly as they waited in an empty room that pulsed with the distant heartbeat she had heard when they first entered the House of Pain. "Is it all over?"

The knight stood erect, resting his hands on his sword. "The plague is over."

"Thank God." Caitlin wiped away a fugitive tear. "At least I'm not a complete failure." She pulled Liam to her and stroked his head, feeling the weariness sweep over her again.

"You can still leave this place," the knight said.

"I can't. Liam will die if we leave."

"Not him. You."

She glared at the knight. "How can you say that? He's my son."

"Think, Caitlin. You've stopped him from moving on. Do you think this place is good for him? Do you believe it's right to deny him what lies beyond . . . whether eternal rest, or eternal life? Moments frozen in time have no meaning. Only constant change gives us perspective . . . and life. Liam not growing, not having a life, is not Liam. It's just a snapshot. Nothing more."

"Don't you dare lecture me!" she raged. "What right do you have?"

"More right than you might think." He appeared to steady himself, though the armour hid any sense of what was going on inside him. "You asked why I kept coming to you, Caitlin. Here's why." He took off his helmet. "Because I love you . . . and I'll always love you."

The shock was so great that Caitlin staggered, and for a moment she thought she might faint. It was Grant, filled with the flush of life, looking as though he had never succumbed to the ravages of the plague, and for a moment she wondered if her devastating images of burying him in the back garden were just a nightmare.

There was a weight in her chest forcing its way up into her throat, blocking all the words that wanted to come out. Liam cried, "Daddy!" and ran to throw his arms around his father's waist, and then Caitlin thought the rock would burst her chest open. She buried her face in Grant's neck, immersing herself in the fragrance of his skin, something that had been taken for granted for so long and now was as valuable to her as all the riches of the world. She didn't want to lose that simple aroma ever again. It brought with it a rush of such overpowering memories that she was carried away: the two of them sitting in Roundhay Park when Grant gave up his career and his ambitions for her; their marriage, seeing Grant waiting at the end of the aisle, looking so handsome, so special; Liam's birth, the baby on her chest, Grant holding her hand, tears in his eyes, too choked to speak; and more, every precious moment that had made up their lives together, now more precious than ever.

And by the end of it, all the suffering and the harrowing experiences on the road from their village to the House of Pain had been forgotten, and once again she was the woman she had been, Caitlin Shepherd, GP. Not a Sister of Dragons, not a saviour of the world. Just a person; and that was enough.

"I don't understand . . . how you can be here . . ." she said.

"Come on," he replied. "We've got a lot to talk about."

He led her to the entrance, where they sat just inside so they could look at the slowly setting sun playing across the plain, and the night drawing in, with a full moon and a spread of glittering stars providing a wonder to the darkness. They talked about everything, exhausting all the questions Caitlin had and the issues that needed resolving that she had thought would hang over her for the rest of her days; and they played with Liam, and kissed him and hugged each other. And when the sun came up, they were a family again.

But then Grant's face grew serious and he took Caitlin's hand. "You know we can't stay like this."

"Why not?" she replied, knowing the answer to her question, not wanting to hear it.

"This is all fake, Caitlin, sitting here in the shadow of this nightmare place, and we can't pretend it's anything else. There won't be any happiness here—no shared moments, no joyful experiences, no growth. What we have had is a second chance to put things right. We wiped away all the things that can hang around after a death and spoil a life. That's a tremendous gift, more than other people get."

"It's not enough!"

"It is, Caitlin. Really. It's hard for you, being alone in the world, but the fact that I'm here now should tell you something. To stay here is to offer victory to the House of Pain and what lies behind it, because it's a mockery of all the things that make life so wonderful. It's not life, it's anti-life—it's what the Void stands for."

"Don't go," she pleaded. "Don't leave me alone."

"You won't be alone. You'll find more love in the world . . ." She went to protest, but he silenced her with a finger to her lips. "You might not want to consider that now, when you're here with us, but it's important that you know I'm happy with it. Having someone who loves you, and loving somebody, is the most valuable thing there is—that's what Existence is all about, when you come down to it. It might sound stupid, and soppy, and you know I've never been a great romantic, but it's the truth. The only truth."

His tone calmed her enough to take his hand. "I know you're right . . . I don't want you to be, but I know. I'll do my best to cope. Really . . . for you, and Liam. I'll miss you . . . both of you."

"You've had a glimpse of the rules that underpin everything, Caitlin. You know there is no beginning and no end, that everything is connected, that emotions are more powerful than concrete things, that reality is just what we make it. You know all that, and that will give you the strength to keep going . . . until we see each other again."

He held her for a long moment and she didn't want to let go, but she did. "There's one thing . . . You said I could leave here, but I can't. The House of Pain has changed me to make me survive here. There's a cold that keeps crawling up my body—I can feel it coming back now—and it's stopping me from walking away. I can't leave of my own accord. It's making sure I'm going to be the queen here forever."

Grant smiled and ran his fingers through her hair. "Wait and see. You may not have to leave on your own."

"What do you mean?"

"Wait and see."

"I don't want to see you both leave."

"Then close your eyes. Remember us both sitting here now and that thought will stay with you forever." He touched her forehead. "Just here."

She closed her eyes. And when she opened them again, they were both gone.

chapter nineteen

OF LOVE AND OTHER THINGS

"Just as the health of a forest or a fragrant meadow can be measured by the number of different insects and plants and creatures that successfully make it their home, so only by an extraordinary abundance of disparate spiritual and philosophic paths will human beings navigate a pathway through the dark and swirling storms that mark our current era."

Margot Adler

With the dull heat of a new day starting to build, Caitlin finally left her position at the entrance to the House of Pain and wandered back toward the source of despair, her new home. The cold was already working its way up her legs. But she hadn't gone far when she heard the sound of two sets of feet approaching from the darkness.

"She's here! Look, she's here!"

Caitlin was so surprised to see another person in that place that it took her a second to realise who was running toward her.

"Bloody hell! I thought we were going to be searching this bastard place until I'd worn my legs to stumps," Harvey said in his thick Birmingham accent. He threw his arms round her with unrestrained joy and then backed off suddenly. "You're not going to go all psycho on me, are you?"

The second person emerged more slowly, but he was grinning broadly. It was Thackeray. "See, I told you we'd find her."

Harvey jerked a thumb in Thackeray's direction and said to Caitlin conspiratorially, "Blind optimism . . . that's true love for you."

Thackeray walked up to Caitlin and stood with his arms folded, his grin now lazy. "How are you?"

"What are you doing here?" she asked in amazement.

"It was something to do," Thackeray said. "And we thought it would be better than Birmingham."

Harvey rolled his eyes. "I have never been so shit-scared in my life. This bastard owes me big time for keeping him company."

"But how did you manage to survive?" Caitlin said. "I mean . . . the things out there . . ."

"Don't," Harvey said, uneasily. "I don't want to think about it."

"On the way across the plain up here, we met this scary woman, all black hair and wild eyes, and she said, *The gods look after fools and lovers*, so I suppose that covers all the bases."

"We followed you out of New Street Station," Harvey said, "once I'd convinced Thackeray what an idiot he was being to let you go—"

"I didn't need much convincing," Thackeray said shyly.

"—but you were walking like a mad thing and we couldn't catch up," Harvey continued. "Nearly, but . . . then we saw you go through that big, blue, flashing doorway thing and . . . well, I was ready to turn back then, but he hurled me through." He glared at Thackeray. "Bastard."

"The things we've seen." Thackeray stared into the middle distance as the memories surfaced. "A few times I thought we weren't going to get through . . ."

Harvey blanched and looked at the floor.

"There was one time, just before we got here, on this plain with cairns everywhere. Shit, I thought our number was up there. And then these freaky sand things dressed like samurai turned up and said we'd got safe passage . . . and . . ."

"And here we are," Harvey said.

Caitlin smiled. She was pleased to see them. "So are you going to get me out of here?"

"You bet," Harvey said. "I just hope the journey home isn't as bad. I don't think my nerves can take it."

As they walked toward the door, they talked, and Thackeray told Caitlin how they'd met Mahalia, Jack, and Crowther when they entered the House of Pain. "They said they were going to lose themselves out there somewhere," Thackeray said. "Lie low for a while . . . find a little magic, they said. The old bloke looked really happy."

"They all did," Harvey said.

Caitlin told them the whole story of the plague and the quest, and at the end of it the full gravity of what had happened descended on her. "I don't know what's going to happen," she said, worried. "The Brothers and Sisters of Dragons are the last line of defence against the Void. But I've failed . . . I'm not one anymore. If there isn't the right number, the whole system won't work!"

"Ah, something will turn up," Thackeray said.

"How can you be so blasé about it?"

"Well, you know . . . things do turn up. That's life. That evil bastard . . . the Void. It could be here tomorrow, but it might be a million years away. Why worry about it? If I sat around worrying about dying I'd never enjoy life. Don't think of it as a big threat. Think of it as a . . . as a metaphor."

"Thackeray," Harvey said wearily, "I keep telling you, nobody likes a smart arse."

They reached the doorway and Caitlin hesitated, the cold in her limbs freezing her to the spot. Thackeray took her hand and led her across the threshold. Once she was outside, a faint flush of warmth eased into her heart. Slowly it began to drive the cold out.

Before them, the Land of Always Summer stretched out, filled with wonder and magic, and somewhere, a place that would allow them to get back home.

"Come on," Thackeray said. "Let's get out of Birmingham."

If you would like to know more about the world of
The Queen of Sinister, seek out the other books in
The Dark Age sequence:
The Devil in Green
and
The Hounds of Avalon
and
The Age of Misrule trilogy:
World's End
Darkest Hour
and
Always Forever

AFTERWORD

This book is one part of a puzzle.

A puzzle that draws on clues scattered across more than two thousand years of human history. In the alignments of stone circles, and mysteries encoded in the great cathedrals and castles. The secrets locked into old fairy tales and ancient mythologies. The learnings of seers, magicians, and philosophers. And, too, the kind of clues you might find scattered through a detective novel, which point into the dark recesses of the human mind.

More than ten years ago now, I found myself on a sun-drenched island three miles off the coast of Wales. I'd reached something of a turning point in my life, or so I felt, and I was thinking about the path ahead, and all that had come before.

Sitting on the beach, looking across the stretch of water to the pastel-painted houses of the resort town of Tenby, it felt the perfect place for reflection. If you visit Caldey Island today, you'll notice, I'm sure, a peculiar atmosphere—one of great peace, evident under the dark canopy of the woods that run down to the shore and the hidden coves, as well as, surprisingly, on the wind-swept cliffs where the waves crash relentlessly. It's only a tiny island. You can walk around it in a morning.

Caldey is owned and managed by a small community of monks resident at the white-walled Cistercian monastery that sits at the heart of the island. There's a handful of other residents who help work the fields, but that's it apart from the tourists who make the short boat trip from Tenby—only twenty minutes away, but the two places might as well be a world apart.

The monastery is relatively modern, with the current order moving to Caldey in 1929. But as I explored, I discovered that other religious people had been drawn here too—a group of monks came in 1906, a Benedictine foundation was established in 1136, and a Celtic monastery had been founded as long ago as the sixth century. The beauty of the island and the relative isolation made it attractive, I supposed.

But then I came across other information that made me think deeper. A strange inscription in the mysterious Ogham alphabet had been left on Caldey. Ogham is a secret writing, possibly invented by the druids, with only four hundred surviving inscriptions, mostly in Ireland.

And then I found the cave, partially excavated by archaeologists. They'd uncovered flints and bones suggesting humans had come to this place more than twelve thousand years ago. And there was evidence, too, of rituals and funerary practices on Caldey throughout the later Stone Age. Neolithic people also found something special in that place.

What was it about Caldey Island that drew people there across thousands of years, from different belief systems? Was that potent atmosphere more than just the sum of trees and rocks and sand and sea? Something buried in the very fabric of the island itself? I wondered.

Stories start with the smallest of thoughts.

Feverishly, I sketched out an epic story that would take in the full sweep of human history, ancient mysteries and occult secrets, and the world's great mythologies too, tumbling across three separate worlds—our own, modern-day world, the mystical Celtic Otherworld, and the world beyond death. The detailed research would take months on the road around Britain, and then across the globe, visiting mysterious places, reading old texts and scholarly papers, and talking to the contemporary custodians of that information.

This sprawling story would eventually be told across nine books—a trilogy of trilogies that could, just about, be consumed in any order, complete in and of themselves. But read together the three trilogies would reveal an even greater story.

The Dark Age is one of those trilogies, and, as I mentioned at the start, part of a puzzle. As you move from *The Devil in Green* to *The Queen of Sinister*, it is not immediately obvious how this story hangs together, but the clues are there. All is revealed in the final book, *The Hounds of Avalon*, but you may enjoy trying to work it out for yourself as you go along.

If you want to know how the world of The Dark Age came about, read the three books of The Age of Misrule (also published by Pyr)—*World's End, Darkest Hour*, and *Always Forever*. This series tells of magic returning to our modern world, and five unlikely people who came together as champions, known as Brothers and Sisters of Dragons, to fight a terrible threat. They are Jack Churchill, the troubled leader of the group; Ruth Gallagher, a lawyer who learns to wield old magic; Ryan Veitch, a reformed criminal; Shavi, a mystic; and Laura DuSantiago, which may or may not be her real name, who has a big mouth and a strange destiny. Their shadow falls across The Dark Age, if you look carefully.

Many strange events and odd coincidences dogged my trail while I was researching this story. One of them even cropped up while I checked my facts for this afterword: the Welsh name for Caldey Island, I just discovered, is Ynys Byr, meaning Pyr's Island. Now check the spine of this book.

There are puzzles and mysteries everywhere.

ABOUT THE AUTHOR

A two-time winner of the prestigious British Fantasy Award, Mark Chadbourn has published his epic, imaginative novels in many countries around the world. He grew up in the mining community of the English Midlands and was the first person in his family to go to university. After studying economic history at Leeds, he became a successful journalist, writing for several of the UK's renowned national newspapers as well as contributing to magazines and TV.

When his first short story won *Fear* magazine's Best New Author award, he was snapped up by an agent and subsequently published his first novel, *Underground*, a supernatural thriller set in the coalfields of his youth. Quitting journalism to become a full-time author, he has written stories that have transcended genre boundaries, but is perhaps best known in the fantasy field.

Mark has also forged a parallel career as a screenwriter with many hours of produced work for British television. He is a senior writer for BBC Drama and is also developing new shows for the UK and the US.

An expert on British folklore and mythology, he has held several varied and colorful jobs, including independent record company boss, band manager, production line worker, engineer's "mate," and media consultant.

Having traveled extensively around the world, he has now settled in a rambling house in the middle of a forest not far from where he was born.

For information about the author and his work:

www.markchadbourn.net
www.jackofravens.com
www.myspace.com/markchadbourn

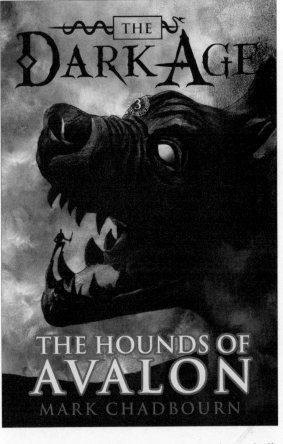